'Another moving and thought-provoking read, this lives up to expectations' *Cosmopolitan*

'If you only do one thing this weekend, read this book. It's another utterly brilliant psychological thriller from the author and we one hundred per cent recommend it' *Sun*

'Powerful thriller about a woman's life unravelling . . . We were hooked from the start' *Company*

'I enjoyed the passion and power with which Koomson writes, and her portrayal of an emotional underworld in which nothing is clear-cut and the line between guilty and inno-cent is blurred' *Daily Mail*

'Another masterpiece from Dorothy Koomson. A must-read that will have you gripped' * * * * * *Heat*

'Cleverly told by three female narrators, this is a complex tale of a terrible crime . . . I was gripped from the start of this book and desperate to uncover the truth' *Woman Magazine*

'An excellent roller-coaster ride of a book, which keeps you guessing until the very end' *Bello*

D0190777

Also by Dorothy Koomson

DOROTHY KOOMSON
The Rose Petal Beach

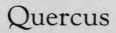

Quercus

First published in Great Britain in 2012 by Quercus

This paperback edition published in 2013 by

55 Baker Street
7th Floor, South Block
London W1U 8EW

Copyright © 2012 Dorothy Koomson

The moral right of Dorothy Koomson to be
identified as the author of this work has been
asserted in accordance with the Copyright,
Designs and Patents Act, 1988.

All rights reserved. No part of this publication
may be reproduced or transmitted in any form
or by any means, electronic or mechanical,
including photocopy, recording, or any
information storage and retrieval system,
without permission in writing from the publisher.

A CIP catalogue record for this book is available
from the British Library

ISBN 978 1 78087 499 9
EBOOK ISBN 978 1 78087 498 2

This book is a work of fiction. Names, characters,
businesses, organizations, places and events are
either the product of the author's imagination
or are used fictitiously. Any resemblance to
actual persons, living or dead, events or
locales is entirely coincidental.

10 9 8 7 6 5 4 3 2 1

Printed and bound in Great Britain by Clays Ltd, St Ives plc

Typeset by Ellipsis Digital Limited, Glasgow

For
G & E
Always.

Prologue

Have you heard the story of The Rose Petal Beach?

The legend of the woman who gave up her whole life for love? She walked around and across the expanse of a deserted island, looking for her beloved who had been lost at sea. Her love was so rare and wondrous, so deep and beautiful and pure, that as she walked her feet were cut by the sharp pebbles on the beach and every drop of blood turned into a rose petal until the beach became a blanket of perfect red petals.

Have you heard the story of The Rose Petal Beach?

Is it a story worth killing for?

Tami

This is where my life begins.

Not thirty-six years ago in a hospital in London. Not seventeen years ago when I moved out of my parents' house to live in a smart but compact bedsit all on my own. Not fourteen years ago when I moved to Brighton. Not twelve years ago when I married my husband. Not even nine years ago when I had my first child. Not seven years ago when I had my second child. My life begins now.

With two burly, uniformed policemen, and one slender plain-clothes policewoman standing in my living room, about to arrest my husband.

Five minutes ago
Five minutes ago, Cora, my eight-year-old, was on her hands and upside down. She was showing her dad what she had done at school that day in gymnastics. 'I want to go to the Olympics one day,' she'd said. Her curly hair, folded into two neat plaits, hung on each side of her face while her almost concave stomach strained as her arms trembled with the effort of being upside down for so long. Anansy, our six-year-old, was cuddled up in the corner of the large leather sofa, wearing her pink, brushed-cotton sheep-covered pyjamas, while telling a knock-knock joke.

Scott had finally laid aside his mobile and BlackBerry, both of which he'd been on since he walked in the door, all during dinner, and now in the minutes we had together before the girls were meant to head upstairs to bed. I had been tempted by that point of the evening to calmly walk over to him, take both his phones from his hands and then just as serenely put my heel through the screen of each of them. Maybe if I broke the link, severed his connection with the office, he would finally leave work and his mind would join his body in the house.

Three minutes ago
Three minutes ago, I was nearest the living-room door, so when the doorbell sounded, followed by a short, loud knock, and I had watched Cora collapse happily – but safely – onto the floor, I went to the blue front door. I wasn't expecting anyone because everyone we knew would ring first – even the neighbours who would drop by had been 'trained' to send a text or call beforehand – no one turned up without notice any more. I'd walked to the door with anxiety on my heels. I'd seen a single magpie sitting on the fence this morning as I washed up after breakfast. Then another of those black and white birds was hopping around the garden when I came in from the school run.

When I opened the door and saw who was standing there, three people who had no real business being on my doorstep, I remembered the salt I spilt at dinner the other night that I'd simply brushed away instead of chucking a pinch of over my shoulder. I thought of the ladder I walked under last month before I even realised I'd done it. I recalled all the

6

cracks in all the pavements I'd been stepping on all my life without a single thought for what they might do, how they might fracture my world at some undefined point in the future.

One minute ago

One minute ago, I thought to myself, *Who's died?* at exactly the same time the policewoman said, 'Hello, Mrs Challey. Is your husband in?'

I nodded, and they didn't wait to be asked in, they entered and went straight for the living room as if they'd been there before, as if they regularly came storming into my life and my home without needing an invitation.

Now

And here we are, in the present, at that moment where my life is about to begin. I know it is about to begin because I can feel the world around me shifting: the air is different; the room that is like any other living room with a sofa and two armchairs, a rug and fireplace, and more pictures of the children than is strictly necessary gracing the walls, feels somehow altered now that these people are here. These *police officers* are here. My life is about to begin because I can feel around me the threads of my reality unravelling, waiting to be re-sewn into a new, unfamiliar tapestry.

'Mr Scott Challey,' the policewoman says, her mouth working in an odd fast-slow motion.

Everything has slowed down so it takes me an age to reach Cora and Anansy, to gather them to me, to hold them close while the policewoman speaks. And everything has speeded up, so a second ago the police officers were on the doorstep, now they are taking Scott's hands and handcuffing him.

The police officer continues, 'I am arresting you on suspicion of—' She stops then, pauses at the accusation, the crime that has caused all this. She doesn't seem the nervous or shy type, but apparently she is the sensitive type. She didn't seem to notice Cora and Anansy before, but now she stops and shifts her eyes slowly but briefly in their direction before giving Scott a look. An intimate stare from a complete stranger that says they share something that does not need to be spoken; theirs is a connection that does not need words. In response, Scott, whose hands are now ringed by handcuffs, whose body is rigid and upright, nods at her. He is agreeing that she will not voice it in front of the children, he is accepting that she does not need to because he already knows what this is about.

Of course he knows what this is about. In the unfolding nightmare, in the girls clinging to me, in trying to comfort them while attempting to take in everything that is happening, I have missed Scott's reaction to this: his face is anxious, unsettled – but not *horrified.* He is not responding like the rest of us are because he knew it would happen.

What is going on?

My fingers are ice-cold as I try to turn Cora's head into my body; Anansy, who has been terrified of the police since I told her if she stole something from the corner shop again they would come and take her away, has already buried her face in my side, her tears shaking my body.

'You do not have to say anything,' the policewoman continues, her eyes focused on my husband. 'But it will harm your defence if you do not mention when questioned, something which you later rely on in court.'

Will this really get to court? Surely it's a mistake? Surely.

'Anything you do say may be given in evidence.'

Scott's impassive eyes watch her as she speaks.

'Do you understand these rights as I have read them to you?' she asks. Scott replies with a half-nod, then his eyes are on me. He knows what is going on, he knew this was coming and he didn't bother to warn me.

Why? I think at him. *Why wouldn't you tell me this was going to happen?*

He doesn't reply to my silent question, instead he looks away, back to the door through which they are about to lead him.

When they have gone, I lower myself onto my knees and pull Cora and Anansy closer to me, bringing them as near as I can to make them feel safe, to make me feel safe, to protect us from the world around us that is unravelling so fast I cannot keep up.

This is where my life begins: with the sound of my daughters crying and the knowledge that my life is coming undone.

Tami

Twenty-five years ago
'What are you here for?' Scott Challey asked me. I wasn't the sort of eleven-year-old who was usually to be found waiting in the corridor to see the headmaster, so it wasn't a surprise that he asked me that.

'They want me to be on the team for something the school is taking part in for the first time ever. It's a great honour.' I was a swot. I had friends who were swots and I was in all the top sets at school. I didn't mind being a swot, it was just the way things were. 'What about you?'

'Same,' he said, shrugging and looking away.

Scott Challey was not a swot. I knew that about Scott Challey. He was clever and in all the top sets, but he was a Challey, and everyone knew the Challey family. My mum always made sure none of us left the house without an ironed uniform, perfect hair and a bag of books filled with neatly completed homework. Scott's parents thought their job was done because he was often seen at school and the letters they got home about his behaviour were proof that he went there at all (Mum said).

Whenever Mum or Dad saw one of the Challeys in the street they'd talk about them quietly afterwards but not so quietly we didn't hear. We knew that they were people you crossed over the road to avoid. But you had to pretend that wasn't why you crossed the road – they'd do you over if they thought you'd done that. They'd do you over for most things, I'd heard, but definitely for that because, I'd heard, you'd have made them work – i.e. cross the street to get you – to give you a beating, rather than just give you the beating you might have got from simply walking past them.

I wasn't sure if I believed that the school would really ask Scott to do this. He was always in trouble. Like, last week in physics Mr McCoy asked Scott to answer a question in front of everyone on the blackboard. When Scott did it, Mr McCoy said that he'd got it wrong. A few people had snickered and Scott, with his eyes all wide and wild and angry, turned around and glared at us all. Everyone stopped laughing straight away. I hadn't laughed because I knew Scott was right and Mr McCoy was wrong. When someone else put up their hand and said so, Mr McCoy had been embarrassed and said sorry to Scott. But Scott, now with his eyes narrow and mean, said, 'If you ever do that to me again, I'll cut your heart out with a spoon and feed it to my dog.' Mr McCoy didn't say or do anything. If it'd been anyone else he'd have shouted or sent them to the headmaster's office but 'cos it was Scott, he knew that Scott *would* do it if he got him into trouble. And if Scott didn't do it, he had a family who would.

'Have the school really asked you to do this thing or are you joking with me?' I asked him.

'They really asked me. What would be funny about that?'

I shrugged. 'I didn't think you'd want to do it.'

We stood in silence, listening to the voices on the other side of the headmaster's door. 'Why did you say that spoon

14

thing to Mr McCoy?' I asked Scott. I couldn't help myself. I had to know why someone would say such a thing.

'He made everyone laugh at me.'

'Not everyone laughed. I didn't laugh. Loads of people didn't laugh. More people didn't laugh than did laugh.'

'It felt like it.'

'But why did you say that? It's horrible.'

Scott shrugged. 'Something I heard my brother say.'

'But it's horrible.'

'So's my brother, I suppose.'

'OK.'

We didn't say anything again for a long time. Then I said, 'Just because your brother's horrible, doesn't mean you have to be.'

Scott stared at me. 'Doesn't it?'

'No,' I replied. 'You can be nice if you want to. Or you can be not horrible. Like, see, my sister loves teddy bears, even though she's miles older than me. I don't have to like teddy bears because she does. You don't have to be horrible because your brother is. You can be whoever you want.'

He frowned at me for ages like I'd spoken to him in another language that he didn't understand. 'Do you really think so?'

'Yeah, course.'

We didn't say anything to each other for ages and ages then I said, 'Are you going to do this thing then?'

'Dunno. Depends what my parents say. Are you?'

'I don't know, depends what my parents say.'

'So you're doing it then,' Scott told me.

'Yes, I suppose I am. And you're not doing it then,' I told him.

'No, I don't suppose I am.'

The sound of chairs moving on the other side of the door stopped me from leaning against the wall and to stand up straight instead. Scott Challey didn't, he kept leaning against the wall, because he didn't care what anyone thought of him and what he did. As the door handle turned, I saw from the corner of my eye that he pushed himself off the wall. He took his hands out of his pockets, tucked in the front of his off-white shirt, which had been hanging out like a tongue, and he stood up straight.

'Oi,' he said.

I looked at him.

He tipped his chin up at me.

I grinned at him in return. He was all right. For a Challey.

Beatrix

Call me Beatrix. All my friends do. Some of them call me Bea, of course, but that's only when they've known me a while and since we've only just met, if you don't mind, I'd like you to call me Beatrix.

It's amazing the amount of people who'll shorten your name without so much as a by your leave when they've only just met you. It's a bit of a liberty, wouldn't you say? Not that I think you'd ever take liberties like that. I simply want it to be clear that right now, I'd prefer if you called me Beatrix. Once we get to know each other, you can shorten my name, or lengthen it – but I probably won't answer if you call me Trixie. (My best friend in school, Eilise Watford, had a dog and they called it Trixie, so you can understand why I won't be answering to *that*.)

This is what I'm going to say to the man opposite me if he slips and calls me Bea. Although, out of all of the men I've met online, he's the best so far.

Yes, I'm internet dating. Well, dabbling in it. No, it's not really worked out for me. Yet. I've met four men after 'talking' to loads: one turned out to be twenty years older than he claimed to be (he'd sent me an old picture, too), one decided to tell me on our first date that he was addicted to visiting prostitutes but was sure the love of a good woman would help him to kick the habit, one claimed to be single but hadn't bothered to cover up the pale band of skin where his wedding ring usually sat, and the fourth is sitting opposite me.

Never thought I'd be doing this still, to be honest. Even after my husband ran off with some*whore* – I mean some*one* else – I thought ... I don't know, I just didn't think I'd *still* be doing this.

This man opposite me seems normal. When we 'met' online he'd been witty, he hadn't started any sex talk and had completely understood when I asked for a picture of him with a copy of that day's newspaper. I also quizzed him relentlessly about his marital status and he'd been honest enough to say he'd been married and divorced and would bring the paperwork with him if necessary to clear up any ambiguity.

This is our first 'in real life' date, and in the flesh, he's pretty hot.

We're in a very expensive restaurant in Brighton – I'm not a name-dropper so I won't tell you which – and this is the truly impressive part, he's got us a booth. You have to *know* people to get a booth, especially at such short notice, so kudos goes to him for that.

'So, Beatrix, tell me about yourself,' he says.

And I smile at him, knowing I'm going to do anything but.

Tami

I'm still shaking.

It's been two hours but I'm still shaking.

I was able to put it to one side while I held the girls and kissed them and told them it was OK. I was able to hide the shaking and confusion and the fear as they clung to me, sobbing and whimpering at what they had witnessed.

They let me take them upstairs and put them in the big bed, and they sobbed and clung to me a while longer as I sat between them, stroking both their heads until slowly, carefully, the sobbing stopped and they drifted off to sleep.

I used to love this happening when they were littlies and neither of them would sleep through the night: we'd all end up in the big bed, a tessellation – complex and delicate – of bodies needing sleep. Scott hated having to sleep on the edge of the bed but I secretly loved it. Yes, I could never allow myself to fall into a deep sleep in case one of them rolled over or crawled off the bed but we were all together, all close, all sharing our time together even though we weren't awake.

After climbing out of the space between them, I sat on the top step, where I haven't moved from, my mobile on one side of me, the house phone on the other, shaking. I curl my fingers into my palms to stop my hands trembling, but the rest of me is still at it.

I don't need to glance down at either phone to know that Scott hasn't rung or texted me. I don't need to, but I do, in case I've missed something, in case I didn't hear.

The look on his face as they led him away . . . There was something on his face, in his eyes, latticed in the language of his body. My mind won't settle long enough for me to decipher what it was, but it was there and it should not have been. The Scott I knew, loved, married, had children with would not have had that look. My brain is racing ahead, racing back. Whizzing and popping, too much, too fast for me to keep a single thought for too long. This is too much. I unfurl my hands, watch them quiver in the half-light of the hallway.

I need to do something. Anything. Sitting here, waiting, is going to cause my mind to implode. The trembling stops when I pick up my mobile and log onto the internet, find the number for Brighton Police Station. There are two, one in Hove, the other in Brighton. Where would they have taken him? Hove is nearer but Brighton is bigger.

Distance wins over size. The shaking returns, though, as I dial the number. It increases as the person who answers the phone checks to see if he's there. He's not. He must be at Brighton. I call the other number. They can confirm he's there. I cannot speak to him. They will not tell me why he was arrested, they will not let me know if he has been charged. They cannot tell me when or if he'll be released. The only thing they'll tell me is that he is there. I need to know more.

Should I go down there? is the punctuation to every heartbeat. *They won't be able to ignore someone who's right in front of them.*

22

It's late, there are only two people near enough who can sit with the girls at such short notice. Beatrix, the one they've known the longest and who lives at the diagonal opposite side of our bottle-shaped road, is out on a date tonight. I've tried her phone anyway on the off-chance her date's been cancelled or she's come home early, but it keeps saying her phone is switched off and you can't leave a message. If she was here instead of me and the girls woke up, they'd be fine. They've known her all their lives, they call her Bix, she's Anansy's godmother and they both miss her when she's not here. I'd have no worries about not being here if she was.

The other person is Mirabelle. The girls love her, in a different way to Beatrix. They call her Auntie Mirabelle but she's only been in their lives for two years, since she and I became friends. She works with Scott and spends time here with the girls, but never without me somewhere nearby. I'm not sure how they'd react to her being here if they woke up, nor how she would react to having to comfort them at a time like this.

The silent phones continue their passive mocking of my ignorance. I have no choice. If I want to know what's going on, I'm going to have to go down there. Maybe the shaking will stop if I find out more – if I do something.

I call up Mirabelle's number on my mobile, then press dial. The phone rings out and then, 'Hi, this is Mirabelle, leave me a message.' I hang up. Then try again. Nothing. I try again. Nothing. The fourth time, her distracted voice answers, 'Hello?'

'Mirabelle, it's me,' I say, so relieved tears cram themselves into my eyes. 'Thank God you're there.'

'Tami?' she asks cautiously. 'What's up?'

The familiarity of her voice causes tears to overwhelm my vocal cords, my words, my ability to speak. It's replaying on loop in my head: the handcuffs on his wrists, the police officers leading him away, the look on his face I cannot name. 'I, erm, I need your help,' I say, trying to control myself, trying to bury the fragile, fractured, almost broken tone in my voice. I want to be stronger than this. I want to take charge and show no weakness.

'What's the matter?' she asks carefully. I can imagine her light hazel eyes narrowing in the dark skin of her face as she awaits my answer.

'I—I . . . Can you come over? It'll be easier face to face.'

'Well, um, not really, I'm not exactly dressed to go out. Can't you tell me what's wrong on the phone?'

'Um . . . No. Please, I really need your help.'

'I . . . um . . . Are you alone?'

'No, the girls are here, but Scott's not.' I say his name and crack myself. Break myself into tiny little fragments that glint from their scattered places on the corridor floor. I am sobbing silently, the inhalations of my tears, soft enough not to wake the girls, but strong enough to be heard on the phone.

'OK, I'm coming,' she says. 'Just give me a chance to get dressed.'

I can't even say thank you as I hang up the phone.

Twenty-four years ago

It didn't seem fair. I was the only girl in the class to not get a Valentine's card. Even Kim Meekson who sat at the back of the class picking her nose and eating the bogeys got a card but not me. Genevieve, my sister, had five pushed through the door this morning and Sarto, my brother, had eight. I had a big fat zero. I thought maybe when they opened the red postbox that sat next to my form tutor Miss Harliss's desk, there might be at least one for me. Nope. Nothing there, either.

After the box was emptied and there was none for me, I looked around, saw that I was different and felt really small inside. My throat got lumpy but I couldn't let anyone see it mattered. Phyllis Latan, my best friend, who sat next to me, said, 'You can share mine.' I didn't want to, hers was from Harry Nantes who smelt because he didn't wash his hair, but it was nice of her, so I held the card for a bit then had to give it back because I could tell she thought I was going to keep it.

No one liked me. No one. I didn't really want boys to like me like that, but I didn't want no one to like me so I was the only person who didn't get a card. I was probably the only girl in the whole of the school who didn't get one.

I dragged my feet going home and as I turned the corner to my road, I knew Genevieve and Sarto were going to laugh at me for weeks and weeks. It was bad enough I was the youngest, this was going to be the newest thing to make fun of me about.

Scott was suddenly there. He was standing in front of me as scruffy as he always was: I mean, there was no point in him wearing his tie when it was almost off, and his shirt – peeking out from under his school coat – had mud smudges all over it. His red jumper was tied around his waist and his grey trousers were mud-smudged, too.

He didn't say or do anything for a few seconds, then 'Here,' he said, shoving a red envelope at me. I didn't even get the chance to say, 'What is it?' before he took off, his black leather Head bag, slung on his shoulder with football boots tied to the handle, bobbing as he ran. I stood watching him go, and didn't look down at the envelope until he'd turned the corner at the end of my street.

I opened the envelope and inside was a card with a white bear holding a big red heart on the front. 'Happy Valentine's Day,' the front read. 'Your secret admirer' it continued inside.

Scott had neatly written:

You're all right, you.

I knew what he meant: he didn't like me like Harry liked Phyllis, he just didn't want me to be sad or be the only girl in the world without any Valentine cards.

Coat. Shoes. Bag. Mobile. Purse. Cash. Keys.

Twenty-four years ago

'What were you doing with that Challey boy?' Genevieve asked me after dinner.

'What do you mean?'

'I saw you, from the bedroom window. He was standing there talking to you. It looked like he gave you a card. What were you doing with him?'

'Nothing,' I said.

'Stay away from him, Tami,' she said.

'I'm not coming near him. He was outside when I got home.'

'Did he ask you out?'

'No!'

'Look, stay away from him or I'll tell Mummy and Daddy.'

'Tell them what you want!' I said. 'I haven't done anything.'

'His family are really racist, you know.'

'Why does that matter to me? I've only spoken to him once in my life and then earlier. That's all.'

'Tami, trust me, he's trouble. Just stay away from him.'

I shrugged at her because my big sister knew nothing when it came to this. I didn't like him, he didn't like me. We hadn't spoken since the day outside the headmaster's office and we wouldn't speak again, probably. He was just being nice, that's all. Yes, he was a Challey and yes, they were all – including him – nothing but trouble, but even a Challey was allowed to be nice at least once in their lives, weren't they?

Mirabelle arrives at the house sooner than I thought she would. She is in the gold jogging suit I dared her to buy when we were out looking for a new running outfit for me.

'I have no shame, surely you know that by now,' she'd said and found her size on the rail.

'What, you going to get a gold tooth to match that?' I'd said to her.

'Don't tempt me,' she'd replied.

Over her jogging suit she has tied up her bright red mac and she has grey furry Ugg boots on her feet, her masses of curly hair is pulled up and back, secured with a scrunchie so her hair falls like water from a fountain all over her head. I can tell she's just washed her face. Probably getting ready for bed when I called.

'What's happened?' she asks. Her concern turns to alarm when she sees I'm in my black mac with my red and white trainers on my feet. 'Where are you going?'

I have called a taxi instead of driving because I don't think I could stop myself shaking long enough to get the key into the ignition let alone select the right gear, remember to use my mirror or even recall what to do at junctions.

The taxi draws up outside, and I wave to the driver over Mirabelle's shoulder. She turns to look at the white-haired man who nods in reply to my wave and sits patiently in the driver's seat waiting for me.

'What is going on? Where are you going?'

'Scott's been arrested,' I state. See, if I state things, say them matter-of-factly, they won't break me.

'What?' She draws back. 'What?'

'Scott's been arrested.' Simple statement. No shattering. 'I don't know what for, but I'm going to the police station.' Simple-ish statement. 'I need you to stay here in case the girls wake up before I get back.' Slightly complex statement, but still not falling apart.

'What? No.' She shakes her head firmly, decidedly. 'No.'

'Please, you have to. I won't be long.' *I hope.* 'If they wake up, call me and I'll dash back.'

'Didn't you hear me? No. You can't ask me to do this,' she says, her bewilderment clear. 'I don't want to be involved in this.'

'Please, there's no one else. I'll be as quick as I can. They'll most likely sleep through. Please.' I am halfway out of the door. She has to do this for me: I would do it for her in a heartbeat. Friendships grow from small acts of kindness as well as from big favours and we are friends – she has to do this, there really is no one else I would trust with the girls.

'This isn't right or fair you know, Tami.'

'I'm sorry, I'm sorry. I'll make it up to you. Help yourself to anything in the kitchen. I'll be back as soon as I can. I promise. Thank you. Thank you. Thank you.'

I dash down the path and into the taxi before she has a chance to tell me no again. Because if she does that, this time, I may just believe her.

Eighteen years ago

'Hello, Tamia Berize, you all right?' he said to me. I was at one of the more pleasant bus stops in Lewisham – there were only two spots of chewing gum on the cloudy, cracked plastic 'glass' of the shelter, the seats were only a little drawn on and dirtied, two of the posters were still intact.

My face beamed when I saw him. 'Wow, talk about a blast from the past,' I said, my grin growing wider. I hadn't seen him in years. 'How you doing?'

'Good, good.' Scott Challey, all grown up. I hadn't seen him since we both finished our GCSEs and I went off to sixth-form college and he stayed on at school. From the little boy who could never stay clean and tidy, he'd grown into a young man who dressed well – smart, navy blue jeans, a white T-shirt and long, black coat. His once-wild hair was now tamed with a stylish long-on-top cut. I'd heard he'd gone to university from my mother who'd said in despair that she couldn't understand how someone from his family went while I didn't. I'd heard from other people I went to school with that his family hadn't wanted him to go. When he'd brought his UCAS form home it'd got thrown out with the rubbish. When his teachers tried to explain that it was an opportunity like no other, they'd been thrown out with a fair few swearwords lining their ears. It was only his grandmother who intervened. She wielded the ultimate power in that family, apparently. When she spoke – which hadn't been frequently – they listened and they did. 'Young Scott's going to university,' I heard, she'd said. And that was that.

'You look all grown up. Am quite impressed.'

'I look grown up? You're a full-formed adult. I suppose that's because you've got a job and can afford to buy clothes and things.'

'You're not exactly naked, are you?'

'Ahh, but it's different when you're working. How did your parents take you not going to university?'

I shrugged. 'Still haven't calmed down. I think they've convinced themselves I'm going to see how hard it is working and decide to go to university next year.'

'And will you?'

'Erm . . . no. I've got a great job. Lots of chances for advancement. I'm really enjoying it. But if it makes them happy to think that uni is on the cards, who am I to disabuse them of those ideas?'

'"Disabuse". Look at you with your fancy words. So what's this job of yours then? Compiling a dictionary? Are you going to be moving on to the thesaurus department next?'

I laughed. 'No, I work in the corporate communications department of TelmeCo.'

'The huge phone company?'

'Phones, mobile phones and the world wide web thing.'

'Wow, I am seriously impressed. What do you do, make tea?'

'Yes, and the rest, you cheeky sod.'

'Seriously, what do you do?'

'Lots of little things, mainly helping out, but I've been given the newsletter to write. I have to do it on the computer and on their intranet. It's great fun. Plus I'm learning so much. If I keep my head down, focus, I reckon I could be running the place in, ohhhh, six months.'

His laughter was a thick and throaty sound that lit up his face in a way I hadn't seen him illuminated before. 'Shift up,' he instructed as he plonked himself down beside me.

'And how's university treating you?'

'Yeah, it's good, it's good. Great chance to reinvent yourself, university. Not many people know what the Challey name means over there. I like that a lot.'

'I take it you're back to visit the folks, though?'

'Yeah. Something like that. Actually, it's my grandmother's funeral.'

'Oh, I'm sorry.'

'It's fine,' he said. 'She was the main reason I used to visit. Now, I've got no real reason to. Every time I come back I'm reminded why I left in the first place and why I never want to return.'

'It's not that bad,' I said, nudging him with my shoulder.

It was that bad, from everything I'd heard, but I didn't like the sheer agony talking about it dragged across his face.

He raised his dark eyebrows at me. 'Isn't it?'

'I'd hope not,' I conceded.

'Funny, isn't it?' Scott said. 'We've both let our families down in pretty significant ways – and we didn't even need to go to prison to do it.'

I laughed again. 'You're not wrong, are you? Sometimes I do have to remind myself that I haven't actually committed a crime, the way my parents carry on.'

'Me too. Except that's the disappointing thing.'

'Misfits and outcasts, that's me and you.'

'Yeah.'

'The problem, though, as far as my parents are concerned, is that I don't actually care that I haven't lived up to their expectations. They think I wasted my brain and all the sacrifices they made for me to go to school. But like I said to you way back when, you don't have to do something just because someone else wants you to do it. You can be whoever you want to be.'

'You know, TB, you changed my life when you said that to me. I asked Grandma Cora if you were right and she said yes. I said could I go to university one day then and she said yes. It was her who told my parents I was going and there were to be no arguments. Even though they wanted me out bringing in money, they agreed. All thanks to you.'

'That's me all over – life changer, parent disappointer.'

'All round perfect woman.'

I burst out laughing, it sounded so ridiculous coming

32

from his mouth. 'Good one! I may have that put on a T-shirt.'
I moved my hand in front of my chest. '"All round perfect
woman". I like that. I like that a lot.'

'See, there was a reason I went to uni.'

'OK,' I said to him, 'here's my bus. I'm off into Croydon
to find a killer outfit that won't cost the Earth for tonight.'

'Why, what's tonight?'

'First date with the most gorgeous man in the world,' I
said, standing.

'Really? I didn't know we were going out tonight.'

'You!'

'Can I come with you? Give you a man's eye view on what
you choose?'

'Sure. But you're going to be so bored. I always go back
and forth to a million shops before I buy the first thing I
tried on in the first shop I went into.'

'That's OK, I'm not busy till later, either.'

'Ohhhh ... Date with a gorgeous woman?'

'Oh yes,' he replied, a filthy grin spreading across his face.

'One of those sort of dates, I see?'

'Yep,' he replied.

'Well good for you.'

'Good for both of us, it seems, TB. Good for both of us.'

In my life, I haven't had much cause to be involved with the
police. I haven't been the victim of a crime I would consider
reporting – someone once stole some change and a satnav
out of my car when I didn't properly shut the driver-side door
– and I haven't committed a crime that I could be arrested

for. Yet, here I am walking through the automatic glass doors into a large reception area at the police station in Brighton. It is a huge beige and white building that from the outside looks like a long, low block of flats.

Steeling myself, forcing the shaking away, I walk up to the large, curved wooden counter that seems designed to put the average person at a disadvantage – you have to look up slightly to talk to the person behind it. And they look down on you to speak.

'Hello,' I say to the man behind the desk.

He is older than me, probably not far off retirement. His jowls are starting to show beneath the soft lines of his pale, aged face. His head is covered with grey-white hair and he is slightly overweight, but not so he'd need to do anything drastic. He leans on the desk and raises his white eyebrows at me rather than speak.

'My husband was brought in earlier, erm, under arrest. I was wondering if I could see him?'

The policeman puts his head to one side and looks at me with what are kindly eyes; he seems to have the capacity to be gentle and probably calming, too.

'What's his name?' he asks.

'Scott Challey.' A lump closes up my throat the second those words are out of my mouth. Scott Challey. Scott Challey. Scott Challey.

'Ah, yes, Mr Challey. Brought in a couple of hours ago,' he says without looking at his computer or the book I'd imagined they had for writing down who they'd carted off in front of their family. 'Yes, he's here.'

I didn't ask that, I asked if I could see him, I think. 'Can I see him?'

His expression becomes the equivalent of someone taking your hand before they impart bad news as he shakes his head slightly and he says, 'I'm sorry, Madam, that won't be possible, he's still being questioned.'

'What's he being questioned for?' I ask. 'And how much longer will it take?'

'I'm afraid I can't tell you either of those things,' he replies.

'Can't or won't?' I reply, in frustration.

'I'm sorry, Madam.'

I curl my hands into my palms again, to stop myself shaking and to stop myself wailing. I want to throw my head back and let out a huge, primal scream that empties my body and soul of all the emotions racing around them. I don't understand why this is happening, why my life is unravelling, and I don't understand why this man won't help me.

'Can I at least see the detective who arrested him?' I ask.

'I'd imagine she is questioning your husband right now.'

'Please? I only want to talk to her. If I can't talk to him then she'll have to do. I just want to know from someone who's seen him that he's OK. If she tells me he's all right, I can go and take care of my children and wait for him to come home. Please? Please?' I don't like to beg, but sometimes, that's all you can do. Sometimes, the ends justify the means.

The Kindly Policeman's kindly eyes study me for a few long moments. He can see the panic, fear and confusion on my face. Part of me still thinks this is not happening, that I am not standing in a police station asking a kindly policeman to let me speak to the detective that arrested my husband. I do not live the sort of life where my husband is arrested, so that's why I am still struggling to believe this is happening.

'I'll see what I can do,' the Kindly Policeman says, 'please take a seat.' He nods towards the bank of seats near the door. I need to keep upright – I'll seem weaker, less effective if I sit down. He nods again towards the seats and I know I have to do as he asks or he won't try very hard at all to see what he can do. Not so kindly after all, then.

I go to the seats, settle myself between a man so thin and ravaged – probably by drugs and drink – I'm not sure how he walks without snapping, and a white-bearded man who is wide in girth because he is wearing everything he owns. Every item the white-bearded man wears is encrusted with black dirt, as are his hands, fingerless gloves and shabby, holey shoes. He's giving off a smell combination of stale urine, sweat, dirt and beer that hits the back of my throat and then trickles down, turning my stomach every time I breathe in.

The policeman actually waits for me to sit before raising the handset of the phone beside him. He stares at me as he pushes three buttons, then continues to stare at me until the phone is answered. Then, he twists away while he talks quietly into the phone, presumably so I can't read his lips and find out what he's saying.

I feel sick.

Properly sick, not just a bit nauseous – I am seconds away from throwing up. It's not only because of the man sitting next to me, it's the slow, creeping dawn of reality: Scott has been arrested and the children have been traumatised by seeing that. I want to call Mirabelle and find out if the girls are OK, but I daren't in case they wake up and I'm forced to go home before I can get some idea of what exactly is happening.

My eyes lock with the Kindly Policeman's and his register pity. Pure, unadulterated pity. '*I've seen this a million times before,*' his expression is saying. '*Some poor deluded wife who has no idea what her husband is like, coming here, wanting to make sure he's OK, when all along he is a prolific criminal with a double life; someone who deserves to be behind bars.*'

I want to say in reply that he has no idea about me or my life, that I am not easily deluded and Scott is not a criminal. He may have come from criminal stock, but he is not one. But that look, that unnameable look I saw on Scott's face, keeps barging its way into my mind. I lower my gaze because there is something going on that I don't yet know about.

'Mrs Challey?' the policeman says.

My two companions turn their heads towards me in unison, then both jerk their heads towards the Kindly Policeman, telling me I am being called, and to go find out why.

'You'll be all right, girl,' says the thin man.

'Tell 'em nothing,' says the many-layered man.

Rising from my seat, I walk on rubberised legs towards the desk.

'Detective Sergeant Harvan said it's highly unusual but she'll be with you as soon as she can,' he tells me.

'Thank you,' I reply.

'Take a seat.'

I nod, and return to my crew. 'Told you you'd be all right,' the thin man says as I sit down again.

'Good girl, you didn't tell them anything did you?' says the many-layered man.

Scott and I are going to laugh about this one day. We're going to laugh and laugh and laugh.

Seventeen years ago
'Aren't you sick of just being friends?' he asked me.

We were in my bedsit, a nicely-decorated large room with separate bathroom and loo, and a kitchen area – which had really classy wooden worktops – that I could screen off from the main sitting room/bedroom with a large, cream curtain. Living with my parents had got too much since it'd dawned on them that I definitely wasn't going to university. Sarto was still living there, enjoying all the benefits while he went to medical school, and that was fine. Anyone could live there relatively unbothered if they were studying, but I was not doing that. I was a constant reminder of how they had failed – the one who found book stuff the easiest was the one who had turned her back on it. I loved working, I loved my job, and I'd been promoted several times in the last eighteen months but that all counted for nothing – as far as my parents were concerned – because I was without a degree.

Whenever Scott returned to London from university in Essex, he would find me. We would spend our free time together, mainly hanging out in my bedsit, eating crisps and watching videos, then at the end of the holidays he would go back to university and we wouldn't keep in touch. It wasn't that kind of friendship.

'How can I be sick of being friends?' I replied. 'You're a wonderful friend.'

His dark eyes grew a bit wider, and his lips entwined themselves into a wry little smile. 'I mean, don't you fancy having sex with me? Once or maybe even a few times? But you knew that's what I meant, didn't you?'

'Yes, I knew that.'

'You just wanted me to say it out loud?'

'Partly. I also wanted to give myself the chance to think about whether I wanted to have sex with you.'

'And?'

'I don't think I do, actually.'

He was surprised and then immediately hurt, his face flushing red. 'Not even a little bit?' he asked, a tad less confidently. 'I get vibes off you sometimes . . . I was wrong?'

'No, no.' I rested my hand on his arm and a streak of desire shot through me, pooling in the space beneath my ribcage and between my legs. Scott did that to me even when I wasn't touching him. 'You're not in any way wrong. I . . . I think I'm having too much fun seeing different people to want to, you know, have a boyfriend. Settle down. Especially with a guy who isn't here most of the time.'

'I wasn't talking about that.'

'Yes you were.'

His soft, pink lips twisted a little more. 'Yes, I was. But not intentionally.'

I took my hand away, sat back on the beanbag and picked up my packet of crisps. 'That's not for me right now. Sorry.'

'You don't see yourself going out with a white man, let alone settling down with him, do you?' Scott said.

I couldn't help but sigh. He had to bring it up, didn't he? He couldn't leave it as it stood that I didn't want to sleep with him. 'I don't think of you as a white person. You're just Scott.'

'But it's true, isn't it? If I was black, you'd think a bit more deeply about going out with me.'

'And if I was white, you'd have asked me out properly instead of asking about sex, wouldn't you?' I snapped back. This was not a conversation I wanted to have, but he'd pushed it, he'd gone onto that precarious-looking spot of an old, rickety floor and had caused the whole thing to cave in. And because of that, we were tumbling through space with no idea where and when we were going to land, nor how we were going to be damaged by the fall. 'Because in your head, if it doesn't work out the way you want it to, you can always say it was just sex – nothing important, nothing to get upset about. You wouldn't try to bed a white girl in the way you've tried to bed me so please don't try to turn this on me.'

He pressed his lips even tighter together, his gaze holding mine. I challenged him in return to deny it, to say that wasn't the case.

I circled my finger around the room, encompassing us in the invisible shape that I was drawing. 'This whole thing, our friendship, our spending time together here, it's all because you're not comfortable with being seen with me. I'd even go as far as to say you're ashamed of being seen with me.'

'No!' he protested. 'That's not true at all. It's got nothing to do with being ashamed of being seen with you.'

'Then what is it?' I replied. 'Because it's something to do with me being black. I'd say it's to do with you being white, but you don't see that as an issue, so I'm guessing you see me as the "problem".'

'There is no problem. I . . . I just find it hard, how we're treated when we're together. All my life, I've either had people be afraid of me because of my family, or treat me like anybody else because no one in Essex really knows what the Challeys are all about. But when I'm with you ... I've never been treated with such rudeness and disregard as I am when I'm around you. The way people ignore you, or say things right to your face. It makes me so angry. And I don't like to be angry. I find it hard to control myself when I'm angry.'

'Fair enough,' I replied.

'So, no, it's not you. It's everyone else.'

'OK.'

'I'd be proud to be your boyfriend. If you'd have me.'

His skin was smooth, warm, silky almost, as I stroked my thumb across his cheekbone. Desire thunderbolted through me again. 'Not right now, eh?' I said, the gentlest way I could think of letting him down. He wasn't being completely honest with me. What he said might have been partially the truth, but it wasn't all of it and I wasn't getting involved with a man who wouldn't be one hundred per cent honest with me, no matter how unpalatable that truth was. That path was the one taken by women who wanted to have their hearts broken and their minds messed with. I wanted neither for myself. 'There are loads of women out there who are desperate to be with you, let's carry on having fun as friends and leave it at that for now, eh?'

Scott's brown eyes lowered themselves from my gaze and then he shifted in his seat to face and watch the television. 'OK. Sure. Fine,' he mumbled.

*

I have lived and waited a lifetime in the two hours I've been here. All the while avoiding my phone. It is burning an accusatory hole in my bag. I should have called Mirabelle by now. I texted her when I got out of the taxi to say where I was, then I texted her half an hour later to ask if the girls were still asleep, and she replied 'yes'. Now it is over an hour later and I don't know what is going on either here or there.

I should not be here. I know that. I should be at home, but I can't go home until I know he is OK. As long as they stay asleep, they'll be fine. I so want to sleep. I so want to curl up and sleep and know this is not happening in my life.

Sixteen years ago
'What are you doing with *that*?' he said to Scott. His sneer smeared his words, curled up his lip and caused his eyes to snake nastily over me.

Scott and I were leaning against a wall, waiting for a bus into Wimbledon. I seemed to do nothing but wait for buses in my life outside of work, and when Scott was back from college that didn't change.

'What did you say?' Scott asked conversationally, the barest hint of an edge to his voice.

His brother repeated his scrutiny, the disgust of his gaze sliming over me once again. I didn't glance away, as he expected. I wasn't an idiot so I didn't glare at him or narrow my eyes at him – didn't want to aggravate him further – but I wasn't going to let him intimidate me. 'What. Are. You. Doing. With. That,' he said again.

Scott glared at his brother, a fox-faced man who wore the

ravages of his life on his face: he'd been glassed or slashed on more than one occasion and as a result his left cheekbone was a patchwork of badly put together stitches, while the bottom of the right side of his jaw held a puckering of scarred skin. His right eyebrow was dissected in three places.

Scott leaned over to me, looked into my eyes for a moment too brief for me to communicate anything, and he covered my lips with his. His kiss went on a fraction too long, his lips a bit too insistent and firm against mine, for him to be just making a point to the man in front of us.

'You mean my girlfriend?' Scott replied as he straightened up, staring down his older sibling.

The sneer on his brother's face deepened, but he'd stopped staring at me, he was focusing on Scott. 'What's the matter, can't get one of your own kind to suck your cock so you have to go slumming it?' His brother was being quite restrained, I suspected, because there were people – also known as witnesses – at the bus stop. He wouldn't think we were worth going back to prison for.

'At least my own kind are humans,' Scott replied. 'Out of interest, which species of animal are you getting your kicks from nowadays?'

His brother's entire body became a rigid mass of anger, his face filling with puce-red rage. 'Say that again,' he snarled.

'Why, too clever for you?'

'You're not too big for me to put you down, *boy*, don't forget that.'

'Yeah, funny how you stopped doing that the second I got big enough to hit back,' Scott replied. His voice, which had

43

been smoothed and shaped by his time in university, had taken a step back into his youth, to the part of London where we'd grown up.

'Don't push me, *boy*,' his brother growled.

'Who's pushing?'

'I see you with *that* again, you're going to wish you'd never been born,' his brother said. As punctuation to his threat, he snorted then spat at our feet.

'Scared, that's me,' Scott replied.

'You've been warned, *boy*. Just watch yourself.' That last sentence was aimed at both of us before he marched away.

I finally understood what it was about Scott. I reached out and took his hand in mine. I finally understood that it wasn't everyone else that made him so cautious about going out with me, it was his family and what they might do to me.

As soon as my flat door shut behind us, the world – his family – firmly on the other side, we reached for each other; moving at exactly the same time, our lips meeting at exactly the centre of the space between us. Our mouths kissed slowly as we undressed each other; nothing rushed or forced, just fluid, and simple; uncluttered by talk and plans and thoughts of what next.

In the bed, we gently groaned as we became one. We clung to each other, afraid to let each other go; afraid to let anything, even air, come between us and break, for even a second, our connection. We whispered into each other's skin; we moaned each other's names, turning them into epitaphs of pleasure; we moved our bodies together, trying to stay as one.

'I really didn't want that to end,' Scott said to me afterwards, his hand lazily stroking my stomach while his fingers inter-mittently circled my belly button.

'Hmmm,' I heard myself reply, my hand slowly tracing a path back and forth across the hair-covered line of his inner left thigh.

'It's OK, isn't it, that I've fallen in love with you?' he asked.

'Hmmmm,' I replied, dreamily, ignoring the unease that flurried mutely but resolutely at the pit of my stomach. Scott immediately turned his head towards me, leaving a deep groove in the under-stuffed pillow he rested on.

'Regrets?' he asked, sounding small and scared. Nothing like the man who'd faced down his terrifying brother earlier.

'No,' I replied, turning my head towards him. He was vulner-able, unsure, so unlike the man I'd come to know. He usually had the confidence of someone who'd had to stand up for himself from an early age. I put my hand on his face, to reas-sure him, to touch him, to get back what we'd been sharing a few minutes ago. 'No regrets.' *I just wish we'd done that for us. That we hadn't been pushed into it because of your idiot brother.* But then, what were we waiting for? What difference would a month or a year make? Except to waste more time. If we did this now, we could be over in the blink of an eye. We could be the itch that we'd both needed to scratch for a while. And once that itch was scratched, we could leave it behind us.

'It's OK, isn't it, that I've fallen in love with you?' he repeated.

No scratches here. No leaving this behind. Just this: us.

'Yes,' I replied. 'I think I've fallen in love with you, too.'

*

45

My two mates have gone; the many-layered one was turfed out, the thin one was taken into the back. I never knew what they were here for, but without them, I'm lonely. This waiting is not good for my mind. Too much time to think unravels more of the denial I have been hiding in.

If it's all a mistake, why isn't he out yet? The longer he's in there, the worse it feels.

Last time I waited this long was when Cora had to have surgery last year. I thought I was going to go crazy, sitting in her room, waiting to find out what was happening. Scott had been called in to work at the last minute, my parents were looking after Anansy, so I was on my own then, too. On my own, waiting to hear if one of the people I loved most in the world would be returned to me in one piece.

BUZZZ! of the door beside the reception desk makes me look up. And the policewoman who read Scott his rights and ordered him to be taken away is there. She meets my eye across the reception and her face softens into a small, sad smile.

That smile, its sympathy and understanding, hits me in the centre of my chest and I physically recoil. I wasn't expecting that. Surely police officers don't smile like that at the wives of men they've arrested?

'Mrs Challey,' she says warmly as she comes towards me. 'I'm so sorry to have kept you waiting. I was tied up and really couldn't get away. I'm sorry.'

'How's Scott?' I ask. The words are too heavy for my wafer-thin voice to project: they sink in the silence of the empty reception area once they leave my mouth.

She draws herself a little more upright, inhales deeply,

then exhales deeply. 'He's . . . he's all right, under the circumstances.'

'Will he be able to come home soon?' I ask. 'I mean, what time should I book the taxi for?'

Her forehead becomes a confused frown, and her eyes level on mine. 'Um . . .' She grimaces slightly, then points to the seating area. 'Come take a seat, Mrs Challey.'

'I don't want to take a seat, I've been sitting here all night. My children are traumatised, and I need to be with them. But first, I need to know when I can take my husband home and when this dreadful mess is going to be sorted out.'

'Mrs Challey—'

'Stop saying my name like that.'

'Like what?' she asks, alarmed.

'Like . . . Like I'm simple and won't understand things unless you speak very carefully.'

'I'm sorry, I didn't realise I was doing that.'

'Well you are. You're treating me like I'm an idiot. I don't know why, but I want you to stop it. I am not an idiot.'

'I know you're not. I'm sorry that this is happening to you, I really am. But . . .' She seems unsure of herself again. There was none of this earlier when she was reading Scott his rights, but this confusion, hesitancy, does seem genuine, as if she doesn't want to do this. 'Your husband is being kept in overnight and will be questioned again in the morning. We want to give him a chance to change his mind and get a solicitor. After that, it's likely he'll be sent to court for arraignment, which is the formal reading of charges.'

'What?' I ask. I'm suddenly in a long, wide tunnel and feeling the vibrations of speech through the air, not really hearing them. 'What?' I repeat. 'He's being charged? Sent to court? What? What is going on? What are you—' My bag slips from my fingers to the ground, and I push my hands into my hair. 'What are you saying to me? He's getting—' I tug on handfuls of my shoulder-length twists, feeling the pain of it in my scalp. 'He's being held overnight and getting sent to court because of a speeding ticket?'

'Speeding ticket?' she repeats.

'I know Scott drives too fast, and he's been caught a few times on cameras and he doesn't always pay his fines on time but this isn't . . . Unless . . .' I lower my hands as a new thought grows in my mind. 'Did he hit someone? Is that what this is about? Did he hit someone and they're badly hurt? Because, you know, I can promise you that he wouldn't have meant it. It would have been a complete accident. You can't keep—'

'Mrs Challey,' the police officer cuts in, sternly. This time she says my name like she knows she isn't dealing with an idiot – she simply wants to stop my rambling. 'I'm sorry to have to tell you this but your husband isn't being held because of speeding, and as far as we know, he hasn't hit anyone with his car.'

I am silent as she shifts uncomfortably from one foot to the other. The ponytail of smooth, chestnut hair she had earlier is gone: her hair is messy and scatty – as if she's been in a fight.

My mind is already racing through all the other crimes he could have been capable of because there aren't that many that Scott could have committed. Maybe Grand Larceny, but we have money. I know how much he earns, how much I earn, that we have enough to live a fantastic life on – he wouldn't need to steal it. Surely?

Detective Sergeant Harvan pauses a moment longer before she tells me what my husband has been accused of. And as she talks, the words echoing to me through that long, wide tunnel again, my body grows still and cold. With every word I become frozen, petrified. When she has finished, she asks if I am OK, if I understand what she has said to me, and because I am unable to move under my own steam, she takes my arm and walks me to the seats, deposits me there before leaving me alone.

This is not happening. I have accidentally stepped into someone else's life and this should all be happening to them and their family, not to me and mine.

The policewoman is gone, the Kindly Policeman behind the counter is watching me warily in case I freak out. But I am not going to do that, I am not going to freak out. Why would I? This is not my life, this is not happening.

Suddenly I am on my feet, darting across the reception area to snatch up my bag, and then fleeing into the night. Running away from the police station and down the hill towards the train station where I can get a taxi. I am too scared to call for one, I am too scared to stop for a moment because it may not be my life, it should be happening to someone else, but until I get my life back, until this is happening to the person it is meant to be happening to, I have to deal with this. I have to live in this life. I have to get home.

As I run, my body cutting through the cool night air, my heart too scared to beat properly in my chest, the policewoman's words still resonate through me. They drive every step, pushing me to sprint faster than I have ever done in my life.

'I'm very sorry to have to tell you this, Mrs Challey, but your husband is being questioned in connection with a very serious crime. He has been arrested for a serious sexual assault. What I'm saying is, he's most likely going to be charged with the attempted rape of his work colleague and neighbour, Mirabelle Kemini.'

Beatrix

'So, Beatrix, tell me about yourself,' he asks.

'I'm not going to do that,' I reply with a grin. 'It's all a bit fake when people do that. I prefer to get to know people over time, slowly.'

You want to know what he looks like? He's tall, taller than me, but that doesn't mean much because I only just clear 5ft 4 myself. He's got a nice body, not gym-sculpted or anything extreme, his body shows he is comfortable in his own skin, if that makes sense? He's got a slight paunch, but that adds to the 'real' quality he has. His hair is black, his skin is white – pink, but you know what I mean – and his eyes are brown. His arrangement of features is one that definitely places him in the 'hot' category of men, but it's hard to get across that he's ordinary-looking too: straight nose, nice-shaped eyes, normal mouth. He's nice, is what I'm trying to say.

I would sleep with him, is what I'm really trying to say, if it was only down to looks and how he comes across on the Net. In real life, it's all a bit flat. I was expecting fireworks, or at least a spark. Flatline, instead.

'I take your point,' he says. 'You see, from that, I could infer that you want to see me again, I could grasp that and cling to it, thinking that you might have changed your mind in the last few minutes.'

'Changed my mind about what?'

'Me. You. The possibilities of anything happening beyond tonight.'

'Ah. You felt the absence of a spark, too?'

'Not at all. I'm sparking all over the place. However, your face and your body language told me from the moment you walked in that you were disappointed.'

'I'm not disappointed,' I protest.

He doesn't believe me and lowers his gaze, pretending to scan the menu, a bit hurt that I won't be honest.

'It's not disappointment,' I say, covering his hand with mine. 'Honestly. I don't know what I expected doing this dating thing, but it's lost its shine for me. I've become jaded. I suppose my problem is I'm looking for love at first sight so we can leapfrog over all the getting to know each other stuff and skip to the end.'

'Ah, Last Page Syndrome,' he says with a nod and a refusal to meet my eye. 'That thing where you don't like the hard work involved in finding out the truth about something, you just want to know right now so you read the last page before you should.'

I do that with books all the time. Don't most people? 'But sometimes you need to know if a book is worth sticking with, otherwise you could be wasting your time only to be bitterly disappointed at the end,' I say. 'Plus, what if you get run over by a bus? You'll die not knowing how the story ended. I knew a boy in sixth form who used to eat his dessert first for that reason.'

'What, he feared getting hit by a bus every time he ate his dinner? Where was he eating it, in a bus lane?'

I laugh. I can't help myself. It feels like I haven't laughed properly in an age and I'm not entirely sure why since I have a great life.

'Seriously though, Beatrix, what if the important part of the story happened much earlier? Would you keep flicking backwards to find it, or would you take a chance and read the book?'

'I don't know, I've never really thought about it. I've done it, sure, I've flicked backwards searching for the last mention of a name, but it's never occurred to me that if I don't find what I'm looking for straight away, like on the last page, I should simply read it properly.'

'Honestly?'

'Yes. I suppose it's the same with the dating thing. If I can't skip to the end in my imagination and see us together in "X" amount of time, I don't really bother to think about dating a few more times.'

'Don't you worry you're missing out on whole new dating experiences doing that?'

'No,' I reply with a shrug. 'I remind myself that life is too short to bother with pointless encounters with people you can't get on with and ditch them after the first date.'

'Ouch,' he says.

'Don't "Ouch" me. You haven't been ditched.' Our eyes meet.

'I sense a yet coming on.'

'You sense wrong,' I reply.

'I'm in with a chance then?'

'I haven't skipped to the end yet, let's leave it at that and see how the night goes.'

'Sounds fair enough to me,' he says with a smile.

I smile back. I'm surprised to find that it's a genuine smile. Like the laugh from earlier, this is a smile that comes from enjoying myself. Usually my smiles are rustled up to fit the cleavage, tight dress and 'sex kitten' image, or if I'm at work to fit the 'trust me, you want to buy this' persona I've created. This smile is neither. It's mine, it's real. I seemed to have mislaid it somewhere along the journey of my life that has led to here. This man has helped me find it.

'So, Beatrix, what looks tempting to you on the menu?' he asks.

'Call me Bea,' I tell him.

His name is Rufus, by the way.

Tami

Two years ago

The road we lived on, Providence Close, was shaped like the top half of a wine bottle. Our house was at the part of the bottle where the wine label would start on the left, and today I was heading for a flat on the far right side of our road where the 'lip' of the bottle was. As I turned the corner at what would have been the neck of the bottle, a tall woman was coming out of her corner-plot house to deposit a black bin bag into the green wheelie bin on her gravelled driveway.

I glanced away quickly, recognising her from somewhere other than the Close. Another couple of steps and I knew where she was from: she worked with Scott at The Look Is The Idea, the international design agency where he was CEO. A lot of the people who worked there lived around here, and I was constantly running into them on the school run, or down on the high street, or on my road. Another step closer and I remembered who she really was and my heart sank – she was his second in command: Miriam or Mylene or something.

'Do I know you?' she called as I passed her property.

'Yes and no,' I said, stopping. 'I'm Tamia Challey, Scott's wife.'

'Oh yes,' she said, cautiously, in that way people tended to do when they met the boss's wife. 'It's nice to meet you.'

'Yes, you, too. Sorry, I don't know your name.'

'Mirabelle Kemini.'

Unbidden, the theme tune of *Mama Mirabelle's Home Movies*, the show about a world-travelling cartoon elephant, started up in my head. It'd been Cora's then Anansy's favourite programme for years.

'You've got the theme tune to that elephant programme in your head, haven't you?' she asked.

I nodded. 'Sorry.'

'Happens all the time.' She shook her head and rolled her eyes good-naturedly. 'Of all the names in all the world, they had to give the cartoon elephant mine.'

I pinched my lips together to stop myself from laughing.

'Why haven't you got any shoes on, Mrs Challey?' Mirabelle asked me, reminding me where I was going and, more importantly, what I looked like.

I was wearing a bleach-flecked black Goonies T-shirt that Scott had brought me back from a trip to America last year under my big Aran cardie I usually wore in bed, and fluff-speckled joggers that sagged at the bottom, oh and odd socks.

'Well, it's a long story,' I replied. 'But the short version is I was in a rush to finish a project I'm working on but I kept looking out of my office window at the bins sitting outside the house, from the bin men earlier, cluttering up the pavement. It was bugging me so I decided to go out and bring the bins in. I got two steps outside when the door blew shut, locking me out. Actually, that was a pretty long version. So, the upshot is I'm going around the corner to my friend

Beatrix's house to see if I can call my husband to send some keys home in a taxi.'

'I'm on holiday but I'll drive you to the office if you'd like?' she offered.

'No, I can't show my face looking like this.'

'What's wrong with your face?' she asked.

'I'm not exactly dressed for the TLTI offices, am I?' I replied. The office was now a sleek, chrome and glass nirvana – completely different to how it had been when I worked there. If you were employed there now, you had to look perfect every day or you'd be encouraged to consider how your personal appearance helped to broadcast the company ethos of beautiful design and superior presentation (i.e. sent home to change). That was the edict from the current CEO, who I happened to be married to. Me turning up in my current state would probably give him an aneurysm.

Mirabelle's eyes fluttered suspiciously over me, as if confused. 'You look fine to me, but if you don't want to go in, I can drive in and get them for you. Or you can come in and ring your husband?' She indicated to her house behind her. *I bet she put the snib on*, I thought darkly.

'If you don't mind, that'd be great.'

Up close to her, I was struck by her beauty. Plenty of women were good-looking, radiating their inner allure, but this woman was beguiling. Her skin was the colour and texture of dark hot chocolate, so smooth and well hydrated it seemed almost liquid. Her lips were gorgeous and full. And her slightly cat-like eyes were a pale hazel colour – a striking shock against the darkness of her skin.

'They're contacts,' she said.

'Pardon?' I replied, embarrassed at being caught staring.

'Most people avoid direct eye contact because a black woman shouldn't have such light-coloured eyes.' She wrinkled up one side of her face in a half-grimace. 'I kind of like the effect it has. I wasn't too sure when I first got them – on a whim – but then I noticed how they effected people and, well, I couldn't help myself. The contacts stayed, my self-consciousness left.'

'They do stand out,' I told her. 'In a good way.'

'Thank you.'

Scott used to talk about Mirabelle quite a lot, to the point where I asked him if he had a tiny crush on her. Then he simply stopped. When it occurred to me he hadn't mentioned her name in a while, I asked if she'd left the company. 'No, worse luck,' he said. 'She used to be brilliant but lately her work's gone off. If she doesn't buck up her ideas I think it might go to disciplinary.' I'd been taken aback that it was possible to go from being the most amazing worker since, well, him (he'd actually said that) to being in line for disciplinary action.

'Coffee?' she asked. 'I'm sorry I don't have any hot chocolate or marshmallows to go in it, but I do have coconut milk instead of cow's milk if you'd prefer that?'

'What makes you say that?' I asked, spooked that she knew what drink I actually wanted without me having to tell her.

'I don't know,' she curved the corner of her lip in a knowing smile, 'something about you suggests that's the sort of thing you'd like.'

'Did Scott moan about me drinking that?' I asked.

'Honestly, no. You simply look like that's the sort of thing you like.' Her smile spread across her face until it became a grin. 'I'm sorry I can't offer you that, but what about a chai latte?'

'Made from scratch?' I asked.

'No, from a packet. But we can both pretend I made it from scratch and that I even milked a coconut if you so wish?'

'No, a coffee will do me,' I say.

'Coffee it is. Strong, touch of milk, one sugar?'

'Yes, how did you . . . don't tell me, I look the type?'

She grinned again and nodded. 'Make yourself at home.'

Alone in her room, I felt shy about sitting down – it was too pristine, minimalist and perfect to be cluttered up by me. She had stripped floorboards, a huge cream rug with fibres the width of my little finger. On opposite sides of the room sat two bespoke-looking leather sofas. Dominating the room, though, the item that drew your attention to it the second you walked in, was the huge painting that hung on the wall above the fireplace. It was at odds with the modern pieces in the room, despite its chrome, bevelled-edge frame.

I walked towards the painting, drawn to it by its composition and the need it instantly instilled in me to continually scan its brushstrokes for a new piece of information, a different element I may have missed.

The setting of the painting was a deserted beach. Not anywhere I had been because the background also had palm trees, thin brown stems topped with fat green leaves that dipped towards the sea. The water was a pale cerulean, slightly darker than the sky. Standing in the water was a slender woman wearing a white dress that flowed down her body in fluid lines until it disappeared into the water that surrounded the woman's calves. The woman's hands were crammed with blood-red rose petals as if she was in the process of scattering the petals on the sea, while a few had already escaped and rested on the water's surface. Behind the woman, on the beach of beige, white and grey-black pebbles were more blood-red rose petals, covering the beach like a crimson path. I leaned closer, scrutinising them, noting how each rose petal had been individually painted into the image, and how every single one of them looked velvety, pliable, luscious. Before I could stop myself, my fingers were reaching for the beach, wanting to stroke the petals that covered the pebbles. My body sagged a little in disappointment that they were not what they looked like. Instead of being strokeable, they were stiff, hardened puddles of paint. In the corner of the painting was an artist's squiggle, not a name I could decipher enough to see if I recognised it. But at the bottom of the centre, painted in the sea in one shade lighter than the water, were the words: 'Have You Heard The Story Of The Rose Petal Beach?'.

My eyes moved from the words, to the petal-bedecked beach, to the woman's face. What she looked like was mostly hidden by swathes and swathes of long, curly black hair but she reminded me of Mirabelle. The way she stood and held herself – confident but relaxed. The smooth dark brown of her skin, the shape of her neck as it was turned away from the painter as she looked deeper into the scene, searching for someone who was out of sight.

'Everyone does that,' Mirabelle said as she returned to the room. 'I say everyone, I mean, most people do that. They can't help themselves touching the rose petals. They look divine, don't they?'

Guiltily, sheepishly, I took my hand away from the picture. 'Sorry,' I said as she handed me a duck-egg-blue mug, so wide and large it was almost like a soup bowl with a handle. The warmth of the coffee, the sweetness of the sugar wafted out to me a comfort that I didn't even realise I needed. 'Thanks.'

'Don't be sorry,' she said, holding onto her mug, my mug's twin, with both hands. 'I'm not surprised, it's a gorgeous painting.'

'Did you do it?'

'Me? No! I told the artist the story and this is what she came up with.'

'Is the story a well-known one, because I don't think I've heard it?'

Her face relaxed into her customary smile. 'No, not many people have heard it,' she said dreamily, her fluid body moving almost weightlessly as she crossed the room and sat on the uncomfortable-looking sofa nearest the window and pulled her feet up underneath her. She was barefoot, and comfortable considering how austere her surroundings were. Her eyes never left the painting, which she was regarding with a sense of wonder, contemplation and adoration. 'It's something I heard years ago that really spoke to me.'

'Is that you in the picture?' I asked her.

'Yes,' she replied. 'Can't believe you noticed, you're the first person to do so. I knew the artist so I posed for her.'

'It really is a beautiful painting,' I replied. I almost said that it was made all the more striking by having her in it, but that would be inappropriate considering who she was. 'Look, sorry

61

to bother you, but can I use your phone to call Scott?'

'Of course, of course.' She held out her phone to me, but didn't release it straight away to my grasp. 'I'm glad you got locked out,' she said, 'because it's given me a chance to meet you. Scott talks about you a bit but it's good to meet you properly.'

'I'm glad I got to meet you, too,' I replied, 'although I wouldn't say I was happy at all about being locked out.'

'You're not at all what I expected.'

'That's a good thing?' I replied.

Her nod was enthusiastic and genuine. 'Oh, that's a really, really good thing.'

Mirabelle is sitting on the stairs when I open the front door. She is still in her coat, her phone is in her hand and she does not look like she has stepped into the house, gone upstairs, or even moved the whole time I have been away.

As I shut the door as quietly as possible, she stands, raising herself to her full height so she towers over me. She is statuesque, her demeanour almost always easy and open.

We stare at each other across the gap of the corridor like two animals thrown into a cage and forced to fight their way out. I examine her again, seeing her clearly now when I didn't really notice before: her stance is closed and defensive, her mouth a black-brown line of silence, her light-coloured eyes warily watching my every move.

My eyes look past her upstairs, straining to catch even the tiniest sound that tells me they're safe and she hasn't harmed them.

'I haven't done anything to them,' she says. 'I didn't move from here. And they haven't stirred since you left.'

When I was tearing home, the terror and desperation to get her away from our children spurring me on, I hadn't thought of what I was going to say to her. I suppose a part of me thought I'd be ripping her away from the girls' bedside, where she would be, what – standing over them, pillow in hand – then fighting her, not talking to her. It all seems ludicrous now, seeing that she has simply sat waiting for me to return.

I saw Mirabelle yesterday. Yesterday. She was on her way to the shops, dressed in her midnight-blue tracksuit, white and silver trainers on her feet, her hair wound up in a bun, sunglasses on her face. I'd been struck by the oddness of her walking on the other side of the street to our house, almost as if she was trying to avoid what actually happened – me popping out to bring in the recycling bins and seeing her.

She seemed to see me but instead of coming over to have a chat, she'd hurried along the road, her pace increasing. I'd called to her, asking why she wasn't in work, and she'd turned, grinned at me, but did not stop. Instead, a point at her bare wrist and a wave were thrown my way, before she increased her speed again and disappeared around the bend into the next street.

I'd wondered why she hadn't come over and now I knew: she couldn't talk to the wife of the man she'd reported to the police.

Did she know they would arrest him last night, in front of the children? Did she know what she would be doing to my life?

Mirabelle, my husband's accuser, stands perfectly still, as if petrified by this moment. But coiled, too. Ready to fight if she needs to. She's my mirror image, of course. I'm frozen too, solidified but also ready to defend myself if necessary.

Her gaze shifts to the door a few times and it dawns on me that she is waiting for me to move away before she leaves the third step of my staircase, before she closes the gap between us for long enough for her to leave.

Mirabelle is scared. Of me? Of being here? Or of how plausible her case would be if the police found out she was in her alleged attacker's house taking care of his children the night he was arrested?

I step aside, her body tenses in response, broadcasting that she is scared of me. Me. I take another step left, away from the door, and she moves right, off the step. We continue to move like that, almost circling each other, keeping our eyes firmly on our opponent, careful not to give the other even the slightest advantage, until I am on the stairs and she is in front of the door.

Without taking her eyes off me, she reaches behind herself and releases the catch on the door.

'Why did you even answer the phone to me, knowing what you'd done?' I ask before she escapes.

'You wouldn't understand,' she says.

She's probably right, I wouldn't. I don't. I don't understand any of this.

I say nothing to her.

The silence in our house is so large, so all-consuming, the click of the door shutting behind her sounds like a bomb going off.

Beatrix

He was nice, I had a nice evening. Will I be reading the book that is Rufus? At one time, maybe, but now? Probably not. Or maybe, I don't know. He was nice, he made me laugh, I smiled a lot, but the spark just wasn't there.

Now, don't be thinking I'm one of those women who has her head in the clouds and doesn't know a good thing when she dates it. I do. But, well, last page and all that. He walked me to the taxi rank down by the bottom of the Lanes and we stood there awkwardly, not sure if we should kiss or not. He would have kissed me, but I wasn't sure if it was a good idea. Then the moment passed, so I stood on tiptoes – more for effect than need since I was in these killer heels – and pressed my lips onto his cheek. His arm slid around my waist, holding me close as I kissed him.

'Am I ditched?' he asked as I stepped back and he reluctantly took his arm away.

'Not yet,' I said because, well, what else am I going to say when he's standing right there? *'Sorry, mate, it's a no-goer, I'm afraid.'* Not my style.

The taxi turns into Providence Close at the end that's nearest Tami and Scotty's house. I'm surprised Tami hasn't called or texted, actually. Usually when I'm on a date she checks in to make sure I'm safe (she really is like my big sister sometimes, honestly). In fact, my phone's been pretty silent all night. I reach into my bag and rummage around until I find it. I pull it out and the screen is black. A few attempts to turn it on tell me that the battery is flat. Stupid phone is banjanxed. I only charged it this afternoon. But, hey, that's something, I must have had a better time than I realised if I didn't even notice my phone wasn't working. Usually, shamefully some might say, I'm glued to my phone – yes, even in company.

If there are lights on in the Challey house I'll stop, I decide as the taxi driver slows for the bend. I peer out and see the house is in darkness. I check the LCD clock of the taxi: 22:55. That's way too early for them *all* to be asleep. Usually Tami's up in her office working on her latest project that's going to transform the image of some small or even large company from 'very nice looking' to 'extremely slick and stylish', while Scotty's messing about on his computer somewhere.

I wonder if something's happened?

The taxi driver continues on his route to my house.

I'm not sure what could have happened on a Thursday evening in Hove that would cause them to go to bed so early, but if something has, I'm sure I'll find out about it soon enough. Nothing stays secret on the Close for long.

Tami

'Are you sure?' Scott said to me.

'Yes. I wouldn't have told you if I wasn't sure, would I?'

'And you've done a test?'

Reaching out, I picked up my cloth bag, delved inside and pulled out the white sticks to show him. 'Try six tests. And, funnily enough, they all say the same thing.'

He brought the heels of his hands up to his face, pressed them on his eyes. 'Ah ... *Man!*' Scott had just watched his dreams of continuing to better himself with an MBA disappear in a cloud of nappies, late-night feeds and Babygros. While watching his future plans disappear he was also wondering if he did in fact love me, if he'd made a mistake about that and how it might be possible to get out of it.

I sat with my bag on the floor between my feet, the tests burning a hole in my hand, watching him go through the same process I had done hours earlier: I had watched my next promotion to head of the Corporate Communications department shimmer and disintegrate in my mind's eye, then had questioned my feelings for him. That had lasted for seconds, a minute at the most, certainly less time than his questioning seemed to last.

'I thought you were on the Pill,' Scott eventually said, his

67

accusation buried deep in his tone, but plain in his phrasing.

'I am. But that's only ninety-nine per cent effective. Meet the lucky one per cent. I should buy a lottery ticket.'

'This isn't funny.'

'Actually, it is.' He sat in the only armchair he had in his bedsit, his legs curled up under him, his face chiselled from stone. 'It's bloody hysterical. It's going to get a whole lot funnier if you ask me if I'm sure it's yours.'

He redirected his line of sight, even though his face remained like stone, telling me I was right, he had wanted to ask.

'You're a bastard, you know that?' I said. 'I can't believe I fell for all that talk of love when you're just a complete bastard.'

Leave, Tami, just leave, I told myself. *Get out of here and start to make your plans.*

I carefully laid the six white sticks on the edge of the bed, picked up my bag while I stood up and pulled myself together. 'I'll see you around,' I threw at him, knowing I wouldn't. I wouldn't see him again. Even if he did try to change the course of this, if he did try to make things right, I wouldn't want to see him again. 'Maybe.'

When the front door to his flat clicked shut behind me and wasn't immediately whipped open again by him asking me to come back, my heart fell. I stood for a few seconds, gathering myself together again. I had to have lunch with my family, I couldn't go there in a state, I had to strengthen myself against this. I had to ignore the hollow space where my heart should be, concentrate on the future that was growing inside me instead.

*

In the darkness of the room, I stare out of the window, with the unsynchronised breathing of Cora and Anansy as the soundtrack of my thoughts. I watch a taxi turn into our road and then move at a snail's pace up towards Mirabelle's house. I'm sifting through my life, the mine of my memories, trying to find that imperfect jewel that has been hidden in my past, mostly ignored, but holds the vital clue as to why he is in a police cell and I am in a life that feels a lot like hell.

Fifteen years ago
'I can't believe you forgot to get chips for me,' Sarto said, pouting. The oldest of us three children – a man in his late twenties – and he still had it in him to pout.

'You can share mine,' I told him, pushing the splayed open white paper towards him. 'I've said you can share mine.' Once every few weeks we had a family lunch where we all pretended that we hadn't deeply disappointed our parents in different ways: me with the university thing, Genevieve with the eloping to get married in Las Vegas thing, and Sarto with the taking his time to finish medical school thing. Genevieve and I came over (Sarto *still* lived there), and usually Mum cooked. Today, not long after Genevieve got there, she had said she would take care of the meal. We'd stared at her in amazement that she was going to cook. She, in return, gave us all scathing 'as if' looks and went to the chippy. Returning without any chips for Sarto.

'That's not the point, though, is it?' Sarto complained. 'My sister goes to the shop and comes back with food for everyone except me. What am I supposed to think about that? I'm a man, I should be served, not forgotten.'

I turned my laugh into a cough, knowing that was probably why Genevieve had done it. The things he said often brought out the radical feminist in her: I simply ignored him, which actually bugged him more than trying to get one over on him.

'Silly me,' Genevieve simpered. 'Silly female me. Never mind, next time you should send a man to the chip shop and maybe he'd remember how superior you are to every woman on Earth.'

'When will you learn, dear sister, I'm not superior to every woman on earth, I'm superior to everyone on Earth.'

The doorbell interrupted us. All eyes automatically turned to me, because I was the youngest and answering the door, washing up, doing whatever the others would have me do was my role. I focused on my chips, using a fork and my fingers to scoop them onto the waiting plate. Scott's reaction to the news I was pregnant was still smarting two hours later, I wasn't about to let myself be pushed around by this lot, too.

Ding-dong, the doorbell chimed again. I licked oil off my fingers and reached nonchalantly for the tomato ketchup and salad cream.

'This family is out of order,' Sarto said, pushing out his chair and stomping to the door. 'You're all out of order.'

Genevieve smirked and I smiled to myself. Poor Sarto was really feeling it today. 'Tam-*mia*!' he called a few seconds later. 'Door.'

The way he said my name told me who it was. I couldn't quite believe he had the audacity to show up knowing most people didn't welcome his type (Challey) round these parts.

'Tam-*mia!*' Sarto called again, louder this time. 'Scott Challey's here to see you.' He did that to let those at the table know what I was up to, who I was fraternising with. As he guessed it would, his pronouncement caused everyone to look at me, blinking in shock.

'A Challey?' Dad said quietly.

'Here?' Mum said just as quietly.

Genevieve did not speak, she simply pushed the waves of her long, black hair off her face and glared at me until I met her eye. Her expression softened from shock into deep, sorrowful disappointment. *Has this been going on since you were twelve?* she was asking me silently.

'Don't let Sarto eat all my chips,' I said to fill the hole that shock had blasted into the room. 'I only said he could have some of them, not all of them.'

'I'll guard them with my very life,' Genevieve replied, now unable to even look in my direction. She had joined my parents in feeling disappointed in me. She had no idea how disappointed I actually felt in myself – becoming involved with someone I knew I shouldn't have then discovering after I'd fallen in love and had become pregnant, that he wasn't the person I thought he was after all.

With their eyes on me, I stood shakily and left.

While I grabbed my coat, Sarto muttered darkly, 'Your lunch is waiting. Don't be long.'

'You're not my father, Sarto, in case you'd forgotten,' I replied, stepping over the threshold to leave.

'Things would be very different if I was,' Sarto called as I shut the door in his face.

'Are you mad, coming here?' I hissed to Scott when we

were clear of the front path and on the pavement. I daren't look back at the house in case they were all in the front-room window watching us. I marched quickly up the road out of sight. 'My whole family were in there and now they all think ...' *The truth*, I realised so stopped talking.

'Sorry, sorry, I had to see you. I came after you but you'd gone. You weren't at your flat and I remembered you said about your Saturday lunches here so obviously ...'

'Obviously what? What do you want?'

'I'm sorry. I'm sorry. I'm so, so sorry. I behaved very badly. Of course I love you. Of course I know the baby's mine. You're the best thing that has happened to me, and the baby will be too if you want to keep him or her. If you don't, that's fine, too. But whatever you decide, I'll support you. I'm sorry I didn't say all that before.'

'Thing is Scott ...'

'No, no. No, don't.' He stopped walking and threw himself to his knees. 'Please don't say "thing is" and my name in that tone of voice because that means it's over. And I can't stand the thought of that. I wish I had been a better man, but I'm here now. I want to be with you. I want to support you. Please give me one more chance. I probably deserve to be – what's that thing they say on *Jerry Springer* – "kicked to the kerb" but please don't.'

'Why shouldn't I?'

'Because I love you. Because we're good together. Because every time we're apart it feels as if there's a piece of me missing. Because I love you.'

'Yeah, well, sometimes love isn't enough, you know? How do I know you aren't going to freak out again about something we're both responsible for? Or suddenly start questioning if I've been sleeping around? A baby puts all kinds of pressure on people and if you can't handle it, I'd rather you weren't around.'

'Please, I'm begging you. I'll do anything to make this work. Anything. You name it, I'll do it. Just don't give up on me, please.'

I could feel people in the street staring at us from behind their net curtains, formulating their gossip as fast as they could: the Challey boy on his knees in front of the Berize girl, hands clasped together as he begged her for something.

'Get up, Scott.'

'No. No, I can't until I've made you understand how sorry I am and how much I love you and how much it would kill me if you didn't give me a second chance.'

'People are staring at us.'

He looked around, the street was empty but the weight of a dozen pairs of eyes was still upon us. 'I don't care. I love you and I don't care who knows it.' He opened his arms wide, threw his head back. 'I LOVE TAMIA BERIZE!' he bellowed suddenly. He lowered his head. 'See? I don't care who knows it. I'm yours from now until eternity. And I want to be the baby's, too.'

Around us, front doors were opening and net curtains were being pulled back as people who hadn't been watching came to see what the shouting was about.

'Right, listen, I'll give you another chance. But only one more chance, Scott – anything remotely bastard-like and I am gone. Do you understand me?'

'I won't need another chance, I'm not going to mess up

like this ever again.' He got to his feet, grinning from one ear to the other. He kissed me in front of all our neighbours, his hand resting on my abdomen, completing the circle that made us a family.

My mobile bleeps on my lap. My heart leaps and I immediately check it hasn't woken Cora and Anansy. Their two forms lie undisturbed under the chocolate-brown duvet. It won't be Scott. I know he's not getting out tonight, his mobiles are downstairs and what could he say in a text that would possibly explain what happened tonight? Without checking who the sender is, I turn off my phone, pull my legs up to my chest and tell myself I need to sleep.

Fifteen years ago

She was gentle and kind, her calmness filtered through the fug of pain and exhaustion. 'How are you feeling, Miss Berize?'

'OK, I suppose,' I murmured through my blue-tinged lips. The tiredness wouldn't allow me to keep my eyes open for more than a few seconds at a time; they kept slipping shut while the rest of me tried to drift off to sleep.

'You've lost a lot of blood so I wouldn't be surprised if you're feeling exhausted right now.'

I nodded. Exhausted, devastated.

Scott's hand was curled around mine like a sleeping cat laced around the feet of its beloved owner. He hadn't let go in the time we'd been waiting in this cubicle.

'I'm sorry,' her gentleness continued. 'There's nothing we can do. I'm so sorry.'

'You can't save the baby?' he asked.

'Not at such an early stage. We're not sure what causes this to happen, often it's just one of those things. I'm truly sorry.'

I nodded.

'Because of how much blood you've lost we're going to have to admit you until we're sure the process is complete. Is that OK?'

I nodded again, too drained and broken to say anything.

Scott's tears crawled down his face in an unstoppable flow. He didn't let go of my hand to wipe away his tears, he held onto me and let the world see how his heart was breaking too.

Fourteen years ago
'Come outside,' Scott said to me in the middle of the night. He tugged at the corner of the red and white eiderdown on our bed, untucking it from where I'd wrapped it around myself.

Scott had stayed over to take care of me when I came home from hospital after the . . . *miscarriage*, and never really left again. Working in bars to fund his studies meant he kept odd hours sometimes but he always came back to me. Always crept into bed and curled up around me, the cold of his body often shocking me awake for a few moments before the comfort of his familiar shape let me drift back to sleep. *'Love you, TB,'* he'd always whisper into my ear. *'You're everything to me.'*

'No way!' I replied, turning over, trying to find that lovely warm spot I'd created. 'There's all sorts out there.'

'Just come outside for one minute. I promise you won't regret it.'

Huffing and puffing, I sat up and threw back the covers. 'This had better be good, Challey boy.'

Standing at the foot of the bed, he was still wearing his black overcoat and still had his grey scarf wrapped around his neck. In his hands he held my long, grey coat. I gratefully slipped into it. The heating in the building was off till the morning and the chill of the February night had seeped inside. At the front door he handed me my snow boots, even though it wasn't snowing outside.

'Do I have to close my eyes or something?' I asked, as we stood at the top of the stairs that led down from my flat.

'If you want, but if you fall down them that's your look out,' he said, laughing to himself.

'You!' I said and gave his shoulder a playful shove.

Outside, the crisp, clean atmosphere chased away any remnants of sleep that might have been lurking in my head and I was suddenly wide awake.

'Tah-dah!' he said, his hands pointing in TV-presenter fashion at the car that sat directly outside the flat. It looked older than either of us, was probably more rust than anything else, but was clean and shiny.

'What's that?'

'A car! *The* car! I bought you a car.'

I blinked in surprise. 'You what?'

'I bought you a car.'

'Wow,' I said, staring at the shiny burgundy surfaces of the car in front of me. I didn't even know what make it was but it was a car. 'I can't believe . . . Where did you get the money?'

'I earned and saved every single penny,' he said, immediately on defensive. 'If you don't believe me—'

'I do believe you,' I cut in. 'Of course I believe you. I'm only curious how you could afford a car when you're working at two different bars just to keep your head above water and afford college as it is.'

'I've been working extra shifts during the day so I could save for this.' He draped his arms over my shoulders like a casually thrown-on cardigan. 'Do you like it?'

'I love it,' I replied. 'But ... How can you take on more daytime shifts if you're in college most days?'

'I took a break for a while. I'll go back to it soon.'

'Scott! College is important.'

'Says the woman who didn't even go.'

'Yeah, well, I can always go another time. You're already there, you don't want to throw away that opportunity.'

'Do you know why I bought you a car?' he asked, changing the subject.

'Ummm, no.'

'Because I think we should do it. I think we should go to Brighton with that promotion you were offered.'

'No, we already talk—'

'No, no, look, staying here because of me is stupid. And, no matter what you say, it is because of me.'

'There'll be other opportunities.'

'TB, you've got a promotion to become head of Corporate Communications for a multinational company, and you'll be the youngest person to hold that position in their history. Do you have any idea how proud of you I am? You can't throw that away for a boyfriend.'

I leant my head back so I could look up at him, he bent his head to look down at me. 'You're not just a boyfriend,' I said. What happened had fundamentally changed us and how we were together. Our love was never hidden, always spoken, always shown. Our time together was always relished and revelled in.

'I say, we pack up everything in this car, and we head on down to Brighton. We get there, get settled and then, you know, think about trying again in a couple of years.' I knew exactly what he meant: we both wanted to try for another baby, we both knew we were scared in case it happened again. We would, though, when the time was right, when everything was in place. 'I can always use the car to come back for college until I find another course down there.'

'Will you marry me?' I asked.

His whole face softened into a smile I had never seen before. It needed to be remembered in paints, on a canvas, anything, because it showed the texture of happiness. 'Yes,' he replied. 'Yes, I will. Can't believe it's taken you so long to ask.'

'Well, I had to be sure, didn't I?' I joked before returning my gaze to the car. *Our* car. 'This is so special,' I said. 'This is a present with a whole new life attached to it.'

'You deserve it, my love.'

'You do realise I can't drive, don't you?'

'What?' He was stricken. 'I thought you could. Oh, great, typical Scott, buy a present without checking the person can actually use it.'

'Just tricking you!' I laughed.

'You!' he laughed and tickled and tickled me until, gasping with laughter, I agreed never to trick him again.

My fingers close around the smooth metal of my platinum wedding ring. I rotate it back and forth around my finger. Nothing makes sense. In all of this, nothing is making any sense.

4

Beatrix

Here's the thing I don't like about being single: waking up alone. The rest of it I really can handle, no matter what other people might try to tell me. It's this part I find hardest.

I long to have someone to sleep with. You can get sex anywhere, it's all around you and you can pluck it out of the air almost – if you're willing to compromise (a lot) on quality, usually – but it's difficult, really difficult to find someone you connect with enough to sleep with.

I love waking up with a man's arms around me and his body next to mine, feeling like I am part of something whole instead of mostly incomplete. I like it and I crave it, sometimes more than sex. It doesn't seem to work as well with one-night stands, not sure why. Maybe it's because you can't pretend too hard? You can't allow yourself to relax and sleep properly if you know at the end of it he's probably going to be gone very early the next day, if he stays more than a few hours at all. Even if he stays till dawn, even if you have that connection that leads to morning sex, you know he's leaving and never coming back. When you crave the intimacy of sleeping with someone, having it faked for only a few hours is worse than not having it at all.

I've opened my eyes this morning feeling flat. My mobile is definitely banjanxed, which means I have to go to the office when I'd planned on working from home today. I could do without driving all the way to Kent now, but they've got no way to get in touch unless it's by email and for some reason that's not enough for my company. They need to know they can talk to me at whatever time they want.

My limbs don't come anywhere near the edges of the bed, my body is not enough to fill it up on its own.

Tami and Scotty pop into my mind. I bet they're waking up right about now, curled up together, their skin so close it could almost be that they're one person. I bet he kisses her on the top of her head as I've seen him do a million times, I bet she smiles and snuggles into the crook of his neck. I sound so jealous, and that's because I am. I am of pretty much every couple who sleep together, not just Tami and Scotty.

I've mentioned them a couple of times now, so I'm sure you're curious about how I know them. Well, about nine years ago, the banker who lived at number eighteen Providence Close lost his job – couldn't have happened to a nicer wanker, sorry, banker, if you ask me. I knew him because I used to work in the City and he'd been on the fiddle for years. Anyways, he had to sell his house pretty quickly, so when this couple came along with a huge deposit and the ability to move quickly he sold it to them and never looked back.

Nine years ago
Whenever I saw the neighbours who I talked to on the Close they'd always have a different story about who was about to move into number eighteen. Gus at number forty-eight said

it was a widower and his six children, Leenie at number three said it was a single mother who'd won the lottery, Cleo at number ninety-six said it was the banker who'd had to sell the house in the first place under a different name so he could cheat the tax man. So when I saw the new owner coming out of the house, dressed in a dust-smeared T-shirt, old jeans, and wild, 'manual labour' hair, I kind of guessed he was none of these things.

'Hi,' he said, a grin taking over his face when he saw me.

'Moving in, I see,' I replied, pausing outside the small iron gate and then leaning against the gatepost.

'Yes, a very long process, considering I'm moving a one-bedroom flat into a five-bedroom house. There's so much stuff.' He shrugged. 'It doesn't make sense, you know?'

He had this cute way of wrinkling his nose to emphasise how baffling things seemed to him. And his habit – which is what I could tell it was from the way he did it – of running his right hand through his brown locks started a tingling in my stomach. But it was his smile, the way it was a little bit higher on one side of his mouth than the other, that made me fall for him. In my head, we'd kissed, made love, set up home, got engaged, had a huge wedding and were trying for a baby by the time he'd said 'you know?'

I nodded at him.

'So it's only you moving in, then?' I said, trying to hide my hope. One-bedroom flat, no visible sign of anyone else helping with the moving process, all on his own at what seems a crucial phase . . . Ergo, moving in alone. Single. Available. As was I. Available, that is.

'No. God, no. I couldn't live in a house this big on my

own. My wife is at home directing the packing. She's six months pregnant and would be here doing this bit herself, too, if I'd let her. She's pretty amazing. I can't get her to slow down.' Ah, married. The second he said that, I switched off the 'available' light I'd been metaphorically flashing and focused on his wedding ring – pretty unusual it was – and, most importantly, backed off. I liked the thrill of the chase, I liked that bit when you meet someone and you know it could go any way, but, as I said to you a minute ago, I'd been cheated on, my husband did it to me, my husband left me for someone else so I was not going to 'go there'.

I met Tami a little while later and I've been grateful ever since they're in my life, that I'm like family to them, and them to me.

The spurt of water on my tired body is a divine experience. There's nothing like the first shower of the day to wake you up and get you going. To tell you the truth, I'm a bit unnerved about driving past Tami and Scotty's last night and the lights being off. It's so not like them. The last time that happened was when Cora's appendix burst and she had to be rushed in for emergency surgery.

I haven't got time to drop in on the way to work, so it'll have to be afterwards. Although once I'm in the office who knows what time I'll leave? I've just got this nagging feeling that all is not well over there. I've got a feeling . . . Ahh, you'll probably laugh at me, so I won't finish what I was thinking. I'd better get on with this shower and then hit the road to Kent. Joy, joy, joy.

Tami

'Rice Pops? Again?' Cora protests when her bowl is full to the brim with small pieces of cereal.

'You didn't have Rice Pops yesterday, did you?' I ask. Yesterday morning seems an age away.

'No,' she replies.

'So what's the problem?'

'We always have Rice Pops.'

'Apart from yesterday. And, if I recall correctly, the day before, as well. In fact, this is the first time you've had them all week.'

'We always have Rice Pops,' she repeats.

'OK, Ansy, would you like Rice Pops?' I ask, reaching for the pink-and-white-spotted bowl in front of her to swap with Cora's blue and white striped one.

'OK, Mama,' Ansy replies. 'But I don't want the ga-ga spoon, I want the BIG Wallace and Gromit one. Not the little one, the big one.'

I make the swap and return my attention to Cora. 'What would you like instead?'

Her large brown eyes are swimming with tears, her mouth is turned down, while her pulled-in chin is wobbling.

'What's the matter?' I ask.

'I don't want that bowl. It's the baby bowl.'

This morning they woke up within minutes of each other in the big bed and both lay very still, looking around them, taking in the surroundings. They looked suspiciously at each other, then reached under the covers – and Cora discovered she was still wearing her jeans and Olympics T-shirt. Anansy, who always puts her pyjamas on the moment she comes in from school to save time later, discovered she was still wearing her red towelling dressing gown.

'Good morning, sleepyheads,' I said brightly, trying to crowbar some normality into the day before fragments of last night came crashing in. I'd sat between them all night, drifting in and out of sleep, waiting for something to tell me that I'd imagined everything that had happened.

'Morning, Mama,' they mumbled, stretching and unknotting their young bodies. Slowly, their expressions changed and I could see what happened last night was playing in their minds. I put my arms around and hugged them. 'We're going to be OK,' I said to them, dropping a kiss on each of their heads. 'So will Dad. He'll be OK, too, I promise.' In response, they wrapped their arms around me, managing to avoid each other's arms, and clung on.

Right now, Cora and Anansy are telling me in their own ways that they didn't believe me.

'Here we go.' I decant the Rice Pops from Cora's bowl into Anansy's. I know this will not be enough for the tall eight-year-old with two shoulder-length plaits on either side of her head. It'll still have yuckiness in it so won't be fit for any other cereal. Taking the bowl, I go to the sink, pausing to open the dishwasher and pluck out the requested spoon. I wash both items with washing-up liquid and the green sponge, making a big show of it so neither can protest on its level of yuck-freeness.

'OK, what would you like?' I ask Cora.

I see it in her eyes, in the way she moves her face, I hear it, too, in the short breath she takes before she mumbles, 'Cornflakes.' What would she like? Her daddy back, please.

'Me, too,' I say to her and fill up my own bowl with corn-flakes, too. She knows what I mean, what I am saying.

Fourteen years ago

'Do you ever trace your name in the stars?' Scott asked me.

We lay on the beach, our second night in Brighton, and stared up at the sky: ink-black and endless; a bottomless ocean suspended above our world. It was cold and we were freezing, but it'd seemed criminal not to come out here to see the black sea up close.

'No, I've never done that.'

'Look, it's easy.' He raised his hand, curled his other digits inwards, making a pencil out of his index finger. 'See?' His hand moved in big strokes, taking in multiple stars, multiple galaxies. A stroke down and then across: 'T'. A diagonal sweep up, a diagonal sweep down, one across: 'A'. A sweep up, then down a fraction, up a fraction, then a long sweep down: 'M'. A sweep down, two small sweeps top and bottom: 'I'. A diagonal sweep up, a diagonal sweep down, one across: 'A. TAMIA.' As he wrote, I could see it, I could see the invisible line that joined up the heavens until they were all about me. Until me, my name, filled the sky. 'Can you see it? Can you see your name up there?'

'Yes, yes I can,' I breathed.

'OK, hold onto that, see it really clearly, and then close your eyes, take a picture of your name in the stars and store it here.' He brushed his fingertips on my forehead. 'And here.' He pressed his fingers to my chest, over my heart. 'Never let it go.'

My eyes lingered shut as I willed my mind to hold onto the memory, begging my heart to do the same.

After it was there, branded deep into me, I turned my head to him, watching him with his eyes closed, taking a picture and storing it too. I did the same to him: his wild brown hair, his smooth skin, his straight, narrow nose, his long, dark eyelashes, his wide, almost perfect mouth. I fixed the image in my head, then I closed my eyes and took a picture for my head and for my heart of the boy who gave me the stars.

After both of them have milk, their favoured spoon and the correct channel on TV, I sit at my place and pick up my spoon. I haven't got any kind of appetite, but I can't encourage them to eat if I don't at least attempt mine.

Silence is unnatural at this table, especially on a school day when chattering and speculating on who will get into trouble or who will be awarded the much-coveted 'star of the day' often overtakes everything. They usually need to be mentally herded back to eating.

Carefully, I lay down my spoon beside my bowl. I need to say something, anything, that will crack the dome of anxiety that is shrouding us. 'Dad is—'

Into the gap between words, a key is inserted into the lock

of the front door. Then comes the groaning yawn of the front door being opened, footsteps inside the house, feet being wiped on the mat – one foot, other foot, both feet in quick time, and then feet walking along the tiled hall, turning, walking . . .

'DAD!' Cora and Anansy both scream, slipping down from their seats and tearing across the kitchen to him. They run to him and he drops to his knees, taking them both into his arms and hugging them close. He buries his face in the space between them and draws them closer still.

I stand watching them, waiting. Patiently waiting for that thing to kick in where I want to throw myself at him, hug him close, check with a thousand kisses that he is in one piece, he is safe, he is all right. I'm still waiting as the girls' relieved chatter fills the room. Waiting, waiting, waiting.

Scott lied to them. He took them off to school with lies sitting in their ears that soothed their troubled minds, settled their fears. I'm sure he thought he was doing it for the best, to reassure them, but a lie is a lie is a lie.

'Why did the policemen take you away, Daddy?' Anansy had asked. 'Did you do something naughty?'

'No, no,' he said, dropping kisses on each of their heads – first Cora then Anansy. 'No, no. I'm sorry you had to see that.' Kiss. Kiss. 'It was a mistake. They thought I was someone else.' Kiss. Kiss. 'They said sorry and that it won't happen again.'

I knew he was lying because of what the policewoman told me. I knew he was lying because he would not look at me. In fact, at that moment, it felt like I knew he was lying because his lips were moving. I stood back and let it happen because sometimes all you want is to hear the lie when you know the truth is too awful to bear.

He told them to finish their breakfast while he had a shower and then as a special treat he was going to take them to school.

They'd done as they were told and I'd forced a smile on my face to see them off at the door. Any minute now he'll be back. I'm not sure which I'd like to do first: tear a strip off for him lying to them, or scream at him for putting us in this position in the first place.

As it turns out, when I see him I do neither of those things: I stare at him across the kitchen for long seconds, then I walk towards him and put my arms around him, the relief so huge it almost drowns me.

My husband clings to me in return and we don't say anything, we simply stand holding one another as the world carries on around us.

Twelve years ago
'We don't actually need to spend so much on our wedding rings,' I reminded Scott. Probably not what the jeweller we were standing in front of wanted to hear, but it was the truth. The ring, the dress, the venue, the food – it was all pretty and lovely but the truth of it was, if we had to wear jeans with a Hula Hoop on each of our ring fingers it'd still be special because marrying Scott in six months' time was the most important thing of all.

Sometimes he didn't seem to understand that. I didn't care about the rest of it as much as he seemed to. He kept pushing the budget, going for the most expensive option, as if he wanted to *prove* that we'd done well for ourselves. People looked down their noses at us, certainly, especially in the posher places we visited, but it didn't bother me, I simply wouldn't use that person. It got to Scott though, it needled him and caused him to want to make big, showy gestures.

'I know,' Scott said. 'But I want to spend so much on our wedding rings. It'll be a symbol of how far we've come and how far we've got to go – together. When we were growing up in our tiny houses and with my family and you not going to college ... did you ever think we'd be able to afford to walk into a shop like this, let alone buy something, let alone something so ...' He paused to look at the bloated, balding man standing on the other side of the counter listening avidly to us, then tugged me a little way away to give us some privacy in a shop that was only slightly bigger than the size of our living room but was still classily crammed with cases of unusual and gorgeous jewellery. 'Let alone something so unique and pricey,' Scott whispered, standing close to me. He found my eyes with his. 'Let's do this. We've both got good jobs, let's splash out on this and show people how important we are now,' Scott said.

I glanced back at the rings, resting on top of the counter on a large piece of purple velvet. They were platinum creations that fitted together to make one ring. The top ring, the woman's ring, had a straight upper edge, the lower edge a wavy line with hidden notches that connected it to the lower ring. The lower ring, the man's ring, had a straight bottom edge, with the upper edge swirled in a similar way and with corresponding notches to allow the woman's ring to sit upon it and become one ring. The jeweller had explained that once you owned it, the rings were resized together to make sure they still fitted together as well as on your finger. They were beautiful. And nearly three grand each. I had money, Scott had finished studying and was earning, but still ...

'TB, I want to do this.'

'I'm not sure. It's so much money.'

'Look, we have to do this. Actually, we are doing this. We deserve nice things so we're doing this. OK?' He lowered his head to be nearer to my face. 'OK?'

I nodded. 'OK.'

He grinned that grin that always made my stomach flip and took his credit card out of his wallet. The rings were too expensive, but if I divided the price by the number of years we were going to be together, it'd be hardly anything at all.

'This is such a nightmare,' are Scott's first words as he sits back on his preferred part of the sofa (nearest the living room door with the plumpest cushions). 'I never thought this could happen to me.'

'What is happening to you?' I ask. I am in my preferred seat, which is the armchair nearest the door. I can't relax, I want to be doing something. I'm not entirely sure what, just something physical that will displace some of the anxiety.

'The detective said she'd spoken to you, told you what I've been accused of and by who?'

'Yes, and that was all she would tell me. I don't know details or anything like that.'

'Well neither do I. It didn't happen so how can I know details?'

'So she's lying? My best friend has made it all up for fun, is that what you're saying?'

'So I did it, is that what you're saying?'

'No, Scott, I'm saying I want to know what's going on.'

He sits forward, agitated, his features pinched as he holds back anger. 'Look, her work hasn't been up to standard recently. She's sloppy, misses deadlines, can't seem to come up with any original ideas. I've been calling her on it, you know I don't carry passengers in business, and she's pissed off at me.'

'There's pissed off, which you take to industrial tribunal, and then there's this.'

'She said she was going to get me back, this is obviously it.'

'It doesn't make sense . . .'

'We work a lot of late nights together, and she can't get at me by sabotaging my work, so yeah, why wouldn't she make something up like that? As you can see, it's had the desired effect – I've been arrested and you're doubting me.'

'*Women don't do that,*' I say in my head. '*They just don't.*'

'There's more to this, Scott, and you are not telling me what.'

The cogs of his mind whirl and click as he waits for me to drop it. I simply wait. Scott doesn't operate well with silence, he needs to keep talking until he knows you're so tied up in knots you give in. I, on the other hand, can wait. I am good at waiting.

'All right,' he says, lowering his gaze to the spot he was

standing when he was arrested last night. 'All right. She might have come onto me.'

'*What?*'

He is on his feet, his hands out to calm me, to stop me losing the plot. 'It was just a little banter that went a bit too far. I stopped it when I realised she was taking it too seriously.'

'You should have told me this,' I say.

'I know, I know, but I was so embarrassed and ashamed that she got it so wrong from my behaviour. But you know I'm always like this so it was a shock to realise that someone was taking me seriously. And now she's resigned I won't have to see her again.'

'She's resigned?'

'Yeah, two days ago, turned up and handed in her notice, said she had a month's holiday owing and she was off. Just like that, no talking about it, no discussion about handing over to a replacement. This accusation was obviously her parting shot.'

'Did you tell the police this?'

'Sort of.'

'What do you mean "sort of"?'

'I think it's best to keep my head down and let it go away.'

'What? Who has a plan like that? Look, what does your solicitor say about it all?'

'I haven't got a solicitor, I don't need one, I have nothing to hide.'

'But Scott, don't you—'

'No, look, TB, I don't want to talk about this any more. You just have to trust me that it's going to work out. I mean, they let me go without charge, without needing bail or anything because they haven't got a thing on me. They said they need to make further enquiries, but I know and they know there's nothing on me. I don't need a solicitor. This is all going to go away, I promise you.'

'What if I want to talk about it and keep talking about it until I understand what's going on?'

He raises his hands and opens his mouth as if about to speak, then decides against it. 'You're supposed to trust me,' he says. 'Look, never mind, I'm going to sleep. If I stay here, I'm going to say something I regret.'

With that, he exits the room and climbs the stairs. Leaving me to deal with the feeling that I am the one who has brought our family to this point.

Seven years ago
Scott was comfortable in front of the crowd of fifty or so people assembled at The Look Is The Idea, about to give a speech. I kept looking around at the faces, so proud of all of them and how far we had come. When I moved down I had come to work in the Corporate Communications department of TelemeCo. Through many, many late nights working together, Terry Cranson, the man who had originally employed me in London, and I had come up with a plan to take the department and make it into its own business. We would work on financing to make it a separate entity that would then do work for TelemeCo and other businesses. It'd take us time to make a profit, but we were sure TelemeCo would go for it since there would be no overheads for them.

Five years later and we had made the kind of profit we

hadn't even dreamed of. Scott was Customer Relations Manager, having been recommended for the job by me, Terry was President and sat on the board, and I was CEO.

'Thank you, everyone, for taking time out of your extremely hectic schedules to come here today to say goodbye to Tami Challey,' Scott said, graciously.

He had asked Terry if he could make the speech today. Scott paused while a few people clapped and I smiled, embarrassed. I'd never liked being the centre of attention, even if it was only for a few minutes. 'It's not often a man gets to admit he's sleeping with the boss and keep his job,' Scott continued, eliciting the laughter he'd wanted, 'but I'm lucky like that. I'm even luckier that Tami is going to be having our second child in just under a month, but it's very sad for all of us here that she won't be returning to work afterwards. Tami feels she can't concentrate on looking after our children as well as single-handedly running the company here – don't tell Terry I said that, obviously.' More laughter. 'So she is stepping down. But I'll still be here to give you regular updates on the progress of our family and my amazing wife.' A few awwws from around the room. 'I'd like to say how proud I am of Tami. When I first decided to move down here to study for my MBA and Tami, rather wonderfully, agreed to move with me so we could stay together, I had no idea what she would do with the job transfer she requested.' I didn't know where Terry was in the room, but I knew beneath his face of stone he would be staring at Scott with incredulous eyes. 'Tami – and Terry, of course – have created something wonderful here and I think we can all say how grateful we are to them for having the vision to see it through.

So, in conclusion, I'd like to ask you to raise your glasses to Tami Challey.' From wherever he was, I could feel Terry's eyes on me now, trying to remind me of the conversation we'd had yesterday, and I heard his voice, louder than the rest, as they chorused, 'Tami Challey.'

Terry had been trying to persuade me to stay, to work part-time, to not give up work completely – he'd even called in to see me at home yesterday, knowing Scott was out. I couldn't stay, I missed Cora in a way I didn't know was possible and wanted to see more of her before the baby was born and afterwards, too.

As I moved to waddle my way to the front to say a few words, Scott's voice rose again, 'I know Tami won't mind me telling you that she's rather shy at public speaking so she's decided not to make a speech but instead to say goodbye to you all individually if she can.'

I knew why he'd done that – to stop me correcting his reinterpretation of how we ended up in Brighton. I wouldn't have done, that wasn't my style, but it was Scott's and Scott assumed everyone thought like he did.

As people came to talk to me, what Terry said to me yesterday replayed itself in my head: *'He's good at his job, I'll give him that, but we both know he'd stab anyone in the back to get ahead. You'd do well to keep Scott at home while you work, Tami. We both know where the talent lies in your partnership.'*

'Please don't say that about him,' I'd said to Terry. *'He's a brilliant husband and father. And he'd never do anything to hurt me. That's what's important.'*

*

'Let's not fight,' Scott says to me sometime later. I have been pulling up weeds in the garden. I didn't mean to, I just saw them, peeking out among the flowers that were trying to grow, and they annoyed me. Had induced a blind rage inside that made me throw myself onto my knees and rip at them. Those weeds, those spindly green monstrosities, reminded me of the things in life that came along, muscling in where they weren't wanted, ruining the things that you knew to be perfect. I went at them by the handful. Tugging and tugging until they gave way in my hands. I know you're supposed to dig them up to make sure you've got all the roots, or use a weed-killer to make sure there's no trace of them left, but I wanted them gone right that second. Out of my garden, out of my sight, out of my life. They were strangling the life out of the flowers, and I needed them to stop. I needed them to disappear, even for a little while.

'Please, Tami,' he says, his hands on my shoulders. 'Please. I really need you right now. I really need you to tell me you know I didn't do this thing.'

I say nothing. Because I know I need the same from him. I need him to tell me he didn't do it. He hasn't said that. He's said they have nothing on him, he's said it didn't happen, he's said it will all go away, but at no point has he said, 'I didn't do this thing.'

He gently tugs me to my feet, spins me to look at him.

'We have to be a team now. For us, for the girls. We have to trust and lean on each other. We've survived people saying we shouldn't be together, we've been through so much, we can't let this tear us apart.'

We can't. He's right. When I think back over the years,

over our lives, I know who he is. I know what he's capable of. And this is something he is not capable of. I know him, the world out there doesn't. He would not do this. The boy who gave me the stars would not do this.

'No,' I say, slipping my arms around him and letting him draw me in for a hug. 'We can't let this tear us apart.'

'I love you so much, Tami,' my husband says. 'I don't know what I'd do without you.'

'Me too,' I say.

I know he would not do this. But why did he go so quietly? Why didn't the police officer need to tell him what he was being arrested for? It was almost as if, when he saw the police in our living room, he knew what he had been accused of, and by whom. If he was innocent, why would his arrest not have been a surprise?

You know why, is what I say to myself in the quietest whisper the delicate state of my mind can bear. *Because he is no longer the boy who gave you the stars. He's the man who was arrested in front of his children and didn't even have to ask why.*

Beatrix

G'day Challeys! Am at Gatwick airport and I'm getting on a plane. Have a last-minute crisis meeting up in Glasgow. Won't be back till next Monday. Haven't heard from you all since Thursday so hope all is well? Have met a man at the airport. He is HOT. We've been getting on like a house on fire. Sending you hugs and love and big kisses. Bea x

And SEND. Perfect. It'll let them know I'm thinking of them, but won't make a big deal of how they haven't been in touch in four days and that it's making me really uneasy. Two days without a text message is unheard of, more than half a week is . . . well, it hasn't happened in a long time.

I can imagine Tami's face when she gets that text. She'll roll her big, black-brown eyes and then use her hand to twirl up her shoulder-length twists – not dreads as I once called them – into a big bun on her head, before letting them fall. She'll shake her head briefly, then sit and play with her wedding ring while deciding what to reply. Then she'll text me back a neutral-ish reply wishing me luck and will somehow manage to avoid telling me to be careful while getting her point across.

Tami really does treat me like her little sister sometimes:

calling me to see how I am, asking me over to dinner to make sure I've eaten properly at least once every two weeks. She even made me godmother to Ansy, the most perfect six-year-old in the universe. She really is. I knew Cora when she was six and she wasn't perfect. Oh, look, don't get upset with me and think I'm a snide cow, I didn't mean it like that. Cora's beautiful, she's warm, and funny and has an amazing spirit. Anansy's so squidgy and humorous and she's really come into her own as a six-year-old. That's all I meant: Anansy's the perfect six-year-old, Cora is the perfect nine-year-old.

I sit up straight as my new travelling companion approaches, rearrange my posture to stick out my chest a bit more, flash my slender waist. I knew wearing the push-up bra and this Lycra top would pay off. *'Seriously, Beatrix, you'd travel for hours in underwire and what is essentially a giant elastic bandage on the off-chance you get some male attention?'* Tami would say if she could see me now.

For men like this one, I would. This hive of travellers and travelling is messy with people, trolleys, bags, the boom of security announcements and the constant flickering of arrival and departure screens but this man stands out among it all. My travelling companion is carrying a white and green cardboard cup of chai latte in each hand. It's dreadful stuff, truly, but he drinks it. I've only got three hours tops to get him to see he wants to spend the next few days in Glasgow with me, no matter what other plans he thinks he has. To do that, I have to show him he and I are made for each other because our interests and lists of likes are mirrors of each other. If that means drinking spiced warm milk, so be it.

I moisten my lips with the tip of my tongue, giving him

a taster of what he could have in store if he plays his cards right.

'One chai latte,' he says, handing me the white and green cardboard cup from his left hand.

'I love this stuff, don't you?' I smile at him as he settles himself beside me. Not close enough for me to press my body against him and make my presence felt, remind him I am a warm, welcoming body, though. Despite that, I can feel a connection forming. He talks with confidence and intelligence. He holds himself comfortably and he has a warm smile with a laugh that could start to tingle my stomach if he does it enough.

'Actually,' he says, 'I can't stand it. I drank it because my ex liked it. When I got up to the counter I thought, actually, I hate this stuff. I'm drinking it out of habit. I'll have a chamomile tea instead.'

'Oh. Right,' I say. I'm going to have to work at this, and I like that. Actually, I LOVE that. I love the thrill of this particular type of chase.

Tami

I wonder if other people feel like this? If they feel completely removed from the world they are living in.

It's Monday morning and I am sitting on a bench on the seafront. If I were to turn my head to the left, I would see two large buildings, then the line of beach huts, with their brightly coloured doors, leading like a string of rainbow beads towards Brighton. I would also see Brighton Pier, and the sweep of beach that makes this part of the UK look like a Mediterranean Riviera. I would see the people who come and go almost like a slow-moving tide on the land. If I were to turn my head to the right, I would see the building that has been rescued from ruin and restored by developers, the back of the public swimming baths, the café that sells homemade ice-cream that people queue around the block for. I would see the little shelter with its smeared windows and peeling paint that looks like something from a movie set in the 1950s. I would see the evenly spaced groynes reaching out into the sea like fingers of the land, and the short platform with its orange and white lifebelt, and I would see the sea in its peaceful, blown-glass state.

I look neither left nor right. I sit on the bench with my legs pulled up to my chest, my eyes fixed on the expanse of water in front of me. There are people in the sea. Even on days when it's too cold to go out without a few layers, a scarf, and gloves, people seem to brave the icy waters. People only avoid the sea, it seems, when there is snow on the ground.

Do other people feel like I feel? As if they've landed in an alien life. As if they are a paper cut-out in the world that is real and whole and three-dimensional. Or is that the other way around? Is the world made of paper since it is so easily re-ordered to not make sense, and I am the three-dimensional dolly that needs to be moulded over time to fit in?

I've come here after the school run to escape the atmosphere in the house. I cannot think in the house, I cannot think with Scott around. And he is around. After a weekend where we've not talked about The Big Thing That Happened, and instead have focused on the girls and making sure they are OK, Scott has decided to work at home this week. I was hanging on for today, desperate to have some time alone so I could think without feeling guilty or feeling as if I was betraying him. I can't do that now. Every time I turn around he is there. Even if he isn't in the same room, there are pictures of him – smiling with the girls, with me – under magnets on the fridge, there are framed photos of him on the surfaces. And even if it's not his pictures, it's his mug, his slippers, his newspaper, his phone charger, his letters, his unread books, his socks, his clothes, his imprint in a chair. He is everywhere because it is his home. And I can't think surrounded by him.

I don't know what to think. I can admit that to myself out here.

I believe him when he says he didn't do it.

I believe every woman when she says she's been attacked.

This is what is frying my brain. I believe them both – when one of them *must* be lying.

And I can't see either of them lying about this.

Fifteen months ago

'Come jogging with me,' she said to me. We'd been meeting up for chats and coffee for months and I could not get over how similar we were. How we clicked on almost every level. We understood what it was like to live with the constant disapproval of our parents hanging over us, to be happy with who you were even if it wasn't what you could have been.

'No!' I said, affronted.

'Why not?' she replied, her usual smile on her face.

'Why would I is the question you should be asking,' I replied. 'Jogging. As. If.'

'Come jogging with me,' she repeated. 'It'll be fun.'

'No way!' I replied. 'Have you seen me run? This body,' I indicated to myself, 'and these lungs were not made for running.'

'Come jogging with me. I do it every morning before work, but you can just come once a week at first.'

'At first?'

'Once you get into it you'll want to come out with me every day.'

'I really won't. Besides, I've got two children to get to school, mornings are a no-no.'

'Why can't Scott do it?'

'Because he's got work.'

'So have you.'

'But ...' I stopped talking as it occurred to me that I did have work. I did work, and I worked very hard. Before Scott's last three promotions, which all happened in quick succession, and so increased his earnings by a significant amount in a short period of time, it was my earnings and savings that kept us afloat, allowed us to afford the house. I made decent money, and I worked long hours if you took into account the things I did when the girls were asleep. It'd just become a given that I would do the school run every day, that I would pick them up, and I would take time off if they were sick, had doctor's appointments, needed extra bits for school. Scott had stopped doing those things the more he earned – without either of us noticing it seemed. I simply worked around everyone, keeping the house going and earning money.

Him doing the school run one day a week, or even just getting up with the girls and getting them washed, dressed and making their breakfast, shouldn't be a big deal.

'Come running with me,' Mirabelle said, the grin on her face growing wider with every second.

'OK,' I said. 'OK.'

Fourteen months ago
'Come on, girl, you can do it. Keep going.'

Mirabelle was obviously mistaking me for someone who managed to go five minutes without stopping.

'Come on.' She was clapping her hands and running backwards, regularly stopping to bounce up and down on the spot to wait for me to catch up, while I dragged myself along the promenade, barely able to keep upright let alone run.

111

I hadn't realised how unfit I was, now I was feeling it in every cell of my body. My skin hurt, tingled under my clothes like a million needles were pricking me. *How did I manage to get talked into this?* I'd asked myself many times over the last few runs. I never had a definitive answer: it was something to do with fun, and enjoying being around Mirabelle and her energy. And her belief in me, I suppose. It'd been something I hadn't had in so long – I hadn't even noticed that until she encouraged me to run. Putting one foot in front of the other was a challenge that I'd never set myself but I was enjoying on many levels – most of them masochistic.

I stopped, placed both palms on my grey jogging-bottom-covered thighs and heaved as much breath into my lungs as I could manage. My running gear was pristine because it was only used once a week, Mirabelle's running gear was pristine because she had a lot of running clothes.

There were other people around, of course. None of them seemed to be as unfit as me. I would watch them jog, their heads held high, their bodies at ease, and would wonder how they managed to jump from my stage to their stage, and when that transition would happen for me.

'Come on, just a bit further,' she cajoled. Sometimes I wanted to take the batteries out of her, she was so exhausting.

'Nah,' I replied, and staggered a bit further to collapse on a wooden bench.

Mirabelle came and stood in front of me, a grin on her face, still bouncing so she wouldn't cool down. 'You're doing so well.'

'Whatevs, as the young people say,' I replied. 'Why so early today?'

'I wanted to show you something,' she replied, the gold edging on her clothes and her trainers shining clearly in the gloom of the September morning.

'What's that?' I replied.

She turned towards Brighton, the place we were heading to, and smiled again, not speaking for long seconds. 'That,' she said quietly and full of pride. I followed the line of her long, lithe arm to where, over the sea, over the Pier, the world started to glow. Peach, pink, amber, were rapidly bleeding onto the horizon, paving the way for the sun to make its entrance.

It felt like the world was beginning from scratch and I was there to bear witness to it. I was watching one of life's miracles I regularly took for granted: the sun rising.

I gasped.

'You've never seen the sun rise like that, have you?'

I hadn't. I'd never been outside and watched the sun rise, I'd never sat up all night in the open air and watched the breaking of light in the distance. It was different than watching it rise behind glass, but I hadn't even done that very many times. How was it possible that I had never watched a new day being born au naturel?

'This is how I always think the day starts on the Rose Petal Beach,' Mirabelle whispered.

'You'll have to tell me that story one day,' I said.

'One day,' she said. 'But not today.' Instead of offering me the story of the picture that hung in her living room, she held out her hand to me. I took it, her hand was smooth and soft, not at all the hands of a woman who spent her days washing up, cleaning up and forgetting to use hand cream, like me. I was envious of her hands, like I was envious of her hair. She had grown her beautiful, shiny black hair to the middle of her back without chemical straightening because she had time to take care of it properly. I washed and twisted my hair every two weeks and wound it back off my face because that fitted in with my lifestyle. She lavished care and attention on her hair that made it one of her most outstanding features. Mirabelle hauled me to my feet. The strength of the sun seemed to suddenly flow through my bones, tingling my limbs back to life. Upright, I felt strong again, capable of running to Brighton Pier and back. This was what she'd meant, of course. This was the fun part. Not the joking with her, talking with her, the being with her – it was the finding me in all of the daily busy-ness of my life. It was carving out a few precious minutes to be able to be Tamia. I wasn't mother, wife, self-employed consultant, woman, Hove resident, non-graduate, breaker of my parents' hearts when I was running. I was Tamia. Unlabelled, unique, complete. Being myself was the most fun I'd had in a long time.

Mirabelle gave my hand a determined squeeze, and I squeezed back.

We ran towards Brighton, away from our homes, chasing the rising sun. Holding hands most of the way.

This is the bench I collapsed on that day. I stop here often if I am walking into Brighton to remember that day and how it marked the turning point in my relationship with myself. That day, I started to believe I was important, I had the right to take care of myself as well as my family.

114

I've been aware of her walking past several times but not stopping until this trip, when she slides onto the edge of the bench furthest away from me.

I do not look at her. I cannot look at her. Instead, I pull my legs in closer, hugging myself tighter. I'm not sure I want to talk to her. I know I don't want to talk to Scott, but that's because he's always there, the whole of my existence is full of him, but not so much with her. She was so important to me, though. She brought running into my life. And running was something that was purely for me. Mirabelle had started my own little revolution in my mind, my heart, my life. Now she seemed to be instrumental in breaking everything apart.

'I often come and sit on this bench to think,' she says. 'I think of it as our bench.'

My head turns towards her, wondering if she's really talking to me as if nothing is wrong. As if she hasn't labelled my husband a rapist.

Her expression pulls in tight, her distress apparent when she sees my face, presumably noticing the remnants of the tears I've been crying while I have been sitting here. Ashamed at being seen by her of all people, I use the heel of my hand to roughly wipe my face dry, while turning back to the sea.

'I'm so sorry,' she says. 'I thought about it for so long before I reported it. I almost didn't because of what it would do to you. I'm so sorry you had to find out that he's done this.'

'Has he though?' I ask without looking at her.

A moment of agony passes between us, her hurt exploding outwards and stabbing me in the very centre of my heart. 'You don't believe me,' she replies. Her words are followed

115

by a short, dry laugh. 'I really hoped you'd be different.'

'Different? Different to who? Have you done this before?'

'No, I haven't "done this before". But I have been sexually harassed before. And it's amazing how many women who were your friends will develop "belief issues" when you stop accepting the harassment.'

I look away.

'That's why I didn't report Scott for sexual harassment. I thought if I kept my head down, got on with my work, avoided him as much as possible, it would all go away. Except it didn't, it got worse until—'

'Why didn't you ever say anything to me? This is what I don't understand. If it's true—'

'It is,' she cuts in.

'Then why be my friend all this time and not say a word?'

'Would you have believed me?'

'*Yes, of course,*' I'm meant to say, and the words are teetering on the edge of my tongue, but they don't fall. Not when the man she is talking about is a man I have known for half my life.

'No, didn't think so,' she says.

Silence comes to us again, weaves its tendrils between us, binding us together tighter and tighter with every passing second. The sound of the waves takes up the space where the words should be.

I eventually ask again the question I asked the other night: 'Why did you even answer the phone to me, knowing what you'd done?'

For a moment I think she's going to give me that answer she did the other night in my hallway. Then her black eyes

– for she is no longer wearing her contacts – close wearily. 'Because for a brief moment I thought – hoped – you were calling to tell me that you believed me. It was a stupid thing to think, to hope for, but there you go. I almost didn't answer but the part of me that was hoping, would always have wondered if you did believe me.'

It doesn't make sense, though, how could she agree to look after the children of the man she claims tried to ... 'You could have said no,' I tell her.

'Think back to that conversation, Tami, at what point could I have said no so you would have listened? You were on the verge of hysteria and I did keep saying no and you kept on at me until I gave in.'

I do not like what she is saying. In another context, it sounds like ... Is it really that easy to force your will upon someone else without even realising what you are doing? I needed her help so I kept on at her until I got it. It never occurred to me there might have been a reason for her reticence. I simply carried on until I got what I wanted.

I have to speak to Scott. I jump to my feet. I have to speak to him, and he has to tell me everything. Something is not right about this. I trust Scott, I trust Mirabelle, but there is something not right here and I need to find out what it is.

Tami

My house is alive when I insert the key into the lock.

The sleek stereo, which lives in the kitchen, is filling the house with Luther Vandross. The Hoover is droning on as it is being pushed around upstairs, above the sound of it is Scott's singing voice, accompanying Luther.

Would a guilty man be so blasé that he does housework and sings along to love songs? Would he not be formulating a plan to get off with his crime? Would an innocent man be doing these things? Would he not be worrying that he was going to get sent away? Wouldn't he have got himself a solicitor and be going over everything to sort out his defence?

Not bothering to take off my shoes, I head to flick off the music, to bring silence so I can tell him I'm here without having to call him. My hand hovers over the stop button of the iPod sitting in the dock of the stereo as I cast my gaze around the kitchen. He has cleaned. Scott has cleaned the kitchen. Every surface has been cleared, tidied and wiped. There are no dishes in the sink or on the side. He's vacuumed and mopped the floor. The back doors even look like they've been given a wipe. I can't remember the last time he did any of those things, let alone *all* of those things.

Is this Scott's equivalent of a man bringing home flowers

for his wife because he's done something wrong? Luther is crowding me, he is filling my brain with the words he's singing, his voice vibrating my body, when what I want – what I *need* – is clarity. I need to think. To listen. To understand. Because nothing is making sense.

I hit the stop button, cutting Luther off mid-word. The word hangs there for a moment but is finished by my husband singing upstairs. He continues to sing for a few seconds before realising his backing vocal has gone. He switches off the Hoover and then nothing. Probably waiting to hear if there is someone else in the house, if I am home.

His footsteps are on the stairs, almost skipping as he comes down to put his music back on, to fill the house with his happiness. I cannot understand it. He was arrested five days ago and he is acting as if nothing has happened, like all is well in his world.

He enters the kitchen, humming 'Give Me The Reason' but stops, saying, 'Oh,' when he sees me standing there. 'I didn't realise you were back.'

When I say nothing, he waves his hand around the kitchen. 'Ta-dah! What do you think? I couldn't concentrate on work so thought I'd make use of this time and help out a little. I quite enjoyed it actually.'

I continue to stare at him. He isn't the man I thought he was. Literally. Physically, I haven't looked at him for a long time. Where did that muscular frame come from? He was always a little on the slender side of normal – all muscles, but lean. Where did that haircut come from? He always used to have it buzzed to a grade two or wavy and wild. At some point my husband has begun gelling his hair back off his face. I have noticed but not really registered. Where did the sheen of a tan and 'products' come from? The Scott I know, the Scott I married and have been living with all this time, always had smooth, youthful skin – not this faux healthiness that he seems to exude.

'We need to talk, don't we?' he says to my contemplative silence.

I nod. 'You need to tell me the whole truth.'

In our living room Scott tells me everything. As he does so, he dismantles every piece of my soul.

Three years ago

'What are you doing?' I asked Scott, coming into the office in the loft that we'd just had installed. It'd been a huge job and we'd been driven to the edge of insanity while the builders were in, but it was complete. The walls were the same butter-yellow as the rest of the house, the carpet the same oatmeal. There was a huge desk under the skylights upon which sat the computer, the printer, the scanner and the fax machine. Along one wall, we'd had floor-to-ceiling bookcases installed, and a comfy chair plus beanbag so it could be a reading area. There was even a padded-top boxseat that doubled as a toy box. Pictures of the girls were leant up against the walls, waiting to be put up to complete the room. It'd been designed so one of us, usually Scott, could work on the main computer while the other would still have oodles of space to work on their laptop. It'd be great, too, for the girls to come up here and play on the computer or in the reading area while one of us worked.

'Oh, nothing,' he said and clicked a button on his mouse

to change the screen as I stepped into the room.

'I thought you were coming to bed,' I said, snaking my hand across his collarbone and around his neck.

'I am,' he replied, tensing ever so slightly at my touch.

Ignoring the trickle of hurt that caused, I slung an arm around his neck and tipped myself onto his lap. 'I thought we were going to celebrate your promotion the old-fashioned way?' I said. I felt the rigidity of his erection and the raw edge of his open fly beneath me, and turned to look at him quizzically.

'We are,' he said, his mouth finding a smile, 'I just need to finish up here.'

I moved my gaze from him to the computer, then clicked the mouse to bring up the screen he'd hidden as I came in.

My body and mind reared back at the movie, paused and frozen, that filled the screen. I studied the image, a sickness stirring in the space beneath my ribcage. It wasn't *that* extreme, it wasn't *that* unusual an act, the woman even had a smile on her face while the two men had lecherous sneers, but it was the look in the woman's eyes that I was forced towards. The vacant despair she couldn't hide behind that smile; the unending torment that lived in her eyes and probably in her soul.

As suddenly as those people, those porn stars, were there, they were gone again, clicked away by my husband. I slid off his lap and stood facing the bookcase while I heard him zip himself up. When I could brave seeing him again, he was a little sheepish, a tad embarrassed, but otherwise normal.

'We were about to have sex,' I said to him, confused.

'I know, but ...' There was no end to that sentence, no reason for being up there doing that when we were 'on a promise' as he'd been calling it all day. He'd just been promoted, he was now 'King of the Universe' as I labelled him. He was one step away from being CEO of TLITI, two steps away from partner and the Board. All his dreams had come true. We were going to bed with a bottle of expensive champagne to *celebrate*. He'd only nipped up here to check his emails and hadn't returned.

'How long have you been using this stuff?' I asked when it was apparent the sentence wasn't going to be completed, his actions weren't going to be explained.

'I've only been up here ten minutes.'

'You know what I mean.' This explained why sometimes I would walk into a room and there would be the faint odour of sex in the air. I'd always tell myself that I was crazy because why would the living room – any room – smell of sex when we hadn't had sex in there?

His sigh moved his body, he chewed on his bottom lip, ran his hand through his hair, all the while avoiding visual contact with me. 'It's only a bit of porn, Tami, don't make it into a big incident. It really is no big deal.'

'Actually, it's a huge deal. I didn't know you looked at this stuff, I thought you had more respect for women.'

In an over-exaggerated manner, Scott rolled his eyes at me. 'All men look at porn. It doesn't mean they don't respect women.'

'So why didn't you tell me about it if it's so normal?'

'Why didn't you ask if you've got such an issue with it?'

'Because I thought you had a lot more respect for women.'

Another eye roll, another sigh, another facial expression that dismissed what I was saying.

'Is this why we haven't had sex in weeks?' I asked. 'Because you've been getting your kicks by doing this?'

'No, you being constantly tired and tied up with the girls and snowed under with work is why we haven't had sex for weeks.'

'That's not true. Not completely, anyway. I've tried to initiate it and you haven't really responded.'

'I've responded, but not as enthusiastically as I should because I could tell your heart wasn't in it.'

'It was.'

'It doesn't feel like it, Tami. I don't get the feeling that you, you know, want me as much as you used to. It sometimes feels as if you're doing it because you feel you have to.'

'That's not true. You know that's not true.'

'That's how it feels.'

'So wanking off to dirty movies is better, is it?'

'Not better, easier. I know they're not going to reject me.'

'I never reject you.'

'It feels like it.'

Inhaling a few times, I stared at him wondering if he really felt rejected or if he was doing that old Scott trick of turning it onto me to win the argument, or if it was a bit of both. I'd never know, of course. 'Look, I don't like you watching this stuff, I'd *really* rather you didn't. But if you're going to do it, make sure the girls never see it. I can't believe you've got it on this computer when Cora could easily click on it.'

His eyes dipped and his head lowered while a modicum of shame emanated from him. At least he could see how wrong he was to do that.

'If you're going to use it, then I can't stop you, but if the girls ever see even one image, I will divorce you.'

His head snapped up at that. 'It's only a bit of porn.'

'If the girls see it,' I repeated slowly so he could understand, 'I will divorce you. I'm telling you this now so there'll be no arguments should it happen. OK?'

He nodded.

As I turned to leave, he said, 'Get the champagne open, I'll be down in two ticks.'

I spun to look at him, to check if he was in any way joking. 'Take your time,' I said when I realised he wasn't. He actually thought we'd be doing it after what I'd just discovered. Astounding. 'Take all the time you want. I'm going to sleep.'

No matter how hard I tried to doze off, I couldn't. The image of the woman with the rictus smile and torment etched into the windows to her soul was something that kept waking me up before I could properly sleep.

This is how I know I am still alive: it hurts. My life hurts.

There is a huge gaping hole in my chest where my heart used to be, and it is so big I could put my whole fist in there and it would not touch the sides.

This is how I know I am still alive: his words are killing me. His words are like a truck that has hit me full-force without slowing first, and I am nearly gone but not quite because it hurts, and everything that comes out of his mouth is killing me.

I am sitting on the armchair in our living room, knowing I should be somewhere else. Knowing that none of this would be happening if I wasn't living someone else's life.

In my mind, I see Scott holding his hand out to me as I reach him at the end of the aisle. He has a smile on his face, and tears streaming down his face. In my mind, I feel his hand tighten around mine and I know he will never let me go. In my mind, I hear him say, *until death us do part.* In my mind I relax and let go because this is forever.

Scott has been having an affair with Mirabelle.

This is what he has just told me.

'I didn't want to tell you this,' he'd said to me when he first started talking. We sat in our living room, in our favourite places, both of us on the edge of our seats. 'I really hoped . . .' He'd paused, squeezed the bridge of his nose between his thumb and forefinger, his eyes brimming with tears. 'I didn't want you to find out like this.' Isn't that the sort of thing that Mirabelle said to me? *'I'm sorry you had to find out like this.'* Neither of them had said they were sorry for what they had done, they were just sorry I had to find out. 'It was a flirtation that got out of control. Me and you weren't getting on that well, I felt shut out from the life you had with the girls, you had no time for me. I felt really . . . *lonely*, yeah, lonely in our marriage. I threw myself into work to try to block it out, and she was there. We started off just as friends, then we started spending more time together, mainly working, and we started to chat about non-work stuff, and one thing led to another. I didn't mean for it to happen. But

125

after that, it became impossible to end it. Every time I tried she threatened to tell you. She said she'd ruin my life if I finished with her, she'd tell you everything and would make out that I was going to leave you for her. That was never going to happen, please believe me.

'I felt so trapped. And then we were getting on again, you started to be like you again, you seemed so much happier, and I felt so dreadful, so awful. So I finished with her once and for all. Told her that I didn't care if she told you because I'd take my chances. I told her I was going to tell you myself. And she went crazy. She called me all sorts and said she was going to ruin my life just as I'd ruined hers. She said she was going to do something that would make sure everyone hated me. Three days later I was arrested.'

I always thought that if I was cheated on, if the man I loved slept with someone else behind my back, I would lose the plot. I would shout and scream and throw him out. I would then hurl his stuff out the window, still screaming abuse, still making my feelings known, and then, when he was removed from the house, I would call a divorce lawyer. I never thought that it would happen with Scott, of course, but it's one of those things that crosses your mind; that you'd talk about – like you'd imagine what you'd do if you won the lottery even though you don't buy tickets. It's a hypothetical situation that wouldn't ever happen, but if it did you're pretty sure, knowing your own personality, how you would respond.

So why am I sitting here, a chain of knots linking my chest and my stomach, my body frozen in horror, my mouth filling and refilling with bile, my mind racing and suspended at the same time?

'I didn't ever want you to find out,' Scott is saying to my silence. I have been unable to speak since he started to because every word has been slicing me apart; dismantling everything I thought about us, about our lives, about him, about me.

'Do you love her?' My voice has asked this all on its own. I don't remember instructing it to, it just did it.

'No. God, no. It was a horrible, horrible mistake. Especially with what's happened in the past few days. I've been hoping that she'll go to the police and tell the truth. That's why I didn't get a solicitor. I know she's not going to let it go that far. She'll tell the truth and all this will go away. I really didn't want you to find out like this.'

'How many times did you make love to her?' I ask.

'It wasn't lovemaking, it was . . . It was stupidity. A hideous mistake.'

'How many times did this hideous mistake happen?' My lips feel odd, like they're not attached to my body; numb and cold.

'You don't want to know that,' he says.

'I do. How many times?'

'Tami, believe me, you don't want to know.'

'Stop telling me what I do and don't want to know. How many times?'

'I don't remember,' he replies.

'When was the first time?'

He shrugs, looks away. 'I really don't remember, Tami.'

'You don't remember the first time you slept with the woman who you've thrown your marriage away for, but you've never once forgotten your boss's daughter's birthday? Don't give me that. When was the first time?'

127

'Eighteen months ago,' he replies. More than a year. More than a year ago he started to lie to me. He started to deceive me. And I'm sure he remembers how many times, too. Even if it was once a month, it would have been at least eighteen times. Eighteen times. And I know what Scott is like, what anyone is like when they start something new, it wouldn't have been once a month. It would have been more. It would have been as many times as possible.

'Where was the first time?' I ask. I need to get the picture right in my head. I need to fix it there so I can understand all this. Because until I hear it, I don't think I'll really believe it. I don't think I'll be able to frame this as something that's really possible.

He stares at the fireplace in response to my question. He'd wanted that fireplace. I'd thought it was too big and imposing, the marble too wishy-washy amongst the cream walls, ,beige carpet and tan leather sofas. I'd wanted a solid black one, one that would stand out, make a statement in this otherwise bland room. But no, Scott had insisted. 'I know best,' he'd said. 'It's going to look fantastic.' And it hadn't. It'd looked bland. I'd never said that. I'd never say that. I have a sudden urge to tell him that now. To put him in his place. To let him know that he wasn't always right. In fact, sometimes he could be downright wrong.

'Where?' I ask him. I have a horrible creeping suspicion that it was here. In our bed. I have a deep, seasick-type fear that the first time he cheated on me he used my sheets, my pillows, my home. She probably showered in my shower afterwards, as well. Dried herself on my towels. Probably went through my belongings and had a laugh about my assortment of dull, ordinary, black knickers. My range of dull, ordinary, black bras. My average clothes. My run-of-the-mill hair products. If I was screwing someone's husband, I would probably go through her things and laugh at her too. What would stop me when I'd already crossed such a huge line?

'Where?' I ask again. The feeling is coming back to my lips. Feeling is flowing through my body again, crashing and crashing through me in hot, foamy waves of anger.

He hangs his head, a puppy dog in need of some reassurance that he isn't completely bad, he isn't totally naughty.

'*Where?*' The word is forced out through gritted teeth and burning lips.

'I don't think you—'

'Where. Just tell me where. Why is that so hard? You did it, so now tell me about it. Where, where, where, where?'

'In her kitchen,' he says loudly to drown me out. 'Up against the sink. Over before it even started. Does that make you feel better? Is that what you wanted to hear?'

Colours are exploding behind my eyelids. That truck has hit me again. The hole where my heart should be has exploded again. My body is numb and on fire at the same time. I cannot get air into my lungs. I cannot breathe in one smooth movement. Every breath is a short, forced gasp. I press my hand over my chest, I push the other hand over my stomach. I cannot breathe.

One year ago

'Is Scott a good husband?' Mirabelle asked me.

'What an odd question.'

129

'Not really. Just wondering if he is or not. I might ask him one day if he thinks you're a good wife.'

'Go right ahead. I have no worries that he'll tell you I'm the best wife a man has ever had. Why wouldn't he?'

'But you can't say the same thing about him as a husband?'

'Of course I can,' I replied. 'He's wonderful.'

She grinned at me. 'You went all gooey when you said that.'

'Well, I'm allowed. He's, you know, he's my man. He does that to me.'

'I was married once,' she said.

'You? How come you've never mentioned that before, Mirabelle Kemini?'

'It was a long time ago.'

'What went wrong?'

She stared off into the distance for a while, looking at where we'd just come from on our run. 'Lots of things. But mainly it was my fault. I got married too young to the wrong person. I was bound not to stay, always chasing the impossible dream, me.'

'Which is?'

'Love, of course. What else is there in life that is worth chasing?'

'And you didn't love your husband?'

'Oh, I loved him all right. Just not enough. Not in the right way. Especially when my impossible dream was out there somewhere.'

She stood upright, stretching, and as her running top rode upwards, it showed off her smooth, flat stomach and the diamond body bar inserted into the skin below her belly button.

130

'Come on, we've got to get showered and on with the day. Have you finished your stretches yet?'

'Did you cheat on your husband?' I asked.

She stopped her final stretches and lowered her arms to look at me, a haunted look on her face. 'I suppose I did, if I'm honest. But not necessarily in the way you mean. I do know I did some things I wasn't proud of. And I need to come to terms with that. Which I will one day. I'm trying not to be the sort of person who would do what I did back then. I'm trying to be a better person.'

'I think you're a great person,' I said.

'Thanks, honey,' she replied, tugging affectionately on one of my twists that had escaped my ponytail before securing it behind my ear. 'You're great too. I hope Scott knows how lucky he is to have you.'

Beep-beep-beep-beep!

My phone in my pocket makes me jump. My eyes go to the clock on the mantelpiece. Two-fifty. My ten-minute warning, a reminder that I need to be on the way to pick up the girls from school in no more than ten minutes.

Scott has his hands in his hair, staring down at the carpet. I need this to be over. I need to rewind time and for him to have not told me, or further, for him not to have done it. I remember that first time we did it. He always called it making love. He always made it seem special, like he'd never do that with anyone else. He always said he didn't want anyone else. Liar.

LIAR!

My legs felt like jelly when he first told me, my body seemed carved from stone, too, but now I am standing, I discover my body can support itself, my limbs can move.

'I have to go and get the girls,' I say. I have to put this all in a box because I cannot handle this right now. If I think it through any longer, if I talk any longer about this, I will not be able to do anything else. I will not be able to keep on walking and thinking, and the girls don't need that. They don't deserve to have me falling apart because I was stupid enough to marry their father, and befriend his mistress.

'I didn't mean for any of this to happen,' Scott says as I am about to leave the room. 'I really didn't mean for you to find out.'

I'm sure you didn't, I think to myself.

He didn't say he was sorry. He didn't beg forgiveness for sleeping with someone else. In Scott's mind, our biggest problem was me finding out he'd been cheating.

That was the thought that haunted me as I hurried to school.

My husband was sorry to be caught, not for doing what he did in the first place.

Tami

'Where do the clouds sleep, Mama?' Anansy asks.

We're at the beach, eating fish and chips for dinner. I am a bad mother, yes, for doing this to them, but the thought of going back to the house with *him* is unacceptable at the moment. It's slightly chilly, especially with the wind down here on the front, and night will start to ink itself onto the sky soon, but a few more minutes here, and then home and straight upstairs for homework and then bed will help me.

I look up at the clouds above us and those suspended over the sea.

'I don't know,' I say to her. 'Do you know, Cora?'

'No, I don't know either,' she says.

'Maybe Dad will know,' Anansy says.

'Maybe,' I reply. 'Maybe.'

I relieve them of their greasy chip papers and scrunch them up, place them on top of my untouched chips. 'Let's go, homework, bath, bed.'

'Is Dad going to read us a story?' Anansy asks as they gather up their book bags and normal bags. My hands are cold, almost numb. The girls are cold to the touch, but not cold. They never seem to feel the cold, it's always a battle to get them to wear coats or do them up because they are always so warm.

'Maybe,' I say, as non-committal with the word as I can make it. *Maybe he'll read you a story, then come back to finish torturing me with the story of his affair.*

Tami

He didn't know where clouds sleep, apparently. They asked him and he didn't know. He also didn't read them a story because that would mean leaving the safety of the loft room where he has been hiding all this time.

I'm curled up in the dark, waiting for something.

I'm not sure exactly what, but I am waiting, my breathing pausing and waiting with me until I have no choice but to breathe out.

I can't quite bring myself to think about it. It is too big, too scary, too unreal. Maybe that's what I am waiting for. Maybe I am waiting for the reality to hit so my mind will accept that Scott cheated and Mirabelle lied. It doesn't seem possible.

The bedroom door opens and he slides in through the gap, trying to keep the room dark and not wake me. Usually, lately, he hasn't been that bothered about waking me when he comes to bed after me. He didn't want me to go running with Mirabelle. He'd sulked and complained about it when I told him he had to get the girls ready one morning a week until I said, 'What's wrong with you looking after *your* children for two hours one morning a week?' and since the only answer was 'nothing' he'd let the matter drop. Instead, it felt as if he had been trying to sabotage my running but

135

didn't quite have the courage to go all the way: he didn't mind waking me up so I'd be tired and might cry off the run, but he stopped short at doing something overt like arranging an early meeting. Of course, now I know what that's been all about. He wanted to keep us apart, scared that his secret would leak out.

Scott's clothes rustle loudly in the quiet as he removes them and leaves them in a pile on the floor on his side of the bed. I can tell from here, without even looking, the order of the pile: shirt, trousers, T-shirt, underpants, socks. It is virtually the same every night – sometimes with a suit jacket, sometimes with a jumper, but usually as it is now. He takes off his clothes in the same order every night, then drops them on the floor for me to put in the laundry hamper. It's not an overt act, of course, it's simply a habit: he leaves them there because I will clear them away. It didn't used to be like this. I don't know when it changed, when he became too important to put his clothes in the hamper and when I became so unimportant I let him get away with it.

His body is warm in the bed. A familiar, solid presence I've come to expect over the years. Well of course I have, he's my husband. He's the man I've pledged to spend the rest of my life with. Where else would his lean, muscular body be at night except in bed with me? Where else? Up the road and round the corner, in the big house with the drive and gorgeous owner. Scott moves across the bed, edging closer and closer until his body is near mine, and then it is touching me, and then he is beside me, his body curled around mine, making the other part of the 99 quote we always used to be.

'Remember the nights you used to come home after working in

the bar and would curl up behind me, and I'd wake up for a second and then fall asleep again because now I could sleep properly because you were home?' I want to say to him. *'Remember how we were the perfect 99, then?'* And I want to say, *'Were you fucking someone else then, too? Did you lie about working late nights so you could orgasm inside someone else's body?'* And I want to say, *'Can you finish cutting out my heart with a spoon and feed it to your dog because this job you've left unfinished is so incredibly painful? I'd rather you did it and it killed me so I don't have to feel this.'* And I want to say so many other disjointed, unpleasant, hurtful, painful, desperate things that I'm glad I can't speak.

'I'm sorry I hurt you,' he murmurs. We used to whisper when the girls were babies and slept in our room. 'I'm so sorry. I didn't think about what I was doing. It was a stupid, stupid mistake because I was so weak and lonely. I can't think or function properly if we're not getting on, if we're not working together as a team. It was such a huge mistake . . . I'm so sorry.'

I want him; ache for him. In my chest, between my legs, at the back of my mouth I long for him. I need him to be a part of me so that he can be mine again and that will somehow undo him being with her. His body can belong to me again, as he pledged it to me on the day we got married, like it has been all these years. I reach for him, my hand knowing exactly where to touch to let him know what I want: him. I bet she doesn't know. I bet she goes for the obvious place to initiate sex, but if I touch Scott there, he knows what it means.

In response to my fingers on his skin, to our physical shorthand, he moves from behind me, and as I roll onto my back, he climbs on top of me. He briefly kisses me, our lips meeting in an exchange of understanding, of acceptance of what is about to happen.

Scott, erect and firm, pushes into me and the ache doesn't recede into nothingness like I thought it would once we were together. It explodes, becoming more urgent, more agonising. I arch my back, pull him closer to me, digging my hands into the flesh of his back as I try to claw him back. I want all of him. It's what I had, it's what I want back.

I want him back.

I draw him nearer still, the memory of the first time we did this, the intensity, the closeness, the desperation to not allow anything to come between us flashes through my mind as he starts to move harder.

He did this with her.

The thought slams into my head, my chest, my heart at the same time. And then it ploughs into my hands, which rip themselves away from clinging onto him and are suddenly on his chest, pushing at him, while my body twists away, rejecting him, distancing him.

'Stop,' I almost scream. 'Stop. Stop. Get off me.'

Without question, in an instant, he is rolling away and off me.

The tears are huge and constant as I grab the duvet, tug it up over me, hiding my body from him. I don't want him to see me, not even the outline of me. I don't want him to think of me naked when I know he'll be comparing that image to her. And I'll be found wanting, of course. Because I'm not good enough for him any more. Maybe at one time he looked at me and couldn't imagine being with anyone else, maybe at one time he thought that my body and who

I am were what he wanted, but now I know different. In this moment, I realise I am not enough. He looks at porn and he had an affair. I am not enough for him.

If I was, he wouldn't have done what he did.

'I'm sorry,' he whispers.

Scott reaches out to comfort me as I sob, but I shrink away from him. I don't want him now. I don't want him to touch me at all. I have heard half a story, have had half an explanation and I can't let him touch me again until I hear it all. Until he talks and talks at me and I understand. Until I know *why*. And *when*. And *how*. *How* he could do this to me.

'I need to have a shower,' I say between sobbing breaths. I can't believe I did that. I can't believe I tried to reclaim my husband from someone else. I can't believe I had sex with the person who has hurt me more than anyone has in my life. I need to cleanse myself of that. 'I need a shower. Please look away.'

'Why?' he asks, confused.

'I don't want you to see me naked.'

'I've been seeing you naked for sixteen years,' he replies.

'You don't get it, do you?' The sobs are subsiding, calmness is starting to enter my body. 'Just look away, Scott. Please.'

He starts to protest, I can tell in the way he takes a breath, then he obviously changes his mind. When I see he is staring at the wall of wardrobes opposite, I slip out of bed and grab my dressing gown off the metal hook on the back of the door. The towelling material feels scratchy, like needles against my over-sensitised skin.

My hand is on the door handle when he speaks again.

139

'Are you going to make me leave?' he asks, his voice small and fragile and frightened. I haven't heard him sound like that since the night of the miscarriage when he asked the doctor if there was any hope of the baby being saved. Scott hasn't shown that type of fear, *real fear*, since then. He might have felt it, but not shown it.

'How can I make you leave, Scott?' I say through the broken glass in my mouth. 'You've already gone.'

Eighteen months ago
'I've invited Mirabelle over for dinner tomorrow night as well as Beatrix,' I said to Scott as he sat reading reports in bed.

'What?' he replied, lowering the piece of paper in his hand, slipping off his reading glasses. 'You *what*?'

'You know Beatrix is coming over? Well, Mirabelle's at a loose end so I said she should come, too.'

'No,' Scott said. 'That's not happening. Isn't it enough for you two that I have to work with her all day, do I really have to eat with her after hours, too?'

'No, you don't, actually. You can sit up here and I'll bring your meal up to you if you feel that strongly about it.'

'You know what I mean, TB. It's enough that she comes over and sees you and plays with the girls. Why does she have to keep invading our family time, too?'

'"Keep"? This is the first time I've invited her.'

'I don't want her in this house when I'm here,' he said firmly. He used that tone with his not very competent juniors at work, with difficult clients, with tradespeople who hadn't delivered the things we'd ordered and were trying to wriggle out of it. He had clearly forgotten that I

140

was his wife. I didn't need that tone – about anything.

'Well I do, and in case you'd forgotten, it's my house too. And in case you'd forgotten something else – you're not *actually* the boss of me, as the young people say.' I mimicked him: '"I don't want her in this house when I'm here." Who do you think you're talking to?'

'You're not being very fair on me, you know,' he said sadly. 'I come home from work to get away from the office, not to have to put on the face that I use there. This is my refuge from all the shit I have to put up with every day. I'm gutted you can't see that I need a break from my work and that having her here puts me under pressure. You did this job once, I'd have thought you'd remember what that was like.'

'I'm sorry,' I said to him, feeling ashamed. 'I didn't think. You're right, of course. I'll get out of it somehow.'

'Thanks, gorgeous, I really appreciate it.'

Sorry lovely, is it ok if you don't come to
dinner tomorrow night?
Bea has some private stuff she
wants to chat about. Will reschedule. X

No problem, gorgeous. Hope she's OK. Lots of love
M x

PS Remember that programme No Problem?
Loved that show! M x

*

Scott creeps down the stairs to find me because I haven't returned to bed. I wanted to be down here rather than the spare room because I feel safer in here, in the kitchen. Wearing only my dressing gown, I am cuddled up on the sofa watching a gambling show on the television.

'Come back to bed,' he tells me, standing beside me as I stare across the room at the wall-hung TV.

I ignore him, concentrate on the television. I have the sound down because I do not want to wake the girls whose rooms are above the kitchen, and I do not need the sound to watch this. I'm fascinated by what these people are doing, which is risking it all. Who would risk it all? Who would look at a set of numbers and decide to scoop up their whole life – house, spouse, children, job, future – and place it on a bet? A sure thing. Except there are no sure things when it comes to taking a gamble. Even cheaters eventually get caught out.

'Come back to bed,' he urges. When I do not respond he marches across the room and switches off the television.

'Come back to bed,' he insists.

'No,' I said.

'Tami, you can't sleep down here, I won't let you.'

'Leave me alone.'

'I can't. You're not behaving rationally. I need you to come back to bed. I'll go and sleep in the spare room ... Look, please. I can't stand the thought of you down here all alone all night. Please.'

He doesn't even know he's doing it: '*I need you to come back to bed.*' '*I can't stand the thought ...*' I laugh at him: 'It's not concern for me at all, is it? It's all about you. Even something as simple as me sleeping on the sofa is all about you because you can't stand the thought of me being down here. You need me to do what you want me to do.'

'I didn't mean it like that,' he says.

'Leave me alone.'

'TB—'

'Don't call me that,' I hiss loudly. 'Don't you dare call me that! Leave me alone before I decide to go and sleep in the car and all the neighbours see.' That gives him pause, especially after his arrest.

'I'll go and sleep in the spare room anyway, in case you change your mind,' he eventually says.

'I won't,' I reply under my breath. Once I am alone, I go back to watching the gambling show, this time with the screen off.

Tami

'You have to go to the police and tell the truth,' I say to Mirabelle.

When she opened the door just now I'd had a visceral reaction to her, my body clenching in on itself. Her hair was in large twists and swept back with a headband she usually used for running. Her face was free of make-up and showed many imperfections – blotches and pimple scars as well as dark circles under her eyes. Her eyes were bloodshot and puffy, almost as if she had been crying. Unusually, she wasn't clothed in a form-fitting outfit but in a baggy grey sweatshirt and over-size jeans.

Last night, all night, from my place on the sofa, I kept thinking about who was most important in all of this and one answer kept coming back to me: Cora and Anansy. They did not need to have their father labelled a 'pervert', 'criminal', 'rapist' and every other name used to describe what he had been accused of. It didn't matter if I'd been hurt in all of this, I was an adult, I could take care of myself. My children needed me to look after them. And that meant talking to Mirabelle and getting her to retract her statement.

I waited for Scott to take the girls to school and came here. Every step has been an ordeal. I did not want to be here. I did not want to look in her face and imagine it as she went down on my husband. I did not want to see her hands and imagine them hooked into his hair as he pleasured her with his tongue. I did not want to see her body and imagine it moving beside and with his.

My husband's mistress is puzzled for a moment as she stares at me. 'I did go to the police,' she replies. 'And I did tell the truth.'

Surprise blossoms on my face. 'What did they say when you told them why you'd made it up?'

'Nothing, because I haven't told them that. I told them what happened, what he did to me.'

'Please, Mirabelle ... Look, I know, all right? I know all about you and him and—'

'What do you know about me and him?'

I sigh. 'He told me. He told me about the affair and how you said you'd get even with him for dumping you. I know and I'm devastated. I don't think our marriage will survive. You got what you wanted so now call this whole thing off.'

She stares at me, her dark eyes fixed on my face for an eternity. I am willing to beg if that will make it easier for her. I will do virtually anything to stop the girls finding out this horrible thing.

Mirabelle throws her head back and starts to laugh. It's genuine laughter, not something she's forcing. Soon she's clutching her sides, bent forwards as she continues to laugh. Suddenly she straightens up and refocuses on me. 'Me and him? An affair? I wouldn't touch him with yours!' she shrieks, shaking her head.

'How can you behave like this after what you've done to

me?' I say. *How can she act like this when she's helped him to smash up my family?*

'How can I behave like this?' She sighs. 'Actually, I'm not talking about this on the doorstep,' she says. 'Either come in and we'll talk about this properly or go away.'

'Fine, I'll go.'

'Your choice.'

'Yeah, my choice.'

I turn on my heels and start to march away, indignation burning through my veins. *Who does she think she is?* The woman who is holding the future of my family in the palm of her hand, that's who.

She opens the door as I reach it, steps aside to let me in without looking at me. I know I'm stepping into the lion's den. And I know there's absolutely nothing I can do about it.

The hit-by-a-truck feeling is back. It crashed into me without slowing the second Mirabelle turned left towards her kitchen. I have to hold onto the wall for support as my knees soften. I have been in that room countless times in the last eighteen months, not knowing it was where they first did it. Did that give her some sort of thrill, to have me in there while she replayed the first time my husband made love to her? Did she smile to herself knowing she'd got one over on me?

I can't go in there. If I do, I know I'll be confronted with full-on images of them. Of her pressed up against the kitchen sink, her pencil skirt shoved up around her waist, her knickers on the floor, his trousers and underpants around his ankles, the pair of them rutting, moaning loudly with each stroke.

One of the truck's wheels is resting on my chest and I can't seem to breathe properly.

'Are you all right?' she asks, returning to the corridor when she sees I am not following her. 'Do you need a drink or something?'

I shake my head, while trying to summon my anger again. 'I'm fine,' I say, straightening up, letting go of the wall. 'I want to get this over with.'

She comes closer to me, lowering her voice. 'I take it he told you that nonsense about me and him having an affair?' she says.

'Of course. And I know it's not nonsense.'

'How . . . I mean . . . Do you really think I'd do that to you?' she says. 'I'm your friend, why would I sleep with your man?'

'Why would you accuse him of . . . of what you've accused him of?'

'Because he did it.'

I shake my head at her. I don't believe it. Not because I don't believe her, I just don't believe it was Scott. That doesn't make sense, I know, but it's the only thing that works in my brain at the moment.

'You really can't see what he's like, can you?'

'I know what he's like, I married him, remember?'

She inhales deeply, and then exhales loudly through her nose. 'Tami, if I told you someone had tried to . . . to . . . mug me, would you believe me? Would you comfort me and support me?'

'Yes, of course I would.'

'And if I told you someone else had tried to break into my house and rob me, would you believe and support me?'

'Yes, I would.'

'And if I told you someone had punched me in the face for no reason whatsoever, would you believe me?'

'Yes, I would.'

'And if I told you someone else had tried to ... to ... had sexually assaulted me, would you believe me?'

'Yes.'

'So why would you believe someone else had done that but not him?'

'Because I don't know the other person.'

'So only a man you don't know is capable of that?'

I stay silent because there's no real answer to that question, is there? I've known other people – people I went to school with, people I've worked with – who were accused of various crimes and who were often found guilty. I just know that Scott couldn't have done this. The stilled porn film I saw flashes up in my mind. That was years ago. And it has no connection to this at all.

'Tami, listen to me, I wasn't having an affair with him. I have never had one and I never will have one. He tried to ... He tried ... ' She always seems to run away from that word.

'Put yourself in my position for a moment,' I cut in. 'Would you rather the man you loved was accused of doing something hideous to someone else you love or would you rather he was having an affair with her?'

'I would rather he was loving, faithful and not a monster,' she replies flippantly.

'Well that's not an option for me right now, is it?' I snap in retaliation.

Impasse. We stand in the corridor, facing each other, both of us on the defensive.

'You really can't see what he's like, can you?' Mirabelle says. 'He has such an overblown sense of entitlement. And his arrogance . . . I thought I was bad, but he is out of control. He demands nothing short of devotion, he almost spells out that he expects to be worshipped or there will be consequences. And of course, he thinks every woman on Earth adores him and if you don't, you're obviously frigid or a dyke.'

'That's the father of my children you're talking about,' I say quietly.

'And I'm sorry about that. But it's true. And it's true what he did to me.'

I shake my head. It's not true, it can't be.

'I'm not a liar, Tami.'

'I didn't say you were.'

'Yes, you did. This whole thing is you calling me a liar.'

Without thinking, I bring my hands up to my mouth, clasping my left hand over my right fist I shove my left thumb into my mouth and bite down on the knuckle in an attempt to stop myself from breaking down. I want to shove my whole fist into my mouth as far as it will go and scream. I want to scream so loud it cracks the world.

'This whole thing started when he made a pass at me about six months after we started working together. I let him down as gently as possible and he laughed it off so I thought he was all right about it. He really seemed OK with it, then the comments about my work started. Then the giving me a verbal dressing down in front of people in meetings.

Then the comments when we were alone. Not constant, just every now and again so I wouldn't be expecting it. I couldn't ever relax because I didn't know when he was going to get nasty again.

'And, you know, when you and I became friends he seemed to chill out a bit. Maybe he was scared of what I might tell you, but things settled down and I started to enjoy work again.

'Then we started running. Which must have pissed him off or something because it started up once more, the comments, the put-downs, the digs, but worse than before. And this time, there was also the porn talk.'

'The what?'

'Yeah, into the mix of everything else he was putting me through, he started asking my opinion on the films he'd watched. He'd describe the scenarios in detail and ask me what I thought.'

'That doesn't sound right.'

'Of course it wasn't right. None of it was right. He put those scenarios there in my head and I couldn't get them out. I tried to avoid being alone with him, but he made it so difficult. I still have the images in my head, you know, and I can't get them out.

'That night, he asked me in front of everyone to stay back so we could work on the take-over bid. He asked in front of everyone so it would look like I wasn't devoted to my job, wasn't as committed to the company's expansion as he and everyone else was, if I said no.'

I know the bid she is talking about. Scott had asked me to look it over when it was done to make sure it was perfect.

It'd been brilliant, so creative and, mean as it sounded, I knew it hadn't been his work. He didn't even pretend it was – he said Mirabelle and his team had worked on it, and he'd been so determined to get the niche firm to become part of the TLITI portfolio. If he landed that, then he would definitely be made partner, he said.

'I was so anxious because if I didn't do it, I'd be out of a job. If I did, he might try it on again.'

'Is that what really happened?' I say. 'Did he make a pass at you that, horrible as it is for me, you didn't welcome so you've blown it out of proportion? Is that it?'

Her face closes in on itself, her lips twist themselves together briefly before she opens her mouth: 'He waited until everyone had gone home. Until we'd eaten our food, until I had started to let my guard down slightly because we'd been alone for hours and nothing had happened. And when I started to relax a little he grabbed me, slammed me onto his desk and ripped three buttons on my shirt trying to get it open. Then he tore half the cup off my bra, all the while holding me down and saying this disgusting stuff I've never heard a man say before.'

Like a creature that is about to become road kill, I stare at her wide-eyed and mute with horror at what is bearing down on me.

'Is that how he made a pass at you the first time? Just curious, in case I've blown it out of proportion.'

I don't think my body can move, even though I want it to. I want my body to move because I want to get away from here, from what she is saying to me.

'And did he tear the button on your trousers, while his

hand forced its way into your knickers? Did he keep up the stream of filth, telling you what he was going to do to you, while he's at it? Did he start—'

'Stop, please, stop,' I manage to utter. 'Please, stop, I can't listen to any more. Please. Please.'

Her eyes are full of tears, her face is no longer twisted in disgust, it is drenched in agony. 'I'm not a liar. I am not making it up. I only just got away from him. If I hadn't . . . I'm not a liar.'

It sounds true, and I'd know it was true if it wasn't for the fact she is talking about Scott.

'You know what he can be like. Deep down, in that place inside that you avoid visiting because that's where all your bad thoughts and experiences live, you know, don't you?'

My memory flickers with that time. That time I said yes, when I felt yes. But . . . there had been the act that I had not been expecting, had not wanted. There had been the words he'd never used before. There was the bruising on my body afterwards because that was the roughest he'd ever been. It'd been rough before, it'd been getting marginally rougher over time, but that was the worst, the most painful. Then there had been afterwards: when he'd been tender, and caring and close. And the holding afterwards, which had been becoming shorter and shorter, again by increments, was longer this time. Afterwards I felt loved, wanted, adored. And scared, scarred, hollow, insecure, *used*. 'That was amazing, TB, wasn't it?' he said. I had closed my eyes so I wouldn't have to look at his face, I tightened my grip so I wouldn't push him away, and I inhaled his scent so I would be reminded what the man I loved had always smelled like, and I murmured, 'Hmmm' so he wouldn't know how horrible it had been.

That was that, though, it wasn't like what Mirabelle was saying. What she has been saying makes him a criminal and a monster. What I have been remembering was a time of yes, of consent and of misunderstanding. The two are completely different.

She crumples a little, the corners of her mouth turning down. 'Oh, Tami, he did it to you, too, didn't he?'

'No, he didn't. There's a difference between rough sex and . . . and what you're talking about.'

'Yes, yes, there is. Who doesn't like rough sex every now and again? As long as it's what you wanted?'

Was it what I wanted? I don't remember. Does anybody remember what sex they wanted each and every time they do it?

'Was it?' she asks my silence. 'Was it what you wanted or was it what your sex life had become?'

'This has nothing to do with that,' I tell her.

'God, Tami, all the time we've been friends, all the chats we've had I've known there was something wrong. He's got worse, hasn't he? The higher his star rises, the worse he treats you. He's probably been dominating you and pushing your boundaries for ages. I didn't realise it'd got to the point where he's ra—'

'Don't say that. Don't say that word. He hasn't done that to me so don't say it.'

'I love you, Tami,' she says. 'You're one of my best friends, you're one of the most amazing people I've ever met, I just wish you would wake up and see what he's really like. What he's doing to you and what he's done to me.'

I have to get out of here. I have to leave because if I stay any longer, if I'm around her any longer, if I listen any longer, I'll start to hear her. I'll start to remember elements of my marriage differently, I'll start to pick it apart to fit what she's saying. That's what the human mind does, it finds evidence to back up the things we believe. If I do not leave, I will start to believe what she is saying. 'Stop it. Just stop it. I'm not listening to any more of this.'

I turn without another word to her. As I open the door, she comes up behind me. 'Every time I see you, I realise I did the right thing going to the police,' she says. 'Not only for my sake, but also for yours.'

As I step out of the house into the driveway, fury rises up inside me. I haven't got her to retract her allegation, I am actually leaving with more doubts than when I entered.

The car that has pulled up from the road is silver and older than either of the two cars sitting on Mirabelle's driveway. I'm sure it's in good working order and will pass all the necessary checks. It has to: it is a police car. One of the police officers is in the process of getting out when I exit the house, the other was obviously going to wait in the car. But now, when he sees me, he opens his car door and exits too.

'Mrs Challey, I'm surprised to see you here,' Detective Sergeant Harvan says, coldly. The warmth and concern she showed me the other night is long gone, probably spirited away on having to release Scott without charge.

'Hope you're not trying to coerce or in any way intimidate our witness,' the male officer says. He is tall and muscular with black hair, dark skin and the biggest pair of brown eyes I have ever seen on a man. Both police officers look from me to the woman behind for a microsecond before returning to me. Almost synchronised.

'Of course not. We were just . . . We were just talking.'

As one person, they again move their line of sight to Mirabelle.

'Erm . . . yes, just talking,' Mirabelle says. Mirabelle and I have duplicate echoes of anxiety and nervousness in our speech. We sound as if we have something to hide.

'Well, in the future, don't "just talk",' Harvan says.

'Just stay away from each other,' the policeman adds.

'We don't want any misunderstandings to occur,' Harvan says.

'That could jeopardise the case,' the policeman adds.

'I wouldn't do that,' I say. 'I'm not like that.'

'No one ever is,' Harvan replies.

'Until they are,' the policeman adds.

'Do you two do a double act on the stage or something?' Mirabelle snaps. I was thinking the same thing but would never say it. 'Because what you're doing – all the finishing of each other's sentences – it's not endearing, it's not funny, it's irritating.'

I certainly wouldn't have gone that far had I been inspired to say anything at all, but I suppose she can say that sort of thing, she's the victim after all. She can do and say whatever she likes. It's me that can't step out of line.

'Can I go?' I ask the officers.

'Of course,' Harvan replies. 'Just don't let me catch you

here again.' She smiles a smile that would curdle milk. The policeman doesn't smile. He stares at me with cold eyes that are accusing me of something I know I haven't done.

Beatrix

It didn't happen with the man from the plane. He was nice, but not interested. I hope that's not a smirk on your face there. It was only a little flirtation, I wouldn't have done anything so don't get all judgy and think I need to be taken down a peg or two. I suppose, since my husband left, I've been desperate to know I'm attractive to men.

I mean, I know it, I do look in mirrors, I do go out of my way to dress well, but it's nice to have external validation every now and again.

To know I'm not all those things he said when he left. Did I mention he left me for some*whore* – sorry, some*one* – else? She wasn't even that much prettier than me. Oh, I don't know. I do know that some days it's a wonder I get out of bed at all. The things he said about my body and our sex life and pretty much the whole of who I am scored me deep. It was like he took a branding iron to my soul, burnishing every criticism there for eternity.

I suppose any man who looks at me or shows interest in me is kind of proving him wrong, is rubbing out all those things he said. That does make me sound desperate. But before you start to look down on me, look at yourself. I bet you do it too. And if you don't, I really, really envy you.

Still nothing from the Challeys. I'm almost too scared to call now because if something has gone wrong, it'll be a very big wrong.

Tami

'Thank you for coming in to see us, Mrs Challey,' the police-woman says.

I didn't have much choice in the matter. They followed me down from Mirabelle's and stopped me outside my house and said they would like to talk to me. I'd been given the choice of coming down to the police station there and then or for them to come visit me at home at some point in the near future. The way DS Harvan spoke, she made it abundantly obvious she was pushing my buttons, using my weakness – Cora and Anansy – to get me to do what she wanted and come to the station. *Then* it would be official; they could record the conversation, they could sit me in a room like the ones they reserved for criminals and they could be in charge. Which is currently what is happening. Me installed in an interview room on one side of the table, them on the other, recording machine on.

Not what I wanted, but after what happened last week, I didn't want there to be even the slightest chance that the girls would see them. Neither Cora nor Anansy have mentioned it again, but I know the memory is still there: that the experience probably stalks their nightmares in the same way it fuels their need to know where Dad is every moment of the day. I did not want them to see me being questioned, too.

'That's OK,' I reply, shifting uncomfortably on the seat. Considering how long people must sit on these things, they're pretty unforgiving, no seat pads, no comforting lines you can mould your body to. That's most likely the point: you're not there to be comfortable, you're there to suffer until you confess – whether you're guilty or not.

'We're trying to get some background information to help us with our enquiries,' Harvan says. I get the impression that she's in charge although I may be wrong and her colleague is the more senior of them and likes to take a back seat to watch their suspects' responses.

I nod at her.

'What's your relationship with your husband like, Mrs Challey?'

'*Normal, fine, OK. Not perfect, but which relationship is perfect? It's all right, you know? We have our ups and downs but none of that matters because we love each other, we've been together since the dawn of time and we're going to grow old together.*' That is the reply I should have been able to give. I would have given a week ago, six days ago, even.

'Not great at the moment,' I reply, pulling the sleeves of my fuchsia cardigan over my hands and then picking at the edges of the cuffs with opposite hands. One of the threads on the right-hand cuff has worked its way loose, so the seam is slightly unravelled.

'And why's that?' she asks, as if she doesn't know.

'Something to do with him being arrested and me finding out he was having an affair with one of my friends. Doesn't make for a great time as a couple.'

'So you had no idea he was allegedly having an

extramarital relationship with Ms Kemini?'

I shake my head. I really didn't. I have been too trusting. Too gullible. Too blinded to whatever it was that was going on under my nose.

'How often do you have sex with your husband, Mrs Challey?'

What? I think. 'What?' I say, shrinking back in my seat. My gaze flies from her to him. They stare back at me with twin expressions of nonchalance.

'How often do you have sex with your husband?' she repeats.

'That's none of your business,' I reply, lowering my head and picking harder at the unravelled thread.

'I'm sorry you feel that way, but it would really help your husband if you could give us as full a picture of him as possible.'

'I'm not answering that question,' I state. That memory, the one that talking to Mirabelle dislodged, is fighting to be released. It wants me to look at it again, examine it, explore it, experience it – then explain to myself why I have been avoiding thinking about it. Why, apart from the night when he told me about the affair, I haven't had sex with Scott since. Nearly four months and we haven't made love. I find that hard to admit, even in the privacy of my own thoughts. That time, the time of yes that felt like a no, killed any desire I had for him, and it put a barrier between us in our bed, in our lives. We didn't talk about it, but I think we both knew that sex was not on the cards for the foreseeable.

'That's your right, Mrs Challey,' she says with a small, hardly noticeable smile. Triumph. She thinks I've proved her point. She's going to use my refusal to answer the question as evidence to say that he did it. He wasn't getting it at home so he had to go out and force it on someone else.

In my memory Scott's hands are gripping me, controlling me, then he's hurting me; in the echoes of my mind his voice is breathing out words I can't believe he'd ever say; in my body, the shaking is back. With force, I push them – the memories, the feelings, the shaking – all away. I shove it all behind me and slam shut the door. *Concentrate on what is happening now*, I order myself.

'Does your husband look at pornography?' she asks.

'Don't all men?' I reply.

'No,' she says with a shake of her head, 'they don't.'

'I don't,' the policeman, Detective Wade he told me his name was in the car over here, says. He seems a normal man, not inhibited or overly 'in touch with his feminine side'.

'I assumed all men did,' I state. I sound pathetic. Clueless and pathetic. I don't even believe that. I tell myself that to make it OK that Scott *still* does it. Even though he knows I hate it, he still does it and does it regularly.

'Not all men get aroused watching women being brutalised,' Harvan says.

'What? Looking at porn doesn't mean you get aroused by women being brutalised.'

'Read around the subject, Mrs Challey, I think you'll find out a lot of the stuff is made in disgracefully unethical ways,' Wade says. 'And a lot of the images that are out there are of women being degraded, humiliated and, yes, brutalised.'

I can't read around it, it's bad enough I know it exists; it's bad enough that periodically that woman's face I saw for a fraction of a moment on that film all those years ago wells up in my mind and I briefly imagine what she is going through, what she is feeling, what happened in her life so she smiles while she is obviously being hurt. I can't read any more about the subject. What would I do with that knowledge? How would that make Scott any better in my eyes?

'Does your husband masturbate to rape pornography?' Harvan asks.

'*What?* No. Absolutely no.'

'You sound very sure, have you checked?'

'No, but he wouldn't. OK? He wouldn't.'

'Are you sure? Most men start with very vanilla types of porn, the so-called "tame" stuff, but their tastes become more extreme as the need for a bigger hit increases.'

'He wouldn't do that.'

'Like he wouldn't attack a woman?' she says.

'Like he wouldn't have an affair?' Wade says. Their tag-team is back.

'Depending on whose version of events you wish to believe,' she says.

'Either way, it's not looking good for your husband, is it, Mrs Challey?' he says.

'Being a cheat and looking at porn doesn't make you a . . . doesn't make you guilty of what you're accusing him of.'

'You'd be surprised,' she says.

'It wouldn't be the first time we've seen it,' he says.

'That's why we're asking you about it,' she says.

'The wives often know more than they realise. If they would just put the pieces together.'

'And look at the bigger picture.' She lowers her voice to a concerned level. 'Mrs Challey, has your husband ever hurt you during sex? Intentionally or unintentionally?'

'I told you, I'm not answering those questions.' The look again, this time without the smile, but still the same, still deciding what she can glean from my refusal to answer.

'Do you have any other questions?' I want this to end. 'Because I have work to do and children to pick up from school.'

'Where were you on the night of April eighth this year?'

'Do I need an alibi or something?' I reply. That's the first time I've heard the date. Obviously Scott hasn't told me the date because it never happened.

'No, we're interested in your husband's emotional state when he came home that day.'

'Erm . . . Eighth April? What day of the week was that?'

'A Monday.'

'Oh, well, I probably didn't see him. I go running on a Tuesday morning so I go to bed early.'

'Do you go running alone?' she asks.

'No, I'm sure you know I go running with Mirabelle.'

'Did you go running with Ms Kemini, the morning after eighth April?'

The tingling starts on my scalp then shimmers down my spine, radiating out over my body. That was the week before last, the only time Mirabelle hasn't turned up for a run without cancelling way in advance. I shake my head.

'Why not?'

My tongue feels stuck to the roof of my mouth and I'm finding it hard to speak. 'She didn't turn up.'

'Any idea why?'

I'd waited and waited in the usual place at the edge of

164

the Close, I jogged up and down on the spot until it was ten minutes after our usual start time. I had my phone on me, strapped to my bicep, and I kept checking it for text messages or missed calls but nothing. After ten minutes I called her but she didn't answer either of her phones. And then I jogged round to her house, to see if she'd overslept, but she didn't answer the door. I was worried. The blinds were down but I could sense she was in the house.

I paced around outside for a bit, wondering what to do. What if she'd had an accident and was there all alone and unable to get help? Should I get help? But what if she'd met someone and had brought him back? The last thing she'd want is to have me sending in the cavalry while she was mid-coitus.

I tried calling again but no reply.

A few seconds later my phone bleeped.

Overslept. Go without me.

That was it. Not her usual type of text message which were always sunny and signed off with a kiss.

Does that mean . . .

'Mrs Challey, you haven't told us why you went running alone the morning following the alleged attack on Ms Kemini?'

'She, erm, said she'd overslept.'

Which had seemed ludicrous because in all the time I'd known her Mirabelle had never overslept or been late for anything. Later in the day she'd texted to say she'd hurt her leg so couldn't go running for a while.

'Did you go to her house and check?'

'Why would I?'

'Did you believe her?'

'Why wouldn't I?'

The policewoman's smile returns. 'Why indeed?'

I look down, still worrying at the cuff of my sleeve. More of the sleeve is unravelling. Unravelling. Everything unravelling.

'Overslept. Go without me.'

is written in large letters in my mind.

'Thank you for your time, Mrs Challey,' Detective Sergeant Harvan says, holding out her hand. 'That's all for now.'

The words of Mirabelle's last text swim before my eyes. I stand and accept her hand. It is a firm handshake, one that challenges me to show what I am made of – am I wimp or am I strong woman? I return the handshake in the spirit it is given, I am not a wimp.

'I'm sure we don't have to remind you to stay away from Ms Kemini,' Harvan says.

'If she is threatened in any way we will be forced to take action,' Wade adds.

'Why would I threaten her? I know Scott's innocent.' That sounds hollow to me, probably sounds even worse to them. 'I know the truth will come out eventually.'

'You're right there, Mrs Challey,' Harvan says.

'But still stay away from her,' Wade ends.

Tami

I am watching the equivalent of hell on film.

After Harvan's question, the look on her face as she asked me if I was sure he didn't masturbate to this stuff, I thought I'd better have a look. After all, I had been equally sure he would be faithful and he had confessed he hadn't been.

When I came home and went from room to room, searching for him, but couldn't find him, I decided this was as good a time as any to take a quick peek: I was in the loft room – the last place I looked for him – so I might as well refute the ridiculous thought that Harvan had planted in my head.

The folder wasn't that well hidden, but it had over a hundred sub-folders. And each sub-folder had over a hundred images or video clips.

I clicked on one movie without a proper title and began this nightmare. I kept choosing random movies, random files, hoping that they would be different, they would be 'tame'.

Instead, I am watching the end of my marriage played out on the screen in front of me. This is hell. This is what hell would look like to every woman I know. And it looks real. It feels and plays like what is happening in front of me is not happening to an actress, someone who is performing and will be paid for her trouble, it is actually happening to a woman who looks like an ordinary person. Someone like me. Someone like me is being brutalised, battered, *raped* on film.

And my husband has downloaded this 'film' so he can watch it whenever he likes. He has downloaded film after film after film of this. The ones I have seen are playing in loop in my head. And it is there: that act, what happened the night of yes that felt like a no. And it is there: what Mirabelle described to me.

He did it.

My stomach spikes as it twists painfully and I wrench the cable from the back of the computer, hoping I have fried the hard-drive, fearing I haven't, before I have to run through the house to the toilet and throw up everything I haven't eaten. My retching is dry and painful, my stomach almost cut in two with each one, but eventually there is nothing, not even pale, slimy bile, and I collapse on the floor beside the bath. I put a trembling hand to my mouth, and scream into the silent void. It's over. He did it. They weren't having an affair, he did it. He tried to rape her.

Fully clothed, I step into the shower and turn on the water. I want to wash this away too. Like last night, like what I did, I want to remove all this filth clinging to me, I want to feel clean again.

Tami

The shaking is getting worse.

Everything I do, I have to will my body to settle itself so I won't shake. The horror of what I saw on the computer earlier has lodged an unmoveable ball of nausea firmly in my solar plexus. I have tried making myself sick again, I have tried drinking water, I have tried forcing down food but it is still there. It is embedded behind that smooth, flat piece of skin equidistant from each of my breasts, in front of my spine, cleaving apart the prongs of my ribs.

The girls are talking ten to the dozen. They have been talking since I pulled together the pieces of myself and collected them from school. It was a burbling I couldn't decipher, I smiled and nodded in what I hoped were the right places and said, 'Is it?' a lot. They might have told me they had visited the moon, but I could not have understood.

I keep looking around at our house, at the items we own, the knick-knacks and *things* that we have collected over the years that have slotted together to make our home, and I wonder why? And when? And how?

How has Scott become the type of man who can do that? Not even the crime, how can he orgasm to moving images

– faked or real, I do not know – of women being brutalised? *When* did he progress to the real thing? *Why* didn't I notice? *Why, why, why?*

'Burble, burble, burble,' the girls continue at the table behind me. We need to leave. I need to pack up and take the girls. Now. Right.

I cut the flame that is heating water to cook pasta. I need to be quick. I will pack the bare minimum and when we get to wherever it is we're going, we can—

'Hello everybody!' He beams at them and I know with absolute certainty that I have got it wrong: he can't have done it.

'Hi Dad,' they say at different times.

'Come on, get ready, I'm taking you all out for a slap-up dinner,' he says. And I know with absolute certainty that I have got it right: *he did do it.*

'Yeah!' the girls say as they jump down from their chairs and hurry to get changed.

'They haven't done their homework,' I say, trembling, still trembling.

'It's one time. They can start it when we get back and finish it in the morning.' *He can't have done it.*

'Well, you mind they do, because it's me who has to deal with any letters home from the Head.'

'They'll be fine. I was always having letters sent home from the Head, never did me any harm.' *He did do it.*

'If you say so.'

'Look, Tami, about yesterday—'

I raise my hand to halt him. 'I don't even want to think about it.' I don't want to think about whether I had sex with a . . . 'I just want to concentrate on the girls. Anything else is not important.'

'I'm sorry I hurt you,' he mumbles.

'No you're not, you're only sorry you got caught. Now leave me alone.' What has he been caught for, though? Cheating or rape?

I go towards the door and he grabs my arm. 'Do you still think I did this thing? Do you still believe I'm a rapist?'

I tug my arm free. Glaring at him but saying nothing, I leave the room.

Nearly three years ago

'Are you sick of me, Scott?' I asked him once the girls were tucked up in bed and, having finished our meal, he was about to head out to the gym.

Pocketing his mobile, he stopped walking through the door and revolved slowly on the spot to face me. Irritation slithered over his features, answering my question more clearly than his words ever could.

'Why would you ask me something like that?'

'Because . . .' My courage failed me. We had barely spoken during dinner, just like every night he was home in time for us to eat together – he seemed to be here but not here. He was busy, he had visitors from America he had to entertain, he had a project that could make the company millions if he pulled it off, his life was away from me. But it'd been like that many times in the past and it hadn't felt like this. I had to know if it was me that he was sick of, fed up with. If it was me that needed replacing. I wanted to know, but after I asked, I thought of all the things that would end when he answered that question. No more seeing the girls every day, no more ticking the married box on forms, no more financial security, no more house probably because it'd be hard to keep it going on just my earnings. No more having someone who came home to me. No more looking at the sleeping face of the man I loved and wondering who he had become. The answer would lead to the end, I was sure of that. Was I ready for that?

'Never mind,' I replied. 'It's not important.' I picked up the salad dressing, the homemade hot pepper sauce and the low-fat mayonnaise from the table and returned them to the fridge. 'I'll see you later. Have a good time at the gym.'

'Is this about going to counselling again?' he asked, his disdain as apparent as daylight.

I kept my head in the fridge, the air cooling my burning, humiliated skin; tranquillising the raw edges of my nerves. 'No. It's nothing. Ignore me.' *Like you often do.*

'TB, I don't understand what you're saying.'

'I'm saying nothing. Nothing at all. I think I need an early night or something.'

'Do you want me to stay home and not go to the gym tonight?' he asked.

'Absolutely not. You go. I'll see you later or tomorrow if I manage to get an early night.'

Scott did nothing for a few seconds, he seemed to be deciding something. Eventually he came to me, still hiding in the fridge, and pressed his lips against my cheek. 'You try to get some sleep, OK? Take good care of yourself, you belong to me, don't forget.'

My face found a smile but I couldn't look at him, nor

leave the fridge until I heard the front door click shut behind him. After he was gone, I picked up my black Mulberry bag and returned to my place at the table. I had the almost full glass of water I'd poured with my dinner. From my bag I retrieved the white paper bag from the pharmacist. Curling back the top, I took from it the box of citalopram, the anti-depressant my doctor had prescribed. I sat staring at it, knowing what I had to do.

The sadness, the anxiety, the hopeless had to stop. It was no good for the girls, it was no good for me, it was no good if I wanted to rescue my relationship. I couldn't help but look at the door, seeing the Scott-shaped hole that he'd left when he departed. I was trying to save that all on my own, though, wasn't I?

'Mama,' Cora called from upstairs. 'Mama, I need some water.'

Stuffing the box and paper bag back in my bag, I decided that tonight wasn't going to be the night I started these. I'd give it a little while longer and if I still felt like this, if the despair and hollowness continued, I'd take them. I'd claw my way back to normality and then deal with things from there.

'Mama!'

'Coming, Cora, coming.'

This is my third large glass of wine since we've been home, the only thing that will stop the shaking.

'Where were you earlier? I waited and waited to see if you'd come back before I left, but you didn't.' Scott asks. His approach has been silent, as if to try to catch me out or something.

Was it this morning I went to see Mirabelle and defended him? Was it this morning I went to the police station and defended him again? I know it was this afternoon that I found out that he likes to watch criminal sexual acts upstairs in our house.

'Tami, where were you?' Scott asks.

'At the police station,' I say on the crest of a sigh as I lower the glass from my lips. His eyes alight on the glass but he says nothing. Then his eyes alight on my ring finger. It is missing its ring. I took it off this afternoon. Affair or attack, there was no way I could stay married to him now.

'Why were you at the police station?' he asks.

'They saw me walking down the road and asked me to come in for a chat. They wanted me to verify your story for the night in question, among other things.'

'And did you?'

'How could I verify your story when you have no story except she's out to get you but it'll all go away so you don't need a solicitor?'

'Right. Right.'

'But it was super fun to be questioned about our sex life and your porn habit. I think I'm going to ask to have that happen again and again.'

'I'm sorry you had to go through that,' he says, quietly.

'Are you, are you really? Or is that simply something for you to say in this situation?'

'Tami, if I had known it would turn out like this ... I'm sorry, I'm truly sorry.'

I rest my head back, close my eyes. I would love to feel the sun on my face, I would love for it to warm me up. I would love for it to make me believe that he couldn't have done this thing, I would love for it to burn away the images my husband's porn has put into my mind.

'Did they . . . Did they give you any idea of where they are with their investigation?'

'No, but they seem to be looking at this from all angles. From the way they were acting, I think they may have some proof.'

'How can they have proof when it didn't happen?' he asks.

'I'm only telling you what I thought after the conversation with them.' *I'm not telling you I have seen that act carried out on one of your films, nor that I know the date now so it can all be verified.*

'Do you think I did it?' he asks.

My eyes fly open. I stare up at the ceiling, a bright white that surprisingly hasn't been coated with deposits from food condensation.

'Your silence speaks volumes,' he says after a while, his hurt evident.

'What is it that you want from me, Scott?' I continue to stare up, to wonder how I can escape into the world up there. 'The best-case scenario right now is that you were cheating on me. That's the very best-case scenario.'

'That doesn't answer the question. Do you think I did it?'

'No. No, I don't think you did it.'

'Yes. Yes, I do think you did it.'

'Well, at least I know where I stand,' he says. The sound of wood on tile fills the air as he stands. 'I didn't want to

175

do this,' he says. 'I didn't want to show you these and I didn't think I'd have to because you'd believe me. But here. Proof of what I'm saying. Proof that we were . . . together.' The clatter of his BlackBerry on the wooden table. 'They're in the saved messages folder. I'm sorry for what you're about to read. It's not . . . I'm sorry.'

He leaves me then. He leaves me alone to go through another life-changing agony.

7 January
I love you. I have never loved anyone like I love you. Why can't you see that? M x

21 January
I'm not asking you to leave the three of them behind, I would never ask that of you, I just want more of you. Is that too much to ask? M x

4 February
I can still taste you. M x

7 February
I can still feel your fingers inside me. M x

15 February
I would never look at anyone else. Why can't you understand that? I'm yours. Always. M x

15 February
Always. M x

25 February

Please stop saying that. It's you that I love. It's you that I want. M x

1 March

Of course I want us to be together, but I'm not going to ask you to leave. I've left before, it's a horrible thing to do, I'd never ask another person to do that. Not even you. M x

3 March

Do you know what I was thinking about today? Our first kiss. I could actually feel your lips on mine, the way you gently bit my bottom lip. Pleasure and pain, wasn't that what you said? You're pure pleasure, no pain. M x

6 March

You tasted incredible yesterday. I just wanted you to know that. M x

9 March

You're mine. Don't care what you say, you're mine. I'll fight to keep you. M x

15 March

I've never been fucked like that before. No one who fucks me like that will ever be out of my life. M x

20 March

I know it's wrong but I can't help feeling how I do. I know you're married, but I'm willing to wait. I'd wait a lifetime for you to be ready to be with me properly. It'll cause a lot of hurt, and I'm not proud of that, but I love you. M x

I keep checking back, I keep calling up her number on my phone and it's hers. It's hers. She sent these little notelets of love and lust and sex. To Scott. To my husband.

My husband was having an affair with my best friend. They were in love. She was trying to get him to leave me.

My best friend was having an affair with my husband. They were in love. He fucked her like she'd never been fucked before.

My husband and my best friend were having an affair.
My husband and my best friend were having an affair.
My husband and my best friend were having an affair.
My husband and my best friend were having an affair.
My husband and my best friend were having an affair.
My husband and my best friend were having an affair.
I have to keep saying it until I can believe it.

Tami

I want to go for a run. I want the unyielding ground beneath my trainer-covered feet as I pound it with all the strength I have in my legs, and I want the wind, usually strong and unforgiving on the seafront, to slam into me, clearing my head and freeing my body.

I want to feel each knot of anxiety untwisting itself as I run down the streets to the seafront, then run on with the Pier in my sights, then the hills of Rottingdean as my destination and then keep on running to whatever is beyond. I have only run to the Marina before, then turned back to run the 10km to Shoreham Lighthouse. Today, I want to run and run and not turn back. I want to keep going until my body collapses, until the physical pain erases all the emotional agony that is excavating my heart.

Instead, I walk around my office, trying to tidy up. My office was once the smallest bedroom on the first floor, but now it is my space. It has a huge noticeboard that takes up one wall, upon which are newspaper cuttings, postcards, images I like, font examples, a timetable and deadlines of work that is to be done, as well as pictures of my family. On my desk are piles of mess: unopened trade magazines, invoices I have produced but not posted, letters – probably some containing cheques – and ordinary post. Things that I have

179

been mentally brushing aside to get through the last few days.

My body aches with the loss of running from my life. My limbs are cold and barely responsive, my torso feels solid and leaden, my head is a mass of cotton wool. Physically, I am like a classic car kept on the driveway that is stiffening, seizing up because it hasn't been taken out for a long drive that will blow away the cobwebs, will encourage the parts to work as they are lubricated, oiled and forced to move.

My husband has been having an affair with my best friend.

That is why I want to run. I want to escape from all of this.

However, fear and shame and gossip are holding me hostage in my house. We are being studied, scrutinised, observed. Those who saw Mr Challey being carted off are probably waiting for the next instalment. The voices of a dozen whispers – speculating, wondering, condemning – are deafening in the still of the street. I'm not sure how it doesn't bother Scott, when he is now so obsessed with the outward appearance of things, but it doesn't. He's taken the girls to school today and is going to drop into his office to pick up a few files. He told me this when the girls were there so I wouldn't tell him to fuck off speaking to me like everything was normal; to stop behaving as if anything could be all right between us ever again.

The gossip bothers me. It bothers me enough to stop me running and to have me doing this necessary clear-out of my workspace. It bothers me that people might have seen him going into her house and thought it odd. It bothers me that people out there might have known what was going on and looked at me pityingly: Tami Challey, the pathetic wife who knew nothing.

DING-DONG! KNOCK-KNOCK! Then the metallic creak of the letterbox, followed by a call of 'Hell-oooh!'

Beatrix.

She's on her second 'Hell-oooh!' as I run down the corridor, down the stairs to the front door. I snatch it open before she's had a chance to straighten up and she almost falls through the door, barrelling into me. I stumble backwards, but manage to keep my balance. I throw myself at her, forcing her to take me in her arms.

'I take it you're pleased to see me, then,' she says, as I practically swamp her slender frame.

'You have no idea,' I say.

'Oh dear,' she replies. 'This doesn't sound good. Come on, cup of char and a sit down then you can tell me everything.'

Instead of letting her go and walking through to the kitchen, I hang onto my friend. She's the one sane person in this whole mess. It takes seconds to soak through her shoulder and she doesn't even complain.

'This is horrific,' she says. 'My goodness, Tami, it's a wonder you're still standing. You should have called me.'

I shake my head. 'What could you have done?'

'Lots of things,' she replies. 'Look at my shoulder, for instance, it's perfect for soaking up tears. And I could have had the girls for sleepovers so you could talk to him. Where is he, by the way?'

'Work, picking up files.'

'At a time like this? When he should be here trying to

talk to you?' She shakes her head. 'I'll tell you what else I could have done, I could have warned off her ladyship.'

'I don't want that,' I say. 'And, if there's any warning off to be done, I'll do it. There's no need for you to fall out with her, too.'

Her green eyes bulge out of her head. 'No need to fall out with her?' she shrieks, but quietly as if there is someone else in the house. 'She's practically ruined your family. There's every need to fall out with her. I can't think of a time when there's ever been more of a need to fall out with someone.'

My mouth curls upwards in a smile of sorts, I feel so heavy and sad. Bereaved, almost. 'Scott did that,' I say to her. 'He's ruined this family. Whatever's gone on, it's all down to the choices that Scott's made.'

'I hear you.' Beatrix reaches across the table and carefully wraps her long slender hands over my hands. 'I totally understand.'

I'm not sure I do, to be honest, I think as I watch her hands. Her fingers are about two-thirds the width of mine so her hands are smaller, narrower. It seems odd to get comfort from someone who seems so much less substantial than me.

'What do you think happened then?' she asks, picking up her mug and tipping it to take a sip. She's doing that to avoid making direct eye contact but still watching me and my reactions.

'I don't know what I think any more,' I say to Beatrix. 'This whole thing is trashing my life. I keep thinking that I don't deserve this.' Or do I? Is this the price I pay for not listening to my parents? Is this what I deserve for marrying someone from a 'bad' family who none of my family approved of, and for not going to university, and for not staying in London, and for taking pride in having gorgeous children who are the light of my life? Is this what happens when you think you know best and try to live your life as you please? You're forced to live with the consequences, as huge or insignificant as they may be. In this case, those consequences are ginormous-antic, as Anansy would say. They are so huge they blot out the solar system, the stars he once wrote my name in.

Beatrix nods sadly. 'I know what you mean,' she says. 'When my husband left after giving me the old "I love you but I'm not in love with you" speech which was actually a lie, he was simply shagging some*whore* – I mean, someone else – I wished more than anything that I could have another reason for the end of my marriage. I wanted him to have had a knock on the head so he wasn't himself, or something, anything that would mean the man I knew and loved wouldn't be capable of cheating on me and then leaving.'

'I hate him for what he's done to me,' I confess. 'I hate both of them for what they've done. Sometimes I get so angry about it all, I swear I could kill them both with my bare hands.'

Beatrix nods. 'I felt like that, too. It's all normal. When my husband decided to come back for a while because he thought we could make things work – in other words his whore got cold feet about leaving her husband so he panicked – I remember wishing as I was making him dinner one night that I had time to grind up some glass and mix it in his food. I was being the perfect wife, you know, so that he wouldn't leave me again, but I still had these flashes of intense hatred and anger where I could have murdered him. So I get what you're saying, totally.'

It's hard to think of Beatrix as someone who would feel such rage. She's always been so calm and fun, she fills her world with dating and fine wine, yoga and zumba, Pilates and football. Her existence is the perfect balance of the single life interspersed with a taste of family life with us, which I think she must sometimes crave from the way she looks so hungrily at the girls. Plus she lives in her huge flat she has decorated exactly as she's wanted. No ugly fireplaces for her. It's difficult to imagine her having thoughts as murderous as mine have been over the past few hours.

I look her over, imagining myself feeling that comfortable again. Her features that are as fine-boned as the rest of her body, giving her a china-doll-like appearance; her complexion that's always had that strawberries-and-cream look to it with or without make-up, her hair — whoa!

'What happened to you?' I shriek. Her hair used to be a mass of shiny red curls that spiralled all the way down her back, now she has a platinum blonde, chin-length bob. How did I not notice that? I must be so mired in my problems I didn't even look at her.

Her face creases with a grin. 'You like?' she says, scrunching her fingers through the silky length of her tresses.

'Yes, yes, I like,' I reply. 'When did that happen?'

'This week. I walked past a hairdresser's in Glasgow and I thought, I'm going for a change. I've been a bit flat lately so I thought this might liven me up. It's worked a treat.' She scrunches her fingers through her hair again. 'You really like?'

'Yes, I really like.' I reply. She's a different person, of course. You don't go from red and long to short and blonde and stay the same. But it's not a bad thing, at all. 'It really suits you.'

'I did a Skype call with Mum the other day and she hates it. But I told her, "Gentlemen prefer blondes don't you know, Mother? I've listened to what you said about me needing a man and it's the only way to get one." Soon shut her up. Her husband couldn't stop laughing.'

'How is Mrs Beatrix's Mum?'

'Fine. She drives me potty, and I wish she didn't live all the way over there in Sydney but she's happy and I can't wish for more than that, can I?' Beatrix says, a huge smile on her face.

'No,' I reply.

'It'll be all right,' she reassures me. 'All this stuff with Scotty and Mirabelle will work itself out for the best and everything will be OK.'

'I hope you're right,' I say.

'It will, but let me say one thing: don't let yourself be pushed around on this. If you need Scotty to leave while you get your head together, you make him do that. My biggest regret from when my husband did this to me was that I didn't throw him out the second I found out. He might have come back then, if I removed that option.'

'We'll see.'

'I'm not saying you should do it, I'm just saying if that's what you want, don't be afraid of doing it. It'd serve him right.'

'Enough about me,' I say to her because making him leave

is not something I've even considered. 'Tell me everything about your date and the man from the plane.'

'You are so going to regret saying that,' she says.

For the next two hours, she takes me away from here and everything going on, and carries me on the waves of her words to another life that has nothing to do with me. It feels like the best two hours I've had in months.

Beatrix

You have a lot of explaining to do. Call me as soon as poss. Bea x

I LOVE Tami. She's like the sister I never had. She's such a warm, giving person. That makes it all the harder to say this, but I think she's brought a lot of this on herself. *Urgh*. I feel *awful* even thinking that. But – hear me out now – if you look at the facts of the matter, it's true. I wish it wasn't. I wish I could look at their relationship from the outside and say it was a surprise, that he was insane to stray, but I can't say those things without my pants instantly catching fire.

They've been barely surviving as a couple. When I met her, she was seven months gone with Cora and glowing. Remember, I'd met Scotty before and he'd dropped into conversation his wife was pregnant? I'd been keeping my eye out for her every time I passed their house on the way to George Street, the main street in Hove, but actually saw her coming out of WHSmith down there. She was wearing big sunglasses, her hair was loose, and she was grinning at people as she walked along, her hand constantly rubbing her large baby-filled stomach. I noticed her because of her smile – always at hand – brightened the already luminescent beauty of her face even behind the sunglasses.

She was in front of me as I wandered home and my heart sort of skipped when she turned into Providence Close because I knew by sight most people who lived there, which meant she was probably *her*. The woman Scotty was married to.

'Hi ya,' I called as she was about to push her key into the front door lock. She turned and looked at me.

'Hi,' she said, and pushed her sunglasses onto the top of her head, her smile back on her face.

'You're Scotty's wife?' I said.

'Yes, and you must be the friendly neighbour, Beatrix?' she said.

'Guilty.'

She grinned, although I didn't think it was possible for her smile to get any wider, or for her to look any more radiant.

'I've finally met one neighbour who's my age now,' she said. 'I'm Tami.'

'Oh, yeah, this road full of old giffers. I mean that in the nicest possible way, of course,' I added, in case she thought I was a bitch. 'So pleased you and Scotty have moved in.'

'So pleased to be here. Can you come in for a coffee? It'd be nice to get to know you.'

I was meant to get back to work, my sales reports weren't going to write themselves, but I wanted to look around the house and I wanted to talk to this woman. I wanted to know what sort of woman Scotty married, and what sort of woman chose a man like Scotty.

The afternoon was lost in laughing and joking and

drinking cups of tea in the shell of their kitchen which was being remodelled. We sat there for so long that Scotty came home. Her whole body seemed to light up when she heard his key in the lock, and when he kissed her after kissing the baby hello, I noticed how her hand lingered on him, wanting to keep touching him for as long as possible.

Contrast that with now. When was the last time I saw a smile on Tami's face about something that Scotty had done or simply who he was? She didn't become radiant and luminescent around him or when talking about him any more. Sometimes, I'd be sitting at the dinner table and she would barely glance in his direction. She would serve him his meal and there'd be no secret smile to tell him she loved him, no extra portion to show he was number one, no surreptitious wink to reveal she thought he was the sexiest man alive.

Over the years, Tami has become all about the kids. All about feeding them, getting them ready for school, homework, activities, play, development, bed, Cora, Anansy, Cora, Anansy, Cora, Anansy. Where was the space for Scotty? Where did he fit in with the grand scheme?

I'd asked them both that question about two-and-a-half years ago, when I was trying desperately to get them to see their relationship was under threat.

'Nowhere, clearly,' Scott said so dejectedly I thought my heart would break for him.

'Where does Scott fit in?' Tami replied. 'Where do I or the girls fit in with his life is what you should be asking.'

'But he feels shut out of everything here, I'm sure of it.'

'So you think I should peel his grapes and suck his cock a bit more to change that?' she said, shocking me with her language. That wasn't what I'd expected from her at all. 'What about me? I do all the housework and all the child-care as well as working. Are you saying on top of all that I'm expected to make sure he's feeling loved and valued, too? Who's meant to do that for me?'

I shrugged at her because she sort of had a point.

'Scott is the love of my life. But I can't help thinking if he was more involved with day-to-day family life – you know, doing the laundry or Hoovering once in a while, even being home in time to put the girls to bed – he might feel more a part of things. Plus we'd both have more time for each other.'

I wish I'd made her listen, I wish I'd made her see that a man like Scotty needs adulation to feel complete. He needs to feel wanted and needed. Hoovering, laundry and putting the girls to bed wasn't going to change the basic fact that Scotty was an alpha male and alpha males need to be as close to worshipped as they can get.

He wasn't completely blameless, oh no. He should have taken more of an interest in her: bought her flowers, little presents, even a bit of sexy underwear. I told him this. He'd squeezed his face and said she'd flip if he bought her underwear because then she'd have to have sex with him and that wouldn't happen. If they'd both tried, they wouldn't be here today.

Don't even think of ignoring me, Scotty. This isn't going to go away. Bea x

I knew, too, that this thing with Mirabelle was going to blow up. A few weeks back, Scotty managed to get us tickets to one of the Premier League end-of-season matches up in London. We didn't support either of the teams, can barely remember who it was that was playing come to think of it, but they were corporate tickets for the private box and it was a chance to see a live match and you just don't pass up those opportunities. We went up on the train because we both fancied a drink with the posh lunch we were going to be served. A few people from his work were going too, so we'd had to dress up for the occasion. I'd said I'd look after the girls so Tami could go, but she'd said, 'I'd rather stick knitting needles in my eyes' so I'd gone. Which I was secretly pleased about since I LOVE football. On the way there and during the match he'd seemed happy and unburdened. We drank, laughed, joked – even managed to watch some of the game – and then we had to get a car back on the company account because we missed the train home. The closer we drew to Brighton the quieter he became until he confessed – after much prompting from me – he was dreading going home, dreading seeing Mirabelle at work on Monday or on the street any time.

'Why, Scotty?' I asked, concerned by how down he seemed.

'She's . . . She's been giving me the come on,' he said. 'I'm finding it hard to say no.'

'What, you're into her?' I asked, horrified. 'You want to start something up with her?'

'Of course not,' he reassured, 'I'm just finding it hard to get her to leave me alone. Tami has no idea what she's really like.'

'What are you going to do?'

'Get tough with her,' he said, like it was some great effort.

191

A person like him didn't run an international company by being squeamish. 'I'm scared, though, she's going to go crying sexual harassment or something.'

'Urgh! Women like that make me sick. They make it hard for all of us women in business.'

Scotty's gaze rested quite affectionately on me but he didn't say anything.

'Why are you looking at me like that?' I asked.

'Tami wouldn't see it that way. She'd be asking without asking if there was any truth in Mirabelle's claims. She thinks women have it tough in the corporate world.'

'Only if you choose to be a victim,' I said to him.

'Exactly,' he said. 'That's exactly it. It's nice to talk to someone who understands for a change.'

I can't abide women like Mirabelle. I can't abide Mirabelle herself, either. Tami tried several times to get us to be all matey but I couldn't stick her. Maybe it's because even back then I got a sense Mirabelle was after Scotty.

OK, seeing as you can't seem to find your dialling or texting finger, I'll just go out with the new guy at work instead of babysitting the girls like I planned so you can go out to talk. It's fine if I'm the only one wanting to save things here. I'll leave you alone now. Bea x

Once again it's me who can see what a mess they've got themselves into and it's me who has the solution. Anyone would think it was my marriage.

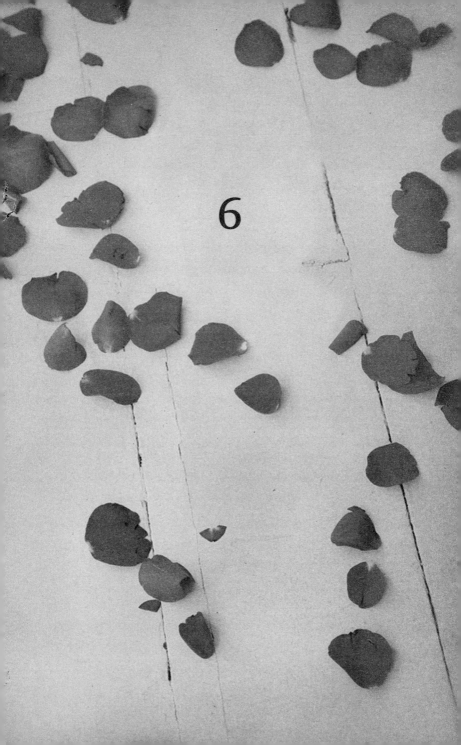

6

Tami

Anansy and Cora are tucked up in their beds, so excited they can hardly keep still. Beatrix is looking after them tonight so she's brought over a sleeping bag to use on the roll-out bed we have between their beds.

'You're not going to sleep tonight, are you?' I say to the three of them as they peek out from under their rainbow of covers.

'We will,' they reply in unison – even Beatrix.

My body sags in defeat at how this is going to pan out. 'All three of you are going to be a mess tomorrow,' I state. 'I'm going to suffer for this when you all get really tired really early and nothing I do will be good enough.'

'We're going to be good,' Cora says, her mouth hidden by her yellow duvet, but her little nose and tapered, large brown eyes shining with unvented exhilaration.

'Very good,' Anansy, with her pink duvet tucked under chin, her expression the mirror image of Cora's, adds.

'Really, very good,' Beatrix ends. Her eyes are green, her hair is blonde, her skin is pale but she looks exactly like the girls – as if the intoxicating thrill of Christmas, their birthdays and every holiday ever been on have been torturous compared to this.

'Right. I trust you.' Said by me with a hitch of my eyebrows and the quiet resignation of a person who knows their kids and knows her friend. I don't, of course, trust them. I don't think I'll ever completely trust another human being again after what he has done. This is what this is about: Scott has asked me – begged, actually – to talk. I do not want to talk. I want to forget this awful thing is happening, I want to skip to the future when we've dealt with it; or I want to go back in time to the point where my marriage was so horrible that he had to look elsewhere and stop it from happening at all. I don't know when that moment was. I can guess, I can imagine, I can think I feel it but I don't know. I have no way at all to place the pad of my finger at that location on the map of my life and know that's where it all started to fall apart.

'I love you, see you tomorrow.' I kiss Cora. 'I love you, see you tomorrow.' I kiss Anansy. 'I love *you*, thank you and see you tomorrow.' I smile at Beatrix. She offers me back concern and courage wrapped in a smile.

'You'll be all right,' she mouths at me.

I nod, knowing I won't be.

We haven't spoken as we walk into town. Scott has been taking his laptop with him on the school run these past couple of days, looking like a packhorse with his workbag, his laptop bag and the girls' bags hanging off him, so he can stay out of the way until the girls are home and he can have them as a barrier to me ignoring him. So he'd had to ring earlier to ask what sort of food I fancied while we talked. I'd hung up on him in reply.

I cannot speak to him. Every time I try to, a text message

will pop into my head, the image it conjures up like a knife to the guts. I'm not sure which causes more trauma, more bruising: the emotional messages or the sexual ones. But they all hurt, they all bring me up short.

'Are we not going to speak at all?' he eventually says. Scott can't handle silence, which is why he has been trying to get me to talk, why he needs the girls to be around before he is alone with me. 'We can't carry on like this, we need to talk.'

'About?'

'TB—'

'I've told you not to call me that. I know I can't ask much of you, but I'd really rather like it if you didn't insult me by calling me things that remind me of the life we once had.'

'What's that supposed to mean?'

'What is there to talk about, Scott?'

'How we're going to repair this marriage. Unless you want to break up our family without even trying?'

We're walking along Church Road, the road that feeds another road that feeds another road all the way into Brighton. Usually we'd walk along the seafront, we'd pause and stare at the water as we talked, we'd casually sling our arms around each other, move in close to share body heat, gaze at each other and kiss, stupid grins on our faces. Scott had been heading there, but I had set the route, up here, with the darkened shops, and odd splashes of light from a restaurant or a shop with their lights left on all night. It seemed appropriate: sombre with an unsubtle hint of hope-lessness.

I have not answered his question by the time we pass

Tesco, which is brightly lit, full of people who seem to move slowly and aimlessly like zombies gathering supplies, and move on towards the end of George Street. I am reticent and hesitant about answering because I do not know if I want to save this relationship.

'Do you want to save this relationship or not?' he asks, indignantly. 'Because we both have to work on it, we both have to make changes.'

'I don't know if I do want to save it, actually.'

Outside the Italian restaurant that hugs the corner of Ventnor Villas and Church Road, Scott halts.

'You don't know if you want to save us?' He is incredulous. A tremor of anxiety trickles through his surprise.

Before stopping too I shift to one side so a young couple, arms linked, bodies close, can pass us. I gaze longingly at them as they pass – so much ahead of them, so much innocence. I am standing in the island of light the lamppost casts and Scott joins me, putting us under a spotlight. My line of vision strays to the restaurant, to the diners who are seated in there. Eating, drinking, living. I wonder how many of them are cheating? How many of them have been cheated on. How many of them feel the absolute agony of loving the one person they can't be with any more? 'No, I don't.'

'What about what I want? Does that count?'

Yours are the only wants that have counted for a long time, I say in my head. But I would never hurt him by saying that, especially not when his body is so tense and fretful, his hands are itching to grab me, shake sense into me, make me rethink what I am saying.

'Look.' I speak like him. More than I should, more than I

want to. I'm sure it's because we grew up in the same place, I'm sure it's not because I've lost my identity, being with him. 'Our situation is too damaged, it can't be fixed.'

'You're not being fair. You're deciding to break up our family without giving us a chance.'

'I wondered when you would come out with that and admit you think it's my fault that you cheated.'

'I wouldn't have looked somewhere else if I was happy in the relationship,' he states, far less desperate and far more righteous now.

Those words aren't unexpected, I knew he was going to throw them at me because he's been throwing variations of them at me since he told me the truth, but to hear them is a different experience altogether. I am suddenly outside of myself, I am perched atop the lamppost, looking at the two of us, and I can see myself clearly. My hair needs washing and re-twisting to smooth away the escaping strands. My skin is dull and blemished, my eyes are beleaguered and red from the constant rubbing, my lips are dry from constantly being bitten and mashed together in anxiety, my body has shed weight so my clothes are starting to swamp me. This is what Scott sees, this is what he is telling me he has been seeing and has found wanting. This is the woman who wasn't enough for him so he had to look elsewhere. This is who I am.

'Do you know, I expected you to say that. And if the man I married, the man I loved all these years, had said it, it would have devastated me, but from you, it's water off a duck's back.'

'What are you talking about? I am the man you married.'

It's my turn to sneer, whether I do so on my face or not, I'm not sure. 'The man I married wasn't a porn user, obsessed with money and making sure he looked good at all costs. He was kind and had a hug or kiss for me that wouldn't always have to lead to sex. Porn-style sex, obviously. The man I married listened when I talked, he cried when his daughters were born and he held my hand sometimes just for the sake of it. The man I married once gave a *Big Issue* seller his last fiver because it was cold and he wanted the man to have enough for a cup of coffee. The man I married wrote my name in the stars. He found me one hundred pebbles on Brighton beach just because, then put them all back where he found them because he didn't want to further ruin the miniature ecosystem of the beach. The man I married once played horsey with his girls in the garden even though it was more mud than grass and so had to bin his favourite pair of trousers. And he stayed up every night for a week when one of his daughters had chickenpox to stop her from scratching, to keep an eye on her temperature and to read her stories. You are not that man.

'I don't know where the Scott Challey I married went, but it's not you. It's like every day you killed the real Scott Challey a tiny little bit until he completely disappeared and all that is left is a man who could have an affair and would behave in ways that would not only see him arrested for sexual assault but would make me think he was capable of it. You've taken away my best friend, my lover and the father of my children.'

All those words have not been formed like that in my mind before. I didn't realise that was how I felt until I was

200

telling him those things. It's true, though. I don't know who he is any more. What has happened has dragged me out of denial, out of that comfortable coma of getting through the day, into the waking world of living with a complete stranger.

Scott has been taking in what I have been saying with an impassive face. He is not incredulous or shocked any longer, he has stepped back to anger. And I see him again: the boy who told Mr McCoy he would cut out his heart with a spoon and feed it to his dog. He rears up in Scott's body, unveiling himself on his face, in the sinews of his body, in the way he stands and breathes. His hands curl into fists as his face twists and he opens his mouth.

'You're so hard done by, aren't you?' he jeers. 'So hard done by but you have no problem spending my money, living in my house, driving my car, do you? And what about me? The person I married was this cool, laid-back woman who was hot and sexy and up for trying out different things. She was funny and welcoming and I could trust her. And now I have to live with this neurotic, frumpy prude who can't be bothered to put on a bit of lippy so she doesn't show me up when we're out together. And sex? What's that? There's not a man out there who would put up with no sex like I've had to. And let's not even bother thinking about you doing something for me without first fretting about how it'll affect the kids. Because that's all you care about, isn't it? Your ridiculous need to micro-manage every aspect of the children's lives at the expense of our life together. When was the last time we even had a decent conversation, hmm, Tami? Are you at all surprised I needed someone else to rely on? To hold me? To make love to? I was getting none of that at home, from the person who was meant to give me all that.' He comes right up to me, his face is contorted with anger, accentuated by the orangey light of the lamppost, and his voice a vicious snarl. 'Why wouldn't I look elsewhere when I've got a wallflower at my table and an ice block in my bed?'

His words settle like dust all over us, another layer of accusation and hurt upon what I have said. There is an oddly satisfying irony to this: he started the conversation to make me agree to 'rescuing' our marriage, and now he's come round to the same conclusion as I have.

'So you agree, we've nothing left to save?' I say. 'We can get on with the process of splitting up?'

Scott immediately pulls back, physically, emotionally. His body changes, his face alters, his whole manner is now conciliatory. 'No, I'm not saying that. I'm not saying that at all. I'm saying that neither of us is perfect. I don't want to split up.'

'Why not?' I shriek at him. 'I'm terrible, I'm awful, I'm a frigid frump, why don't you want to split up? This is your chance to start again with your perfect woman who's interesting inside and outside of the bedroom. You can go be with her.' With Mirabelle. Even though it'll be a knife through my heart if I have to see them together, and the children will not understand why he's living there and not with us, but I will get used to it, we will get used to it. 'This is your chance at the life you obviously don't have with me.'

'I don't want to split up,' he insists. He is calmer, gentler, softer. 'I want us to work this out, not to split up.'

I want to work it out, too, of course I do. I love him. I'm not sure how my life would function without him in it. How

202

I would wake up each morning and be able to breathe without him there or knowing he was going to be there. Even in all this misery, I still see flashes of the old Scott, the real Scott. But if I stay, it will be more of the same. Too much of the new Scott, slivers of the old Scott, and always the knowledge that he was capable of giving himself to someone else. Body, soul, heart. What was left for me were the entrails of his personality. Even in everything, *everything* I know I deserve better, more.

My feet take charge, turning me around and continuing the walk towards Brighton, towards our destination. Scott is forced to follow. We have to talk about this some more, I have to make him see that splitting up is the only way I will be able to stay sane.

We've walked together, we've sat down together in this restaurant, but we have not talked together since we were standing outside the other restaurant. I am thinking about the dissolution of our lives. I am thinking about divorce.

There is so much to sort out, the house, my work, telling people. Telling the girls. Every time I think about that my brain veers away from the realities, the practicalities of separating.

Divorce. The word is a nightmare all on its own. It is huge, and frightening and insurmountable. I am standing at the bottom, staring up and up and up but I still cannot see the top. How can I climb it when I have no realistic concept of how big it is? From my position at the foot of this Everest-type word I lower my head, turn to my right, trying to see to the end of it, trying to see how far it stretches, to see if

I can see the final 'E', but no, it is too far away, it goes on for too long. How can I even begin to think about going around it if I cannot see how long it goes on for? There is no way to get over it, or around it, I have to go through it. And it looks terrifying in there. It looks like I will be battling through long, lightless tunnels, feeling my way as I go, stumbling, falling, hurting myself and knowing that to turn back will only mean I will probably have to go through it again, and this time it will seem even scarier because I will not know how to get to the other side.

I am getting divorced. This was not meant to happen to me. To us. To our relationship. To our family.

'Remember that time we had that two-day stopover in Turkey on the way to Egypt?' Scott says to me.

I nod, my gaze lowered to the stiff white tablecloth underneath my bread plate, butter knife and little rectangle of pale, unsalted butter. 'Yes,' I mumble.

'Remember when we got to the hotel and they refused to give us a double room because we weren't married and they didn't want us lowering the reputation of their flea-pit hotel by us sleeping in the same room?'

I nod again, the smile nudging at the edges of my mouth as the memory is ignited and I'm being tugged back to the sights, sounds and smells of that time.

'And remember, after you'd given them the dressing down to end all dressing downs, they totally backed off but would only give us a twin room?'

The smile wants to get bigger, to show itself on my face, in the movements of my body.

'And remember we went out to get some food and ended

up eating in the equivalent of that horrible greasy spoon in Brighton? And then when we came back to the hotel we found that a cat had got in through the open window and peed on your bed? And we were scrunched up in my little bed and you kept going, "I *know* I shut that window before we went out. Do you think they let the cat in on purpose and just opened the window to cover their backs?" And I kept saying, "You're really very optimistic to think it's a cat. I mean, how would a *cat* know to pee on your bed and not mine?"'

We'd talked and laughed, our bodies spooned together but both still hanging a little over the edge of the bed. Those were the types of memories that welled up when you thought of all the reasons why you loved someone.

'Remember?' Scott asks.

'Yes, I remember, Scott, what's that got to do with anything?'

'I . . . Just . . . Splitting up . . . Tami, I know you don't want this, and I don't want this. Please. We had something so good, so special. Somewhere along the line we lost sight of that. But I think we should fight for what we had, what we could have again.'

I shake my head. I don't want to fight. I don't want all those memories, like the ones he's just talked about to be rewritten, *unwritten* actually, by the process of staying together in the reality of an affair. An affair is like unpicking the thread that binds your marriage then using that thread to make something completely new and, of course, tainted. Our relationship is tainted, no matter how we move on from here, and if I have to look at him every day, finding out new things about how and when he betrayed me, I know my memories will not withstand the invalidation of significant or even subtle rewrites. I don't want to fight to stop any unpicking, unmaking, undoing. I want to keep what I have intact and to do that, I have to walk away now.

'We can't do this to the children,' Scott says, 'without knowing we tried *everything* to make it work.'

I think of telling the girls that Mama and Dad wouldn't be living together any more. That they wouldn't see both of us every day from now on. I can't imagine the look on their faces, the horror that will slowly dawn on them that their family is over. They have friends with divorced parents, who have two homes and who are fine. They are happy, healthy, thriving. But did they get that way instantly? How did they feel in the first few weeks, days, hours? How did they manage to make sense of it? I conjure up Cora's face, how she will shut down, stiffen her lips and knit her forehead together in a frown; I picture Anansy's face, how her eyes will widen and her mouth will open as she starts to breathe fast and anxiously. Can I really do this to them without trying everything first?

'Let's go for couples counselling. Find a way to talk to each other about this, find out how we can fix it,' he says.

I think about the girls growing up and finding the understanding that I walked away without trying counselling, without giving their father the chance to put things right.

'Tami, I will do anything to put this right. Anything. Just tell me what you need from me and it's yours. Anything.' He pauses. 'Even if we can't make it work, let's at least go to counselling to find a way to split up amicably. Please, we can't end like this.'

'Why now?' I ask him. 'Why now after you said no again when I asked you for the second time last year to go to counselling?' I suggested counselling again even after his reaction the first time *('Don't be stupid, Tami. Why the fucking fuck should I fucking pay to fucking talk? People pay me to talk, not the other way around. Counselling, like gambling, is a fucking mug's game. You should know better, you really should.')* because his behaviour had reached new lows and I couldn't stand it. A stark realisation hits me between the eyes: but of course he was being awful, of course he'd graduated from subtle put-downs to overt ones, of course he'd increased his preening – that was when he started unpicking the thread of our marriage with his affair.

'I, erm, I wasn't being . . . I had a different mind-set back then, I was—'

I raise my hand to stop him. I don't want him to carry on, we both know why. Anything else he says will just sound like trying to explain it away. Not only the affair, the behaviour that went with it.

'Things are different now,' he says. 'I want this to work. I know it's going to work.' He says that as if he can just erase the past few days of hell, the past eighteen months or so of his affair, the last four years of appalling, entitled behaviour by sheer force of will. He can't, of course, but I want to try for Cora and Anansy, to spare them any unnecessary pain.

'OK, I'll give it a try. But I'm making no promises. We're just going to find someone and see if it might help us.'

His body visibly relaxes. 'Oh thank God,' he says. 'Thank you. I know we can make it work, I know we can.' His hand moves towards mine, wanting to slip his fingers between mine. I jerk my hand, my body, backwards away from him. The bruises of the things he said in the street are still there on my skin – not visible to the naked eye, but still there. Still painful to the touch. My words don't seem to have hurt him, he has brushed them off and thinks it's normal for us to have said those things to each other, that we can rebuild something after all that. For someone whose character was assassinated not even an hour ago, he seems remarkably fine.

'Right, OK, I think we can class this an emergency. I'll be fine to take time off work this week or next week. Hopefully they'll have someone this week. Just let me know what day, what time and where and I'll be there.'

I blink at him, wondering if he is serious. He can't be, can he? He must surely be pulling my leg. *Surely*. I say nothing, my eyes wandering idly over his face.

He is silent. I remember something I should have said to him earlier: the man I married would never have treated me like his personal assistant at best, his servant at worst.

'I'm not arranging counselling,' I state. 'Why would I when I don't even want to go and, more importantly, *I wasn't the one who had an affair*.'

I watch as the realisation dawns on his face and his eyes slip shut in regret.

'Nice sense of entitlement you've got going on there, Scott,' I say.

'Don't do that,' he says sharply.

'Don't do what?'

'Don't be snide. If we're going to work this out, we have to at least try to be kind to each other, be understanding until we can get ourselves a counsellor who can help us communicate better.'

He's right, of course. But it still niggles. Maybe that's why we need counselling so it doesn't feel wrong to try to be kind to him.

'You have to give up the porn,' I say.

'Pardon?'

'You said you'd do anything and I want you to give up the porn.'

Scott's tensed body is telling him to refuse, to deny me this request. 'Right. OK, all right. I'll stop watching it.'

'And delete all the files you've got saved. On your PC, laptop, iPad and mobiles.'

His head nods as if in contemplation but he doesn't make eye contact.

'Is there a problem?' I ask.

'No. No. There's no problem. I'll do it. Of course, I'll do it.' Scott's dark eyes stray to my hands, laced together in my lap. I've noticed him staring at my hands a lot these past few days. 'And you have to put your wedding ring back on.'

I may not wear it, but I keep it with me every day. I put it in my pocket and if what I am wearing doesn't have pockets, I slip it into my bra. I like to have it close, even though I don't wear it. When we were first married I could hardly wear it for more than a few hours because it irritated the skin on my finger. I had to keep taking it off and putting it back on until my hand got used to the metal constantly rubbing against it; until my body got used to being married. As it is, around the base of my ring finger there is a smooth, darkened band of skin from where the ring won its battle to be worn permanently. There is a band of skin that I'm not sure will ever properly fade so I will always be reminded of this marriage, whether it works or not.

'Don't push your luck,' I say to him.

His reply is a small nod.

My fingers curl tightly into my palm, the jagged edges of my picked-apart nails digging in and stopping the tears. The shock is wearing off, the numbness thawing throughout my body. And all around me I can feel the thread of my past, the tapestry of the history of my one true love and marriage being unpicked, undone and callously rewoven.

Tami

Two weeks have passed.

Two weeks where we are more fragile, but putting on a front for the girls. Beatrix comes over every three or four days, trying to take the tension out of us being together. Scott is back at work and I have the house to myself during the day.

Scott is trying. He takes the girls to school every day now, he is home for dinner with them and he helps with the bedtime routine. He washes up after dinner, he puts on the laundry, he hangs it out before he goes to bed, he cleans the bathroom on the weekend. He checks the fridge and cupboards to see what is missing and picks it up on the way home. Every other day when we are eating dinner he Hoovers the house. He is here. Present. No more texting or emailing on his phones when he's sitting at the table or with the girls. He focuses on them and them alone. He is the model husband and father.

I hate him for it almost as much as I hate him for the affair. He knew what he should be doing, he knew how removed he was from us and yet it took the end – virtually – for him to be here again. For him to return to his family rather than sending the shell of himself home every night.

Right now, we're going to the doctors for a check-up with

213

Anansy who has an ear infection. Scott is here and he is coming with us. Normally he wouldn't have been here, let alone come with us. Obviously, this is when the inevitable happens. We don't live in the biggest place in the world, and she clearly isn't going to hide away, like I would if I had done what she has done.

Mirabelle is coming towards us on the road. Seeing her is a trip back to the messages, to the passion and the lust, to the images of them together that have snagged themselves into my mind like those little plant spores with hooks and barbs that snare themselves on your clothing and you can only remove by picking them off individually. These memories will not go away by themselves, they will need to be plucked out one by one and destroyed.

Mirabelle – her name pools nausea at the back of my throat – is on our side of the road. As if she hasn't betrayed me and condemned Scott, she was about to walk past our house.

Scott and Mirabelle both falter and then pause in the step they were both about to take when they see each other. What must it be like, being confronted by your lover now that the person you were betraying knows?

Unaware of what is going on, Anansy screams, 'Auntie Mirabelle!' before darting off towards her. She throws herself at Mirabelle's legs, encompasses them with her arms and squeezes. 'Auntie Mirabelle, where've you been? I've missed you so much.'

I knew they liked her, but not this much. They saw her regularly because she would often drop by for coffee over the weekend, when Scott was out at the gym or some kind of trade fair where he'd pick up business contacts. She would sit with them and play with them, and chat with me afterwards. Our lives were so much more intertwined, interwoven, than I had thought. It will take some time to unstitch her from my life, from our life.

Mirabelle's face, adorned with far too much foundation and eye shadow and eyeliner in an attempt to look normal, creases with a smile. She lowers herself to her knees and takes Anansy in her arms. I want to rip my child away from her. I want to scream at her to get away from my daughter. I can't do that, of course, without scaring Anansy and alerting Cora that Mirabelle is something to do with the tension in the house.

'Hi, Aunt Mirabelle,' Cora says, moving closer shyly until she is near enough for Mirabelle to reach out and tug her into the hug, too. The urge almost overwhelms me this time, and I actually step forwards to rip them away. Then I stop. The look on her face is so bereft. I remember once asking her if she wanted to have children.

'Me? Children?' she said and smiled that secret smile of hers, the one that would sit on her lips the second she was about to become mysterious.

'Yes, you. Do you want to have children?' I repeated, determined not to be put off.

'Want to? Maybe. Need to? Yes.'

'What does that mean?'

'It means I feel the need to have children. And if you're asking because you can see I'm not exactly relaxed around your children even though I adore them, I just, I get scared I'm going to break them, I suppose.'

'Most people get over that after the newborn stage.'

'Yes, but for me, it's a never-ending fear. You can break children without meaning to. I don't just mean physically, either.'

Mirabelle does not look at Scott. Since my step forward, he is behind me and possibly looking at her, I do not know. Is he staring at her and reminding himself of what they had, what they did, how they fitted together in their desire for each other? Is he wondering if he has made the right choice?

'I hope you girls are being good,' she says.

'We are,' they chorus.

'When are you coming to our house again, Aunt Mirabelle?' Anansy asks. 'We can't play special tea on the beach without you.'

'Yes,' Cora adds, 'and you have to bring your rose petals so we can play properly.'

'We'll see,' Mirabelle says.

'In other words, "no",' Cora says.

'Did I say no?'

'Yes. "We'll see" is adult speak for "no". Everyone knows that.'

'Why don't you want to play with us?' Anansy asks, affronted and aghast.

'I do, I do, it's just, I'm really busy with work right now and I don't have time to come over to play. It's not that I don't want to, it's that I don't have the time.'

Like Scott, she lies so easily. Lies slip from her tongue as if untruths are nothing to be afraid of. As if they don't live on your shoulders and stain your soul.

'I will come over soon, I promise.' Lie. A lie on a promise.

'Please do,' Anansy says, saddening her eyes, and evoking a straight-mouth smile of yearning.

'Yes, please do,' Cora says, feeling no shame in copying her sister's expression.

Enough. Enough, enough, enough. I take another step towards the three of them. 'Come on now, we've really got to get going,' I say to the girls.

'Awwwww,' they both intone at the same time.

'Now, come on girls, you can't keep your mother waiting.' For a moment, I think she is going to look up at me because she has mentioned me, but she doesn't. I want her to. I want to see what shame looks like, I want to see what lives in the eyes of a liar. I want to see her. With care and attention, she straightens the collar on Anansy's jacket, and tucks one of the stray locks of hair from Cora's plaits behind her ear. 'You be good, as I know you are.'

She brings herself up to her full height, and focuses completely on the girls, does not raise her line of sight from them at all. 'I'll see you soon, gorgeous ones,' she says with an air of finality that twists a little in my stomach. *Where is she going?*

'See you soon,' Cora says.

Anansy raises her hand to her mouth and kisses her palm then ostentatiously throws the kiss towards Mirabelle. She catches it in the palm of her hand. 'Thank you,' she says. 'I'm going to put this in my pocket and keep it for when I feel sad. Is that OK?'

Anansy grins and nods.

'Bye,' she says, grins at them both again, before pulling her Mulberry bag – the twin of mine – onto her shoulder.

She does not look at me or Scott, not even a glance to acknowledge she knows we're there. She steps off the pavement and hurries herself to the other side before carrying on with her journey.

'I miss Auntie Mirabelle,' Anansy decides, slipping her hand into mine.

Me too, I almost say but I catch those words in my throat before they escape.

'I think we should invite her for dinner again. We like her beach and flowers game.'

Scott is silent, his mood has shifted and I can feel his sullenness radiating outwards from him. The police investigation is still ongoing, there is still the threat of divorce hanging over him, seeing Mirabelle must have reminded him of that.

'Why didn't she speak to you and Dad, Mama?' Cora asks as I unlock my car and open the back door for her to climb in.

'*Ask your father,*' the vicious side of me, the side I have had to tame in the name of 'being kind' to the man who has ripped out my heart and stomped on it, wants to say.

'Maybe she was busy,' I reply.

'She can still come to our house to play, can't she?' Anansy asks. 'She said she would.'

'We'll see,' I reply, knowing they will both understand what I mean.

Tami

It's been three days since the 'happy' news that Mirabelle has retracted her statement and so the case has had to be dropped and, yet, I don't feel like celebrating.

Detectives Harvan and Wade told Scott and I that they were going to look into whether there had been any intimidation going on, but I am trying to get back to the place where I was before Scott was arrested. I haven't arrived there yet. I am nowhere near that destination.

'Does Scotty look at porn?' Beatrix asks, a question from left field. The man in question is taking care of the girls this Saturday afternoon because he wants to. He told me to go out and enjoy myself, his benevolence in that regard something I was unused to. I'd wandered down George Street and looked in a couple of shops, and then found myself here at Beatrix's flat, sitting down to coffee from her coffee machine and small pink cupcakes I'd bought at the organic bakery on the high street.

'Why would you ask that?'

'Well, I was reading something the other day that said there's a huge link between secret porn use and infidelity. Something about boundaries and trying it out for real or something. So, does he?'

I'm tempted to say no, to say he's not like that. My instinct, as always, is to protect him. 'Not something I really want to talk about.'

'My husband did. I think that's how it started, you know. How he progressed onto the whore he left me for.'

I have almost erased those horrific images from my head. They have haunted me and now they have stopped because he has stopped looking at them. 'He . . . um . . .' The images don't haunt me any more, but this thought does: did my face look like that woman's in the film where they showed the act that happened the night of yes that felt like a no? Did I look that frightened and horrified and disgusted? 'He doesn't any more.'

Beatrix stands at her kitchen sink, observing me in that quiet way she does when she's about to say something she knows I won't like. 'Are you sure, sweetie?'

My body flushes with heat and indignation. 'Why do you say that? Has Scott told you something? It was a condition of us staying together and going to counselling.' I rub the area where my wedding ring should be. 'He said he would stop.'

'Sweetheart, he's cheated on you for months, he's lied and lied to you, why would he do what he says now and give up porn?'

That is something I've not dared consider. He is being the perfect husband and father, how can I consider that he is still going behind my back and doing that?

'Tami, look,' she comes to the table, pulls out a seat and sits down. She reaches across the table and takes my hands in hers. 'My husband cheated on me, more than once. I think it started with the porn. Or maybe I'm just hoping it was the porn and not just him. But he promised me many, many times he would knock the porn on the head, he would stop cheating. I don't mean sleeping with other people but online flirting, getting pictures, then online sex talk. Every time he lied. He couldn't give up porn, he couldn't give up the thrill of other women. We would recommit ourselves and he would be OK, then it would start again.

'Sweetie, I don't want to upset you more than you're already upset, and you know Scotty's my friend and I love him to pieces, but if he's addicted to porn there's no way he'll have given it up that easily.'

I know she's right. I know I have been fooling myself that he has simply given up his secret sex life because I asked him to.

'Look, I just don't want you to end up like me – with your self-esteem on the floor and your body covered in "consensual" bruises, and him leaving anyway. You need to take charge. You've been blindsided too many times already. And if he's lying to you about that, then he might be lying about being committed to your new start, he might even still be cheating on you.'

I need to know. But do I want to know? A tiny voice inside is telling me it's better not to know, it's better to leave well enough alone. These are the thoughts that Pandora probably had before that moment where she chose poorly.

Beatrix

'Oh, great,' I mumble to myself. 'Just f-ing great.'

Across the gym is that woman. Mirabelle. Even saying her name in my head is like spitting out green, slimy phlegm. She's on the running machine. She has a headband around the front of her hair, the rest of her voluminous curls bunched back into a ponytail. She's wearing a black, long-sleeve tracksuit that looks far too hot for in here and with the way she is running, the anger with which she is pounding the machine, I'm surprised no one has been over to tell her to back off. It's that glass-fronted gym down on the seafront. The running machines are mostly facing the windows so you can run as if you're running outside. There are also stationary bikes and an area at the back for free weights.

I didn't know she came here. She always seemed to be about running outside, rain or shine. Dragged Tami into it, too. I remember asking Tami if she fancied coming to the gym with me a while back, it was something for us to do together, as mates without the girls and without Scotty. She'd nearly burst a lung laughing. 'As if!' she'd gasped between laughs. 'You know me,' she'd said when she saw the hurt on my face, 'I walk to keep fit.' Next thing I know, she's picking out running shoes and a running bra and going out in the filthiest weather to run with Mirabelle. I couldn't believe my ears! We could have had such fun at the gym, but no, when Mirabelle says 'Let's run', Tami goes, 'Where to?' and that's it.

It sounds a bit like I'm jealous, doesn't it? I'm not. Truly, I'm not. Me and Mirabelle, we don't gel. Never have, never will.

Twenty-one months ago

'Aren't we a bit old to be having a sleepover?' I asked Tami. She was all a dither because we were going to be sleeping down in the living room with duvets and popcorn, snacks and champagne cocktails. From the way she was fluttering around, checking she had enough plates for the snack-dinner and glasses for the champagne and the right duvets, and pillows, and an extensive DVD selection, if I didn't know better, I'd have thought she had a girl-crush on Mirabelle. I'd met her a couple of times since she and Tami had become friends, but this was the first time I'd be spending an extended period of time with her.

I knew – *knew* – she and Tami would be falling over them-selves with the in-jokes and talking natural hair and bonding, while I'd be sat there like a lemon. Scotty was away so I couldn't even speak to him as an alternative.

'Who on Earth is ever too old for a sleepover?' Tami said.

'Anyone over twelve?' I said, and it sounded so snarky Tami stopped her fussing and focused on me.

'Sorry, I kind of railroaded you into this, didn't I?'

'Just a bit.'

Tami came over and linked her hand through mine, confirming our friendship with the warmth and surety of her touch. 'Thing is, right, you and Mirabelle are my two best friends. I've known you longer and you're so wonderful, I want her to get to know you like I do. I want you to get to know her. It'd be great if we can do this sort of thing all the time, the three of us.' She stopped while she thought it through. 'To be really, really honest, I don't have that many friends any more. Most of the ones I had were through work. I don't have many people down here I can trust and I'm too much of a wimp to get involved in school-gate politics. I drop the girls off and run. You and Mirabelle are my circle of friends, which makes us more of a triangle, but you know what I mean.'

I did know. A lot of my friends did come and go in my life, drifting in and out like clouds. I sort of admired her for being honest enough to try to change that, to try to hang onto the friendships she had in her life.

'So, will you try? For me?'

I nodded, like a sulky teenage girl. I'm usually far more mature, but I'll admit Mirabelle got my goat because she was prettier than me. There, I've said it. She was better-looking, more striking *and* taller than me. Tami, lovely as she was, was kind of ordinary. In a good way, in a wonderful, earth mother, 'be your best friend who wouldn't steal your man' way. When she smiled she was radiant, but Mirabelle had an edge. She could break a man's balls without even trying. It's awful to admit this, but I liked being the prettiest woman in the room. I generally was, unless Mirabelle was there, too. 'But if she starts tossing her hair and being all, "I'm ever so pretty" I am going home.'

Mirabelle drifted in, the picture of perfection, and I

wanted to swear at her. She'd brought her make-up collection, nail polish, hair stuff. I'd brought a bottle of Blue Nun. Warm.

We had a good time, but whenever Tami was out of the room the chat dried up. I could see how Mirabelle was looking at me when we were alone, her eyes glaring down at me from on high, like she was better than me, so there was no way I was going to talk to her. I had tried, like I promised Tami I would, and this was how she behaved. After that night, I didn't bother again. We even saw each other in the street and pretended we had never met, neither of us were going to make the first move on that score.

She's seen me. She's doing a very good job of looking through me, though. I take my towel and move to the other side of the gym to the cross-trainer at the back, nearest the free weights. She cuts her eyes at me as I go past. The cheek of her! THE FLAMING CHEEK OF HER! She lies and lies about one of the people I'm closest to in this world and then cuts her eyes at me. Unexpectedly, my body is aflame, all at once. How dare she! Who does she think she is?

I'm too angry to move from the spot; I glare at her until she finishes her run and jumps off the treadmill. I watch her hand close around her big, fluffy white towel and head for the changing room. We're the only ones in here, the person behind the desk is out of sight so if I speak to her, give her a piece of my mind, no one will know. It'll be my word against hers if she goes to the police. Since she's a proven liar having retracted her statement, they'll never believe her.

She's still dressed, her face drenched in sweat, her locker door is open as she takes out her rucksack and belongings.

'Who do you think you are?' I say to her.

'Oh, this should be good,' she says, pausing in filling her bag and spinning towards me. 'Have you got something to say to me, *Beatrix*?'

The way she says my name incites a whole new level of rage inside me.

'You are . . . I can't even think of the word. You're a *disgrace*. I've known women who have been—'

'You know women? I seriously doubt that,' she cuts in.

'What's that supposed to mean?'

'You are what people call a handmaiden. You don't like women very much, probably been brought up to think you have to compete with all women or act like a man to get ahead – join in all the derogatory stuff men say in the work-place. And because you're nobody's "victim" you think you're all empowered and feminist. Except you'd never call your-self a feminist because to you that means man-hater. When actually,' she makes her face soft, mockingly understanding and patronising, 'being a feminist means striving towards equality for women. Most feminists have no issue with men at all. Did you understand that, or do I need to repeat it in words of one syllable?'

'Scotty was right about you. You are a—'

'A frigid, man-hating dyke? I think you'll find he says that about any woman who doesn't follow him around with big doe eyes, letting him feel her up whenever the mood takes him. Of course, you wouldn't know what I mean about that, would you, *Beatrix*?'

'If you're implying that I am after Scotty—'

'You wouldn't dream of doing that with dear Scotty, would you, *Beatrix*?'

'You have no idea what you're talking about.'

'You think because Tami hasn't noticed how you are around her husband that no one else has? Newsflash for Beatrix—' She makes a loudhailer out of her hands and calls: 'Everyone knows you fancy him.'

'Oh, fuck off.'

'Or what, you're going to tell your boyfriend on me? Guess what?' She remakes the loudhailer: 'I'm not scared of him.'

If she wasn't so much taller than me, stronger-looking than me, I would have her. I'd grab handfuls of that hair she takes so much pride in and rip it from her head before scratching her eyes out.

She returns to packing her bag, hoists it onto her shoulder and then goes to leave the changing room. It's a small white-tiled space, stolen from the men's changing room because it used to be a men-only gym, so it doesn't take much for me to block the exit.

Anxiety momentarily twirls on her face then she seems to find the idea of me doing her harm hilarious. She literally laughs in my face. 'I wouldn't try anything if I were you, it'll end very badly for you,' she says.

I step aside and without another word she goes, leaving the bitter taste of anger and outrage in my mouth.

I hate her so much I could do her serious harm.

Bitch! Why doesn't she do everyone a favour and just disappear? *Stupid, entitled bitch!* No one speaks to me like that and gets away with it. Especially not someone like her. Mirabelle, the bitch of Providence Close, has a whole world of pain coming her way, I promise you.

Tami

Last night, I slept in my clothes. And I went walking in bare feet. Streaks of dirt and tiny pieces of gravel, which must have been hell to walk on, were stuck to the bottom of my feet when I woke up earlier. I also have scratches on my hands, and my forearms are sore. I may have fallen over or something.

I have no memory of what I did last night.

Well, I remember sitting in the kitchen, listening to Whitney (Houston) and Donna (Summer) and downing glasses of the most expensive wine I could find in Scott's wine store which was once the under-stairs cupboard. The raw edges of my feelings started to abate, the hurt subsiding even as 'Your Love Is My Love', which had been one of the readings at our wedding and our first dance, started. Fury frothed up in the place of the hurt. Blinding, boiling rage, and the need to hurt Scott and Mirabelle was all consuming.

I could almost feel the weight of the pillow in my hands seconds before I pushed down on Scott's face, holding it there until he stopped moving. I could almost feel the silkiness of the chocolate-brown skin of Mirabelle's neck as I closed my hands around it and squeezed. I remember being horrified and fascinated in equal measure that I felt the need to hurt them so acutely it was almost real. It was in me. I had said it to Beatrix, but that was rational, that was explaining a thought I'd had, this was actually feeling the emotion. Knowing that a part of me could actually do it. I was capable of lashing out – physically – with the intention of causing damage.

It's fuzzier, hazier after that. The music stopped, I knew I should go to bed. I'd drunk two bottles of expensive wine on an empty stomach, but I didn't go to bed. I went out. We don't have a gravel path or drive, I do know who does, though. I wouldn't have gone there. Would I?

The orange-red gravel washed down the drain in the shower this morning and now I am here, making breakfast.

I move around the kitchen, getting two bowls out for the girls, making toast. I pour juice into their pink and red beakers, place them in front of their cereal bowls. I take out the milk, put the cereal selection between their two place settings and then I fill the kettle. I am one shallow breath too many away from being sick right now, and two more accidental plate clashes away from my head splitting in two.

I don't make breakfast for Scott any more. I cannot bring myself to do it, and he doesn't seem to expect it.

What Beatrix said the other day about him still looking at porn is playing on my mind. I should check, but I can't bring myself to do that, either. It sounds pathetic but I can't cope with any more, it's all too much already. And what if he is? Will it change anything? Really? I am treading water, waiting for counselling. Waiting to have someone else there so I can explain to him that I want to split up. That is why I am still here. That is why I am being a robot in my own life, and drinking myself to sleep every night. I know splitting up will be bad, but staying together is worse. We are still here, not because I think the girls will be devastated beyond repair; not because I still love him because I feel more hate towards him than anything. It is because if he stays, he will leave me alone. If he goes he will constantly be on my case to make it work again. I'm waiting for counselling to have someone else there when I tell him we can't work this out. Because right now, as things stand, I know he won't accept it and until we've 'tried everything' I can't walk away with a clear conscience.

Standing at the table, I stop. Pause. Let the moments wash over me. I need this stillness, I need nothingness in the chaos of everything.

The thump upstairs tells me the stampede is on its way, breakfast has begun.

'What you thinking about, Mama?' Anansy asks. I have not sat at the table, I am tidying, moving things around, keeping busy so I don't have to sit opposite my husband.

'Nothing,' I reply.

'Are you thinking about chocolate cake?' Cora asks.

'No,' I say.

'Are you thinking about how many stripes a zebra has?' asks Anansy.

'No.'

'Are you thinking about your ring?' Cora says.

Spinning towards the table, I see the pair of them watching me. Scott is staring into his cereal bowl. Now that I have stopped making him breakfast he doesn't seem to mind eating whatever cereal there is available instead of needing a cooked breakfast every day. 'Why would I be thinking about my ring?' I ask.

'Because you're not wearing it any more,' she replies. 'Have you lost it?'

'No, it's in . . .' Where is it? I didn't take it out of the skinny jeans I was wearing yesterday and put it in today's jeans. Actually, I didn't have pockets yesterday, did I? I put it in my bra. 'I don't remember. It's upstairs somewhere, I haven't lost it.'

'OK, who's ready for school, and who's going to be running behind the car like the Pink Panther?' Scott says, almost bounding out of his seat.

My stomach lurches and upends itself as it always does when he speaks. I turn back to the sink to avoid having to engage with him.

'Me! Me!' The girls shout in unison and I'm not sure if they mean they'll be running behind the car or that they're ready, but there is the scrape of chairs and then the thud of feet on tiles before they run out of the room.

'Tick-tock, you're against the clock,' Scott calls jovially. 'How's my gorgeous wife?' he says, coming behind me, linking his arms around my waist and pressing his lips against my neck.

My whole body freezes, unable to respond. This is the first time he has made bodily contact since we had sex that night. I don't know why he has crossed that boundary, why he thinks it's acceptable. The revulsion I feel is in my blood, it is infecting every part of me.

'Tami, I've said I'm sorry,' he says, releasing me, stepping backwards. He's probably buried his hand in his hair, he's probably looking as wounded as he sounds. 'You have to believe me when I say I'm trying really hard. What more do you want from me?'

'You believe me now, don't you?' Mirabelle says in my head. It feels like it was last night she said that. Like she had told me something, explained everything and I knew the truth. Finally I had the truth. And the truth was I believed her.

'I thought we were getting back on track,' he continues to my silence. 'I'm doing everything here. Everything that you wanted and you're giving me nothing. Not even a hug. I can't carry on like this, you know.'

'Is that a threat?' I ask.

'I'm saying I don't know how much more of not getting anything back for the efforts I'm making I can take. You're not completely blameless in this, you know?' he said.

'How many times did you tell her you loved her?' I ask.

Silence is his reply.

'How many times did you make love to her in our bed?'

Silence.

'Were you planning on leaving me?'

Silence.

'See, this is it – I don't know how much more I can take of not knowing the details. I haven't asked because I know you won't tell me. When you feel you can tell me anything I ask, I'll see if I can give you "anything back" for you doing the things you should be doing for your family anyway.'

'You believe me now, don't you?'

'Look, T—'

'Dad, can I sit in the front?' Cora asks as they reappear.

'No way!' he says, slipping smoothly into doting dad mode.

'It's much safer in the back for little tykes!' He scoops her up, I don't need to see it to know that's what he does.

Anansy comes to me, slips her arms around my legs. 'Have a nice day doing your work, Mama,' she says brightly. She is a tiny version of me, sometimes. She thinks the world is a wonderful place, and I can see the sun of life shining deeply, clearly in her eyes. That's how I look sometimes in my head. Like a little girl who thinks the world is full of joy and awe; that there are always new things to discover, there is always fun to be had.

'Aww, thank you,' I say to her, getting down on my knees and wrapping my arms around her. *Thank you for reminding me that there is good in the world. Even if I am not living with it at the moment.*

Afterwards is the calm, the hush. I sit at the kitchen table and stare at my cup. When we first moved in here, I remember Scott and I sat on the floor in the corner by the door, talking and visualising this space so it would be exactly as we wanted it to be. He leant over and placed his hand upon the swell of my stomach, upon our baby, and kissed me. 'Once she's here, I don't think life could get any more perfect,' he said. And I'd started crying because he was right. I was desperate to stay there, to remain in that moment so nothing could change, nothing could go wrong.

The knock on the door renders me immobile. No one visits without calling first. Beatrix did when she returned from working away, but that was a one-off. No one visits without calling first.

If I do not answer the door, nothing else bad can happen.

Especially since I've been so careful with the salt, the cracks, the ladders. Even with greeting magpies. Nothing bad can happen if I do not answer the door.

There is a uniformed police officer on my doorstep. It's happening again, we're back here again.

'Hello, Madam,' he says and from then onwards I do not consciously hear a thing.

Beatrix

Answer your phone! ANSWER YOUR PHONE! I'm not messing about, you need to answer your phone.

Tami

The policeman talked about a crime down the street, asking if I had seen or heard anything last night. He couldn't elaborate on the nature of the crime, simply that it was serious and they were looking for witnesses. I knew nothing and so I told him nothing. I was grateful to be able to shut the door, to not have him storm in looking for Scott.

Almost immediately there is another knock on the door, then the letterbox is being poked open, a rectangle of face visible in the gap. 'Tami, open up, come on, quick,' she hisses.

I open the door and she stumbles in. Looking out into the street as if someone is chasing her, she snaps the door shut quickly, then leans heavily against it. She sighs dramatically.

'Oh, God, it's so awful,' she says. 'Did the police tell you there's been a serious crime up the road?'

'Yes, what's happened?'

Beatrix stops, pauses, then speaks. 'It's Mirabelle,' she says. 'She's been murdered.'

9

Fleur

From The Flower Beach Girl Blog
Things my dad would freak about if he knew:
That I smoke.
That I generally smoke after sex.
That I not only say the word sex, I actually, you know, do it.
That I have sex. (I feel I need to make that clear.)
That I'm thinking of leaving college.

Dad freaks out about a lot of things, though. He's really got to learn to take a chill pill. I'd love to see his face if I ever said that to him.

Smoking is one of those things I shouldn't do. It's one of those things a girl like me shouldn't even think about doing. Except after sex. After sex, lighting up stops me from being that girl. You know, *that* girl. The one who cuddles up to the man she's with and starts running her mouth because she doesn't want him to roll over and go to sleep. She wants to hang onto the stuff they've got now they've been that close. Smoking is the halfway point between getting up, getting dressed and getting the hell out, and cuddling up and letting show how into this thing you are.

If you like a guy, showing how involved you are is *fatal*. I

243

don't like playing games, but sometimes it's necessary. Like my situation with this man here. I've smoked four cigarettes now. That's a lot for me. I *really* like this man. Wish I didn't, do. Really do do do do.

'What's going through your mind?' he asks. The light from the corridor is shining on his skin, highlighting it in a way that makes me want to lick him.

'Lots of things,' I say, as casual as anything. I am not good at casual around this man. I hope he doesn't know it.

I met him six weeks ago at this Old Skool club that's opened up near Elephant & Castle. In the crowd of fine young men, he was the finest. His skin was the divine colour of melted cocoa, his eyes were as dark as midnight. His head was completely shaved, which I don't usually like on a man, but on *this* man, hair would have distracted from the contours of his face. He had cheekbones that looked like they'd been carved by angels, a perfect, wide nose and lips that went on for ever. I didn't think I'd ever seen a man so handsome before.

He, Noah, reclines against the pillows. He's always got pristine sheets on his bed when I'm here, while the rest of his one-bedroom flat is always tidy and clean, too. He can cook, as well – I've never had better joloff rice.

'You know, you're the only person I've ever let smoke in here,' he says, casually.

I freeze, my eyes wide as I stare at the door. 'You don't like smoking?' I say, horrified. I never actually checked. I just lit up and have been lighting up ever since. I'm never usually that rude.

'Not my thing, at all,' he says, his rich, deep voice sending vibrations of pleasure down from the roots of my hair to the tips of my toes. 'Even had to buy an ashtray after the first time you were here.'

Thankfully, I'm sitting on the edge of the bed, looking away from him. '*Oh God, Oh God, Oh God*,' I mouth before saying, 'Oh. I'm sorry. I should have checked. I'm really sorry.' I grind out my cigarette in the ashtray on the bedside table. 'I won't smoke here again. Sorry.' See what I did there? I said 'again', subliminally telling him I'll be back.

'Not a problem,' he says.

In my bag, my mobile starts to vibrate. I've turned the ringer off so I can't tell who it is, and normally I'd ignore it, but I suspect it's Dad and he'll just keep ringing until I answer. He does that. A lot. But he's got his reasons.

'Sorry,' I say to Noah and rifle in my bag until I find my phone. Yup, 'DAD' is flashing up on the screen.

'Hi Dad,' I say into the phone, trying not to sound fed up. Or that I've just had afternoon sex. Or, indeed, that I've had sex at all. Virgin until my wedding day, that's me.

I don't talk much, just listen. And when he's finished talking, when I've told him I'm fine several times, I hang up. I sit stock-still, the phone balanced on my outstretched limp hand, my eyes focused on a point in the distance.

'Is everything all right?' Noah asks when several minutes have passed in silence.

I shake my head, still trying to assimilate it all. Trying to make it all fit together so I can understand what I've just heard. 'No,' I reply. 'Nothing is all right.'

I hear him sit up. His hand is on the small of my back, his chin rests lightly on my shoulder, both actions significant reassurances of his presence. 'What's happened?' he asks.

What has happened? What has happened is this: 'My mother has been murdered.'

Tami

This doesn't seem real. Mirabelle is gone, dead, *murdered*.
Three words that describe the fact that I will never get the
chance to speak to her again.

I thought Beatrix was lying. It was so surreal, and Beatrix
was behaving in a completely inappropriate way. The way
she said it, you'd think she'd been about to tell me that she'd
walked in on the vicar shagging stuck-up Mrs Plake from
two doors down. Not that one of my best friends had been
taken away from me, from life.

I'd actually said, 'Not at all funny.' Her face fell as she
dropped the inappropriateness, and the serious crime chat
I'd had with the police officer came filtering in and suddenly
time seemed to slow right down. I wanted to fall over, fall
down, but I was frozen; every part of me rigid and locked.
It was true. She was dead. I could feel it.

I haven't been able to think or feel properly since then.

Scott came home at lunch, he must have heard, he'd probably tried to ring – the house phone and my mobile had
rung several times – but I couldn't answer either. His eyes
were wide, haunted, as he dropped onto a chair between me
and Beatrix. We all sat in silence, staring at the space in the
centre of the table or into our teacups, trying to make sense
of it.

Last night I had felt murderous towards Mirabelle. Today it had come true. I put that thought 'out there'. I didn't keep those toxic words and dangerous thoughts locked away in the dungeon of my mind, I had set them free into the world and this was what had happened. That wasn't true, of course, but it *felt* true.

The other thing that was niggling at my mind, worrying at the edges of my memory, was the sensation that I saw her in her house. That I was there and she had talked to me. '*You believe me now, don't you?*' I kept hearing in my head. But that couldn't have been right because the last time I was in her house was the last time we argued there. Everything would be a lot clearer if I hadn't drunk myself into oblivion pretty much every night since I found out about the affair.

'*You believe me now, don't you?*' I couldn't nail down when that memory was from.

The phone in my pocket bleeped and the three of us at the table jumped. I got up without saying anything to either of them and picked up my keys and went to get the girls. Halfway down our road, I stopped. I could feel the weight of the police cordon, the investigators meticulously working, and the heavy, clinging sense of a death that they were trying to unravel behind me and I realised I would have to tell Cora and Anansy. I would have to tell them that someone they loved wasn't around any more because if I didn't, someone else would and I couldn't let that happen.

Shaking, because that's all I could do, I turned and went back to my kitchen where Scott was standing staring out of the back door and Beatrix was in front of the boiling kettle, two cups beside it, about to make more tea, which is what she'd done all day. 'You have to come with me,' I said to Scott.

He nodded. 'We'll tell them together,' he said.

'I'll get going,' Beatrix said.

'No,' I said, 'stay. Have dinner with us. We all need to be around each other right now.'

The dinner that night was quiet. Anansy didn't really understand, she nodded and said she was sad, but I could tell she hadn't really grasped the length and permanence of what we were saying; Cora listened and said nothing much, in that way of hers. I told them they could talk to us any time they wanted, that it was OK to cry if they felt sad and that Mirabelle – even saying her name mined deep sorrow at the centre of my being – had loved them both very much.

We were subdued, but Beatrix did her best at carrying the conversation, and then it was bedtime without a bath.

'I think we should say our prayers,' Cora told Anansy before they got into bed.

About a year ago, when they'd seen a young girl in a movie kneeling by her bed at night with her eyes closed and her hands clasped together, they'd asked what she was doing. I explained about praying and I said that when I was younger I had to say my prayers every night. Anansy asked if they had to do it and I had said if they wanted to, they could. If they didn't it was fine, too. They'd done it every night for about a week, then lost interest. This was the first time in a long time that either of them had suggested it.

'OK,' Anansy said and carefully put Fee-Fu, her pink bear, down on her bed and got on her knees, placed her hands together and closed her eyes. Cora came over from her bed and got down on her knees beside her little sister, assuming the position.

'Dear God. Please look after Auntie Mirabelle,' Cora said. 'She's a nice lady. Thank you. Love, Cora.' She waited a few seconds, then used her elbow to nudge Anansy as a prompt.

'Yes. Thank you. Love, Anansy, aged six and a quarter. Which means I'm not quite six and a half, but I will be.'

'God knows that,' Cora hissed at her.

'Oh. Sorry, God,' Anansy whispered to match Cora's tone. 'I forgot you knew everything.'

Cora's body sagged in that despair and loving disappointment she had only for her sister. 'Sorry, God,' she said, earnestly. 'It's just 'cos she's so young.'

'He knows that,' Anansy reminded Cora, still in a whisper.

Cora sighed, then said, 'Goodnight, God. Goodnight, Auntie Mirabelle.'

'Goodnight, God; goodnight, Auntie Mirabelle,' Anansy repeated. They both scrambled upwards, Cora came to me, hugged me and then said, 'Goodnight, Mama,' before returning to her side of the bedroom and slipping under the covers.

Anansy ran to me, threw her arms around me. 'Night, Mama,' she said, before bounding back to bed, picking up Fee-Fu and diving under her covers.

I liked that they had no real idea of what had happened. I turned off their light and sat on the space on the carpet between their two beds. They didn't need me there to go to sleep any more, but that night after Mirabelle was gone I wanted to listen to the unsynchronised hush of their breathing, I needed to feel the almost imperceptible vibrations their presence in the world created. I had to be near them because, at that moment, not being with them would have been a physical impossibility.

Fleur

From The Flower Beach Girl Blog
Things I have to do today:
Book a ticket to Brighton.
Find an outfit for a funeral.

Seriously, if I get anything else done today it'll be a bonus.

I've only ever been to one funeral in all my life.

And that was Dad's friend's third wife who I didn't really know that well. Didn't really think the next funeral I went to would be *hers*. My mother's. I often call her 'her' because I don't know what to call her. 'Mirabelle' feels a bit disrespectful when I've been taught to call people Uncle or Auntie whether they're family friends or relations, and 'Mum' wouldn't feel right 'cos she wasn't. I mean, she was, but then, she wasn't.

That short little word, probably one of the most regularly used words across the world, sticks in my throat. As does 'mother'. She was a good person, so friendly and we got on really well when I got older, but I don't think I loved her as my mother. I'm always wondering if that, not really loving her as my mother, makes me a terrible person.

I'm struggling, though, with what's happened. I feel

churned up inside, like nothing will help me settle. I want to find a way to sit, lay or stand that will stop the churning, will let me feel calm and relaxed like I was before that phone call. If anyone had asked me, I would have told them all about my troubles and anxieties, all about the little things that bug me. Now I realise they weren't that big, I wasn't that stressed. It's weird how I didn't realise how unburdened I was until I wasn't.

Sitting back in this train seat in first class – I treated myself – my concern for Dad starts up in my chest again. I've been worrying about him since I can remember. But this is different. This is all the usual worries with a few more tagged on for good luck. He hadn't wanted me to come to the funeral. Dad doesn't know how much I've been in contact with her, *Mirabelle.*

Dad thinks I've exchanged a few emails with her and met her a couple of times. He doesn't know that we emailed and texted constantly, and that I've been seeing her at least once a month since I was sixteen. For five years, I've been getting to know this woman who is my mother but wasn't my mum, and my dad has no clue about it. He'd only worry himself over it. Seriously, sometimes I have to be grateful that he lets me walk out the door in the morning. Those are the days when he's been particularly anxious or it's coming up to her, Mirabelle's, birthday or something, and he'll want to barricade us in against the outside world. Dad thinks that one day I'm just not going to come back.

'Fleur, you still haven't explained properly why you have to go to the funeral,' he said to me a few days earlier. He took off his glasses and threw them onto the kitchen table.

'It's not as if you knew her very well.' He was growing old, my dad. Him and Mirabelle had me pretty young – they'd both been seventeen – so he hadn't been an old dad. Not like a lot of my friends at school. But now, his mocha-brown skin had lines pressed into it along his forehead, at the eyes and around his mouth. His black hair was going grey at the sides, so he looked a bit like the plastic guy out of Fantastic Four. And he was getting a bit saggy around the middle. He was still good-looking, definitely the best-looking out of all of my friends' dads, simply older, ageing.

'She's my mother,' I said to him. I shrugged. 'She's my mother,' I repeated, in case he didn't understand the significance.

'You'll only be upsetting yourself,' he said. I knew he wanted to mention that she might have been my mother but she still saw fit to leave me but Dad wouldn't ever say something that cruel.

'I can't avoid doing things because they might be upsetting, Dad. You taught me that.'

He shook his head, slowly, obviously regretting saying that to me. 'It's so far to go in one day,' he said, 'especially when you'll only be upsetting yourself.'

Uh-oh, I thought. I hadn't actually mentioned . . . 'Thing is, Daddy, I thought I'd stay down there for a few days.'

His whole body sort of pulled in on itself. I felt his wife, Jocelyn, pause in the middle of what she was doing on the other side of the kitchen and close her eyes. We both knew how what I'd just said would push his buttons.

'I was thinking of coming back straightaway, but then I spoke to her solicitor who said that she'd made a will and that the executor was someone called Tamia Challey and that I was the main beneficiary and he had documents for me to sign and things for me to sort out. I can't do that in one day and it just doesn't make sense to keep going and coming back, so I thought I'd stay down there until Mrs Challey and me put all her financial affairs in order, put the house on the market, and then I can leave it all to Mrs Challey and come back. Then I won't have any reason to go back there.'

I added that last bit to obviously tell him I was coming back. That I wouldn't run away to live in Brighton like my mother did. I wasn't actually my mother.

'I'll come with you,' Dad said in that way that meant that was the end of the matter.

'I don't think that's a good idea,' I said. Mainly because there was no funeral yet. I'd sort of lied about that because I wanted to get down there as soon as possible. There was no one to organise the funeral at the moment, so I thought I'd make contact with Mrs Challey who she, sorry, Mirabelle talked about all the time, and we'd organise the funeral and then I'd see what happened next. What I could find out. If I told Dad that was the plan there'd be no way on Earth he'd let me go. Twenty-one years old and still being forbidden to do stuff by my dad. He had his reasons, but it felt like being in a prison sometimes.

'Neither do I,' Jocelyn said from the other side of the kitchen. Dad twisted in his seat to look from me to her to me again. The only times she and I really ever got on was when we were in agreement about something that Dad shouldn't do. She wasn't a wicked stepmother or anything, we simply didn't have much in common.

'You and her weren't exactly getting on even all these years after she . . . after you got divorced,' I said. 'You don't need to be going down there to upset yourself.'

'You really don't, Donald. It's not fair on Fleur, either. She's going to pay her final respects to her mother, she doesn't need to be worrying about what you might or might not be feeling as well.' Jocelyn came over to him, her apron swamping her tiny frame, and put her arms around his neck, rested her head against his. 'It'd be really selfish to make this about you, Donald. Fleur deserves the chance to do this in her own way.'

Jocelyn's ice-blue eyes never moved from me as she spoke to my dad: she knew I'd been in regular contact with my mother – probably from snooping in my room. That would have upset me once upon a time, now it seemed quite insignificant compared to the fact my mother was gone. Dead.

'Let her go and do what she needs to do in her own time. Then she can come back when she's ready.'

Jocelyn was talking to my dad, but she was telling me not to come back. I'd always known she wasn't thrilled about having me around, she hadn't wanted kids, but she did want my dad so she'd pretended she wanted to be my mother figure. Like I say, she wasn't nasty, more unbothered. Anyone who could see beyond their own hurt at being abandoned by the person they loved, i.e. anyone other than my dad, could see that she was completely uninterested in me. But Jocelyn telling me not to come back was to help me. She was opening the doors to the beautiful, golden cage that I'd lived in all these years and she was telling me to fly away. *Glance back if you need to,* her look was saying, *but don't come back.*

'I suppose you're right,' Dad said, oblivious to what had just happened.

My mother and my stepmother had both helped me to finally have a legitimate reason to leave home and stand on my own two feet. Dad had never entertained the idea of me leaving before, and I didn't want to ever upset him so, you know, I'd just stayed at home, gone to college in London and tried to have as much of a life as I could while still living with my dad.

My mother and my stepmother would have hated each other, I'm sure of that, but without both of them, I would never have had a real chance at freedom.

Beatrix

I didn't wish her dead. I want you to remember that. I was angry, I admit that, and I did think about going for her, but I didn't – that's the important thing. The police are going to question everyone who knew her, but they won't be questioning me. Why would they question me when I barely knew the woman?

Look, it was a stupid row and it didn't even get out of hand. I don't need to tell the police about it and I know they won't find out about it. If I was stupid enough to tell them, they'd think I did it. And you and I both know that I didn't.

I couldn't. I just couldn't.

Fleur

The train is pulling into Brighton station.

I've been here three times in my life. She, sorry, Mirabelle, didn't really like me coming down here. I think she was worried someone would see us together and connect the dots. I think she told maybe one or two people down here that she had a daughter.

I like Brighton. I like this station with the rock face that flanks each side as the train pulls in, and the lines of platforms that lead you towards the station front. I love the high, metal beams that make me feel like I've stepped into an old-fashioned station that should be in black and white.

I gather up my holdall – I'd had to take a smallish bag so Dad wouldn't realise that I was going to stay down here for quite a while – my book, my bottle of water, my bag, and the large white hatbox.

Outside of the station, Brighton sort of hits me in the face. It's all there all at once. Wham! But softly. There's a city right outside the station: a taxi rank, bus stops, traffic, people. They move towards the station, they move away from the station, like a confused tide: unsure which way it is meant to go at any one time.

You can smell the sea in the air, that peculiar scent that has a slight chemical edge even though it's one hundred per cent natural. I stop at the edge of the road by the station, waiting for the green man and taking in lungfuls of Brighton air. This is the air she, sorry, Mirabelle, breathed in for half her life.

It's a comfort in some ways. I'm near where she was. I like that.

The green man appears and I am almost swept off my feet by the people behind me surging forwards. I turn towards the sea, changing my mind about going straight to my B&B. I want to go to the beach. I want to see the water, smell the salty air up close, be outside for as long as possible. I don't often get the chance at home.

Home, college, that's my life. And Noah, of course. He'd started to feature a lot in my life until the phone call.

I still cringe when I think about that. I fell apart in front of him. After being so careful not to be *that* girl, I became a totally different type of girl that no one wants to deal with: Crying Girl.

Can't believe Dad did that to me. I mean, why would he tell me that on the phone? It's so completely not the sort of thing you should tell someone on the phone. What if I'd been all alone and had broken down on the bus or something? Hmmm? What about that?

Actually, that would have been preferable to what *did* happen which was . . . I physically shudder at the memory.

After I told him, I crumpled. He took me in his arms, rocking and hushing me, telling me to cry all I wanted, all I needed. I wanted to stop, but the sobs kept coming through my body, and with each one he held me closer, allowing them to ripple through his body. He held me until I stopped crying, until there was nothing there. Then he asked me if I wanted him to call a taxi to take me home.

I'd nodded in reply, my mouth jammed up with shock.

'Get home safe, yeah?' he said. 'I'll call you.'

I'd nodded, knowing he wouldn't.

He did, of course. 'Cos he's that kind of man. I didn't answer or anything. Instead, I texted him to say thank you. And that my head was mash up so I'd call him when I was feeling better. He'd replied 'not a problem' and had texted every day to see how I was.

So much caring from a man I met at a club six weeks ago.

I saw him on the way in to that Old Skool club and I had one of those moments when I wished I was one of *those* girls who would go up and start churpsing a man without a second thought. The second I clapped eyes on him I turned to Lariska – who was one of those types of girls – and said, 'I saw him first.'

'Who?' she'd asked. Then she'd elbowed me hard in the ribs as she said, 'You are so out of order. I didn't even get a chance.'

'I know. Still mine.'

'But he's the best-looking man here.'

'Still mine.'

'That's out of order,' she said again, shaking her head, 'that's proper out of order.'

I shrugged. 'Still mine.'

She kissed her teeth, then laughed.

He disappeared into the crush of the club, melting away into the background of bodies and clothes and drinks and talk. I thought I'd lost him, that he was probably in the

261

crowd, rubbing up against some girl, or he was already with someone and she was making it known to anyone who even looked his way that he was hers and she'd fight you to the death before she let him out of her clutches. And then he was there, standing beside me, looking down at me with a small, sexy – oh my God how sexy – smile. I was wondering if he was going to try to talk to me when the opening to a Mandrills song came on and he turned to me and, I swear to God this is true, he mouthed: 'Put Your Money Where The Funk Is' at the exact same moment as I did.

We grinned at each other at that and he nodded 'shall we?' towards the dance floor and I shrugged 'OK' back. We moved at the same time, heading for the small patch of wood we could see that wasn't rammed with people. I thought I'd be self-conscious, just dancing like that, but I wasn't. I loved the song, I liked the man and I felt as if I was transported to another world. I didn't have to think about any damn thing apart from moving to the music.

Our bodies were close, as close as a whisper, but not touching. We danced together, separate but joined by the music, which was pulling us together and yet keeping us apart. His body was fluid, agile, supple. Every step, turn, grind caused heat to rush to my face – that was the first time I'd ever realised that dancing was like sex. I knew it – who doesn't know it – but this was the first time I'd experienced it properly. Usually, honestly, it was like someone was dry-humping your hip, but this no touching, this intimate distance was like being stroked, caressed, licked and screwed for real.

As we danced, the smooth sounds weaving some kind of spell around us, we got closer and closer, until it seemed inevitable that we'd touch, come together and kiss. But then he stepped back. Smiled again. Then he stepped forwards, came close to me but not close enough to touch, and said into my ear: 'Coffee? Tomorrow at the bagel shop round the corner? 3pm?'

He leaned away to see if I was up for that. I nodded, even though I had Sunday lunch with my dad and his wife on the other side of London. I'd have to cry off. I could hear Dad's lecture already, but I had a feeling he was worth skipping lunch for. Just the once. I wouldn't make a habit of changing my life for someone I wanted to sleep with. That was *her* trick. And I wasn't like that.

Over coffee he told me that he'd had to leave early to take his grandmother to church that morning, and then have lunch with his sister and her family. I'd so not believed him because, well, who does that? But the more he talked, the more I couldn't help but wonder if he was that man. He seemed so genuine. Coffee led to lunch. Then lunch led to dinner. And a few dates until there we were: amazing sex – better than I'd imagined after the dancing – and me developing a bit of a smoking habit because I needed to be cool, collected and controlled around him.

At the first sign of clinginess, I'd been sure I wouldn't see his firm arse for dust. Obviously all that had changed with my crying episode. I was hanging on, waiting to be dumped but, like I said, he's been texting me every day, asking how I am so maybe there is hope.

I always reply: 'Fine thanks, how are you?'

I wasn't sure if I was fine, but that's what you say, isn't it?

You don't say you've come down here to plan a funeral and to work out how to catch a murderer, do you?

Fleur

I can understand why she loved it here. It is a breathtaking place.

There's something in the atmosphere that makes it special, I think. Every place is special, unique. And this place is the most unique of all. I'm being silly a bit, I think.

My mind is racing and my heart is churning. Maybe coming to the beach wasn't a good idea. Maybe I should have gone to the B&B. I have no clue where it is now. I'd plotted it out on the map from the station but I have no idea how to get there from here. Panic rises inside me and I have to hold onto the railings.

She's dead. She's really dead.

I'm never going to see her again.

Things like this don't happen to me. I am maybe the sort of girl whose mother leaves, and who lights up without asking in the house of the best-looking man she's ever met, but this, it doesn't seem real.

I bend forwards as tears start to cram themselves into my eyes, touching my forehead on the railing.

'Life is full of the unexpected, Fleury, never forget that.' She said that to me when I walked out of the school gates on the last day of my exams and she was leaning against the hood of her car.

265

I'd gone over to speak to her, shell-shocked because she'd all but disappeared from my life four years earlier.

'I didn't expect to see you here,' I said to her instead of 'hello' because I was proper shocked.

'Life is full of the unexpected, Fleury, never forget that.' She smiled at me. She was great at those big grins. Her whole face was, like, a million times better when she smiled like that. She opened her arms cautiously. 'Hug?' she asked.

I half-nodded over my shoulder to my friends who were all waiting to go celebrate.

'Sorry, should have remembered that it's not cool to hug your mum in front of your friends.'

She said that like she was always around, always asking for hugs. 'Do you want me to give you all a lift somewhere? I can fit four of you in?'

Her car was proper kriss: big alloy wheels, a perfect black with silver trim. I peeked inside as she had the hood down. Black leather seats, too. I waved Lariska and Yasmin over.

'This is Lariska and this is Yasmin,' I said to Mirabelle. 'This is . . . ' They knew who she was because I had a picture of her taped into the inside of my diary, which went everywhere with me, but they'd never met her and it didn't feel right to call her my mum. Or my mother.

'Mirabelle,' she said. 'Call me Mirabelle.'

'Like the elephant?' Yasmin said, smirking.

Lariska elbowed her, hard.

'What?' Yasmin said. 'My brother watches it. He loves it.'

'Yes, like the elephant,' Mirabelle said with a smile. 'Now, do you want a lift somewhere to celebrate?'

'Too right!' Yasmin said.

Lariska elbowed her again.

'Girl, if you connect that elbow with my body one more time, you're gonna lose it,' Yasmin snarled.

Mirabelle lowered her head to hide how funny she found Yasmin, then opened her car door and folded the front seat down so those two could climb in the back. With me in the front, she drove us to Ealing High Street and dropped us off just off the main drag.

When the others were out of the car, she gave me a small white card with her digits on it. 'Call me,' she said. 'If you'd like to ever chat or meet up. Just call me.'

I nodded at her, knowing I wouldn't call. It'd hurt my dad too much.

My phone bleeps in my pocket. It's probably Dad, checking I got here OK and when I'll be back.

It isn't Dad, it's Noah.

Let me know when the funeral is. I'd like to come and pay my respects. Noah

I'm so overwhelmed by the generosity of his offer, with the idea that he'd really come all this way to pay respects to a woman he's never met, I call him back straight away. And stand on the beach, talking and talking for nearly an hour.

Fleur

This used to be her house. This used to be the place where she lived.

It's massive.

I can't believe she lived here all by herself, when the house me and Dad lived in could probably fit in the front room alone. It has red bricks and the top part of the front of the house where the roof peaks has bricks or maybe they're tiles that are curved and sit in rows like the tail of a mermaid. All the windows are old-fashioned-looking but look brand-new if that makes sense? She has a black front door and a huge brass number fifty-seven between the top two panels.

I can't go in there, it has police tape all around it. Across the door, across the driveway. Probably across the door to the bathroom, where she died. I wonder if it's still how it was when she died? If they've kept it the same as when it happened, or if they've cleaned up a bit in there? I force myself to look away. I'm trying to work out if the bathroom is at the front of the house, if those are the windows I'm looking at and, seriously, what good would that do me?

It's a nice road, lots of trees, but a bit weird because it's like curved and then straight up and then straight across, and then back down and then another curved bit. When I looked at it on a map it looked like the top of a bottle. She lives at the bit where the curved part hits the neck of the bottle so she has a corner house and a driveway with two cars outside.

I wonder how many people know that one of the cars – the aquamarine Mini – sitting outside her house is mine? She bought it for me. She wasn't trying to buy my affection or anything like that. She just wanted to make up for the fact that Dad wouldn't let me learn to drive. And like every little thing in my life, the reason he wouldn't let me drive is because she left. Driving might give me, like, the ability to drive away and not come back. She, Mirabelle, got the train, she told me, but it was the principle I suppose. It was another means of getting away from him that he had to totally shut down.

Dad does that a lot. It's hard to explain how he does it, really, unless you've lived with him. This time, this block ended up with me getting a car.

One year ago

She, Mirabelle, came up to London to meet me and I'd just had a 'thing' with Dad. He'd already found out that I was smoking. How? By going through my pockets, of course. Sometimes it felt like I was married to him or he was my owner or something. When Lariska was dating someone who turned out to be all shades of psycho, going through her pockets looking for evidence that she was cheating or going somewhere he didn't approve of was one of the things he did. In my case, Dad was trying to make sure I wasn't acting like a bad girl. He told me that from an early age I had to be a good girl. Obviously because my mother hadn't been and she had left, it all fell upon my shoulders.

When he found those cigarettes he went through the roof, into orbit and three times round the solar system he was that angry. I actually thought he might hit me or something the way he was shaking the packet in my face and screaming.

Jocelyn made herself scarce and I stood there and took it. Nothing else I could do. Sometimes I wondered if I wanted to be caught? I was twenty and going through one of my 'brave' phases where I thought, 'I'm twenty I can do what I like.' Even though I did still live in his house. And have an unofficial curfew. He was already on edge with the cigarettes thing, so I probably shouldn't have applied for a provisional licence. It was a normal thing to do at my age and I only vaguely thought it'd be a problem. It's not as if I could really afford lessons on my student income, it was something to have and ID. But I should have known from the passport incident (same as the cigarettes but a lot worse) that would be a no-no.

Dad opened the envelope – he opened all my post, even the stuff marked 'private and confidential' – and left orbit for his round-solar-system journey again. This time, though, I decided not to back down, to not stand there and take it, but to put my point across. I told him that I was going to learn to drive if I wanted to, that it didn't mean anything. And I was the only one of my friends who didn't have a licence or hadn't started lessons. He tried to say it was for my own good, that cars were dangerous, that they were expensive, and I told him I didn't care and I'd still do it. So I did my theory tests, to spite him almost.

I did it so he would know that I was going to do what I wanted. I hadn't actually wanted to do the theory tests. But I passed so it seemed silly not to do the lessons. The day I met Mirabelle, Dad had said that if I could afford lessons then I could afford to pay rent. I said if I was going to pay rent I'd move out and he started on about all the sacrifices he'd made for me, how he could have had a better job but couldn't because he had to make sure he was always home for me. How I was incredibly ungrateful because I had been his life for so long and now I was saying he didn't deserve the common decency for me to trust him when he told me what I was doing wasn't right for me.

On and on he went until I had to get out of there. I was late to meet her because I had to get off the bus after a few stops and sit at the bus stop and cry. I was so frustrated. *Angry!* Why couldn't I just tell him he was wrong and that I was a person in my own right, that I could make my own decisions? That I wasn't going to live my life how he wanted me to. Except I was. And I hated myself for it.

'What's the matter?' she said the moment I sat down in the little café she'd found at the back of the high street in Greenwich. Dad didn't know very many people down here and he certainly never came south of the river unless he absolutely couldn't avoid it, so it was safe. She seemed to know all the coolest, most hidden places. We never went to the same place twice to make sure that people didn't get to know us. She told me that if for whatever reason I ever walked into a place with Dad, she didn't want any of the serving staff to say they knew me or, worse, ask where she was in front of him. 'It could so easily happen,' she'd explained.

This place was tiny with gingham table cloths, decorative plates on the walls, antique (i.e. rickety as hell) furniture and old-fashioned frilled curtains at the windows.

I shrugged at her. 'Nothing,' I lied. Only 'cos I didn't want to talk about it. It was her fault after all. But that's not fair to think like that because it wasn't really her fault. No one says that mothers *have* to stay until their children are old enough to stop ringing them, do they? I mean, I could kid myself that I would be different, but all my friends do it – even the ones who are close to their mothers, they call them when it's convenient for them. They have busy lives – we all do – so our mothers fit in around us. They are the people who are meant to be there when we need them, but what about them? Why do we make them suffer by not being there when they need us? She was allowed to leave me – she didn't stop being a person just because she pushed me out.

I knew all this, I'd told myself all this, but I still blamed her. I still felt resentment towards her. I loved her too, if that makes sense. It was a resonance of that feeling of love, really. I knew I'd felt it once, but it was so long ago, so not relevant in this day and age, it was more dutiful than instinctive. I didn't actively love Jocelyn, either – not as my stepmother or even as a person – I'd managed to settle on 'like' for her. Most of the time, anyway. The rest of the time we kept out of each other's way.

'Tell me,' she, Mirabelle, coaxed. She had this way of sounding like she understood, even if there was no way on Earth she could.

'It's nothing,' I said with another half-shrug. I didn't want to talk about Dad, either. He was always there as it was, a

272

huge object that sat on the table between us, always. Everything we said – both of us – was run through the filter of 'Would Dad/Donald mind if he heard me say this?'

She reached across the table, put her hand on mine and I suddenly felt the tangle of anxiety, anger, frustration and guilt my heart had twisted itself into unwind as the warmth from her body gravitated into mine. 'Tell me,' she said again.

'Dad doesn't want me to learn to drive,' I said, feeling every bit the traitor to the man who'd fed me, clothed me and given me huge amounts of love my whole life. He had never walked away from me, even though it must have been so hard at times.

'Because of what I did?' she asked.

We'd never really discussed it before, had danced around the subject, especially with what happened on that school trip, but never outright said it, despite Dad 'sitting' on the table between us every time we met.

'I suppose so,' I replied and took my hand away. I was feeling better now, I didn't need her to hold onto me any more. I'd had enough of people holding on to me to last a lifetime.

'I'm sure your father just wants what's best for you,' she said.

'What about what I think is best for me, doesn't that mean anything? I still live at home because Dad thought it was for the best. I wanted to do an art or a media course but Dad said it was for the best that I did something I could get a job with so now I'm doing a four-year degree in computer science. I get a passport because I want to go on holiday with my friends and then I don't go because Dad decides it's best

I concentrate on my studies instead of running around with a group of girls who don't think the future is important. And now I'm not allowed to learn to drive because Dad thinks it's best I don't have any means to run away. Even though all I wanted was a provisional licence so I could have one. I didn't even want to learn to drive but now it's another thing on the list of things I'm not allowed to do.'

I risked a look up at her through my eyelashes: she was watching me but trying to keep her face neutral.

'When am I going to be able to live? What, I'm going to get to thirty-five and still have Dad make all my decisions – or rather make me make my own decisions according to what he thinks it's best to do? How am I ever going to get to learn how to make the right decisions if I don't get to make them and get them wrong sometimes? I'm so angry right now I could spit.'

She said nothing, but the gaze of her light brown eyes – contacts – rested carefully on me as I spoke.

'It's not fair that because you left I get no life whatsoever.' I didn't actually mean to say that. Especially when she was listening to me. She couldn't do anything about it. This was the life we had and yes, it was because of the choice she made, but that wasn't entirely her fault. There were some things I didn't like to think, and one of them was this: if Dad was like this with her, it was no wonder that she left. I just wish she'd taken me with her. But I hardly ever thought that. Because it wasn't very fair on Dad. He stayed, she didn't. Where would I be if he had bailed out too? My grandma on Dad's side is gone, but she died when I was young. My grandma and grandpa on Mirabelle's side went back to Nigeria an age ago and occasionally write to me and send me things, but they don't really want to be involved. There was a lot of shame when she left. She was meant to go to university and be a doctor or something, but she got pregnant, got married, and then she ran away. I don't think they ever really recovered – neither personally nor with their standing in the Nigerian community here. She destroyed so many lives when she went.

Dad wasn't always so restrictive either. For a good few years he let me do stuff that other kids could do, but as I got older and wanted to do more things that didn't mean I'd necessarily come home at the end of it, he started up with the control again.

'No, it's not,' she said. 'And I'm sorry. I did a terrible thing and everyone is still suffering for it even now.'

'God, I'm sorry, I shouldn't have said that to you. It's not your fault Dad is trying to control me.' *Was he always like this?* I wanted to ask, but I couldn't because that would be taking my disloyal thoughts to a whole new level and releasing them out into the real world. Once you've done that, made it real, you find it very easy to do it again. The first time is the hardest and after that it gets easier and easier. I didn't want it to be so easy that I would ever say it to his face. I never wanted to hurt my dad that badly. He's my dad.

'Yes, it is,' she replied. 'I could pretend that he was always that controlling and that was why I left, but it wasn't.' She shook her head. 'Your father is probably traumatised by being abandoned by the person he loved most in the world after you. He hated what I did and why I did it. He probably thinks that if he can control every aspect of his life he won't have to go through that again. I don't blame him, it was an awful thing for me to do. I often wish I could take it back. But I can't. And I'm so sorry for what it did to him, to you and to my parents. My whole family has suffered because I was so selfish.'

I reached out to her. 'Sorry, I didn't mean to make you feel bad,' I said.

'No, no, stop. Don't. This isn't about me, it's about you. I'm not going to derail this. You've every right to be angry with me – more so than your father, probably – and you have every right to express that anger. If you want to slap me and call me names, feel free. If you don't want to see me again that's your right, too. Just don't think about my feeling before yours, you're the most important one.'

'I just want some freedom,' I said. 'You know, like the real stuff, not the pretend stuff Dad gives me so I don't rebel over the big stuff.'

'I know, Fleury.' She put her hands over mine again. 'Listen, I'm going to find a way to make this right. If you want, I can speak to your father.'

'No!' I hadn't exactly told him she was back in touch. After she reappeared in my life when I was sixteen, I'd not got in touch with her until I was stranded in central London after a night out when Lariska and Yasmin both tapped off and I didn't. I'd lost my Oyster card and didn't have money for a cab. I knew Dad would go ballistic if I didn't come home before dawn so I called her and she came. She drove all the way up, drove me back to Ealing and then said it was nice to see me. That was all, no telling off or saying I should have known better, no pretence at liking what I'd done, but I knew she'd done worse in her time. So I emailed her to thank her and we started emailing and then texting and then meeting up. Dad knew none of this. He thought she still sent birthday and Christmas cards that he binned.

'All right,' she said, knowing immediately that I hadn't told him about us. 'All right. I'll think of something.'

Two weeks later, when I saw her, she'd bought me a car. She said she'd keep it at her house for when I was ready to tell Dad or passed my test, and that she would teach me.

'You?' I asked.

'Yes. I know it's not the same as having lessons and your father being cool with it, but it's the only thing I could think of right now. You can say no if you want.'

I'd stared at it. Not many women my age had a car, let alone one that was only three years old and pretty cool. 'Thank you!' I squealed, full-on proper squeal, and threw my arms around her.

'I'm so sorry it's been so hard for you, Fleury. I'm going to try to make it better. Every day,' she replied, hugging me back. That was the first time in years that we'd hugged, I realised later. It'd been so instinctive, I hadn't even thought twice about doing it.

Mrs Challey lives down the road. Mirabelle told me that she'd moved here before she got the job with Mrs Challey's husband and meeting Mrs Challey was one of the best things that had happened to her after me getting in touch with her again. I've got to go and see her.

I'll be quite excited to meet her, actually; I think she's the only person on Earth that Mirabelle has *told* about me. 'Cos that's the thing about me and her, Mirabelle. She never wanted to tell anyone she had a daughter. She was, I think, afraid of how they'd judge her when they found out that when her child was six years old, Mirabelle ran away to Brighton and never came back.

Tami

The radio is playing 'Groove Is In The Heart'.

I have turned it up and I am having a dance while I clean the kitchen. It's not dirty, it doesn't need a clean, but I am KEEPING BUSY until Beatrix comes over and we go shoe shopping.

None of us know what is going on with the police investigation. Very few details have been released, all we know for sure is that she was . . . She died in the bath. But it was definitely not an accident. We know it wasn't an accident because they questioned Scott the day after she died. He was the prime suspect, of course. He told me what they'd asked, adding, 'I didn't do it, Tami, you have to believe me,' at the end of his monologue of worry.

I knew he hadn't. Of course he hadn't. He couldn't kill someone and then carry on with everyday life, just like that. Who could?

They'd cleared him almost straight away, eliminated him from their enquiries because his computer records showed that he'd been online around the time she was killed. It was late at night, and he was online. Apparently they could pinpoint where he was in the house at the time and had detailed records of his activities, which websites he visited, how long he spent on them, what he downloaded, and which cookies were left on his computer. The records showed, apparently, that he hadn't just left his computer switched onto the internet while he snuck out to commit the crime, he'd been active. When he'd told me all this, I'd stared at him knowing what he was saying: '*I didn't do it because at the time I was masturbating to porn.*' Probably rape porn. He'd stared back at me, wearing a tinge of guilt. I'd broken eye contact first and pushed the whole matter from my mind after mumbling, 'Whatever,' and leaving the room.

A horrible thing has happened and it has reminded me I need to focus on the now. On life. On being alive. This whole thing has made me reassess my life and I know that I want to live again. I began the process of finding myself when I started running and taking that time for me. I love the roles of my life, but there are huge chunks of me that have faded away because those other parts took over. The faded parts of me need time to find their full colour again. I need to find out who I am – who *all* of me is.

That starts with inappropriate shoes. Mirabelle had some fantastic shoes. She had them all lined up in her walk-in wardrobe upstairs in her house. Once, she'd taken me in there and I'd been momentarily mute with shock at how many clothes she had, and all the rows and rows of shoes she owned. All of them housed in acid-free frosted plastic boxes with a Polaroid of the shoes on the outside. 'I feel like I'm in Wonderland,' I'd said.

'That's the general idea,' she replied. She'd let me try some of them on. Each one felt like it had been made for me. But then they would, they spoke to the side of me that loved clothes, and loved expensive things.

We were going shopping so I could go back to being Tami, fashion addict.

Beatrix is embracing life, as well. She has taken the day off and is going to buy shoes and underwear. 'To match my hair, don't you know.'

'You're going to get in trouble at work,' I'd warned her, thinking of the incomplete projects sitting on my desk and on my computer.

'I won't. I know where the bodies are buried.' She'd gasped silently after saying that. We'd both allowed several seconds of horrified but reverential silence to pass before we pretended she hadn't said that and ploughed on with making arrangements to meet.

A solicitor rang yesterday and said that I was executor of Mirabelle's will and did I want to make an appointment to come in and talk through all the necessary paperwork and duties? That was the last thing on Earth I wanted to do. He said that the other executor was someone called Fleur Stuminer. I'd told him to get her to do it because it was nothing to do with me and had hung up. I did not want to get involved. I did not want to think about sorting out paperwork, poring over the official records of her life and ensuring everyone she was connected to got what they deserved. I did not want to be dealing with the remains of the life of my husband's dead lover.

A letter arrived from them this morning, but I haven't opened it. I have shoved it deep into the bowels of one of the kitchen drawers.

Ding-dong, intones the doorbell.

My heart skips. It always does nowadays. Trouble has

been to my door far too many times in the past few weeks. It's not even a fifty-fifty chance any more that the person standing on the other side is here to drag something else I do not want or need into my life, it's almost a given. Except, this time, it is Beatrix. And we are going shopping.

I grab my bag, flick off the radio and almost dance to the front door. 'Coming,' I call and pause to slip on my sandals and unhook my dark blue mac from the banister.

'Hope you've got your—'

Trouble. There is trouble on my doorstep.

I do not know who she is. She might be a very nice person but she is not the person I was expecting, she is not Beatrix, so she must be trouble.

She is a tall woman, taller than me by almost half a head. She has skin a shade darker than Cora and Anansy, and masses of ringlet hair that is naturally brown, blonde and black in places. And her face, her body, the way she stands is Mirabelle reincarnated. Particularly her eyes. The set of them, the shape of them, the private openness of them.

I am staring into the face of Mirabelle.

Is this what happens when you are taken away too soon, too quickly, before what should have been your time? You slip back almost straight away and take up in the body and face of someone else?

'Hello. Sorry. Hope you can help me,' she says, sounding nothing like Mirabelle at all. She is from London and the accent is branded all the way through her speech. 'My name is Fleur Stuminer. Are you Mrs Challey?'

I nod, cautiously.

She sticks out her hand, and I unthinkingly take it. We shake three times.

'I'm Fleur Stuminer,' she repeats.

'Yes, you said that.'

The smile drains away from her face and she looks down, crestfallen and embarrassed. 'Oh,' she says quietly. 'She didn't tell you about me.'

I shake my head, pretty sure 'she' is Mirabelle but not certain.

'If she was going to tell anyone, I'd have thought it'd be you. Clearly not.' She sticks her hand out again. 'Hello,' she says politely, but a little more cool and businesslike. 'I'm Fleur Stuminer. I'm Mirabelle's daughter.'

Fleur

From The Flower Beach Girl Blog

Things I've been thinking about today:

Why do people lie? Do they want to hurt you or protect you?

Why? It always ends in tears. Always.

Gah!

Just *gah!*

Just when I've convinced myself that I mean something to her, *meant* something to her, things like this happen. I get a two-cheek slap to remind me that I was her dirty little secret.

And she lied to me. She told me that she had told her closest friends about me. Why do I let it hurt? Every time. I am truly stupid.

I remember sitting beside her in my car once as she was going over the driving lesson route we were going to take when a friend of hers spotted us. She waved at us and then came round to the passenger side to speak to her.

'Hi!' her friend said, all bright and breezy. 'Fancy seeing you up here in Kensington? I thought you never left Brighton.'

'Ah, you know, got to visit the Big Smoke now and again,' she, Mirabelle, replied. I was smiling, making eye contact, waiting. Waiting.

'Oh, yes, I could have told you that.'

'You already tell me too much,' she said.

And then her friend was waiting, too. Waiting. Waiting. Waiting for her to turn to me and say, 'This is Fleur, my daughter.'

'So, who's this?' her friend eventually asked because it'd got to that embarrassing point where she either had to walk away or ask.

'Oh, um, this is Roza,' Mirabelle said. 'My cousin's daughter. I'm giving her a quick driving lesson as, um, a favour to my cousin.' It was so easy for her to lie. It just came out of her mouth. Roza is my middle name, her cousin does have a daughter my age – not that I ever see any of that side of the family – and she was indeed teaching me to drive as a favour. The truth ran like a jagged vein through what she said, but it was jagged because it was all mixed up, it wasn't in the right order, it wasn't completely true.

'Nice to meet you, Roza,' the lady said.

And I smiled. Just smiled. I couldn't say anything, could I? I couldn't add to the lie by saying hello or nothing. I wasn't a liar like the woman sitting next to me.

The lady smiled a bit more, then she said, 'Well, see you next week,' and walked off. The woman looked back a couple of times, but Mirabelle didn't start speaking until the woman was out of sight.

She stared out of the windscreen and so did I because I couldn't look at her.

'I'm sorry about that,' she said. 'I panicked. I'm not really ready to share you with other people. I feel like I've only just found you and I want to keep you to myself. You

285

understand, don't you?' She put her hand on my shoulder.

'Course,' I said. I soooo understood. I so understood I was her dirty little secret.

Mrs Challey puts my coffee down on the side table by the sofa. She actually assumed that I drank coffee, like I'm a grown-up. Dad and she, Mirabelle, never offered me coffee if they were making or buying a drink. They allowed me to drink tea, but coffee – noooooo, that's an adult drink and Fleur is a kid. Always a kid. FOREVER!

This woman asked if I wanted tea or coffee or water or juice. And I'd said coffee, not just because I drank gallons of the stuff but also to see if she'd disapprove or ask me if that was really what I wanted. 'Sorry,' she'd said, 'I can't face getting that stupid machine in the kitchen to work, it'll have to be instant.'

She's shaking. She hides it well, but I can still see her trembling hands as she holds her coffee cup and sits down in the armchair. Is she a boozer? She doesn't look it, but then who goes on what you look like these days? On the outside you might look good, but on the inside you could be a secret drinker or heavily into weed. Or have so many secrets you can't keep up with who you've told what.

Mrs Challey has bloodshot eyes like a boozer, but that could be from crying or not sleeping. She's dressed all right, though. She's wearing skinny jeans like she isn't an old lady. And she isn't that old, only a bit younger than Mirabelle was. And her white sleeveless top with the bow at the front shows off her arms. They aren't big or nothing, not skinny like mine and like Mirabelle's. I suppose she's kind of normal.

Her body, her long twists, her clothes, she's kind of normal. A bit like I thought a mum would be, not like Mirabelle and certainly not like my stepmother. The nail polish on Mrs Challey's toenails has badly chipped off – she's like my friends' mothers, she doesn't have time to do those things 'cos she's too busy being a mum.

I'm not looking at the walls in this room on purpose. There are pictures of the children – everywhere. Dad has a couple of me on the mantelpiece in the living room, but this is way beyond that. They've had their photos professionally blown up. Their daughters laughing, the younger one sitting on grass examining a daisy, the older one lying on grass laughing her head off. The older one dressed in a pink tutu for ballet class, the younger one grinning as she sits on top of a red and blue plastic slide. It's like nothing their children do escapes the notice of their camera, and isn't worthy of adorning the walls.

'This must be so hard for you,' Mrs Challey says to me. 'I can't imagine what it feels like to lose your mother. Both my parents are still alive. Both as mad as a box of frogs and still disapproving of everything I do and say in that way that African parents seem to master, but I still have them.' She gives me a genuinely sad smile, it makes my heart feel funny in my chest. It's like this is the first time I've understood what dead means. 'I'm so sorry.'

My heart hurts.

'It's OK. I didn't really know her,' I say. 'Not really. She left when I was six.'

'Six?' Mrs Challey says like she's going to cry or something. 'That's so young.'

'I suppose. I don't really think about it because I don't know any different. I sort of remember her. Bits of her. Like that story she used to tell me every night. I think I knew that story off by heart before I could even speak. After she left, I remember I couldn't sleep for weeks because I didn't hear the story and my dad didn't know it.' *Dad did know it, he just wouldn't tell it to me because he was angry with her.*

'The Rose Petal Beach story?' Mrs Challey asks.

'Yes. Have you heard it? Did she tell you it?'

'Kind of. She told it to my daughters a few times and I overheard. I asked her about it and she elaborated.'

She left because of that story.

'I feel like I know you. She talked about you so much whenever I saw her. She never actually said it but you were her best friend. I could tell.'

Mrs Challey is going to cry. I've said something wrong and she's going to break down. She closes her eyes and takes a deep breath in, trying to calm herself.

'Thank you for saying that,' she says once her eyes are open again. 'You're so very sweet trying to offer me comfort at a time like this.'

Is that what I was doing? I thought I was being honest. 'I really genuinely thought she'd tell you about me. I must have meant less to her than I thought.'

'That's not at all true,' she says, putting down her cup and coming over to sit on the sofa beside me. 'Mirabelle was so complicated. She told me that she'd got married because she got pregnant. And she said it didn't work out, and I assumed she meant she'd miscarried. If I'd pushed her, if I'd asked what she meant, she would have told me, I'm sure she would. It was me making assumptions that stopped her. I mean, why would she tell a mother of two that she'd left her daughter?' Mrs Challey rubs my shoulder, and it's nice. Makes me feel cared for. 'And you know, she told me recently that she'd tried to go home but your father said no. And that it was for the best. Because at the time she was doing it for her and she was being selfish. She also told me that she was trying to be a better person and was going to put right the things she'd done wrong. There are all these things she told me over time that I thought I understood, but piecing it all together I now understand what she was saying.

'She was telling me that she regretted not taking you with her and that she was going to find a way to make it up to you. You meant the world to her, and she was trying to do the right thing.' She rubs my back, probably how she does to her daughters, probably how she reminds them that she'll always be there for them. Everywhere she strokes diffuses warmth, spreads it throughout my body and it eases the aching of my heart. Not completely, but a little. Enough to make a difference. I wonder if she even knows she's doing it.

'You're all right, Mrs C,' I say to her. 'Sorry, Mrs Challey.'

'Call me Tami, everyone else does.'

Again, treating me like an adult. 'Tami,' I say, testing it out a bit like you test a new swearword. It feels so weird! Saying the first name of someone older just like that. Just like that! 'You're all right, Tami.'

'So are you, Fleur, if I may call you Fleur.'

'You may.' Before I can stop myself, I start doing that thing I do. I can't help it.

When I meet a woman old enough to be my mother, I wonder what it'd be like to be her daughter. I wonder if she'd be strict or fun, if she'd make me clear my plate or if she'd let me eat as much as I liked of whatever I wanted. And would she sit me down and do the birds and the bees talk or would she just hand me a book and tell me to ask any questions? Would she want to know if I went on the Pill and if I had a serious boyfriend? Would she snoop in my room and read my diary and go mental if she found something she didn't like or approve of? Would she be my friend first or my mother first? And, most importantly, would she abandon me to chase the lover who first told her the story of The Rose Petal Beach?

With Mrs Challey, Tami, I have a feeling she would be strict but with some fun. She'd encourage me to clear my plate most of the time except when she could tell I really didn't want to. I know she'd shout at me if I was naughty and tired but would feel guilty about it. She'd tell me all about sex and would try to make it sound natural but would also try to make it sound dull so I wouldn't go rushing in to try it. She'd try to talk me out of going on the Pill and sleeping with anyone until I was old enough to handle it. She'd probably be tempted to snoop, but would only do so if she was seriously worried by my secretiveness. She would go radio rental if she found cigarettes or condoms, but would sit me down afterwards and explain that, while it was my life and she knew it was tempting to rush into these things, but to take my time, think about what I was doing and above all have enough respect for myself to take care of myself – physically and emotionally. She would say to me, 'You're my best friend, but I'm still your mother.' And being my mother would trump all roles and would mean she'd make the hard decisions and mete out punishment if it was necessary, but she would also love me unconditionally even if I hurt her.

And she would never leave me. No matter what, no matter who, she would never leave me if she didn't have to.

I have played this game A LOT. And Tami has been the best so far. I want her to be my mother. That role is open in my life again.

My heart aches.

'I don't suppose you could help me to organise the funeral?' I ask her. I want to ask her question after question after question about what the police have said. I want to ask if she has any idea who might have killed her, *Mirabelle*. I want to ask, too, what Mirabelle meant when she said to me a few weeks ago that she was in trouble. Did she mean this? Did she mean that trouble would end up like this? But I daren't. I can't come in here and start playing detective. It's not as if Tami even knew I existed before I showed up on her doorstep. All those questions will keep. It's not as if I've got anything to rush back for. It's not like I'll be able to concentrate at uni. I have time, I have time. 'I have no idea where to start. I've seen some funeral people down the road but I don't know if I can, you know, just turn up. Or do you have to ring first? And how do you pick stuff? Like the, you know, thing she goes in. And the flowers. And which church? Do you think she wanted a church? There's so much and I don't know how to do any of it.' I turn and look at her. 'Will you help me?'

She looks like she's going to cry all over again. Don't know how I'll cope with that, to be honest. I'm not good at the crying thing – with me or other people. Maybe I should call Noah, get him down here right now. He was good at that sort of thing the other time. Me, not so much.

'The thing is, Fleur,' Tami says and my stomach starts churning. 'I don't want to upset you any more, you're going through such a hard time, but I can't lie to you: Mirabelle — your mother and I had a major falling out just before she died. And—'

'What about?'

'It's complicated,' she says. Then she catches herself. 'Actually, do you know, it's not that complicated at all. I found out that my husband was having an affair with your mother.'

Really? *Really?* 'Really?'

'Yes. It was a bit more complicated than that because the police got involved on another matter, which I don't think you should hear about right at this second, but yes, that's the main thing. I'm sorry I've had to tell you. I really wish I hadn't had to, but, we weren't even speaking when . . . And that weighs heavily on my mind and soul, but I can't pretend it was OK between us. I wasn't going to go to the funeral let alone help . . .' She stops talking, closes her eyes really tight, then scrunches her hands up really tight, and then her whole body goes tense. 'I'll help you. Of course I'll help you. It's not your fault what happened. And what sort of a person lets a bereaved young woman do something like that on her own when she doesn't even live in this city? I'll make some calls, make appointments, and I'll come with you and help you as much as I can. You make all the decisions, I'll come along as moral support.'

I get to make decisions? No one has ever let me make major decisions on my own before. I'm not allowed. I'm too young. Not even she, Mirabelle, let me make my own decisions. She acted like she was the Anti-Dad who gave me freedom, but she just listened to a problem then solved it for me, never actually bothering to ask, you know, what I actually wanted to do. Like the driving thing. I tell her Dad won't let me learn to drive so what does she do? She buys me a car and decides to teach me. She didn't think to say, 'Well, here's the money for lessons, and let me know what car you'd like and I'll try and get you one.' I loved the Mini, it was a cool car, and it was a nice colour, but what if I wanted a Jeep or decided a Micra would fit my life better? I never got the chance to make the decision for myself.

The first time I get the chance it's about this. About things to do with her. Isn't that ironic?

'Are you sure, Mrs Challey? I mean, Tami. I don't want to upset you any more.'

'No, no, it's fine. You can't do it alone, I'll help you in any way I can. And I'll pay for it, so don't worry about costs.'

'Thanks, thanks so much.'

'It's OK. I don't want you to have to worry about anything more than you have to.' She rubs my back and a little more of that heart hurt slips away. Only a little. 'Do you want another cup of coffee?'

I shake my head. I don't. Now that it's being offered to me 'cos it's, like, something I'm allowed, I really don't want it. What if that happens with everything? What if, now that I'm not at home and I can do whatever I want out in the open I don't like it any more? Like, smoking? Or sex?

I fumble around in my bag. 'Is it OK if I smoke?' I ask Tami.

'No, sorry, not in the house. You can go outside, but not in the house.'

Oh, God. I actually don't want this cigarette now. What if I lose the taste for it?

'But you shouldn't smoke,' Tami says. 'It's a really bad habit. You really should think about giving up.'

I can almost taste the smoke as it fills my lungs, that sweet, sweet release of tension as it goes down. I am going to enjoy this cigarette, so *so* much.

I put down my bag and look at Tami again.

'There's something I don't get,' I say to her. 'You said your husband had an affair with her, Mirabelle?'

'Yes.'

'But that doesn't make sense.'

'Why?'

Mrs C, Tami, starts to shake again. It's anxiety. I don't think this is the right time. If I want her help, this is probably the worst time to tell her this. 'I, erm, I just didn't think she'd do that to a friend,' I say.

'Me either,' she says as her eyes fill up with tears.

It'll keep. What I have to tell her will keep. And I suppose, me doing that does make me a bit like my mother after all.

10

Tami

Fleur is standing in front of the mirror in our bathroom, practising shaking hands with people. 'Hello, lovely to meet you,' she is saying under her breath. She's dressed in a tight, ankle-length t-shirt cotton stretchy dress she'd brought with her. Her wild mass of ringlets is gathered into a low bun that sits at the nape of her neck. The heels she has on make her tower over almost everyone and I'm working up to suggesting she borrow a pair of my flats.

She reminds me of Anansy and Cora combined. She has Anansy's exuberance and Cora's tenacity. I look into her eyes sometimes and see the six-year-old whose mother left; I see a little girl who is still struggling to come to terms with grieving for someone she didn't really know.

Although, did any of us know Mirabelle? Honestly. How could she have kept this from me? I opened up to her about my whole life, I told her things I hadn't told Scott and she hadn't even shown me anything below the very top layer of who she was. She had a daughter.

'Fleur,' I say to the girl in my bathroom, who I can't help but treat like a third child, 'You can't wear those shoes. Well, actually, you can. But you're going to freak everyone out.'

Today is the funeral.

It hasn't taken us long to arrange, I didn't realise things

could get done so quickly. I didn't want Fleur to feel as if I was taking over but she seemed almost petrified of making a decision. I wanted to talk to her about Mirabelle, I wanted to talk about her life, but we ended up talking mainly about books. She is a voracious reader and loves them because they are her way of escaping from everyday life. She stumbled over revealing that to me, and yet it was obvious she'd needed an escape from her life at home. I read a lot, too, as a child. It was where I learnt about the outside world and decided I wanted to be a part of it. And how I figured out that the sooner I went to work, the sooner I got to leave and be my own person. Anything was better than watching the path of my life being cut out for me in the most pleasant way possible by the last two people on Earth I wanted to hurt, all the while knowing it simply wasn't for me. I wasn't going to university if it meant studying law. English, maybe, but not law.

'I think they're ... pretty,' she says, looking down from her place on top of the mountain where she's currently residing, and twisting her feet back and forth to afford me a more appreciative view. Fleur did that, a lot, too: pausing mid-sentence to think about what she was going to say. Sometimes it was to put a positive spin on life at home, but other times I think it was to find a word that might fit into this old woman's ears and would be understood by her elderly brain. The old woman being me, of course. She was acting as interpreter for 'youff' culture. And making me feel ancient.

'They're absolutely divine. But they're kind of high. I've got some Jimmy Choo flats you can borrow if you want?'

'What, real ones?'

'Yes.'

'What, real-life Jimmy Choos? You lie.'

'No, I don't. They were a present. I hardly wear them, though, 'cos I've not had anywhere to wear such expensive shoes.'

'They are not shoes. They are *shhoooeess*.'

'If you say so.'

'I say so. And I can seriously borrow them?'

She's being Anansy-like again. Her light brown eyes – the colour contacts that Mirabelle used to wear – are dancing, her body is bouncy and her hands want to clap together in excitement. This is her day, poor kid, I can't rip that away from her by telling her to blend in a little, no matter how well-intentioned or small that act is.

'Actually, no,' I say to her. 'You can't.'

'What, why?'

'Because I think you should wear your shoes. You should stand out from everyone else because you're not just anyone. You're her daughter, you should be noticed.'

'You really think so?'

I nod at her. 'Yes, absolutely.'

I hold my hand out to her. 'Come on, let's get going.'

Scott, who can't avoid the funeral without arousing suspicion among his work colleagues, has taken Cora and Anansy out with Beatrix to get them some food before the church.

Fleur's hand slips into mine and she's in Cora mode: shy, reserved but battling with it to give her the confidence to do something she's terrified of. I squeeze her hand like I do one of my two when I hold them. This moment reminds me of Cora's first day at nursery and Anansy's first day at school.

Once I had their hands in mine, I didn't want to let go. All I wanted was to hold on to them forever because if I was with them, nothing bad could ever happen.

Fleur

I'm still a smoker.

I actually thought for a while that hanging out with Mrs C would turn me. She's so 'up for it' and laidback that I have to keep reminding myself that I don't know her. And she ISN'T my mother. Her two, Cora and Anansy, are so lucky. She's just so chilled.

I mean, there's some pretty fucked up stuff going on with her and her man, and that's no lie. She doesn't want to be anywhere near the dude, and I don't blame her. I don't know how long it's been going on for, but since I've been here, he's not come back before the children are in bed once. In more than a week he's been out till late, certainly not back before I leave. Some days I go and come back then go again. Mrs C, I really should call her Tami, but I like calling her Mrs C ('You make me feel like I'm in *Happy Days*,' she said to me, 'And you're The Fonz. Although I always fancied being Claire Huxtable in *The Cosby Show*. She was the coolest mother in TV-land, don't you think?' When I just looked at her 'cos, you know, I had not a clue what she was on about, she rolled her eyes and sighed. 'How is it people your age have a way of making me feel ancient just with that blank expression?'). Anyways, Mrs C, she asks me to stay for dinner most days.

I like eating out, though. Not in posh restaurants, I like

buying fish and chips in that chippie near where they live and then I go down one of those big, wide roads with lots and lots of big posh houses, right to the sea. And I sometimes walk really, really slowly back to my B&B, eating my chips with lots of salt and lots of vinegar. I love Brighton. I feel like I belong here.

Even when it's a bit cooler, it's like I've come to heaven. You do not need to leave the country when you've got the sea right there and all the old-fashioned buildings and all the different people. I can understand why she, Mirabelle, stayed here. It's an amazing place.

When I get back to my B&B it's usually time for Noah to call me. Every night this week we've talked for hours. He's so sweet, just chatting about everything. He's coming today, as well. At least, he said he was coming, but I'm not sure if he will or not. It might have been something to say because what else could he do when I was telling him about the planning I'd been doing with Mrs C. He couldn't listen and go, 'Have fun!' So he might come. Or he might not. He does seem to be one of those people who does what he says he's going to do, though. But we'll see, won't we?

He was well impressed, though, when I told him that Mrs C was paying for it. She's basically planned it all. She didn't take over or anything, she let me do the talking and when it was obvious I didn't have a clue she suggested something. Which was always the right thing.

Mrs C is OK.

There's no way she did it. There's no way on Earth she killed Mirabelle.

*

The other day

'You're Fleur Stuminer, aren't you?' the second-hottest man on Earth said to me four days ago. Noah is obviously the hottest. This man was tall and broad, and had a grade one haircut of his black hair that graduated into nothing at the nape of his neck (I saw this when he turned round to look at the house I'd just come out of).

I didn't answer straightaway. He was hot, but he might be a bit of a psycho if he knew my name and was waiting for me outside Mrs C's house. 'Who wants to know?' I asked instead.

He reached into his pocket and got out a small, black leather wallet which he opened up to show me. It had a white card with his face on it – only a little bit less hot in it – and a police badge on the other side. 'My name is Detective Wade. I'm investigating the death of Mirabelle Kemini.'

I don't like the police. It's nothing personal, it's not like I've ever known any of them properly, but you know, you just gotta be careful about them. I always think they're out to get you, fit you up for something. Yeah, they probably wouldn't, but you never know, do you?

'Mirabelle Kemini is my mother.'

'I know. And I'm very sorry for what has happened to her. We're doing all we can to find her killer.'

'Couldn't it have been an accident? I don't like to think of someone doing that to her.'

She died in the bath, Dad told me. Drowned or something. He hadn't really known the details and there were some news items in the local newspapers that I had kept but couldn't face reading quite yet. I had a vague idea that I could contact the police for more information but

303

a) I didn't like the police

b) I was scared they wouldn't tell me because I wasn't old enough

c) I was worried they would tell my dad I'd been asking and I didn't know what he'd say about that

d) I was scared they would tell me and I would totally freak out because I wasn't old enough

So I left well enough alone. I would find out things as time went on, you always found out things as time went on.

'From the evidence collected and the condition . . . No, I'm sorry,' the policeman said, 'it couldn't have been an accident. I'm really very sorry.'

I felt that pain again, the boom that hurt. I was sure it was my heart but that sounded stupid, that my heart hurt, that it ached when I didn't feel especially sad. It didn't really make sense, either. I knew I should be sad that I'd lost 'my mother' but I didn't feel it. I think most of the time I was behaving how I knew I should be acting – quiet, shaken, upset, agonised. Shaken was the only thing I felt properly, properly, you know? I'd never known someone who was murdered before. I knew hardly anyone who'd died – I'd heard about a couple of people who I went to school with who'd died in car accidents but they were names, vague faces from my past. This person was connected to me. Someone had deliberately hurt and killed her. That's why I was shaken. Something that only happened on TV, on the news, in books, happened to someone I knew.

'How much do you know about the Challeys?' the policeman asked.

My eyes flicked to the car parked a little way up the road,

I think he got out of it and there's a woman in the front. I couldn't see in properly, it was just that bit too far away, but she was white with brownish hair. I bet they took their time working out who would get the most information out of me and decided on the man. They were right, of course. He was hot. But he was still '5-0' as Yasmin calls them. And that question was so a fishing question. He had something to say but he wanted me to tell him stuff, too. I didn't know what he thought I could give them seeing as I'd been here three days, but I wasn't telling him anything. ANY. THING. 'Enough,' I said.

He kind of creased up without creasing up. His cheek-bones, which you could slice cheese with, stood out as he laughed and lowered his gaze and shook his head. He loved himself so much! He thought he could get away with anything with a smile like that. And, let's face it, he probably could. Under normal circumstances. But this was not normal. At all.

'All right, let me ask you this, do you know what your mother's relationship was like with the Challeys before she died?'

'Yes,' I said. He was hinting at something but I wasn't so dim I'd let him know I didn't know. That's not how you found out stuff.

'So you're seriously OK with being around a man who was arrested for sexually assaulting your mother and has been questioned about her murder?'

What was it Mrs C said? Oh yes: *The police got involved on another matter, which I don't think you should hear about right at this second.* I'd been so bowled over by her being nice to me, treating me like an adult and helping with the funeral, that I didn't actually think to ask her about that. A cold, strange sickness flooded my stomach. No wonder Mrs C slept in a separate room to her husband, no wonder she started to get tense when he was due home, no wonder things were so fucked up in that house.

'I'm not around him,' I said, styling it out.

The policeman nodded. 'You spend time with Mrs Challey?'

'Yes, and the children,' I told him. 'She's helping me to organise the funeral.'

'That's what I was afraid of,' he said.

'What do you mean?'

'Have you asked yourself why she's helping you?'

'I know why – I haven't got a clue about organising a funeral.'

'I wish she was so altruistic but it's more likely guilt.'

'Yes, I know they weren't talking when she died, and Mrs C might feel guilty about that, but people fall out all the time. And the good people feel guilty about it.'

'No, it's not only that. Just be careful, yeah? Mrs Challey isn't what she seems.'

'What does that mean?'

He came a bit closer, and then lowered his voice, all dramatic. Anyone would think he was on some kind of spy show. 'I shouldn't really tell you this, but we have evidence that Mrs Challey was in the house the night your mother was killed.' He stopped and waited for a reaction. He didn't get one. I don't tend to react immediately to the things people tell me. So he added, for good measure, 'We think she could know more about your mother's murder than she is telling.'

I took a step back, not wanting to listen to his secrets any more. He was clearly chatting nonsense in my ear. What would Mrs C know that she would keep secret?

'Just be careful, Fleur. I'd hate to see anything bad happen to you. And if you hear or see anything that makes you suspicious or scared, just give me a call and we can talk it through.'

He was asking me to be a spy, to be a police grass. I wasn't either of those things. There's no way I would betray someone as nice as Mrs C by grassing her up to the 5-0. But I still took his business card when he offered it to me. And I didn't tell Mrs C about the conversation. I wasn't sure why I took the card or why I didn't tell Mrs C about the conversation, it just seemed at the time the right thing to do on both counts.

But the more I spent time with Mrs C, the more I realised it was all nonsense. They didn't bring her in for questioning and you had to spend two seconds with her to know it was stupidness. Mrs C wasn't a killer. And she certainly didn't kill Mirabelle. Why would she?

There aren't that many people here.

Maybe fifty? Is that a lot? The place isn't full, anyway. I did think about standing at the door handing out an order of service, which Mrs C designed and had printed, but I didn't know half these people. Actually, I didn't know any of these people and they didn't know me. Another kick-in-the-face reminder of how separate she kept me from her real life. It's taken her death to get me into her world. How messed up is that?

I remember when I was nine I found a birthday card from

her that had been thrown in the bin. It said, 'My darling flower girl. I miss you every day. I'll see you soon. Love, Mummy.' I read it over and over because she said she missed me, that she would see me again soon. I still remembered her really vividly back then, so I could picture the way she sat as she wrote it, how the tip of her tongue would have come out to lick the stamp to go on it. I thought how she would have hugged the card to herself before she posted it, so I hugged it back, even though it'd been in the bin and had some bits of toast and cereal on it. I didn't care. I was hugging my mummy back through the card.

After I stopped hugging the card, I'd read it again and again and again until I could hear her voice, like melted syrup in my ears, and I could smell that scent of rose water she always had, and could feel the warmth of her body as she held me close. When I had her there, as real as if she was really standing in front of me, I had to let her go. All over again. I had to put the card back in the bin just as I found it otherwise Dad would see that I'd taken it out and it would hurt his feelings. She had left and he had stayed, it would break his heart if he thought I was wanting her back.

How can you go from writing cards like that to not telling a single soul about me? How? It doesn't make sense. A lot of things don't make sense, though. I just can't work it all out.

I turn around to look at the arched wooden door to the church, to see who else is arriving, and there he is. My heart – actually all my insides – turn over themselves. He came. He's wearing a charcoal black-grey suit and a black shirt and a black tie. He stops in the doorway and looks around the church hall, which is quite light actually, despite all the stained-glass windows showing the stations of the cross, and finds me. His face, which is appropriately serious, softens a little, if you weren't looking you'd miss it, and the corners of his mouth turn up a bit in a sad-for-you smile.

I should not be feeling this. I should not have butterflies circling my aching heart like the horses on a carousel. I should be feeling nothing but the pain of having lost her. I want to feel it, I really do. I just can't.

I feel myself relaxing as he slips into the seat beside me.

'You all right?' he asks in a low voice, and presses his cheek against mine, kisses the space below my ear. When he sits back to face forwards, he reaches down and picks up my hand. Carefully, gently, telling me he's going to stay with me for as long as I need him.

Ten years ago

'Fleur, we're going to have to do the candles on the cake, people want to go home soon.'

'I just want to wait a bit longer, Daddy. Please? Just a bit longer. She said she was going to be here so can we wait a bit longer?'

'Fleur, little flower, she's not going to come. I'm sorry to have to tell you that, but I think something will have come up and she can't make it.'

I knew Dad was mistaken. Of course she was going to come. She said she would come and be in time to see me blow out my candles. I was nearly a teenager, I had grown up so much, which was why I could invite her to my birthday party. Dad had asked if I was sure that was what I wanted, and I almost told him that's what I'd wished on last year's birthday candles, and every time I got a wish bone from a chicken dinner. I wanted my mum to see me do something special like blow out my birthday candles or dance at the front in ballet or win a medal on sports day. I wanted her to see me do all those things because I did them for her. I did them to make her proud enough to want to come home to us.

'OK, Little Flower, we can wait until four o'clock, but then we have to blow out the candles so everyone can go home.'

I threw my arms around his neck and hugged him. She was going to be there. She said she would so she would.

I look back at Mrs C who has respectfully chosen to sit in the pew behind me, because she, her husband, her daughters and her friend take up a whole row. I thought I minded being alone until Noah turned up. Mrs C is crying. She keeps clasping her hands together as if she's going to pray really hard, then she pushes her linked hands against her lips and then she lets her hands fall into her lap. All the while tears are drizzling out of her eyes as if she doesn't even know she's crying. Her two daughters are next to her, her husband on the other side of their oldest daughter.

Beside him is her best friend. Her other best friend. I keep watching Mrs C and her man, noticing with every passing moment how separated they are. She barely looks at him, and when he looks at her he doesn't seem to see her. It's like he's looking at a stranger suddenly. I'm seriously creeped out by him.

He reaches an arm out, snakes it along the back of the pew to Mrs C's shoulder and gives it a comforting squeeze. She lets his hand rest there for a second then she leans away far enough to force his hand to leave her shoulder, to stop touching her. Her other best friend has seen this too, and we make eye contact.

It's over for these two, we're both thinking. *Their marriage is dead in the water.*

It's a stupid phrase I've used a million times before. This time, though, I crumble at the thought of her like that. Dead. In the water. Not alive. Not around. Not sixty miles down the motorway living a life I can't see, but still living.

His arm is around me seconds after I start to fall apart. He draws me carefully to him, and holds me so gently but firmly I feel safe to do this. I feel safe to cry again for the mother I didn't know, in the arms of a virtual stranger.

Ten years ago

'You can't keep doing this to me, Donald, it's not fair.'

She didn't come. I had to do the candles without her and she didn't come. She didn't ring or anything. Dad had rubbed my back as I cried myself to sleep that night. None of the presents seemed as important as having her there and she hadn't made it. I really thought she would sweep in, a big cloud of perfume around her, looking like a movie star in an expensive dress and a big hat. 'I'm going through a bit of a hat phase,' she'd told me.

I'd wanted to show her off to all my friends and tell them I had a glamorous mother. That, yes, she didn't live with me, but she was still around when it mattered.

'You leaving a six-year-old is what's not fair, *Mirabelle*,' Dad said.

'You made me choose then took away my choices.'

'You should have chosen better.'

Their voices carried up to my bedroom. I wondered if they had any clue I could hear them. I'd heard similar arguments over the years, whenever she got brave enough to turn up. It was the day after my party and here she was. When it didn't matter, didn't count, she'd shown up.

'Does she know that you told me the wrong time, wrong day?' she asked.

'All she knows, all she needs to know, is that you weren't here when you said you would be – that you left and you keep letting her down.'

'I should have known something was suspicious when you were so pleasant to me on the phone, talking about a change of plan. I should have known it was all a ploy to do this again. Do you realise the only person you're hurting here is Fleur?'

'I love my daughter – enough to stick around.'

'She's my daughter, too. And if you carry on like this, I'm going to go through official channels to get things formalised so I can see her regularly.'

'You do that, Mirabelle. I can't wait to tell the world how you left your child for your lover, and I really can't wait to drag up every sick, perverted thing you've ever done. By the time we're finished, Fleur will never speak to you again and the court will ban you from ever seeing her again.'

'You'd really do that, wouldn't you? Despite how much it'd devastate Fleur, you'd do that to hurt me.'

'No, I'd do it to keep you away from her because she doesn't deserve to be anywhere near a pervert like you.'

'I did a really bad thing in letting her grow up with a bigot like you,' she said. 'I thought you were a good man. Even though I couldn't love you the way you wanted me to, I did love you. I would have stayed if—'

'I don't care,' he said. 'Just go.'

'At least let me see her. I'll tell her I got the dates and times mixed up, I won't tell her it was you,' she said. 'Please. I don't want her thinking I completely forgot about her.'

'She's asleep.'

'Please, Donald, please.'

'No. She's asleep, I don't want her any more upset than she already is.'

'At least take her present.'

'Send it yourself.'

'So that it can get lost in the post like all the other letters and presents I've sent over the years?'

'I don't know what you mean. It's not my fault if you've had bad luck with the postal system. Maybe somebody up there doesn't like you.'

'Fleur's not going to stay a child forever. One day I'm going to have that conversation with her and I'm going to tell her everything about who I am, why I left and everything you've done to keep me away. And you won't be able to stop me.'

'Dream on, Mirabelle. I'd see you dead before I let you fill her head with lies.'

'We'll see,' she said. 'When she's twenty-one and finished with college and finally free of you, we'll see how things pan out then.'

I wanted to be twenty-one so I could hear the truth. Instead, I had to pretend to be fast asleep when Dad came in to check on me. I was good at pretending to be asleep, I'd done it for years and years because when I was asleep, I found out things. When I was 'asleep' Dad didn't keep his voice down as much as he should, he didn't speak in adult codes to people on the phone.

I didn't like pretending with Dad, but sometimes I knew that pretending was the only way to get to the truth.

'I don't want to go to the thing back at the house,' I tell Noah as we leave the graveside. I don't want to be surrounded by a bunch of people I don't really know. And it was at the Challeys' house.

'You don't have to do anything you don't want to,' he says.

'Can you take me for a drive?' I ask him.

'Course.'

'Can I drive your car?'

He looks a little unsure, stares warily at me before asking, 'Do you have a licence?'

'Yes. I never told her, Mirabelle, that though. She was teaching me to drive and she did a good job, I passed first time. But I liked spending time with her doing that, so I pretended to fail two tests so she would still teach me. Is that bad of me?'

'Yes, and no. I don't think *pretending* like that is good, but if you didn't think you could tell her outright you wanted to spend time with her, given the facts of your relationship, I can't say it's a hundred per cent wrong, either.'

314

'I really just wanted to spend time with her.'

'I know,' he says, and holds me close. 'Come on, you can drive my car. If you knew how big a moment that was, you'd . . . No one drives The Beast but me, usually.'

Mrs C is still at the graveside and I realise I need to tell her now. Seeing her with her husband I know she needs to know the truth. 'Hang on,' I say to Noah, who dutifully puts his hands in his pockets and waits for me to be finished. I make my way over to Mrs C, who seems lost in a trance.

'Mrs C,' I say and she turns away from the graveside to me.

'It was a beautiful service, Fleur. You did a brilliant job.'

'Thanks, but you did most of it.'

'I didn't, I really didn't.'

'Mrs C, there's something I don't get, which I didn't want to tell you before, but seeing you today . . . You said your husband had an affair with her, Mirabelle.'

She looks around to see who is listening, and when she sees no one is close enough, she steps forwards, lowers her voice: 'Yes.'

'But that doesn't make sense,' I say, as quietly as her. 'If it was you, yes, but not your husband.'

'What are you saying?'

'She,' I'm waving my hands around, trying to get them to say what I can't. It's proper embarrassing talking about this stuff. She might not have felt like it most of the time, but she was still technically my mother and that meant technically I was talking about – agaralggh – 'sex' in relation to her. You don't think about your parents like that, let alone talk about it. Not unless you've got some serious BIG ISSUES. 'She liked women. Loved women.'

'Pardon?' Mrs Challey says.

'That's why she left, you see. She came to Brighton to try to find her first girlfriend. She met her at school and they broke up because she and Mirabelle were caught by Mirabelle's mum. My grandmother. My grandmother nearly had a nervous breakdown. So Mirabelle got with my dad to escape from home. And then her first love disappeared in Brighton, so she came here to look for her. Just like in the story, Mirabelle came to find her lost love. She liked men, but not in *that* way.'

'Are you telling me Mirabelle was gay?' Mrs Challey says.

I nod. 'Yes, yes I am.'

316

Tami

It's just me here at Mirabelle's graveside.

Everyone has drifted away, either to go home, back to work, or back to our house for the wake. Everything is so surreal. We've just buried Mirabelle. She was so *there*, all the time. Vital is the word, I suppose. It doesn't seem possible that this has happened to her.

And she was gay. She was gay and she never told me.

Fleur is gone, too, having delivered the news that has rocked me at a time when I didn't think it was possible to be any more shocked and rocked. I hope she's gone off with that man, I hope he'll take care of her. I can't remember what she called him but she'd mentioned she was seeing someone and it wasn't serious. But I could tell from the way she spoke, the way she lit up, that she was serious about him no matter how he felt. The memory of feeling like that never goes away, it stays there in your heart to help you through the bad times; to see you through to the other side. Although, is there enough left for us? With everything that has happened between Scott and me, I don't think there is enough to see us to the other side. Especially now I know they weren't having an affair.

She was gay.

She was gay; she did not have an affair with my husband.

My mind stops me there, stops me from going to that place, that place where I have to accept what he has done.

Beside the head of the grave there is a gold box of red rose petals, passed around for those in attendance to throw in instead of earth. Crammed in the hands of those who came, then released in sombre, respectful movements, some of the petals danced away on the breeze. Most of the petals have fallen on top of the brown, maple-wood box with the brass plaque declaring her name, and they're going to stay with her forever.

I scoop up as many of the remaining petals as I can from the box, they're satiny and almost weightless against my skin, and drop them in, covering more of the box with red. I want it to be like the story of her beach. I want there to be a velvety, fragrant blanket of rose petals that will cover her while she sleeps. I gather up more of the petals, drop them in. I want her to be always surrounded by roses, to be comforted by them as she begins her journey into eternity. I want Mirabelle to never be on her own.

'That's a lot of rose petals,' someone says to me as I release another handful of petals.

Rubbing at my eyes, wicking away the tears that are falling, I turn to the speaker and it's the policewoman. Detective Sergeant Harvan. Her sidekick is nowhere in sight, but he'll be there somewhere. They seem to travel in pairs, unable to work without each other.

'She liked them,' I say.

'Really? That's interesting. And what about you, Mrs Challey, do you like them?'

I study her for a moment. I know that anything I say will

be noted down somewhere. 'They're all right. But today's not about me, it's about saying goodbye to Mirabelle.'

DS Harvan puts her head to one side and studies me for a few seconds. With her hair pulled back, she seems to be made up of odd, angular lines that come together to create an unusual beauty when she doesn't have a scowl on her face. 'I suppose that's true,' she eventually says.

'I didn't realise the police came to funerals,' I say because it seems expected that I will speak next.

'We go to a lot of funerals when a person has died in suspicious circumstances,' she says, her brown eyes drilling into me. 'You'd be surprised how often the killer will show up at the funeral. It's good to study everyone there when they don't realise they're being watched, then follow that up with a chat with anybody we're interested in.'

'You think Mirabelle's killer was here?' I sound naïve but I'm not, not really. It makes sense, what she's saying, if you think about it.

'Almost certainly,' she says, with a look that would be probing if it wasn't outright accusatory.

'Why are you telling me this?' I ask.

'You asked, Mrs Challey,' she says.

It doesn't feel like I asked. I know I did, but it still feels like she's only telling me this as a subtle means of accusing me of something.

'I'm glad I bumped into you, actually, Mrs Challey,' Harvan says as if we were walking down the road and happened to run into each other. 'I was wondering if you wouldn't mind popping down to the station for a chat in the next couple of days?'

'A chat about what?'

'Just a general chat.'

'Do I need a solicitor?'

She blinks and pulls her face in faux surprise. 'You're not under arrest, Mrs Challey, we just want to clear up a few things. It's a routine, informal chat. Nothing to worry about, I'm sure.'

The kind of chat she invites someone of 'interest' to, I'm guessing. 'Right,' I say.

'Monday, then?'

'I think I might be bus—'

'Monday. Then.'

'OK, Monday.'

'Excellent. See you then.'

I wait until she is out of earshot before I take a final handful of rose petals. 'I'm sorry, Mirabelle,' I say to her. 'I'm sorry, for everything. Sleep in peace.'

There's a hush in the house. People drift from room to room, talking quietly, careful not to break the reverential atmosphere. Did none of these people know about Mirabelle? Did she really keep herself that hidden from everyone? They are all here, though, to remember her, and yet how many of them knew her at all?

I have been avoiding Scott, he has been avoiding me. Our whole life seems to be based on avoiding each other since I told him that I was helping Fleur and we were paying for the funeral. *'Are you insane?'* he'd asked me. *'The woman almost broke us up.'* I noted the 'almost' in his words, the way he assumed things had healed between us.

'How's the porn habit going, Scott?' I'd replied. 'Oh, and have you chased up about our counselling sessions, yet?'

He'd clamped his teeth together so hard the veins in his jaw stood out. 'Suit yourself,' he'd said, then marched away so didn't hear me say: 'I will.'

My eyes sweep the living room again, examining the faces of those who were there. Did they know about the animosity between Scott and Mirabelle, or did they just put it down to a personality clash? Did any of them know that Scott was arrested? Did any of them know that he and I are practically split up?

I used to work among most of these people, I was their boss at one time, but the ones I still know are distant colleagues, they work for Scott, they would turn a blind eye to whatever was going on because that's what you do, isn't it, when you want to keep your job, or you want to do well, or you don't want to be next on the hit list.

I look at Scott, and he's in the corner of the room by the bay window, talking to Terry Cranson, who is now chairman of the board of directors and did away with the role of President when he vacated the position. I secretly think he did that to stop Scott getting the role, but we haven't spoken in years so he wouldn't tell me now if he had.

He's made polite conversation, but I knew he was uncomfortable around me. I wasn't sure if it was because I resisted his attempts to get me to go back to work when Anansy was a year old, or if he still has a deep festering dislike and distrust of Scott and he knew I'd be loyal to my husband no matter what.

I'd never told Scott Terry had been on at me to go back

for ages after I left. Not even when Scott was crowing about his latest success while subtly making digs about whether I could have pulled it off had I 'stuck around', as he put it. Another part of our history he had rewritten that I didn't bother to correct. It didn't matter, I often thought. It wasn't important, I knew the truth and he did too.

As he stands talking to the man whose job he has his eye on, Scott's gaze is constantly drawn across the room. To the fireplace. Where Beatrix is standing, talking to one of Scott's subordinates. Trust Beatrix to go for the best-looking man in the room. She never misses an opportunity to—

'Maybe he's not lying about what he's been up to, just who with? Maybe that's why you're so willing to believe what he's told you because deep down you know he's got someone else.' Mirabelle said that to me. I can remember it as clear as anything. I've got a lot of fuzzy memories from the past few weeks from getting drunk so many times and passing out, but I remember that. We were arguing, she was wearing a dressing gown. No, that's not right, in all the times I've spoken to her since this blew up, she's been fully dressed, not in a dressing gown. I must be remembering it wrong.

But she said that. I look at Scott. He is focused on Beatrix.

Slowly, carefully, so no one else can see, not even the man she's talking to, she shifts her eyes towards Scott and a tiny smile curls the very corner of her mouth before it returns to normal and she focuses again on the man she's flirting with.

'Maybe he's not lying about what he's been up to, just who with?' Mirabelle knew, or at least suspected.

Scott is sleeping with Beatrix.

Beatrix

Can you get away later? Bea x

I've been aware of Scotty's eyes on me all day, checking where I am, what I'm doing, who I'm talking to – like this man, who was at the footie with us a few weeks back. Scotty noticed me talking to him and said to me in the car on the way home he didn't like it. He's the one who's married but he didn't like me legitimately talking to a man who had started a conversation with me. Sometimes his reasoning is very suspect.

Since all this blew up with Mirabelle, Scotty has said we need to cool things off. He wanted to spend more time at home, be there for the kids, calm her down so she wouldn't do anything rash like take the kids and leave. He can't stand the thought of that, that's what keeps him there. I said it was the perfect time to tell her, to go public when there was already so much upheaval. But he'd been convinced the police were trying to stitch him up, that they believed Mirabelle's ludicrous story and were going to get a conviction by any means, so this would be the very worst time to start the split. Even when Mirabelle retracted her statement, it wasn't the right time. I'm wondering what excuse there'll be now she's dead? A less trusting woman than I would think he was stringing her along. I know he wouldn't do that to me. I know because he is watching me talk to this man. He's jealous. He wouldn't be jealous if he didn't want me, need me, *love* me.

I talk to good-looking men and I go on dates because I need Scotty to know that I have options. That other men find me attractive and if Scotty isn't careful, doesn't treat me properly, I might find one of those men attractive too.

Also, he needs reminding that I'm not going to wait forever.

This living room is one of my least favourite rooms in the house – it has so many pictures of them, stark reminders of the family they once had. The family they would still have if they'd paid more attention to each other. It's horrible to think it's all fake – that Scotty has been going through the motions all this time to make sure that he sees the girls.

I don't think she's that vicious, but you never know how someone will take being replaced. I have to stop myself looking at her. She's dressed in black and is so obviously devastated. That woman – Mirabelle – tried to ruin her marriage and she's heartbroken that she's dead. How's that for mixed-up priorities?

Scotty told her he was having an affair with Mirabelle because otherwise she might have looked too deeply into the absences, the 'conferences', the times she's called him at work and he'd been off-site at a meeting, and found out about us. Like I say, a less trusting woman would be worried he had gone to such lengths to stop her finding out about us, but not me.

I turn my head ever so slightly in Scotty's direction, I can feel the weight of his gaze on me, the jealousy in his eyes must be intense, so I move the corner of my mouth up a fraction in a self-satisfied smile. I am not worried. At all.

I'll try. But she's not in a good way. Think I may be sitting up all night with her. Make sure you've got that blue and black thing on. Getting hard thinking about you in it.

Me and Scotty? It wasn't meant to be like this.

Before I explain about that, I want to say I'm sorry I didn't come right out and tell you everything, if this is a bit of a shock to you. I thought you'd have guessed when I said about us coming back late from the football and him saying stuff that wasn't very nice about her and was sort of praising me. I'm not proud of the fact he does that critical/praising thing quite often and I don't pull him up on it. I'm not proud that we sneaked off to the loos to ravish each other during the game. I'm even less proud of him suggesting we check into a hotel for a few hours, which is why we missed our train home. I felt absolutely wretched the next day when she told me Cora had a stomach bug and had been throwing up all afternoon and she'd had to deal with it on her own for longer than expected because we were back so late.

Thinking about it, I also assumed you'd have worked it out when Mirabelle said that stuff about me and Scotty and I didn't properly refute it because it was more true than she knew. And the other not very nice things – like trying to push her into checking to see if he still used porn so she'd, you know, make him leave – I thought they were dead giveaways, too. I'm not proud of myself for doing them, just

325

so you know, but it was necessary.

Well, whether you worked it out or not isn't the problem. The problem is, it wasn't meant to be like this. This wasn't meant to happen. Scotty and I 'clicked' and that was our downfall really.

We supported the same footie team, we drank the same vintage whisky, we liked talking about sports cars and we loved to smoke the odd cigar together.

I got some new lingerie. Stuff that makes the blue & black thing look like a chastity belt. Would you like to see? Bea x

God, don't, you're really turning me on when I can't do anything about it.

That's the general idea. Bea x

If I dare look back on all the things I could have done to stop it happening, all the other paths during this that I could have taken, I always conclude that I had no choice. Once you get to the stage where he's all you think about, when you wear the things you've noticed make his eyes linger on your body, when his name is on your lips when you first wake up because he's been filling your dreams every night, you know that you have no choice. Every other path has disappeared and there's only one left for you to take.

And it's the one that leads you directly to the boy who you're willing to betray your friend for.

*

Twenty-one months ago

There were seconds to go until the final whistle, everyone was holding their breath, every muscle of everyone in the stadium was tensed, poised, waiting to see if he could do it. The referee blew his whistle, then there was the sound of boots on grass, the thwack of leather on leather, the united gasp of thousands of people waiting, and then the glorious release of the ball hitting the net. Then uproar, everyone on their feet, everyone screaming, the jostling, the jubilation. Bodies against bodies, joy hitting joy and then Scotty's arms around me, clutching me close, his screams in my ear, his body moving mine as we jumped and screamed together. And then the moment of realisation, as he looked at me and I looked at him and it seemed the most natural thing in the world to go up onto tiptoes and press my lips against his; it seemed expected for him to lower his head and push his mouth onto mine. We didn't. He let me go and stepped back, embarrassment, shock, guilt showing like watermarks on both our faces.

'Erm, sorry,' I think he mumbled while not making eye contact. I couldn't hear properly with the euphoria around us, but I guessed that was what he was saying because it was what I would be saying if I was him. 'Got a bit carried away.'

'Yeah, me too,' I said.

'Come on, let's get you home,' he shouted. 'I know Tami will be waiting with a bottle of champagne.'

He said her name and put her firmly between us. We both loved her, we both wouldn't want to hurt her. It was the atmosphere, it was the fact we'd been spending time together what with him doing lots of small DIY jobs around my flat. It was Tami being so busy with a huge new project she hardly had time for either of us. It was Tami spending more and more time with Mirabelle and excluding both of us from her life in that way. It was lots of silly little things that were throwing us together. But we loved Tami, we'd never hurt her by doing anything more than be friends. We were just friends.

Think I'll do you over the kitchen table, first.

Really? Well you might want to rethink that. I might have a special something in the bedroom to arouse your interest. Bea x

Eighteen months ago
It'd been a good two months since the football match and we had both kept our distance, shocked as we were by what had almost happened. If I had a DIY issue, I tried to cope without him, but when all four of the spotlights went in the hall and I couldn't reach them, I had to call him to come and change them.

It took him minutes, and afterwards we stood in the kitchen, talking. Awkward, describes it best. Neither of us wanted anything like what had happened at the match to happen again. There was too much to lose. I stood in front of the sink, sipping my glass of water and listening to him speak. I wasn't tracing the lines of his strong face with my eyes. I wasn't imagining my tongue in his mouth, his hands on my bum, his—

'Actually, I should probably head off,' he said, coming

towards me and placing the glass he'd used in the well of the sink. As he pulled his hand away, his fingers brushed accidentally against my hand. I expected him to jerk away, horrified that he'd touched me when we were both so non-verbally clear about the dangers we faced. Slowly, deliberately, he ran his fingers up my bare arm, goosebumps chasing in their wake, until his fingers moved over my shoulder and onto my face. I could tell his gaze never left my lowered eyes. My breathing shallowed the longer he kept his hand on my face and his gaze on my eyes. Summoning my bravery, I raised my eyes to meet his.

'Bea,' he breathed, and I was his. I could not look away, I could not move, I was in his thrall. It felt good to be wanted by a man again. It felt incredible to be wanted by *this* man at all. You know how in school there's always a boy that you fancy that would never even breathe in your direction? He was Scotty.

It was wrong. So delicious and so wrong. When, gaze still connected to mine, he was slipping his hand down the waist-band of my floral skirt and into my lacy black knickers, I knew it was wrong and I should stop it. When he was unzipping himself I knew it was wrong and I should stop it. Even when he was guiding me backwards and entering me, I knew, I knew, I *knew* it was wrong and I should stop it. Should and could are two different entities in moments like that: I should have stopped. I *couldn't* stop. I couldn't physically pull myself away from this man who wanted me.

Eighteen months ago
'We can't let that happen again,' he said to me. It'd been

329

three days and I'd been stuck back there, my body and mind playing on loop that delicious moment where he entered me, the excitement of feeling his body shuddering as he came, the intoxicating purity of my orgasm.

We stood on opposite sides of the kitchen, keeping our distance. That was the problem last time, we got too close, physically and emotionally. If we kept the table between us, we'd be OK. We could talk and we could end this thing before it started. Three days ago, seconds after we finished, he'd done up his trousers and dashed out of there without another word, horror on his face.

I nodded, rationally agreeing to what he was saying when every other part of me was disagreeing. I wanted it to happen again. Who would willingly deny themselves that amount of pleasure? I'd been shocked at myself for crossing that huge boundary with a friend's other half, but it felt *right*, too. It felt like this was always meant to happen, we were always meant to be together.

'I've been with her since forever. I don't want to hurt her,' he said.

'Do you love her?' I asked. He didn't use her name and neither did I. If I said her name she would be real. She'd be the woman who left an important meeting to come to the hospital after I was mugged. She'd be the person who said, 'How would you like to be Anansy's Godmother, so you can be the person she turns to when she's older?' She'd be the friend who told me she'd give me her blessing to have one-night stands if she thought I could handle the emotional fall-out, but because I couldn't, I had to believe her when she said I was worth more than that. She wouldn't be the complication, the bump along my road to love.

His mouth stayed silent while our eyes could not tear themselves away from each other. I could look into his eyes – that shade of brown between chocolate and maple – for ever. 'I don't want to hurt her,' he repeated.

Neither did I. That's the insane part. She was my best friend, she really was. Yet, this was love we were faced with. Love trumps everything, doesn't it?

Suddenly we were moving towards each other, we were grabbing each other, kissing ferociously, hands on faces, in hair, inside clothes. We were tearing at each other's clothes until we were on the floor, and we had access and he was doing it again, he was entering me and that deliciousness was descending again, and he was moving hard inside me and I wanted him to slow down, to be as gentle as he had been the other day but I knew he was excited and it was sort of passionate, and then he was orgasming and I was too.

'That wasn't meant to happen,' he said, genuine regret in his voice. 'I came here to stop this very thing from happening but I can't help myself. I'm weak when I'm around you.'

'It's like you're reading my mind,' I said to him.

'I don't want to lose the girls,' he said. 'She can never find out about this otherwise she will take the girls and leave.'

I sat up, then climbed on top of him. I wanted to do it again, but this time I wanted to control it, I wanted to be in charge of the pleasure. 'I'll never tell her. And this won't happen again after this, so there'll be nothing to tell. Right?'

I cried out a little as I sank down onto him.

'Right,' he replied. 'Absolutely, right.'

*

Tell me what it is, in case I don't make it tonight.

Well you'd better make sure you do make it tonight, otherwise you'll never find out. Bea x

Fifteen months ago

'Do you love Scotty?' I asked her.

Things hadn't gone to plan. Not that there'd ever been a plan. We were simply meant to stop it after that time. But it'd been more than a few times – weeks, actually. All right, it was months. We had been together for months. I avoided her as much as possible and she didn't seem to notice, probably because she spent a lot of time with Mirabelle. But, occasionally, she would ring me to see if I was working at home and would come over like now with coffee and homemade cupcakes.

'Course,' she replied. 'We wouldn't be married if we didn't love each other.'

'Even after all this time you still love each other?'

'Yes. I know we had that conversation a while back where it seemed I couldn't stand him, but that's the way things get sometimes. We're mostly happy.'

'In all areas?'

'If you're asking if we still have a love life, then yes, we do. It's not as frequent as I'd like, but with so little time for each other that's no real surprise. But yes, we, you know, do it.'

'Can you ever imagine your life without him?' I asked. Recently he'd been hinting that he wanted things to move to the next level. He wanted to leave her and be with me.

We'd have to move out of the area, of course. I loved where we lived, but that would be the price we'd have to pay for us to be together because no one would understand. They'd take her side and shun us. The girls wouldn't be able to understand at first why Dad was with me, and we'd probably have to keep it from them for a while. His work could be tricky since a lot of the senior people knew her and still gave her a substantial amount of work. It wasn't impossible, it'd simply be easier if we moved elsewhere while everything settled down. Maybe nearer to Kent, where my head office was.

'No,' she said.

'That's it, no qualification, no explanations, a flat "no"?'

'No, I can't imagine my life without him. Why would I even try?'

You might need to, I thought. My eyes started to sting, guilt started to blossom in my heart. I was doing a terrible thing to a lovely person.

'It's all right, you know,' she said, perplexed by my behaviour. 'It's not going to happen.'

'I'm being silly. Thinking about when my husband left me,' I said. 'It would have been our anniversary today.'

'Oh, I see,' she said, then put her arm around me. 'You'll be OK. Things will get better, I promise.' The explosion of guilt almost stopped my heart.

When she left, I broke down. I sat on the floor of my living room, surrounded by memories of making love to him where I sat, and I cried. I hated what I was doing, how much I was hurting her without her knowledge, but I loved him. I loved him, I loved him, I loved him. I couldn't give him up.

My tears became full-body sobs. What was I going to do? I loved him too much to finish it, but the alternative was hurting someone I cared for deeply. At some point I was going to have to choose: friendship or love?

Even as I sobbed, I knew I was too selfish to choose the option that would cause me the most pain.

That'd be telling. You'll just have to make sure you come over tonight and find out. Bea x

Tease!!!

Always. Bea x

You can't help who you fall in love with. And you can't help, sometimes, who you hurt in the process. I hope she understands that when she finds out, I really do.

Tami

'I'm just nipping out for a bit,' Scott says to me. The girls are in bed and everyone has gone, although a few people did stay behind to make sure the place was cleared and put back together. I can still feel it, the heavy fug of what has happened here today, the sadness and shock over who has been lost.

After everyone left, while Scott put the girls to bed, I seated myself in the living room, on what used to be my favourite seat, and looked around me, taking in the fragments of our lives again. The sofa, the chairs, the ridiculous fireplace, the rug, the carpet, the butter-yellow walls, the wooden-slatted blinds, the ceiling rose, the chrome sockets, the oversize television.

I hate this room now. Everything bad that has happened seems to have happened in this room. Over there, Scott was put in handcuffs. Right here, I sat and listened to him tell me about his affair, not knowing he was lying about who but not what. And right there, in front of the door, I discovered whom he is really sleeping with. I will take a flamethrower to this room one day, I really will. I will raze it to the ground and start again. Much like what I am going to do with my marriage right now.

Scott, my husband, the love of my life, is the picture of

innocence as he checks his messages on his mobile and prepares to go out. He is that hard-edged handsome that unsettles rather than comforts or attracts me. His black suit is expensive, you can tell by looking at it. He fills it well, along with the black silk tie that I can tell – from knowing her – Beatrix bought for him. His white shirt is crisp and still crease-free, it will be another designer label. His shoes are from his collection, probably quite old since no new boxes have appeared on his side of the wardrobe recently. His hair is combed back, styled into place with the products that have been multiplying in the bathroom for months, probably even years now. He looks fake. He is a fake. Everything about him is fake.

'Going over to screw Beatrix, are you?' I ask him, conversationally. I do not feel like I've been hit by a truck this time. For the first time in a long time everything makes sense, the world does not seem to be full of things that don't add up, with inconsistencies that only I seem to see, which must mean it is me who is crazy, out of step with the real world. I have clarity. I was not going mad, I wasn't paranoid, I wasn't selfish and clinging to the past, I wasn't holding up the process of moving on by being cautious and on edge. All of my reactions were normal because I was still being cheated on; disrespected. LIED TO.

'What?' His head jerks up from staring at his mobile. 'What are you talking about?'

'Isn't that what you've been texting about all day? How soon you can get over there and screw her?'

Hurt, shock, a smidgen of anger from him. 'You can't go around accusing me of all sorts because I'm friends with a woman, Tami. You have got to start trusting me again sometime, otherwise what's the point in us trying again? Now, it's been a really long, difficult day, I need to go out and clear my head. When I get back we can talk again about your ridiculous accusations and how you're going to start to put this stuff behind you.'

'Or were you both laughing over how stupid I am not to have seen what was going on *literally* under my nose?'

'I don't know where you've got this idea from but—'

'I know you've been sleeping with Beatrix. Not Mirabelle, Beatrix. It was her all along.'

Scott's light brown eyes are piercing as they try to drill their way into my head to find out what I know and what I am guessing.

He moves to speak, opens his mouth to lie.

'There's no point lying, I know the truth. I saw it with my very own eyes.'

He closes his mouth and slowly, surely he is transformed: his back is a little straighter, his body a little more rigid, his features set themselves into a sneer, and his hands curl into fists. I have seen this man before, of course, but he has rarely been like this with me. Tilting his head to one side slightly, he observes me for long, uncomfortable seconds. 'If you know it all, what are you bothering to ask me about it for?' With his voice the transformation is complete. He is a Challey again. A real Challey with all the sociopathic traits of one.

I should probably be scared, but I'm not. I am a fool, of course. 'I want to know how you got those texts from Mirabelle because they were definitely from her number.'

'What makes you think it wasn't Mirabelle as well?'

337

'I *know* it wasn't Mirabelle as well,' I state. 'She wouldn't do that to me.'

'What, don't think your precious Mirabelle was capable of it?' Scott sneers.

'Mirabelle was gay,' I say to him.

The sneer is washed away by the tidal wave of that revelation. 'What?' he says, jolted to a whisper.

'She. Was. Gay. She said to me that she wouldn't touch you with a barge pole and me, idiot that I am, didn't believe her. I mean, I touched you, so in my brain, obviously a million other women must be as stupid as me. But not Mirabelle, apparently, you're not her type.'

Scott stares wide-eyed at me.

'Tell me how you got those text messages that convinced me you had been sleeping with her and that she was so obsessed with you she would lie to the police? I don't understand how you managed that.'

'Thought you were the person with all the answers.'

'You stole her phone and wrote them all yourself, didn't you? You did that so you could . . . Oh my God. Oh my God. You set up an alibi so you could force yourself onto someone.' Nausea rises through me. My husband is a cold, calculating sexual predator. He's probably done it before. I'm shaking now. The full horror of who I have been living with, sleeping with, *loving*, is revealing itself to me in broad, sickening strokes.

'No, no, I didn't plan it,' he protests. 'I didn't do that and I didn't plan it.'

'Then tell me about the text messages because they're the only things that don't make sense.'

'I, erm, I found her phone—'

'Where? Where did you find it?'

A sigh, a pause. 'On her desk. I went through her office, looking for information. I wanted to find out about her, she was so closed, so guarded. I always thought there was something she was holding back so I went through her desk and found she hadn't taken her phone with her to a meeting. It wasn't password protected despite how paranoid she was, so I looked through it. I saw the text messages and I *knew* it was a married man on the board, maybe even Terry. I wanted time to work out who it was, so I sent the messages to my phone as an insurance policy.'

'Blackmail?' I put my hands to my face in horror. 'Blackmail, infidelity, violent porn, rape—'

'No, no, you can't say that because I didn't do that. I didn't try to rape her. Things got confused. She was sending mixed signals—'

'How could she have been sending you mixed signals? She's gay. She *was* gay.' Was. Was. Was. She *was* gay. She doesn't exist in the present tense any more; she's gone.

'Maybe she was confused about her sexuality,' Scott says. 'But, I thought, you know, she wanted it. I thought if we got it over and done with, things would be more settled between us.'

'Over and done with? Did she have any say in it, or did you just—'

'It wasn't like that. It wasn't how you're making it sound. You weren't there, you don't understand. I thought if it got going, she'd—'

'She'd what, happily accept what was happening? What

you're describing is rape, Scott,' I shout at him. 'And you know that. Any man knows that.'

'It wasn't like that.'

'You need to leave. I need you to pack your things and leave.'

He shakes his head. 'No. I can't.' He shrugs.

'Scott, I need you to leave.'

'That's not going to happen. I can't leave. Where would I go? And I can't be without you all.'

'I need . . .' My voice dries up and I take a moment, a moment to accept what is happening. I knew before, when I realised it was Beatrix not Mirabelle, what he had done, but now it is real. Now it is in front of me, the monster that lives under the bed, the bogeyman that stalks your dreams. They are real and here. My husband is a rapist. He needs to leave. 'You have to leave.'

'I can't,' he says. 'Don't you understand? I can't.'

'Scott, if I told you that your daughters were living with a man who had been arrested for a serious crime that he's all but admitted to, that he was planning on blackmailing someone, that he lied to their mother on a daily basis for years, and was addicted to something that would be harmful to them if they were exposed to it, what would you say? Wouldn't you want that person away from them? Wouldn't you say that he had to leave and sort himself out before he had meaningful contact with them, let alone lived with them and influenced important decisions in their lives?'

His face crumples, he shakes his head. His hands come together as in prayer, as if begging. 'Please, Tami, don't make me go.' He seems small, terrified.

'Scott, please, don't do this. You know you have to leave.'

Suddenly he is a Challey again, his face angry and scornful. 'It's my house, if you've got a problem, then you go. Because I'm going nowhere.'

'OK,' I say. 'OK. I'll take the girls and we'll go to London. We'll stay with my parents.' I start to formulate the plan for the next few weeks. I'd rather not, I know my parents won't make it till the end of the first evening there without telling me 'we told you so' about my life choices, it'll be hell, but at least the girls will be OK. At least I'll have space to think.

'You're not taking my children anywhere,' he spits.

'Try and stop me,' I reply.

Another change: 'Tami,' soft, reasonable, 'it's not as bad as you're making out. I'll get help. I've already broken it off with ... with *her*. I'll get help for my porn habit. I'll get better. But I can't do that without you and the girls. I can't do it if I leave. I need to know that you'll still be here for me at the end of it. What would be the point otherwise? I need you to be there for me.'

'You'll always be the girls' father. They'll always need you in their lives.'

'What about you?' he asks. 'Will you always need me? Will I always be in your life?'

'We're always going to be parents,' I say. 'We still have to bring up the girls together.'

He shakes his head, the tears coming back. 'Don't talk like that's all we'll ever be to each other.'

I say nothing. I can't tell him that we'll ever be together again because right now, we can't. I can't see how I'm going to ever be with him again.

He crumples completely, his knees giving way, leaving him in a heap on the floor. 'Don't send me away. Please don't do this to me. I love you. And I'm sorry. I didn't think. Please don't send me away because I didn't think. I never meant to hurt you.'

Before all this started, before Scott and I became lovers, we used to sit in my bedsit, watching television or videos and eating crisps. And talking. We talked for hours about nothing, creating a friendship from our words. I don't know when it became possible for him to do all the things he's done and I don't know when it became possible for me to watch him cry and not reach out to soothe him. But that is what is happening. I wonder what the Tamia of then would say to the Tamia I am today if I told her where I was, where she would one day be.

'I'm going,' he says to me. Two bags packed, a suit bag draped over the top of the bag that is resting high on his shoulder. He used to carry his schoolbag like that, the memory almost makes me smile. 'I, erm, I'm going to change,' he says to my nod. 'I'm going to be worthy of you again. I promise. I'm going to be a better father and I'm going to be the man I used to be. Do you understand? I'm going to win you back.'

'Do it for yourself,' I say quietly. 'OK?' I add, softening my voice because it sounds as if I don't care. As if this is easy and I have removed myself from his orbit in one easy step. 'Do it for yourself.'

Our eyes meet, and I feel the guillotine fall between us. Severed. Apart. I will never look at him in the same way again. He inhales to speak, and I raise my hand in a stop gesture and shake my head. I don't want to hear those words again. A thousand 'sorrys' will not change this. A million 'I never meant to hurt yous' will not undo this place we are at. One 'I love you' will not alter the damage in our hearts.

'I'll see you, Scott,' I say.

'I'll see you, TB.'

I lower my gaze as I nod, tears collecting on my eyelashes. We used to say that at the end of the holidays, when he was heading back to college. When I knew I'd miss him because he was one of those friends I didn't really think about, didn't hear from, and when he wasn't there it was no big deal, but in the holidays we were inseparable.

I wonder what the Scott of then would say to me if I told him what had happened. I wonder if he'd fix me with his gaze, steady and certain and strong? I wonder if his face would frown as he listened and then would curl up into a smile as he told me I was off my rocker? That he would never do those things, and I would never have allowed things to get so bad.

The front door closing is an explosion that happens deep in my chest.

I want to run after him and tell him to come back, that we'll work it out, that everything will be all right. And that's the reason why he has to go away.

Fleur

'Hi Fleur, it's Tami Challey. I hope you're doing OK, all things considered. I'm actually ringing to apologise to you. I didn't tell you the entire truth about what happened with your mother and my husband. I thought they'd had an affair because the other story was just too awful to contemplate. Basically, my husband was arrested for assaulting your mother. That was very hard for me to accept so I threw myself into believing they had an affair. I didn't tell you the whole truth and that was a terrible and cowardly thing to do because I was trying to protect myself. Which isn't at all fair on you when you already have so much to deal with.

'My husband was also questioned in connection with your mother's death but he has an alibi. I'm going to be questioned, too, but I don't know what they're going to ask or even why they want to talk to me when they know Scott is innocent. Unless they think I'm somehow involved in her death . . . God, I'm just rambling now.

'The point is, I'm sorry. I got the impression that your life has been lived with people not telling you the truth about everything and I shouldn't have done that to you. Fear makes you do stupid things. I really hope you're doing OK. Let me know if you need anything or even if you just want to chat. Bye.'

344

That's the thing about Mrs C, she makes it hard to hate her. Really hard. I didn't really hate her, I did feel betrayed, though. I couldn't understand why she didn't tell me everything until now.

I listen to the message again.

If we were in a film, it'd turn out that she did it all along. Seeing as we're not in a film but in, like, real life, I don't think it's going to pan out like that. Or maybe it will, who knows. The point is, she's apologised and 'fessed up in the end. And she seemed to know that I'd been hearing half-truths all my life and wanted the truth.

I like her. She's the person who's come closest to the idea of what a mum should be. But, still, she stayed with a man who attacked my real mother. I don't think it'd be wise to trust her completely, or at all.

I'm still here in Brighton. So is Noah. He can work from wherever he has his computer because he's a consultant and travels a lot so can be based anywhere. We've moved out of my B&B to a slightly nicer boutique hotel because we wanted more space and much better Wi-Fi for Noah.

He's sitting by the window at the table where we had breakfast, concentrating on his laptop, papers spread around him on the table and the floor so it looks like large, rectangular snowflakes have fallen on him. It's all organised, apparently, and the way he scratches his head, frowns and then searches for a good few minutes for something is just all part of the way he works. It's *nothing* to do with not having organised himself properly.

I smile and go back to painting the toenails of my left foot in rainbow colours. The little toe is red, the next one is orange, the next one is going to be yellow, the next one will be green, my big toe will be blue. Why? Why not? I'm thinking of getting a tattoo done, too – something that starts on my foot and goes up my ankle. Why? Why not?

The sense of peace I feel not having to go back to London just yet is so comforting. Dad's been calling quite a lot and I've only answered half his calls. I'm not being nasty, it's not being able to handle hearing the desperation in his voice – every time it churns it all up again and the guilt starts and I feel like the worst daughter in the world.

Eight years ago
'Are you sure, Fleur, you want to do this?' Dad said to me.

'Yes, Daddy, it'll be fun.'

'I'm not sure it's safe,' he said.

We were the last ones at the coach pick-up point, of course. He'd been saying this all morning as I finished packing for the four-day trip to Spurton Hall in Wales. I would be away for four whole days. Four days. I couldn't imagine it properly. I'd be away from Dad and he couldn't tell me what to do.

'Daddy, it'll be fine.' After a struggle, I managed to get the case out of his hand. 'I'll call you every night and I'll make sure I go to bed really early.'

Dad had only said yes to this because my form tutor, Miss Devendis, and the headmaster, Mr Ratchford, had told him that I wasn't mixing well with the other kids. 'Fleur's work is excellent, but she isn't developing social skills as well as the other pupils because she doesn't seem to participate as much with the other children.' After that meeting I'd been allowed to join the after-school gymnastics club, and now I was allowed to go on this trip.

I hadn't really thought it would happen. Dad said we couldn't afford it first of all, then he changed his mind and said it might be OK. And now we were here. I knew he could change his mind any second and I wouldn't be able to go, but we were here at least, that was something.

'Fleur, I'm so looking forward to you being on this trip,' Miss Devendis said, coming over and taking my bag off me. That was it, I had to go because now Miss Devendis had the bag, Dad would never be so 'rude' as to take it back.

I beamed at her, she knew what my dad was like, I think. I wondered if her dad had been the same.

'Fleur, you be a good girl, now, and do everything your teachers tell you,' Dad said, putting his hand on each of my shoulders.

'I will, Dad, don't you worry.' I threw my arms around him and suddenly didn't want to let go. I didn't want to be away from my dad, actually, what if I came back and he wasn't there? What if he left like she had left and I didn't get to see him for ages and ages? What would happen to me then?

'Come on now, Fleur, you should be going,' Dad said, untangling me from him. He was embarrassed in front of Miss Devendis.

I waved and waved and waved at him from the window of the bus and had to hide my face so others couldn't see that I was crying. Everyone else seemed so happy to be away from their parents and I had been, too. But I didn't think anyone else's mother had gone, which meant their dad could do exactly the same thing and you'd never know the reason why.

'Papa Don't Preach' starts on my mobile phone. It's Dad's ringtone and this is the fifteenth time it's sounded off this morning – and it's not even lunchtime. Noah looks at my mobile and then at me and then goes back to his work. He knows things are complicated with Dad right now – he wants me to come home, which is why most of his calls go to voicemail – but Noah would never comment. Unless I asked him to, in which case I'm sure he'd give me his opinion. Which is maybe why I haven't asked for it. Don't ask, don't tell.

Eight years ago
'Quick, run!'

I didn't stand a chance. I was so not used to doing things like this. Earlier on a few of the boys had snuck into our dorm, and Raymond Rheine had sat on my bed. I really liked Raymond Rheine and he used to stare at me a lot so I think he liked me. He had asked me what football team I supported and I'd said, 'Arsenal, of course.' And he had said, 'I support Liverpool.'

And I shrugged and said, 'Never mind,' and he had laughed and said, 'That's what my older brother says. He supports Manchester United.' Then, I swear, I had no idea he was going to do it, he kissed me on the mouth. I sat really still and frowned at him because it'd been so quick I didn't really get a chance to see if I liked it or not. So I did it to him, just as quickly, and it was nice, it was strange but nice. I wanted to do it again but then his friends were saying they'd found a way outside and we should all go out and have a cigarette.

'Are you coming, Fleur?' he asked me.

I didn't really want to go because I knew we could all get in trouble. But I did want to kiss Raymond again so I said yes and we climbed out of the back window of the dorm and went around to the back of the house. And people started smoking and passing cigarettes around until it got to me. That's when the trouble started and someone heard a teacher, and someone hissed, 'Quick, run!' but I was too late, too shocked. Suddenly the Deputy Head and Miss Devendis were standing in front of me and I was holding a cigarette I had only just put in my mouth.

'Please don't call my dad,' I sobbed as we were standing in the middle of the office. 'Please, please.'

'We have no choice, Fleur,' Miss Devendis said. 'You are the last person we expected this of, I'm so disappointed in you.'

'I'm sorry,' I sobbed.

'Who else was there?' Mr Marmaduke, the deputy head, said. 'If you tell us that, we won't be so hard on you.'

There was no way I was grassing on anyone. My life wouldn't be worth living for one. And it wasn't cool to tell on your mates.

'Please don't tell my dad.'

'We have to. We have to inform your parents of these sort of things so they can punish you as they see fit.'

Parents. They had to inform my parents.

'Can you ring my mum then?' I said. 'They're divorced, but it'll be better if Dad finds out from her.'

'Do you want to have dinner in town tonight?' Noah asks me. He looks up from his screen at me.

It's a bit weird thinking about the first boy I ever kissed when the last boy I've kissed is sitting there across the room.

I nod at him. He's so different to Raymond. But that feeling in your stomach doesn't go away when you like someone, does it? It might over time, but it's that same feeling now as it was then. Sort of like you feel sick and you can't settle but in a good way.

'That's great. So you have to choose where we're going since I decided we're going out.'

I narrow my eyes at him, talk about your rookie mistake.

'What?' he says innocently, shrugging his shoulders. 'You know the rules, babe, one person decides what we're doing for dinner, the other picks.'

'I get all the best jobs,' I say with my eyes still narrowed.

Eight years ago

They called her that night and at six o'clock the next morning she was there. She went in and spoke to them for ages without me in the room, and then she sat next to me and listened as they told me it wasn't going to go on my record, but they were disappointed in me and they were sending me home with my mother. I don't know what she said to them, but it wasn't going to be a permanent problem so Dad wouldn't be able to bring it up all the time. He was never going to let me out of his sight again anyway, there was nothing I could do about that.

'Are you going to tell Dad what happened?' I asked her as we passed more signs for London and I knew we were getting closer and closer to him. I didn't think he would hit me, but he would be so, so cross. I was scared of him being cross but I was more scared of seeing him cry. When he cried, which he did sometimes when I was really naughty, it made my stomach feel all funny. It made me want to cry and to hug him. And to be a good girl all the time.

'Why don't you tell me what happened, Fleur? Then I'll know what I should tell your father.' she said.

'I didn't do anything. I wasn't smoking.'

'Who was, then?'

'Not me,' I said. It was her fault, anyway. If she was around then Dad wouldn't be so sad and cross and expect me to always be good. Dad wouldn't cry if she hadn't left us.

'OK.'

'I didn't do anything wrong,' I told her. *Not like you.*

'OK,' she said.

'It was other people.'

'OK.'

'It *was*! Raymond Rheine was talking to me about football and then he kissed me and it was nice and it made my tummy go all funny in a good way not in the bad way it does when Dad gets cross or when he cries. And then everyone said they knew a way outside and Raymond said I should come and so I went because I'm always the boring one and then they were smoking and I was given it and

351

then the teacher was there and everyone ran before I could and I had the cigarette but I didn't smoke it. I wasn't smoking.'

'Kissing boys and smoking, that's two major things, Fleur, in one night,' she said.

'I wasn't smoking!' I shouted. It wasn't fair that I was being sent home when I didn't do anything. 'I didn't do anything wrong.'

'Actually, you did,' she said. She looked at me really quickly so she could keep driving. 'You shouldn't have gone with them. That's me ignoring you kissing a boy which you're far too young to do, too.'

'I'm not too young. And no one ever asks me to do anything because I'm so boring. Dad never lets me do anything.'

'Boring is good, you know? Boring girls generally do better at school and get to have the freedom to be and do whatever they want when they grow up. Wouldn't you rather live an exciting life then than now?'

'No!' I said to her.

'Yes, stupid question. Fleur, this isn't good. You know how upset your father is going to be.'

'I know.'

'But, more than that, you should want better for yourself. It shouldn't be a case of your dad being upset that stops you from doing things you know aren't right, it needs to come from you.'

My tummy was full of butterflies and I felt a bit sick. I didn't want to see Dad. I didn't want any of this.

'Can I come and live with you?'

'Pardon?'

'Please, Mummy, can I come and live with you?'

She looked in the rear-view mirror and then indicated and then she pulled over right there on the motorway. There weren't lots of cars so it was OK. She didn't turn the car off, she just took off her seatbelt and turned herself around in her seat so she was looking at me.

'Fleur, I would love for you to live with me, but I don't think that's what you really want, is it?'

'Yes, it is,' I said to her. I didn't want to leave Dad but I did want to live with her. Sort of.

'I think you're scared and worried about seeing your dad when he finds out you've been asked to leave the trip. I don't blame you, if it was my dad I would be feeling the same thing, but living with me won't solve the problem. You have to face up to the things you don't want to do. It's a hard lesson to learn, but if you think you're old enough to kiss boys and get into trouble with your friends, you have to take your punishment, like the girl who is old enough to do those things.' She stroked my face. 'It won't be so bad. But, if after you've spoken to your dad and you've sorted things out with him properly, you still want to come and live with me, you can tell me that and I'll talk to your dad about it. Does that sound OK?'

I nodded.

I wonder if Noah is the perfect man? This is so different from anything else I've been involved with before. He's kind of laidback, but not horizontal. You can tell he works hard. The fact he's absolutely gorgeous doesn't hurt, either. He glances away from his computer screen and his face creases up with a smile at me. See? Perfect.

Eight years ago
'You wait here, I'll go and tell your father what's happened,' she said to me. 'Don't worry about anything, it'll all be OK.'

It was early Saturday afternoon so that meant Dad would be watching the football on television and his new friend would be cleaning the house. He always called his girlfriends his friends. I don't know why, I knew they were his girlfriends and I knew what he did with them. That sex thing. Sometimes I would hear and I would hear Dad telling whoever it was to shush because I was asleep and I would put my pillow on my head because it was too disgusting. Usually on a Saturday I would be tidying my room and writing in my diary and doing my homework.

I slid down in my seat so only the top of my head could be seen in the front passenger seat as she walked up the path to the door. She pushed the doorbell and then took a few steps backwards. It took ages for Dad to answer the door and I slid even lower when I saw the look on his face.

She started talking to him and he started to look at the car and I could tell he was really, *really* angry. The butterflies in my stomach got worse and worse.

He started to come to the car and I said, 'No!' and almost threw myself onto the floor. But she stopped him and kept standing in his way, 'cos she was as tall as him, until he stopped trying to come to get me and he stood and talked to her.

He didn't say anything for ages but he kept looking at me

in the car and she kept talking and talking. And then he stopped looking at the car and looked at her and she was still talking. She talked and talked and talked. Then she came over to the car and opened my door and said, 'Come on, it's OK, he's not going to shout at you or stop you going on any more school trips.'

I didn't believe her so I didn't move. I really, really wanted to live with her. I didn't want to go home at all.

She went and got my case from the boot of her car and then she came back and held out her hand. She hadn't asked me to hold her hand since I was a little, little girl.

'Trust me, it's fine,' she said. She smiled at me and it was like I was five again. When I was five and she used to smile at me, I always smiled back. I felt safe when she smiled at me, I felt like she would always protect me. I felt like I was curled up in her arms and she would never let me go. When she smiled at me like that, right then, she felt like my proper mummy all over again.

I took her hand and got out of the car and she led me to where Dad was standing.

'Fleur, I'm very disappointed in you,' Dad said. I knew he was saying that because she was standing there. Usually he'd be shouting at me and telling me what a bad girl I'd been and how he'd made all these sacrifices for me and I was throwing them in his face and trying to hurt him and how I was never to even think about going out again.

'I'm sorry, Dad,' I said.

'I'm going to call the school on Monday and make sure you are given detention for at least a week. I don't think sending you home early is enough of a punishment. But you mustn't get mixed up in something like that again.'

'I won't, Dad.' She was still holding my hand, still making me feel safe, still being my mummy.

'Go to your room and start any homework you have left. I'll bring you a snack later.'

That was it? That was all he was going to say? I looked at Dad and he didn't look angry any more. He looked disappointed, I suppose, but not as angry as he had when she first spoke to him.

I looked at her, wondering what she had said to him.

'OK, Fleury, I'll say goodbye now.' She was still smiling at me like she did when I was five. She bent down and, looking right in my face, she took me in her arms, pulled me close to her. I felt so safe, so wanted and loved. So very loved. She whispered in my ear, 'I love you, baby girl. Don't forget that, don't ever doubt that.'

She stood up and nodded at Dad. 'Donald,' she said, like she was talking to someone very important who she didn't like very much.

'Mirabelle,' he replied.

She smiled at me one last time and then went back to her car. She waved at me and Dad and then she drove away.

I thought Dad would shout at me once she was gone, but he didn't. He told me again to do my homework and he brought me a cheese sandwich a bit later. He didn't mention it again.

Just before I went to bed that night, as I was pulling across the blue and red flowered curtains at the window, I saw someone standing across the road, looking up at my bedroom window. The outline of the person looked like her, but I couldn't see properly because it was dark and she wasn't near a lamppost.

I pulled the curtains across and got into bed, and turned out my lamp and closed my eyes. I tried to go to sleep, but I could feel her out there. I could feel her telling me the story of the Rose Petal Beach, like she did all those years ago. I threw back the covers and ran to the window, opened the curtains then opened the bottom of the window so I could lean out and look across the road properly, see if I could make her out. But she was gone. If it was her. I think it was her because after that day, I didn't see her again for four years.

Noah still has a frown upon his face as he concentrates on his computer. It feels weird to not have anything to do. I do have stuff to do, but I have no inclination to do it. I keep thinking, 'What's the point?' It's not like I love college or anything, and it's not as if there's any point to anything any more. I mean, take her, Mirabelle: she did what she wanted, she dipped in and out of my life, but did it make her happy? Did it stop her from being murdered? No. So what's the point?

I sit back on the bed, staring at the different colours that top my toes. They remind me of the dress she wore that day she came to get me in Wales. It was a long dress, made of strips of the rainbow that clung to her body and ended at her thighs. It showed off her long, slender legs and made her seem even taller than she was. She was a real beauty, my mother. Not many people could have dressed like her and got away with it. The way she hugged me that day was as if she was saying goodbye. It was as if she was showing me all the love she could with a clock hanging over her head. What did she say to Dad that day that made her leave?

Before I think things through properly, I'm picking up my mobile and dialling Dad's number.

He picks up on the first ring. 'Fleur. How are you? When are you coming back?'

'I don't know,' I reply. 'The police haven't allowed me to go into her house yet, so I can't pack up her stuff and get on with preparing it to go on the market. So I'm going to be here a little longer.'

'I think you should come home and then go back when you can get into the house.'

'It could be any day now,' I say to him. 'I'll just hang on and see what happens. Hey, Dad, remember that time I got sent home early from the trip to Wales?'

'Yes,' he says, cautiously, because he hasn't managed to get me to come home.

'What did she, Mirabelle, Mum, say to you to stop you being so cross?'

His silence reverberates down the line and fills the hotel room. I am silent, holding my breath. Noah has stopped working and is looking at me, waiting, too, it seems, for my father's reply. 'I don't remember, Fleur, it was a long time ago.'

'Yes you do, Dad, you remember everything,' I reply. He does. He remembers all sorts of conversations that most people forget.

Noah suddenly hits the save buttons on his laptop, grabs

his two mobile phones and his jacket, then waves at me as he departs. Just before he shuts the white door with the emergency exit instructions hanging on the back, he raises his hand to his head in the 'call me' gesture.

'Why are you asking me this?' Dad says.

'Because I want to know. I was just remembering that time and I know you spoke to her and I need to know what you talked about.'

His silence returns, descends like a blanket of snow upon us. I'm supposed to say, 'It doesn't matter, actually, I'm sure it wasn't important,' right now. I often do that when he goes silent, not just about her, Mirabelle, about everything. But this time I'm not going to do that. Because it doesn't make sense that he wasn't cross. The first time he trusted me I let him down, and he didn't hit the roof, he practically let me get away with it.

'She told me,' he begins slowly and reluctantly, 'that you had been sent away from Spurton Hall because you'd been hanging around with kids who were smoking and you were very sorry and very worried about how cross I was going to be.'

'What else?' I ask.

'That was it, mainly.'

'Please, Dad, what else?' There was definitely more to it than that.

He sighs. 'She said you were so scared of my anger that you had asked to live with her. Did you?' He sounds upset and asks that in the hope that this show of hurt will distract me from questioning him. Which means there's more.

'Yes, I was thirteen and scared. What else?'

'She . . . She said if I gave you a hard time, she would do everything she could to get you to live with her. It was what she wanted more than anything, but she had told you that you had to sort things out with me even though she would have you living with her in an instant. She'd even bought a big house near the sea so you could come and stay with her as I promised you could sometimes.'

'You promised her I could stay sometimes? Why didn't you ever tell me that? Why didn't you let me go?'

'I knew that wasn't what you wanted, Fleur. I knew you didn't really want to go and stay with her and feel like a burden. She had her life down there and she didn't really want you to stay, she just said it to make herself feel better.'

It isn't often my dad lies, he mostly omits things, but this is a lie. No way to style it, he is lying. He is absolutely lying. I know it like I know how to breathe. She did want me to stay with her. She did want me.

'What else did she say?' I ask. My mouth is all dry and my whole body is prickly, like it's going to break out in hives or start itching uncontrollably.

'She told me that I had to give you more freedom. To let you go on school trips and join after-school clubs and the like. She said you should be allowed to sleep over at your friends' houses if you wanted. She said you were a good girl and that you shouldn't suffer because of what she'd done.'

'And what else?'

'She . . . She said if I gave you those freedoms, let you be a normal teenage girl, she'd go away and leave me alone. I mean, leave us alone to get on with our lives.'

I can't say anything. My mouth is choked, my throat is

full, my chest is stuffed with the thought of Dad agreeing to that. *How could he?*

'Why, Dad?' I manage to force out. *Why did you do that?*

'I'm sorry to have to tell you that, Fleur. I know it's hard to accept that she didn't want to be around and that she used this as an excuse to try to stay away. I'm sorry, I don't have the answer to why she did it. I just know that I had to protect you from her coming and going in your life like that.'

That's why after the school trip I didn't see her for four years. I never really understood why she just disappeared and stopped sending me birthday cards and stopped writing to me, and stopped replying to my attempts at contact. I'd never been given them, I found them in the bin or in Dad's room before they were binned. But then they stopped, I never found any more and wondered why. I could never ask Dad, of course. Now I know.

She did want me. And she stopped seeing me to give me a life. Dad did let me go on school trips, he did let me stay at friends' houses sometimes, he did say yes to me joining after-school art and drama as well as after-school gymnastics. As I got older and got used to the freedom, started to stay out a little after curfew and stuff, that's when he started to change again. That's when he started freaking out at what I did, that's when I realised I wasn't going to be allowed to go to university away from London. That's when she wrote to me again and I found the binned letter. I didn't get in touch, but I knew she was in touch. She came back when Dad started to break the deal he made with her. I don't know how she knew he'd broken the deal, but I do know that she did want me.

'Fleur, it must be so hard hearing all this when—'

I click the hang-up button, cut him off. I can't listen to any more of him lying about her. She offered him that and he accepted it and then acted – never said, just *acted* – as if she didn't give a stuff about me. Lying. Absolute lying. And her, why didn't she tell me? She did it for me but in all these years I've been seeing her, why didn't she mention why she walked away from me for a second time?

'Papa Don't Preach' starts to play on my phone and 'DAD' flashes up on the screen.

With shaking, trembling hands I cancel the call.

Immediately 'DAD' flashes up again as his ringtone starts up, the phone buzzing.

I cancel that call.

'Papa Don't Preach' starts again and I cut it off without even looking at the name on the screen. I scramble off the bed, smudging a couple of the not-quite-dry nails on my toes, and dash into the bathroom as the tune starts again. With one shaking hand, I push the metal plug into place in the sink and then turn the hot water tap on. With my other hand, I am cancelling the calls as they come in. Once the sink is full to the overflow hole, I look at the phone in my hand.

'Papa Don't Preach' starts up again and 'DAD' flashes up on my screen.

'Bye, Dad,' I say as I drop the phone into the water. It gurgles for a moment, still playing 'Papa Don't Preach' until the water obviously seeps into the electrics and the song is cut off and the vibrating stops, and the screen goes black instead of saying 'DAD'.

I'm not going back. I thought I'd always have a home there

in case it didn't work out for me down here, but I know one thing for sure at this moment in time, I am never going back. I am never seeing my father again.

11

Tami

'Have you ever seen a dead body, Mrs Challey?' Detective Sergeant Harvan asks, her slender frame seeming much bigger, more threatening while she prowls around the room like a predator assessing its prey. Which would be me. There have been a few pleasantries, all there for the tape, but they were rapidly dispensed with.

I shake my head. Thankfully I never have, hopefully, I never will. 'No.' I am nervous for some reason. I suspect they know something I should know, that this 'chat' is a lot more formal than was hinted at.

'Are you sure?'

'Yes.'

'What about Mirabelle Kemini?' she casually says, like it's every day that someone I care about is deliberately killed, *murdered*.

'No,' I say. I didn't even see her body before the funeral. Fleur and I asked the funeral director to take care of that because we could not do it; neither of us were strong enough. We bought a simple white gown, we described how we wanted her hair and her make-up, how it was necessary to hide any sign of what had happened to her, but neither of us could stand to look at her like that. The funeral director was very understanding, she took photos and slipped them into sealed envelopes in case either of us changed our minds. I haven't. I don't know about Fleur.

'Since you haven't seen a dead body, shall I talk you through what they look like?'

'I'd rather you didn't, thank you.'

'It's not like in the movies.' She is behind me, controlling the situation, my responses, by not sitting still. I am being kept off-balance, on edge. 'It's not all clean and somehow quite beautiful. In the case of Mirabelle Kemini, who, as you know, was strangled while being drowned, it was particularly gruesome.'

'I don't want to know any more,' I protest.

From the corner of my right eye, I see Harvan give Wade a nod. He reaches out for the yellow cardboard folder that lies on the table between him and me, and opens it. I see the corner of what is inside: photographs. They aren't going to show me pictures of her, are they? *Are they?*

I have not known a terror like this. I do not want to see this. I do not want that in my head for the rest of my life, imprinted on the insides of my eyelids, there to greet me every time I try to sleep.

'If you show me those photographs I'll walk out of here right now,' I say, panicked. 'I don't have to be here, you said so yourself.'

Harvan and Wade exchange looks, wondering if I am serious.

'I don't care if you have to arrest me to get me back here, I don't want to see them.' I am ready to run if I need to.

Her hand is heavy on my shoulder, causing me to jump. 'Relax, Mrs Challey, calm down.' She speaks like she is used to calming children, she manipulates her tone like she knows which frequency will lull people. 'We won't show you the pictures, there's no need. I'll tell you instead.'

'No.'

'If you were to look at her body, you would note her upper arms, shoulders and neck are black with bruising – these came out some time after death, when her body was completely cold. Our forensic team tell me she was obviously pushed down into the bath first, probably hitting her head on the bath before the killer's hands slipped around her neck. Then she was probably thrown around like a rag doll while being constantly pushed under the water.' I can picture it and I don't want to. I don't want to imagine Mirabelle being treated like that. 'Are you listening, Mrs Challey, or do you have no need to since you were there?'

'I wasn't there and I don't want to listen any more.'

'Mirabelle was a fighter, though. She didn't go quietly. Her lungs and stomach were filled with water so forensics believe she must have been yelling pretty loudly while fending off the strangulation. The fingernails on her hands were ripped and torn, so she was obviously clawing at the tiles and the bath edge, trying to cling on, trying to hold onto life. Her heels and her calves were severely bruised from kicking. The amount of water on the floor means she probably got away from her killer quite a few times and it was just being in the bath that had her at a disadvantage. She was a fighter, Mrs Challey, she didn't go quietly or easily. But you already know that, since you were there.'

'I wasn't. I've told you already, I wasn't there.' What she has told me is lodged in my mind, playing itself over and over. Her fight, her screams, the non-stop sound of splashing water.

Harvan comes back to the table, back to her seat, and carefully tucks herself in close to the table so that she and Wade are level, a united wall of the law. 'You weren't there, you say?'

'No, I wasn't.'

'Then what's this?' she asks, placing a small clear plastic bag on the table. I look down at the bag. I'm about to say it is a plastic bag and what has it got to do with anything when I see what is inside it: my wedding ring, with its unusual wavy edge where Scott's ring fits into it, creating the ultimate symbol of marriage.

I haven't realised until the ring is in front of me that I have been playing with the space where my wedding ring should be, tracing the wedding ring indentation with my finger. I have periodically looked for it out of general interest, but I accepted it as lost – probably quite symbolic of where we were with our relationship – and would turn up when I was looking for something else.

'For the benefit of the tape, I am showing Mrs Challey a platinum wedding band with the inscription "TB 4 SC" and numerals "21.10.98".'

Are you thinking about your ring? Cora asked out of the blue, the first time I noticed it was missing.

'Is this your wedding ring, Mrs Challey?' Wade asks.

I stare at the ring, my heart beat slowly increasing until it is galloping in my chest, running and running as I have the urge to do now. 'It looks like it,' I say to him.

'Have you recently lost your wedding ring, Mrs Challey?' Harvan asks.

I am in trouble.

'Yes,' I say.

'Aren't you even a little bit curious as to where we found this?' Harvan asks.

'Not even a little bit?' Wade adds.

'Where did you find it?'

'In Mirabelle Kemini's house,' they say together.

I am in real trouble.

'I recognised it straightaway, especially with the inscription. Obviously Wade didn't.' She rests her hand on Wade's shoulder. 'Men don't notice things like that, do they?'

'Some men do,' I reply.

'Well, not our Wade here. But I, I recognised it because it is so unusual. And then, of course, there is the unusual inscription. Not your wedding date, I gather. What is it? First date? A special birthday? First declaration of love? First fuck?'

I say nothing, she does not need to know what it is.

'Come on, Mrs Challey, you can share that little titbit of information with us. We're like old friends.'

My legs start to jiggle with anxiety and I have to place my hands upon them to stop them.

'You do disappoint me. Well, when your ring was found, I thought, "Now, what would Mrs Challey's wedding ring be doing at a crime scene?"'

'I wasn't there.' *At least I don't think I was.*

'Your ring says otherwise,' Wade replies.

'Wade made an interesting point that as you've been friends with Ms Kemini for some time, maybe you dropped it on one of the many other occasions that you'd visited her.'

I look gratefully at him, he returns a blank stare.

'But I remembered that you were wearing it when you came in to talk to us, which was the same time I warned you to stay away from her.'

I am in real trouble.

'That's a strange little habit you have.' She nods to my hands. 'Always playing with your ring. I remember noticing it the first time we met.' I take my hands and knit them together in my lap. 'You were doing it at the cemetery, even though you didn't have a ring on.'

'If it was only the ring, we might not be convinced there's a problem,' Wade says.

'But then there are female-sized footprints on the tiled floor of the corridor,' says Harvan.

'And the black hairs found snagged in the velvet trim of the silk dressing gown found on the floor of Ms Kemini's bathroom.'

'I'm sure you won't mind offering your footprints to help eliminate you from our enquiries. And your hair for DNA analysis.'

They are silent then, their double-act suspended while they await my defence, while they give me the opportunity to explain myself.

'I think I'd better get a solicitor,' I say. I don't remember if I was there or not, that's the problem. That's why my heart is speeding out of control and I know I am in trouble. The night she died was the night I drank two bottles of expensive wine on an empty stomach and tortured mind. The most I'd drunk in a long time. It was the night before the morning I woke up fully clothed with pieces of gravel lodged into the soles of my bare feet and cuts, scrapes and bruises on my hands, forearms and chest. It was around the time I last remember having my ring. These are all the solid facts I have about that time, but the rest, the salient, important parts, I still can't remember. Fragments of that night come to me in flashes – like my arms around her, like shouting at her, fighting her off – but nothing solid. Nothing is coherent or fixed, the events slip away from me like jelly through the holes in my mind. In normal circumstances, that would be fine. At this moment, I am in trouble.

'What happened to "I have nothing to hide, so I don't need a solicitor"?' Wade asks. I'd think he was being snide if I didn't know he was serious.

'No, no, that was Mr Challey who said that,' Harvan corrects. 'He's the other criminal in the Challey household who also made protestations of innocence.'

I *am* innocent. I know I wouldn't do that. Drunk or not, enraged or not, I couldn't – *wouldn't* – do that. I wish I could remember, then I could tell them everything and all of this would go away.

'We always have to wonder about the guilt of a person who refuses to co-operate and decides they suddenly need a solicitor,' Harvan says conversationally to either Wade or me, I'm not sure who.

I link my hands together more tightly, to hold myself together. My hands look like I'm praying – Harvan will notice that. She'll think I'm internally praying, asking for forgiveness and deliverance. I'm not. I immediately separate my fingers. Instead, I lower my head and pick at my cuticles. They are toughened and rough-edged, and do not give no matter how hard I push at them. I concentrate on my hands because it is not a good idea to speak. Where did I hear someone say that a person shouldn't ask a question they don't already know the answer to? I really shouldn't answer a question that I don't already know the answer to, either.

'What are your solicitor's details so we can call them?' Wade asks.

I don't have a solicitor. Why would I need a solicitor? I work from home, I look after my children, I lived with my husband, I bought my house a lifetime ago. Who lives the kind of life where you need to know your solicitor's name at the drop of a hat? Who lives the kind of life where they end up in a police station three times in less than a month?

Me.

'That's OK, Wade,' Harvan says, 'we don't need Mrs Challey's solicitor's details. She can go.' She turns to me. 'You can go.' She returns her look to Wade. 'We know Mrs Challey has a nice life here, she wouldn't dream of going anywhere until we can eliminate her from our enquiries. You know, when we have that court order compelling her to give us a DNA sample, and her footprints, we'll probably have to arrest her to get them. I hope it's not in front of her children, like we had to with Mr Challey.' She shakes her head. 'Those poor children. They'll be so confused about why we have to keep arresting their parents. I wouldn't be surprised if social services were involved.'

In the silence that follows, I keep picking at my nails, my head still lowered. I know what she is trying to do. And it's almost worked. I felt my hackles rise, my muscles tense, ready to go for her, ready to agree to anything if she'd just leave the girls out of it. But, she has to do this. If she had more evidence – *proof* – she would have arrested me already. I have to stay silent. I have to not react. Even if she is trying to use my biggest weakness against me.

After the lifetime that is waiting for her to speak again, she turns to me. 'Oh, Mrs Challey, are you still here? Didn't you hear me, you can go.'

I get up, pull my cardigan closed around me and pick up my bag. I don't even say goodbye, because I do not want them to take that the wrong way as well.

12

Beatrix

I'm getting really worried about you, babe. What's going on? Are you OK? Let me know what I can do to help. Love you. Bea x

I can't bear this any longer. I haven't heard from him in six days. Six days! Even when they're on holiday and she's by his side 24/7 he finds a way to message me: he goes to the bathroom with his phone or he sneaks out of bed in the middle of the night. He'll even send me naked pictures from beside the pool. We once had phone sex while he was in the bedroom and she was showering only a few feet away in their villa in Portugal. This is not a good sign. He's not been into work either and no one seems to want to tell me why. They say he's not available and to leave a message which will be passed on to him upon his return.

'When will he return?' I always ask.

'Soon,' is always the reply.

'Do you know who I am?' I want to scream every time I hear that. 'I'm the next Mrs Challey, I'm the love of his life, and you need to tell me what's going on.'

I can't stand it. I've barely slept or eaten since I last saw him, I've had to call in sick to work because there was no way I could drive all over Kent not knowing what was going on.

That night, when he was meant to come over, I'd sat there, dressed up in killer heels and this red and black Chantilly lace item I'd bought, waiting.

And waiting.

And waiting.

While irritating, I do sort of expect it – the waiting. The having to fit in with whatever else crops up in his main life. It's not great to think of yourself as not part of his main life, but nobody except the seriously obese eats dessert all the time. I'm the treat at the end of a hard day; the excellent bottle of wine you save for best. I am the pleasure that he craves.

I opened a bottle of champagne – Vintage Veuve, his favourite – at nine pm, intending to have one glass because he wouldn't like it if he showed up and I was half cut. I finished that bottle over the course of half an hour. So I started on the second one. Then the bottle was gone. I woke up slumped over the kitchen table, a third bottle in front of me, my muscles frozen and a crick in my neck so severe it would take my chiropractor hours to sort out. And I was alone. Had been all night from the look and feel of the place.

When I checked my phone and there were no messages or texts, incandescent fury ignited in me. I fired off an angry text saying he'd better have had an excellent explanation. Nothing. I called and his phone was switched off. No reply to an email. Nothing on FB or Twitter. Nothing. Nothing, nothing, nothing. Silence and more silence. For six days.

The only explanation for it was that he was dead. There was no way he would not contact me otherwise. And after what happened to Mirabelle, I knew it was a real possibility.

The police had no clues as to who really killed her, so Scotty could have been the next victim. That's when I started to call his wife.

Her. Yes, I know what you're thinking, and you're absolutely right, I am a bitch for calling my lover's wife to find out if he was OK, but I needed to know. I love him. I needed to know if something had happened to him. She didn't answer her mobile after the first two calls, then switched it off. Then when I tried the landline, it had been disconnected. Another pointer to something hideous having happened. I had to find out what was going on, so here I am, walking the long way around the Close to their house because I can't bear walking past the house where Mirabelle died. I know it's ridiculous because I live in a flat in a converted house and almost all the houses on this road are old so people are bound to have died in them at some point, but I didn't actually know any of them, did I?

She may have done a terrible thing, lying like that to get back at Scott, I may have wanted shot of her the last time I saw her, but she didn't deserve that. No one deserved that. Strangled and drowned in your own bath. Left there, naked I presume, for someone to find. No one knows who found her, which is even creepier. Or maybe the police know and aren't telling us because that would cause widespread panic. I shudder. What has happened is already awful, but it comes to mind every time I think about running a bath. I love taking long baths, too. I've not been able to since because the thought of dying like that . . . I shudder again, stronger this time.

At the house I hadn't planned on visiting, but I've been

forced to by the comprehensive silence of all communication channels, I knock quietly, forgetting for a minute that I don't need to. When Cora was first born, I used to ring the doorbell or knock – only for seconds later a cry to rise up from inside the house, followed by the door being snatched open, Tami's face thunderous and tearful in equal measures, while her arms were full with a tiny, squalling bundle with a smattering of black curls. I learnt my lesson: knock quietly or text to say I was outside. I forget sometimes that the girls are at school.

There's no answer. I know she's in because the window to her office is open. She would *never* go out and leave the window open. I emphasise that because it's not in her nature, she's far too conscientious.

Another knock. Louder, this time.

Wait. Wait. *Nothing.*

Doorbell and knock this time.

Wait. Wait. *Nothing.*

I know she's in. I can almost hear her, sitting up there in her turret, ignoring the intrusion because she's so engrossed in her work. How she can be so unbothered when something has happened to her husband? What kind of callousness is that? Please don't think I'm deluded, something *must* have happened to him, because you don't understand the connection we have – he wouldn't cut me off with no explanation. He loves me.

I reach out, place the palm of my hand square in the middle of the doorbell and lean forwards. I keep leaning on the doorbell until I hear footsteps descending the flight of stairs to the hall and then approaching to the door and snatching it open.

'Hi,' I say brightly, taking my hand away from the door-bell. 'Got time for coffee, cake and a chat?' I grin at her. 'Obviously you'll have to provide the coffee and cake since I appear to have forgotten both. I've got a great line in chat, though.'

Her face relaxes for an instant, then slowly winds itself into a small, bitter-looking smile as she slightly tilts her head to one side. She is quietly incredulous, calmly fascinated.

'He's not here,' she eventually says.

'Who isn't?' I reply. I'm keeping my voice bright, my tone light, but fear is uncurling itself inside the ventricles of my heart: she knows. She knows about me and Scotty. What was it? A stray text? A discovered email? An unlogged out instant message conversation?

'He's not here,' she repeats, more firmly this time. I've never experienced this side of her, I don't think. She doesn't take any nonsense in shops and restaurants and the like, and she always gets her point across when it comes to complaining about customer service but I've never had this tone, this face, directed at me. It's unnerving. Actually, it's terrifying. She definitely knows. If she did, though, wouldn't she have attacked me by now? If I found out Scotty had been with someone else, I would be clawing her eyes out for even glancing at him, ripping her hair out to make sure no one else ever looked at her, and smashing her face in for good measure.

'You mean Scotty?'

'It's always bugged me how you call him that,' she says. 'I was never quite sure why the over-familiarity and intimacy of it niggled at me, but I understand now.'

It's always bugged her? *Why?* 'How do you mean?' I ask, thrown by the direction of the conversation.

'The whole world calls him Scott, *everyone* apart from you. Because you're so special, you're so close to him. But, you know, whatever. He's not here.'

'You said that before, but why would he be? He's at work, surely? I was working at home today so I thought I'd come to see you, see how you're getting on.'

She lowers her gaze to the ground. 'How am I getting on?' she says, as if pondering the question. She raises her gaze, inhales heavily, and stares off into the heavens for a moment. 'How am I getting on?' she continues to muse.

'Yes! It's not a trick question,' I say jovially, rattled by the conversation about his name. I always do that. I always shorten or in this case lengthen someone's name in endearment. Don't most people?

There's a small inscrutable smile on her face as she finally returns her gaze to me. 'I'm tired, to tell you the truth. Really, *really* tired. I've been trying these past few weeks to keep my marriage together because my husband was having an affair with my friend and he begged me to give our relationship another chance.'

She hinted before that he'd been the one to beg to stay, and when I asked him, he said he'd had no choice – he couldn't make a move until he had sorted arrangements properly so he wouldn't lose contact with the girls.

'All this has been so hard on you,' I say sympathetically. It's genuine, because I do honestly feel for her. The part of me that is her friend kicks in and I want to hold her, tell her it'll all work out for the best. 'Look,' I say, my body relaxing as I realise I need to forget about him for now, be a proper, supportive friend to this woman who has been through so much hurt, 'why don't you put the kettle on and we can talk about it?' I move to come inside but she does not budge – she remains an immoveable object blocking the entrance to her house.

'Turns out he was screwing you all along,' she says, staring me straight in the face.

'What?' I say, half laughing from the shock of what she said and how she said it. The cold dread starts at the pit of my stomach, spreading quickly and decisively like the tendrils of a fast-growing vine throughout my body.

'Yeah, fancy that, eh? I suspected the wrong friend.'

'What are you talking about?' I manage to choke out through the vines of dread that are rapidly encasing my body.

'You see, that's why I'm tired. I'm so exhausted with feeling all that anger and devastation before, and then with trying to make my marriage work and my friend dying, that I never really recovered. So, things can't get any worse, I think, it's going to get better, I think, but no, I have to make my husband confess who he was really having an affair with, then I have to cope with realising how I've been lied to and manipulated by him and his lover for nearly two years, and *then* I have to deal with making my husband leave, so I'm pretty much incapable of feeling anything but tired right now.

'Anyway, if you wouldn't mind going away and *leaving me the fuck alone*, I'd be ever so grateful.' She steps back and shuts the door before I can say anything else.

Standing on the doorstep, the blue door an unfriendly barrier to the Challey home, I'm not sure what to do.

I never thought what it'd be like that when all was revealed. I thought there would be tears and raised voices and attempts to claw my face right off. I thought after the first few times, where she'd be shouting insults and I'd be shouting explanations, the situation would calm down and I would be able to manage it. I'd time the length and regularity of seeing each other until she got used to it. Until I was able to explain to her that I hadn't set out to hurt her, that what's done was done and we should all try to move on with our lives.

This hadn't been how I expected it to pan out at all.

I didn't think she would be like that, nor that the conversation would be like that. And I thought Scotty – urgh, it feels wrong to call him that now – and me would be together.

If I sift through what she said, it's clear what happened: she somehow found out about us, confronted Scott, who didn't admit it straight away. When he did, he told her everything. And then she asked him to leave. He didn't go quietly, but he did eventually go.

Which begs the question: where is he? Which also begs the other question: why didn't he come to me? Which also begs the third question: why, when everything was revealed, didn't he warn me that she knew?

There is only one answer to all these questions, of course, and obviously you know the answer: he's done a runner, is currently holed up somewhere licking his wounds, having decided it's every person for themselves as soon as the fan got hit.

That, or she's killed him. Which isn't even funny considering what happened down the road.

I turn away from the door, force myself down the path, and pause at the gate. I'm not sure what to do now. Where to go, what to do, what to think.

My eyes alight upon their family car, an ordinary car. Scotty – *Scott* – has a GT-R, a £75,000 car, which he replaces new every year. She has been driving this one for the past five years. She had been planning on buying herself a GT-R at one point because she'd been given an enormous bonus for the way she orchestrated TLITI's transition from being an in-company department to becoming its own company *and* making a huge profit in its first year. She'd wanted a sports car, but decided to put the money into savings as a deposit on a family house. Even though they found the perfect house, and it was an amazing place to bring up their children, she still thinks of the black GT-R she wanted to buy.

I don't know how I know that about her, about her life, but I do. I know lots of tiny, inconsequential details about her that make up her life, make her the person she is.

My mind cycles back to what just happened: she knows.

All things considered, it's amazing I'm still in one piece.

Tami

I like to think of Mirabelle as being surrounded by flowers, roses, of course. I like to think of her lying on that beach of hers, surrounded by rose petals, sleeping. Just sleeping. Maybe she'll be wearing her white dress from the painting, but her face will be soft, her eyelids resting gently closed, those long, black eyelashes of hers sitting on the rise of her perfect cheekbones. Her hair, shiny and curly, framing her face, pooling on her shoulders.

I have to think of her like that. I have to, and I have to make it a clear image I can hold in my head. I have to see the creases of her dress, each seam, the perfectly turned-out hem; I have to picture the smoothness of her flawless complexion; I have to hold onto the twirls and coils that make up her beautiful hair; I have to cling onto the fluid length of her limbs, conjure up the curve of her stomach, the swell of her chest, the slenderness of her neck and her shoulders.

I need to do this every time I think of her because of what that policewoman told me. The details of how she died are scorched into my head and I can't erase them. Like the extreme pornography I saw on Scott's computer, it plays on loop in my head.

The images of her being pushed into the bath, the flailing of limbs, the choked, watery screams, the determined violence of hands around her neck, drowning and strangling her at the same time. Those images work their way through my mind, unspooling themselves over and over. Almost every time, the person whose hands are around her neck are mine.

13

Beatrix

Scott, look, call me, text me, IM me. Anything. I need to know you're ok. Nothing more. Just that you're OK. Bea x

I hate the fact Scotty – Scott – wasn't free when we fell in love. If you knew me, you'd know I'm not like that, this isn't the sort of thing I would normally do. I mean, yes, some might say I have 'previous' when it comes to liaisons with unavailable men. But I don't *mean* to do stuff like that. I promise. And I double promise I'm not a man-stealing slut. Life simply seems to work out that way.

You see, I'm one of those women who get on better with men than women. I'm certainly no 'handmaiden' as Mirabelle said, but it's been like that since I can remember. I have been through phases where I'd accumulate female friends but the rivalry – the trying to outdo each other in looks and clothes and make-up – would become too intense and we'd have to take a break from each other. Then, of course, there was the way they were so suspicious of me because I could hold my own in a conversation about the latest Michael Kors collection *and* about who was going to finish top of the Premier League.

As soon as these 'friends' had fellas and I didn't, it became all-out war. As time went on, I was dropped by a lot of my women friends and I saw more of their husbands at the footie or down the pub. I was being friendly, having a laugh, enjoying my life, nothing more. However, when these men's other halves heard that 'Beatrix' had been there too, there'd be a scene and tears and ultimatums, and most of the blokes would ditch me for the quiet life. EVEN THOUGH WE HADN'T DONE ANYTHING.

The ones who didn't ditch me met up with me in secret. That was when things started to get complicated, the secrecy, the shared worry about being caught . . . The forbidden nature of it . . . All of those things often pushed us closer together.

I hated myself for it, truly I did, and I rarely did it more than a handful of times with these men because I knew what was coming – I knew they would fall in love with me, they would want more and I couldn't give them more because, well, my husband left me for some whore and I would never do that to another woman. I would never let a man leave his wife – and sometimes kids – for me. Screwing them was one thing, breaking up their marriage was another.

After the last one, Craig, a guy I'd got to know first through work and then through going to the footie, did leave his wife even though I'd dumped him, I swore to myself no more.

I'll never forget seeing Craig's wife in Sainsbury's a few weeks after he left. She looked like she'd been hit repeatedly by a bus. Her hair was unwashed and hung in greasy clumps around her face, she was gaunt, her skin almost alabaster white, and her clothes were practically hanging off her. In all the time I'd known her before we drifted apart,

I'd never seen her without make-up and immaculately turned out clothes.

Guilt took the breath right out of my lungs and I stepped behind a woman in white handing out strawberry cheese-cake samples to hide from her. Craig had sworn to her – he told me – there was no one else. 'I told her that I loved her but I wasn't in love with her any more. We can tell everyone that I turned to you for comfort after things had ended,' he'd said to me in my flat the night he left her. 'No one need ever know when we fell in love.'

'But I'm not in love with you,' I'd said to him, confused, wishing he would go. He'd seemed so sexy before when he was off limits, but in leaving his wife he was transformed into a liar and a cheat. Exactly what my ex-husband had been.

'You do love me, I can tell,' he'd said.

'At no point did I mention love. It was a bit of fun, no one was meant to get hurt and you weren't meant to leave your wife. Why did you leave your wife? What did she ever do to deserve that?'

He stayed for what felt like hours, trying to change my mind, until I told him that I would tell his wife if he didn't get the hell out of my flat. He left saying he'd wait for me and I knew I'd have to avoid him. Seeing his wife was horren-dous. I remembered that look well, I remembered how it felt to have your whole world obliterated. To go from being with the man you loved and knew inside and out to dealing with a stranger, one who saw your relationship completely differ-ently to how it actually was.

After that, I promised myself no more married or attached

men. Even if he was divine, even if his other half was controlling him by not letting him be friends with any woman he
wanted to hang out with, I would stay away because of the
devastation it caused.

Everything had been fine, it'd worked, I turned down every
opportunity I had to be with a married or attached man and
felt very proud of myself.

Until there was Scotty.

Tami

The sound of running water scares me. It bubbles an icy fear through my heart.

It's unsettled me since Mirabelle died, but after what DS Harvan did and said, the sound now terrifies me. I get a cold trickle of fear running through my body and I have to stop myself from shaking. I try to conjure up the image of her surrounded by flowers and sometimes it works, the terror banished. Sometimes the images combine and there are rose petals in the water, there is Mirabelle at rest in the water and there is no sound. Other times, it is a pointless exercise. I am enslaved and tortured by it, powerless while it rampages through me.

I think the sound is one I heard that night. The night she was murdered. Since I know I didn't have a bath that night and I don't think Scott did, either, all I can think is ... I might have heard it there. I might have been there when she died.

I'm not sure. That's the worst part, I suppose. Not knowing for sure if I was there while the bath was running; if I crept up behind her, pushed her in and then held her down until she stopped fighting, until she was gone; if that was where the scratches on my arms came from. Could I have done that? I was so angry. Not that night, but every night and every day since Scott's arrest, if I'm honest. I was hurt, horrified, shocked, shaken, scared, but underlying that was anger. Most of it at myself, for not guessing, for not seeing it, but a lot at Scott, at Mirabelle. The result, of course, is I'm now scared of what I am doing – running a bath for my children.

The very act of pushing in the plug, turning the five spindles at the top of the tap with my hand, wrenches and wrings my stomach. I reach out and take the organic bath wash from the window ledge that doubles as a shelf and flip it open. My hand is shaking, of course. I drizzle some into the bath, watching it turn the clear water a milky white that obscures the bottom of the bath and the fish-shaped bathmat. I look away from the bath then. It's always at that point, when clouds of white begin to streak the water before dispersing, that I have to look away. It reminds me of something. I'm not sure if it's real, or if it's something I've conjured up to fit in with the images that the policewoman evoked for me. But it's making something that was a pleasure, a great way for us to spend time together, a fraught experience.

'Are you two ready?' I call out of the bathroom door. I take a deep breath to centre myself, to push away the memories that I am sure are false. I would not do that. I have to keep reminding myself, no matter what I was feeling, no matter how angry I was, I would not KNOWINGLY kill someone. I couldn't.

Could I?

'Ready!' Anansy squeals, arriving in the bathroom first, her towel in hand, still dressed in her pyjamas. Her hair is technically still in the three plaits I'd put in earlier – in reality, strands of her hair are escaping all over her head in a cute, chaotic mess. I remember my mother *despairing* because I would look very similar to Anansy by tea time, no matter how neat I started the day. I don't really remember why, that's just the way it was, to paraphrase Anansy.

'I'm here,' Cora says, sauntering into the bathroom, wearing her fluffy dressing gown, a towel wrapped into a turban around her head. She is so from the wrong era, she should be in 1950s Hollywood, with a cigarette holder suspended between the fingers of one hand and martini glass in the other. I can imagine Mirabelle looking that elegantly glamorous of an evening.

As Cora sheds her dressing gown, I want to grab her, stop her from getting into the bath, stop her meeting the same fate as Mirabelle. That is an irrational reaction and instead I get down on my knees to help Anansy finish getting undressed.

It's OK to put them in the bath. Nothing is going to happen in the bath, nothing bad happens in the bath. What happened to Mirabelle doesn't happen to people that often. People die, yes, but not like that. Not *murdered.*

Anansy is splashing water, Cora is not. I'm surprised that Cora is still willing to share a bath with Anansy, but she doesn't mind. I've asked her more than once if she feels weird at all, or if she'd like to have her own baths, but she looks at me as if I am crazy. She loves spending time with her sister, they really are the best of friends. They've been closer since Scott was arrested and almost inseparable since Scott left.

The sound of water being moved by bodies, warm, living

bodies, is magnified. Deafening. It's like standing on top of the ocean in the middle of a storm, everything sounds rough, dangerous, deadly. I close my eyes because I can't slam my hands over my ears without unnerving the girls, but that, of course, makes it worse. Take away one sense and the others become magnified. I knew that. So why did I do something so stupid, something that almost instantly turned up the volume, brought the ocean crashing all around me?

She sighs. In my head Mirabelle sighs. She looks away over my shoulder as if checking if there is something more interesting out on the street. 'Yes? What do you want?' she asks, hostility in her tone. She was being hostile to me? Me?

'I want you to tell me why you did it.' I slur.

She focuses on me then, stops looking over my shoulder, stops ignoring me and concentrates on me. 'You've been drinking?' she says, suddenly full of concern. And then she looks down at my feet. 'And you've got no shoes on. Oh God, Tami, what are you doing to yourself?'

'Stop pretending you care,' I say to her. I am swaying because I can't stay upright and still.

'Come in here,' she says and before I can properly protest, she takes hold of my arm, pulls me into the house.

'Get off me!' I screech at her, pushing her off. 'Don't touch me! Don't touch me!'

'Mama, what's the matter?' Anansy asks, dragging me back into the bathroom.

I am shaking. My back is flat against the wall. I don't want to rely on gravity and the present to stop me from falling back there. I need to hold on to something.

'Are you OK, Mama?' Cora asks.

Their concerned faces look at me from the bath and I know I am scaring them. 'I'm fine, I'm fine,' I say, taking a chance on letting go of the wall. I'm fine. I'm not falling backwards. 'Nothing's the matter.' I'm fine. Everything is absolutely fine.

'Now, come on, let's get you out of the bath and into bed for storytime.'

I'm fine. Whatever that was, it's from the same place as the running water. It's just my imagination. It is not a piece of the jigsaw that is that night. It is not proof that I did it. It can't be because I wouldn't do that.

Beatrix

Sweetheart, I know she knows. Just talk to me. I think you owe me that much. Bea x

Four months ago

'I want a baby.'

It was early on a Saturday morning, he was officially at the gym, he was actually here, in my bed, making all kinds of delectable love to me. Our bodies were intertwined as we lazily whiled away the morning.

'Come on, Bea, what am I supposed to do with that?' he asked.

'I want a baby, Scotty. I'm not getting any younger and if you can't or won't, I'll have to find someone who will.' I wouldn't, I wanted his baby, no one else's. I hadn't ever felt that urge before, but with him, I wanted him to look at me and love me as the mother of his children. I wanted him to have on his face the expression he had the day I first met him when he talked about her. I wanted him to be like that about me.

'Don't do that,' he said.

'I'm letting you know as a courtesy – I'm officially stopping the Pill, so as of now, you're going to have to take care of contraception.'

'Don't do that,' he repeated.

'I'm not asking your permission. I'm serious – if you want to have sex, then you either wear a condom or take your chances.'

'Bea, this isn't fair. What you're basically saying is I won't get to live with at least one of my children if I keep on making love to you. I'll have to choose between Cora and Anansy or your child. You know I can't give you up.'

'No, what I'm saying is you need to take care of contraception from now on or it's likely I'll get pregnant with your baby.'

'And that's your final word on the matter?' he asked.

'Yes,' I replied.

'OK,' he said. 'OK.'

14

Fleur

From The Flower Beach Girl Blog (drafted in my head)
Things I've been thinking about:
I have to ask again: why do people lie? I don't mean the little lies, I mean the big ones. Is it a case of 'If I'm going to tell a small lie I might as well tell a big one instead'? Or is it that you think you're so important you need to distort reality to fit around you? I don't have all the answers and I know I do it, too. But why do people lie? What good could possibly come from it?

'Can you tell me about my mother?'

I had no choice but to come here. Noah is great, but he doesn't understand. His mother died when he was young and he was brought up by his grandmother and his dad and his sisters. He grew up with a family around him, with people who loved him, who knew him and who didn't lie to him.

Mrs C lied to me, but she admitted it almost straightaway. She's the only person I've met in a while who has been honest with me.

She looked apprehensive when she opened the door, then her face relaxed into a grin as she saw it was me. 'Fleur,' she said, a smile in her voice. 'It's great to see you. I thought I'd alienated you for ever. Come in.'

I asked her if she would tell me about my mother before I stepped in. I was only there to get her to tell me about Mirabelle. Having the knowledge now that she hadn't willingly abandoned me like I thought has been churning me up inside again. I'd been feeling settled, then I discovered the deal she made to get me a better life; the promises she probably made to the school to keep the smoking incident off my record. I had to find out about her. I had to find out what she was like because I only knew her in pieces. I want the whole picture. I need to know about her.

'Of course, I'll tell you anything you want.'

Noah is up in London today at a meeting, so I was at a loose end. I walked around North Laine for a bit, looking in all the little shops, doing that thing where I look for stuff that's going to fit. I need sometimes to buy stuff that will fit in that part of me that is missing a piece. Out there is something that will fill the hole in me; will complete me. Weaving in and out of the shops not finding anything and feeling my anxiety rising, I had to get out. I ended up running to the seafront, getting somewhere that was wide open and free, that had space for me to breathe.

With the strong sea air blowing through me, clearing away the fog and the claustrophobia, I knew I had to find out about her. I was stuck where I was in my life because I didn't know about her. She was gone, and so much was lost to me. Shut away. I had no way of getting her back. The house was still off limits and I couldn't speak to my dad because he was a liar. I was without a phone because he was a liar.

'Please don't lie to me,' I ask her as I follow her into the house.

Her house is so welcoming, so much like a home. My house growing up felt like a home, but it didn't feel like this. There is so much of the people who live here jumping out at me from everywhere. The coats hooked over the banister at the bottom of the stairs, the assortment of shoes at the top end of the tiled corridor, where the overloaded coat stand lives. The large, brass-framed mirror as you walk in that is adorned with small fingerprints. The corridor walls covered with drawings by the girls, each one framed and mounted, with their name and age at the foot of it, a reminder of what they did at different stages of their young lives. The walls in every room I have seen have pictures of the girls. They had a couple of Mrs C and her husband, but not as many as the girls.

She takes me through to the kitchen and pulls out a chair for me to sit on.

On the butter-yellow sofa that is pushed up against the wall, little Anansy is installed under a pink duvet. She has her hair in bunches and she is wearing pink, sheep-covered pjs.

'Hello,' she says, raising her hand briefly before going back to trying to push a large green frog into a small silver box.

'Hello, I'm Fleur.'

'Yes, I remember you. You're Auntie Mirabelle's daughter.'

'That's right,' I say. That thing happens to me where I get a lump in my throat and my heart starts to race. It was so easy for her to say that. She knew it and she said it. It's odd being around people like that.

'Anansy is ill,' Mrs C says with a slight raise of her eyebrows that tells me she thinks Anansy is pulling a fast one but has let her stay off school all the same.

Dutifully, Anansy forces out a little cough and rearranges her face to look pitiful enough to have been let off school.

'I thought it was your tummy that felt funny?' Mrs C says with another raised eyebrow.

'It is, Mama, but my throat is a little bit coughy, too.'

'Right,' Mrs C replies with a 'give me strength' expression. *Just like a real mother would*, I think. I don't remember if she, Mirabelle, was the kind of mother who let me stay off school if I was ill. I reckon she was all, 'Your head has to be falling off before I think about maybe letting you stay off'. Dad was always keen to keep me at home, but only when he had someone to look after me. When he was between 'friends' I had to go in no matter what. I push aside thoughts of him. I bet he's been ringing my phone non-stop. I bet he's getting himself all worked up and probably thinking about coming down here to drag my sorry ass back up to London. Well, that's what happens to you when you're a liar – people stop speaking to you.

'Coffee?' Mrs C asks me.

'Yes, please,' I say. I look at Anansy, and she grins at me, the pitiful look banished in an instant. I look around at Mrs C, to see if she's noticed that her daughter is clearly not ill. Mrs C is at the other end of the kitchen with the kettle in one hand while staring at the tap as if it's going to bite her if she touches it. I return my gaze to Anansy, who tells me to come and sit next to her by doing the 'come here' gesture quickly with her hand so her mother doesn't see.

Doing as I'm told, I go over to the sofa and she scooches up, and grins at me again that I'm playing along. She's cute. Proper cute. There are some girls who are just, you know, cute-looking and pretty-haired, but this one has cuteness running through her. And cheekiness. I'd love to see how Mrs C is going to deal with her when she gets older. There'll be a line of boys outside the house.

'Don't think I haven't noticed you're not too sick to get yourself some company over there, Anansy Challey,' Mrs C says, making both of us jump. We huddle together, pulling 'we're in trouble' faces. Anansy shifts again, this time to put her legs on top of mine then the duvet over the pair of us.

I grin at her and she grins back at me, the hole where her front tooth should be adding to her over-the-top cuteness. She's examining me, I realise. Looking at me like I'm something she's just seen in her storybook for the first time. 'You're the little girl who's like me, aren't you?' she says.

I frown at her, then look at Mrs C, who has apparently got over her fear of the tap and has placed her kettle on its stand, but pauses in switching it on.

Anansy could be right, I maybe looked a little like her when I was growing up, we have similar texture hair, and the same kind of lips, and maybe our eyes are slightly similar in shape, but we're not really that much alike.

'What are you saying, Ansy?' Mrs C asks, her affectionate name for her daughter like a knife in my heart. She, Mirabelle, called me Fleury. And I told her I hated that name so she stopped. It was after the time she called me Roza to her friend. I wanted to hurt her like she had hurt me by not telling people about me so I made her stop. I didn't really hate it, I just wanted her to feel how bad I felt for a moment.

'She's the little girl who's like me,' the six-year-old on the sofa says to her mother. 'Auntie Mirabelle told me.'

'My mother told you I'm like you?'

'She said there was a little girl who looked like me but she had hair that went all gold in the sun. And she said the little girl asked questions all the time and she liked the beach story too. She said she had to tell the little girl the beach story every night to go to sleep.'

'When did she tell you this?' Mrs C asks.

'All the time. She told Cora too, but Cora didn't really like to listen 'cos the little girl wasn't like her, she was like me. Auntie Mirabelle said the little girl used to sometimes get freckles on her nose. And she was always trying to count the stars even though she couldn't see them from her bedroom window.'

That little piece of me that is missing is opening up, it is getting wider and wider inside me. In bed every night I'd tell her I was going to count the stars after I had my story. *How are you going to do that, Fleury-Boo, when you can't see the stars from your bed?* she would ask.

'I know they're there, Mum,' I would say back. *'So I just have to count them in my pretending.'*

'That's a good idea,' she'd say.

'What else did she say?' Mrs C asks, which I'm grateful for because I can't speak.

Anansy shrugs her little pj'd shoulders and goes back to stuffing the frog into the box, even though bits of it keep springing out. 'I think I don't remember, actually.'

'Just try,' Mrs C coaxes.

'OK. She said the little girl liked cows and she used to buy her little toy cows all the time. And I said that wasn't like me because I like sheep. And frogs. And pigs. And rabbits.

And horses. And Auntie Mirabelle said the little girl liked all of those, too, but she liked cows most of all. She said she sewed the little girl a cow blanket that felt all soft like a cow, so the little girl could cuddle it when she went to sleep.'

'I was never there when she said these things,' Mrs C says.

'Yes you were, Mama. She said it all the time. But you were too busy making the dinner, I think.'

'Oh, OK,' Mrs C says.

'I asked if I could play with the little girl but Auntie Mirabelle said she was all grown up now. And I said that doesn't matter I could still play with her. And Auntie Mirabelle said "I would like that, and so would she. I'll ask her one day, shall I?" And I said, yes.' Anansy raises her forefinger to point at me. 'That little girl is you, isn't it?'

My head is nodding because I still can't speak. I feel like my heart is caving in, like everything she is saying is causing me to crumble inside.

'Do you still have your cow blanket?' she asks.

I do, I want to tell her. I packed it up and took it with me. It's so old and the soft furriness of it now threadbare, the black cow splodges almost completely faded out, but I'd had it since I was tiny, and every night I slept at home, I folded it under my chin and would hold onto it. I brought it with me because it was as much a part of me as the skin on my body, but I'd put it away since Noah had arrived. (Didn't want him thinking I was a freak or nothing like that.)

I didn't know she had made it for me. It was obviously hand-made, the seams all crooked and the stitching uneven, but I'd had it as long as I could remember, so just assumed it'd been given to me by a relative who couldn't sew straight. I didn't realise that all these years, I'd had something she had made with love for me. I nod at the little girl again.

'Can I see it?'

'She hasn't got it here, you know, Ansy. Maybe you can see it another time.'

'Would you like to play with me?' Anansy asks, holding out the frog and the little silver box. 'I'm trying to make a frog in a box to surprise Cora. I want it to jump and say boo at her. I have to do the boo bit, but I think I can do it if I get it into the box. Do you want to play?'

'Yes,' I say and have to clear my throat twice of the lump in it to say that word. 'I would like to play with you very much.'

Anansy grins again. 'Auntie Mirabelle was right.'

Sixteen years ago

'Do you want me to tell you the story of The Rose Petal Beach?'

'Yes, yes, yes.'

'Well then, Fleury-Boo, get into bed and I will start. But you mustn't be sad if you fall asleep, I'll tell you the rest tomorrow.'

'I won't fall asleep, Mum.'

'You say that every night and every night you fall asleep.'

'Not tonight, Mum, I promise you.'

'OK, here goes . . .'

*

414

After the children are in bed, Mrs C opens a bottle of wine and we sit at the table in the kitchen with our full glasses in front of us. First coffee, now wine!

Earlier, I used Mrs C's phone to check and Noah is back at the hotel, his was one of the few numbers I knew off by heart before I destroyed my phone. I feel kind of free without it. I can't know what's going on all the time because I'm not constantly plugged into the world. There's no FB, Twitter, no blog, and there's no internet. No texts, no calls, no games. I'm living without the wider world being able to get in touch with me and I love it. I know it can't last forever, the police, for one, have no way of getting in touch to tell me when I can go to her house, but I'm enjoying being out of it all. It's a bit like being from *The Matrix*, you know? I've been unplugged and I get to breathe real air and live out here instead of inside my phone.

'What time is your husband coming home?' I ask her. I want to be gone before he gets back. Can't stand the thought of what he did – being around him is not something I want.

She presses her lips tight together, then puts her glass to them and tries to take a sip. 'He's not,' she says when she seems to have worked out that she can't drink with her mouth closed. 'He's gone. I made him leave. I found out he was lying about pretty much everything and he had to leave.'

My body unclenches a bit. I don't have to worry, don't have to listen out for the key in the door in case it's him. 'Oh,' I say. I'm not much good at this stuff. I'm not very good at giving comfort or finding the right thing to say.

'That's why I let Anansy stay off today. She and Cora are

pretty unsettled by everything that's happened lately so I'm letting them get away with a few things. Not everything, but some things.'

'Has he left for good?'

'I don't want to think about it, let alone talk about it, to be honest, Fleur. It's all such a big mess. Most of it of my making. If I'd been a little less blind and little more brave, a lot of things wouldn't have happened. I wouldn't have fallen out with your mother, for one.'

'I don't know what to say.'

'You don't have to say anything. But I have to tell you that the police think I'm involved with your mother's death.'

The hot policeman told me that. 'Oh,' I say.

'They say they have evidence that puts me in the house the night she, you know. That's what they questioned me about the other day.'

'Did you do it?' The words are out of my mouth just like that! It doesn't feel real, that's why. It's like I'm watching all of this on the telly and I can ask the person next to me, 'Who do you think did it?' and they'll tell me it was the mother of two who seems nice and safe and all that. That's when I'll say, 'It can't have been her because women who wear skinny jeans and give people wine and coffee don't do the crime.'

She stops the glass halfway to her mouth and puts it down again.

'No,' she says, staring at the glass. Slowly she lifts her head and turns to me. 'No, I didn't.'

I want to believe her, I really do. But you know what, I think of all the television shows I've watched and it's almost always the quiet ones. It's almost always the person who sits there and should be innocent, but you can tell by the way they hold themselves, the way their eyes don't settle on anything for too long, the way their hands shake suddenly for no reason, that they have something pretty big to hide.

'OK,' I say.

'Do you want me to tell you about your mother?'

'No,' I say, then gulp a couple of mouthfuls of the wine, which is really nice. It's posh stuff, of course. 'I think I'd better go, Noah's waiting for me.'

She nods and her eyes follow me as I get up and grab my denim jacket which is hanging over the back of the chair and pick up my bag, a knock-off Gucci Yasmin got me from Dubai last year.

'I'll see you, Mrs C,' I say to her at the door.

'Yes, see you. Drop by any time.'

'I will. And say thank you to Anansy for me. She's really made my day.'

She nods and smiles.

I like Mrs C so much, I think as I walk down the road. *I just wish I knew what it was she was hiding.*

15

Beatrix

Scott, I love you. I need you right now. Please. I have two friends and you're one of them. The other one is the woman you're married to. I can't talk to her for obvious reasons, so it'll have to be you. Please, call me. I love you. Bea x

Tami

I didn't expect to miss him.

I didn't expect to wake up every morning and wonder why the other half of the bed felt so deserted; then wish he'd come back to cuddle me, to complete the other half of our 99. I didn't expect to watch the girls do something and immediately grab my phone to text him about it only to remember that wasn't how it worked any more. I'm leaving him alone to get in touch and when he does, we can talk about him seeing the girls. I miss him in the space before I remember *who* he is and *what* he did.

Driving back from dropping the girls at my parents' house for the long May Bank Holiday weekend, the dread starts in my feet. I have three days on my own. I could have stayed, spent time with them, Sarto's and Genevieve's children, but I knew it would be wiser to have time on my own with space to think.

I need to formulate a plan, something I can cling to when it all gets too hard, something that I can call on when I want to let him back. Because I will. Despite everything, I know I will be weak, I will be scared of the future on my own, I will convince myself it is the best thing for the girls when in reality it would be the worst thing ever. If I plan now, when

I still have enough strength to hate him, it will save me from making bad decisions in the future.

'I just need to know why you stabbed me in the back,' I say. These words are reverberating from my memory, a new piece for the jigsaw of that night. I've stopped fighting them now, I've stopped being afraid. It's better to know what really happened, so when these fragments of that night blow across my mind like dust motes, I let them settle and reveal themselves.

'I just need to know why you stabbed me in the back.'

'You can believe whatever else you like about me, but I wouldn't do that to you,' she says. 'Especially not with him.'

'Why would he lie?' I say. I'm too drunk to stay upright, my legs give way and I collapse in a heap on the floor.

She shakes her head at me, such sadness on her face.

'Maybe he's not lying about what he's been up to,' she says, 'just who with? Maybe that's why you're so willing to believe what he's told you because deep down you know he's got someone else.'

'I saw the text messages,' I say to her.

'What text messages? I never sent him any text messages. If you knew how much I hated him, you would know that I wanted nothing to do with him so there's no way on Earth I'd send him text messages.'

'"I know it's wrong but I can't help feeling how I do. I know you're married, but I'm willing to wait. I'd wait a lifetime for you to be ready to be with me properly. It'll cause a lot of hurt, and I'm not proud of that, but I love you",' I say to her. 'You wrote that, didn't you?'

Shocked, she blinks at me.

'You need to leave, right now,' she says and starts to pick me up.

I don't want to be picked up, I am perfectly happy sitting on the floor with the world not spinning. 'Get off me, just get off! I told you not to touch me!' I am hitting back at her, kicking out so she will leave me alone. 'Don't come near me! Just go away! Don't touch me!'

Gone. As suddenly as it came, it is gone and I'm left chasing it, trying to get it back, forcing myself to recall what happened next, wh— There's someone standing in the road! Without thinking I slam on the brakes, and I'm thrown forwards as the car comes to a sudden, emergency stop.

I sit for several seconds, my hands welded to the padded leather steering wheel over which I have been flung, hyperventilating. I almost killed someone. I almost hit them. Sitting back, I try to slow my breathing, settle my hurtling heart. I almost killed someone.

I rest the palm of my hand on my lips then rapidly blow out and inhale deeply, convincing my body to slow down, calm down. It didn't happen; I stopped in time; nobody got hurt today. When my chest loosens and I can breathe normally again, when my mind quietens and I can think again, when my heart resumes its normal beat and the feeling starts to return to my body, I look out of the windscreen. Expecting the person to be long gone, disappeared into the night of Providence Close, unaware how close they came to almost losing their life.

The person is still there. Standing stock-still in the road, looking off down the street and not at the car that almost ended their existence. A shock of platinum blonde hair is illuminated by my headlights, a slender, almost sculpted neck, a petite frame, too. It's her.

'What is wrong with you?' I shout at her once I am out of the car. 'Haven't you done enough to wreck my life already? You want me to go to prison for running you down, too?'

She hasn't moved from the spot in the road where she was when I almost ran her down, but now I have spoken, she revolves slowly until she is facing me. Her eyes are flat and she stares at me as though she is looking without seeing. Automatically I reach for her, to offer comfort before I remember who she is, what she is.

'I don't care what you do, but don't hang around in the road. You're lucky I managed to stop in time, the next driver might not be so lucky. I'd hate for that to happen to them.'

She blinks, suddenly, coming out of the trance she was in, arriving here in the present with an almost audible thud.

'Tami,' she states. 'I was coming over to talk to you but you're here. Thank you. Thanks for coming.'

Beatrix isn't making sense and although she is now here, her eyes are still unconnected, and bloodshot, the black pupils huge. 'Have you been taking something?' I say.

Visibly puzzled by my question she shakes her head, her blonde waves undulating seductively as she moves her head side to side. I can't stop an image of his hand in her hair as they lay entangled together on the bed in the master bedroom of our house flashing up in my mind. My stomach lurches.

'No. Why would I take something?'

'Why am I even talking to you?' I ask her. 'What do I care about your life?' I turn towards my car.

'I'm sorry,' she says loudly. 'That's what I was coming to say to you. I'm sorry. I didn't say it last time we spoke. But I am. I'm sorry.'

425

I stop walking and wait. Wait for her words to sink into my body and to blunt the shards of pain that have been stabbing at my heart. Nothing. It's not enough. I don't know what will be, but not that.

'I need to tell you something,' she calls at me.

I begin to walk again, because there is nothing for me here, and there is nothing she can tell me that will take away what she has done and will make me stop to talk to her. Until she says it. She utters the only words that could stop me in my tracks, cause me to spin on my heels and stare at her.

'I'm having his baby,' she says.

I continue to stare at the woman who is out late on a cool night wearing a yellow, sleeveless summer dress and red flip-flops. I stare because that is not what she said. I thought she was going to say that, I braced myself to hear her say that. But that wasn't it, those weren't the words.

I open my mind again, replay them. And this time I hear them.

What she said is: 'I have breast cancer.'

Beatrix

Do you know, I want to be feisty right now. I want to face this thing head-on, let nothing hold me back. I want to be that woman who stands up in a warrior stance and shouts: 'I am woman. I am Beatrix Carenden, I will not let this defeat me, I will fight this battle and I will be victorious.'

The woman I am wants to curl up into a ball. She wants someone's arms around her, she wants their hushes in her ear as they murmur it will be OK. The woman I am wants to whisper the truth. The truth is: I am scared.

I am scared of pain.

I am scared of being alone.

I am scared of leaving without having made any tangible impression upon the Earth.

I am scared of the end.

I am scared. I am scared. I am scared. I am scared.

I am not cut out for this and I am scared.

Tami

The woman I nearly ran over is sitting in the front passenger seat. I didn't tell her to get in, I simply got in myself then opened the passenger door. Now she is sitting next to me, all clipped in, and I am driving her home.

I steal a glance at her: The Other Woman. My husband's lover. She is diminished. She was always perfect, always on good form, probably always up for it. Until this moment. Now, she is fragile and delicate, silent and shaken, in the front seat of my car.

'Thank you,' she says as I pull up outside her house. 'Really, thank you.'

I drove past Mirabelle's house on the way round. It is empty. You can feel the emptiness of it; even in the car, you can feel the weight of what is missing, who has departed, has been taken. My fingers had crushed themselves into the steering wheel, holding on to tether myself in the present. I did not want to revisit the memories with this other woman around. All the same, Mirabelle was in my mind, at my shoulder, telling me what I had to do: I had done a terrible thing to her so I had to do the right thing now.

'I'll see you then,' she says.

I nod while staring out of the windscreen.

'And I really am sorry.'

I nod again, still not looking at her.

'Tami . . .'

I finish her sentence for her by reaching down and firing the ignition, checking the mirrors and pulling out of my parking spot outside her house.

Beatrix

Hi ya. Could you call me when you get the chance? I don't know what's going on with you, but I could really do with hearing your voice. Love you. Bea x

One year ago

'Your tits are my most favourite part of your body,' he said.

'They're breasts not tits,' I said. 'And thank you, that's one of the nicest things you've ever said to me.'

Scott rolled his eyes. He was emperor of the 'give me strength' eye roll and king of the near-silent, frustrated sigh. 'Don't come over all politically correct on me, I get enough of that at home.'

'"Tits" sounds so ... So ... Dismissive? Is that the word? "Breasts" sounds like sex, "tits" sounds like an unsatisfying quickie.'

His thumbs began stroking my nipples, causing pleasure to ricochet to all the right places. 'I love your breasts, tits, boobs,' he murmured. 'They're my favourite part of your body.'

I lay back on the bed, giving him a full view of my body. 'What about my legs? Aren't they your favourite?' I stroked my hands along the length of them. He shook his head. 'What about my bottom?' I ran my fingers up the sides of my bum. He shook his head. 'What about my stomach?' I stroked along my abdomen. He shook his head. 'What about my arms?' I stretched them out to show him. He shook his head. 'So it's true? These are your most favourite part of my body?' I coyly ran my fingers over the curve of my breasts. The pale skin was smooth to the touch because I kept out of the sun and exfoliated and moisturised every day. Slowly and seductively I circled the small, pink mounds of my nipples and the soft, paler-pink areola with the pads of my fingers. Nobody had said my breasts were their most favourite part of my body before. I liked it, though, that Scotty had said it, that he thought enough about me to have a favourite part of me.

In case you hadn't noticed, I like my body. I *love* my body. It is perfectly proportioned, it is slender and it is curvy and it is basically who I am. Women have all these hang-ups about their bodies, apparently. We worry about the size of our bums, the size of our breasts, the flatness of our stomachs. It's true, I do see this going on around me, but I've never joined in. I don't think like that, fret in that way, because I love my body.

My body hates me.

My body has turned on me. It has turned on me in that sneaky, snide way of a friend who stabs you in the back. It has done this thing to me, it has made this thing in my body and it is slowly destroying me. I don't know how long it's been going on for, but now it is out in the open, it hurts like nothing I have experienced before. Yes, I know my body has done to me what I have done to her, but that doesn't make it right, does it? And I never set out to hurt her.

I love my body, my body is making me suffer.

I wasn't alone when the doctor gently broke the news. The surgeon was there, the specialist nurse was there, too. The specialist nurse sat beside me as the doctor started to talk. I should have known when they both trooped into the room that I wasn't going to be told the blueberry-sized lump I found on the left side of my cleavage was nothing more serious than a cyst. I didn't guess, though, because since I had gone to the clinic for the tests, and had waited around for the preliminary results, my mind kept wandering, going astray like a child let out without reins. At every stage I had to keep bringing my mind back to where I was, what was happening, instead of wondering when Scott was going to get in contact. Which team in the league would go into administration. How many more wears I'd get out of the Prada Mary Janes I'd bought in New York. Every time I forced my mind to focus on what was happening, I discovered this was happening: I was sitting in a room with two people I had been briefly introduced to, being told my body had turned on me.

When the doctor told me, I had a sudden sensation of standing on a desert island, surrounded by sand and sea and knowing I was alone in this. I was stranded and no one could save me, could rescue me.

As I looked up and down the island, searching for a means of escape, I thought of all the people who would try, who would care enough to navigate the sea to get to me, take my hand, let me know I wasn't alone. The sea was empty for a long, long time as the vision played out before my eyes. I was standing alone on that desert island for a lifetime until I saw that person. The one person who would try to save me, who would care enough to want to be with me at a time like this. It wasn't him, but you knew that, didn't you? I knew that, too. He's going through some stuff and needs space right now. If I told him, if he knew, I'm sure he'd want to be here. He'd want to take me in his arms and hold me, and reassure me and tell me it's all going to be OK. He'd tell me he was coming to all my appointments with me, he would promise to hold my hand through all the treatments, and he would look at me and see who he's always seen, the woman he fell for – he won't see the woman I am going to turn into. He won't see the woman whose body has decided it hates her.

The person in the sea, the one who would go through anything, I think, to get me safe and secure again? You know. Of course you know.

Tami places a mug of tea in front of me, and retreats to the other side of her kitchen. She doesn't want to get too close to me, that's clear. Why would she?

But still, she let me in her car, she drove me home – to mine first and then to her home – and she sat me in the kitchen and made me tea. 'The kids are with my parents,' she said as we came in and I tried to shut the door quietly. 'It's just me here.'

'*And me,*' I wanted to pipe up. '*I'm here, too. I'm not gone yet.*'

My eyes automatically go to my mobile on the table in front of me. Nothing.

She stands with her back to the worktop she's in front of, her arms outstretched but gripping onto the solid wood, her head lowered, her body still and tense. 'When did you find out?' she asks.

'Erm . . . I . . . What day is it? Friday?'

She nods without raising her head.

'OK, if it's Friday, then I found out two days ago. On Wednesday.' In about two weeks I should know everything: what type, what grade, the treatment options, apparently. I remember that.

Tami nods again, as if slowly taking in my words with her head trained downwards.

'It only hit me tonight. I heard what the doctor said, I understood it, but it didn't seem real until earlier on when everything sort of snapped into focus and it hit me like a truck.' I take a sip of my drink. 'It's hard to describe that feeling.'

A small, humourless smile fades in and out on her face, and she lifts herself upright and stares out of the blackened glass of the bi-fold doors. 'Yeah,' she says quietly, her gaze still fixed on the doors and not in my direction. 'I know that feeling.'

Tami's been through this, too? Her body has turned on her, too? When? Why didn't I know— She means finding out about me and Scott. About all the stuff that came before when she thought it was Mirabelle and Scott. Although it's not the same, surely? Can you genuinely feel that broken, *traumatised*, by finding out someone you've already fallen out of love with has found love elsewhere? Really?

I want to ask her about him. How he is. How he's coping being away from the girls. I can't ask though. I am in the presence of the one person in the world who has access to the man I love, and I can't ask about him for fear of what it would unleash. *This* is torture.

Why do I keep cycling between feeling scared, sick and falling apart to worrying about him? Not about myself, or Tami or anyone else, just him. It must be because I love him so much, but that doesn't seem a complete enough explanation to me. It doesn't seem to fit. Is this me flitting in and out of denial? Is this me not wanting to face what comes next by concentrating on something else I have absolutely no control over? Do two out of control things make a whole?

'Who have you told?' she asks.

'I, erm, haven't told Scott, if that's what you mean. I haven't spoken to him since he left.'

She shakes her head, still refusing to look in my direction. I can see the lines of her face reflected in the night-blackened doors and she looks a little incredulous. 'No,' she replies, 'that's not what I meant. I . . . I don't actually care if you've spoken to him. That's your business. Since you're here now, with me, of all people, I'm guessing you haven't told that many people or anyone else. I was wondering if there was anyone you wanted me to call to be with you so I could take you home.' That's why she brought me here after stopping outside my house: she didn't want me to be alone. She knew I had no one else, and she didn't want to deliver me into the cold, icy grasp of an empty flat after my diagnosis. She doesn't want to rescue me, she doesn't want to help me, she wants rid of me.

A lump gathers violently in my throat, I can barely swallow

or breathe. Carefully, I place the mug on the table, my eyes going to the silent mobile phone in front of me. She doesn't want me here. Why would she? But I have no one else.

We are breathing in sync, Tami and I. Both of us taking in deep chunks of air and releasing them at length. We are living in time. I wonder if our hearts are beating in time, too? I used to listen to Scott's heartbeat, trying to will it to match mine, trying to confirm that we were meant to be together no matter how much the world said it was wrong. I believe that our soulmate is the person whose heart beats in time with ours, who contracts and expands at the same most basic, vital level with us. Our heartbeats never matched in all the times I got to listen, but that doesn't mean they wouldn't in the future. That one shock that caused one of our hearts to stop for a moment wouldn't result in them beating in time.

Is my heart beating in time with Tami's? Are our hearts beating in time because we loved the same man? Are we soulmates because she's all I have?

Her fingers are curled so tight into the rim of the worktop, I'm sure she's leaving indents. She wants me to leave. The silence, the heavy, relentless silence, is because she wants me to leave. She brought me here, but now she wants me to go. She won't say it, though. She doesn't want to be the one to send me back to an empty home.

I should offer to go, to leave her alone. I'm not going to. I know that makes me a bad person. But I can't be alone right now.

I have cancer. I can't be alone right now. Even if it means being here in complete silence, with only the rhythm of our breathing to link us.

436

Tami

She is asleep on my sofa.

It was obvious she wasn't leaving last night. Even more obvious that she knew I wouldn't make her leave. When did I become this person? When did I become the doormat that people like my husband and his mistress think they can walk all over?

We stood and sat in silence in the kitchen for a long time as I waited for her to get up and leave. Like any other normal person would. Is she a normal person? I'm starting to have my doubts. Who does what she has done to our family and then still wants to be around when the reason for what she did is gone? Or is she still here because she thinks I'll call Scott and tell him and he'll come riding in to save her?

I would do that to get rid of her if it didn't involve the act of calling Scott. I have told Cora and Anansy that he is staying away on business for a long time, and they have seemed fine with it. He calls them on the house phone – I know it's him because I changed the number to stop Beatrix calling – and only he has the number. He tells them he's working hard and misses them and that they should take care of Mummy. He doesn't ask to speak to me and I don't want to talk to him. They haven't asked if he is in prison – which I was expecting – but I suspect they talk about it among themselves. I am trying to fill up their lives with lots of other people, lots of other things so they don't dwell on the atmosphere in the house before their dad left. He's not coming back. I haven't said that to them, yet.

One of the reasons he was not coming back was sitting in the kitchen, desperate not to leave.

After a while, I went upstairs to what used to be the master bedroom – I still hadn't moved back in there – and dragged off the duvet and the pillow. Leaving them in the living room, I went back to the kitchen.

'You can sleep on the sofa,' I said, then left without saying goodnight, left before she thanked me or added another sorry to the list.

She is still asleep. It is nine o'clock and she is still asleep. I did not sleep, the images of her and him drove me from my bed to my office. I sat there working until the birds started to sing and the sun started to bleed into the sky.

I cannot imagine sleeping if I had that news. I don't think I would be able to let go enough to sleep; if I could stand to lose my grip on consciousness knowing I might never regain it. I've often thought that going to sleep was an act of faith, was believing without any proof whatsoever that you would wake up again.

'What time is it?' she asks without opening her eyes. Her dress lies in a pool on top of her flip-flops. How many times has she been like that – naked or as near naked as possible – in this room, in this house?

'Nine,' I reply.

'Can't believe I've slept.' She still has her eyes closed. 'That's the first night's sleep I've had since I found out.'

438

I haven't slept properly since I found out. Enough so I'm not a danger to the children or myself, but nowhere near enough to make me feel healthy, whole, *human*.

'I can't open my eyes because if I see you I'll remember that I need to say sorry to you over and over again.'

'Did you do it in my bed?'

Her eyes open and she takes a few seconds to locate me in the room. 'No, no we didn't,' she says.

'OK,' I reply. 'I've got a lot on today, so . . .' Get dressed and leave.

'Right, of course, of course.' She doesn't move. Simply closes her eyes again and pulls the duvet up towards her ears. She is going nowhere.

Beatrix

I can't believe she'd ask me that.

Of course we made love in her bed. We did it in most of the rooms in this house except the children's room and the downstairs toilet. We even did it in her office. I hated doing that, invading her private space with something so craven, but he'd insisted. I'd cried afterwards because it was a terrible thing to do: sitting on top of him in her chair, making love while looking at the certificates framed on the walls, the awards on the mantelpiece, the organised chaos of piles of work all over the place. The plethora of happy pictures of the children. 'I'm sorry,' he'd said when he realised how upset I was at what I'd let myself be talked into. 'That was a rotten thing to do. I feel awful now. We won't do that again.'

The bed was my preferred place in the house. It made me feel legitimate, as if it was only a matter of time before we'd be in there together, permanently.

It wasn't right, but we all do crazy things when we're in love, please remember that.

Why did she ask, though? It's not as if her knowing the truth would make her feel better.

I can't believe she did that to herself.

Tami

When Cora was about two-and-a-half I had this fantasy that she would allow herself to be 'contained' by a playpen. I had it set up in the kitchen so I could cook while she played with toys, maybe while watching a video or two. She'd still be near me, still see me, but I could get things done. The reality was completely different. The reality was more in keeping with all I'd learnt about parenting – you know absolutely nothing because every child is different so the rules very often don't apply. I would open the gate to the hexagonal playpen, lined with a thick, bouncy cushion – perfect if she wanted to lie down for a nap (I was seriously deluded) – furnished with all her favourite toys, and she would stand in front of me, fingers of one hand laced into the black metal bars, never allowing one foot to leave the tiles of the kitchen floor while her free hand would stretch into the pen, reaching for a toy. 'Just go in,' I would encourage, 'and get the toy.' She would ignore me, reaching and reaching, rather than allow herself to be 'tricked' into going in alone to somewhere she didn't want to be, lest I left her behind.

Beatrix is acting like Cora at two-and-a-half.

I've brought her home, walked with her in silence because it was clear I wasn't going to get rid of her until I took control of the situation. Now she is standing at the door, going through her bag, looking for her keys, even though several times her body has relaxed that fraction we all do when we find what we're looking for. When that can't be drawn out any longer, she puts the key in the lock and tries very hard to find that the key doesn't work. When it does, of course, she takes an age to open the door.

'I'll see you,' I say to her and she swings to me, her eyes wide and horrified. Just like Cora's eyes when I picked her up and tried to place her in the playpen. She would twist her little body, constantly moving her legs so it would be awkward to put her down without hurting her, all the while her eyes wide with the potential betrayal I was attempting to perpetrate upon her.

'Erm . . . I . . .' she says, visibly trembling at the thought of being alone. 'Could you, erm, wait until I get in?'

Scott used to ask taxi drivers to do that for me. *'Could you just wait until she gets in before you drive away?'* he'd say. He knew, even then, that danger could be found right on your doorstep; exactly where you thought you were safe.

'I, erm, get nervous ever since . . . you know, Mirabelle. I don't like being alone.'

That is low, even for someone capable of the low acts I know Beatrix to be capable of (of course she did it in my bed, I just wanted to know how honest she'd be). It's also plausible she could be worried: we don't know why Mirabelle was killed. Mirabelle wasn't . . . Wasn't interfered with sexually before her death, the house wasn't burgled, but it could still have been a random killing, or a killing by someone preying on single women living alone. It could have been an

442

act carried out by a woman who was so drunk and angry she didn't know what she was doing.

I know Beatrix has a right to be scared right now, but she is asking too much of me. She is asking for my help, my companionship. She wants me to be with her while she tries to stay alive. Through all of it. Through going into this flat that maybe has a psycho killer waiting for her to the long journey she is now facing. She hasn't said that, of course, but that's what she's thinking. She doesn't want to go into that playpen on her own.

'You have no right to ask this of me,' I tell her.

'I know,' she says. Her eyes find mine, the corners of her mouth turn down. 'And I'm sorry. I'm truly sorry.'

Mirabelle, she's there again. She's at my shoulder, she's in my head, she's weighing on my conscience over the last time I saw her. 'Just go and get your stuff,' I say to her.

'Thank you,' she says, immediately brimming over with tears. 'Thank you.' She slides her key into the door and dashes off to pack, obviously moving at speed in case I suddenly change my mind.

I won't change my mind. I'm not doing it for her. I'm doing it for the friend I let down.

Beatrix

'I'll take the girls to school on Thursday, if you'd like?' I say to Tami.

She is pushing laundry into the gaping hole of the washing machine. The kitchen and house smell of the chicken roasting in the oven. This is a Saturday job for her. Once the chicken is done, she'll strip it of its meat and put the pieces in separate bags, two for the fridge and the rest will go in the freezer. She'll put the carcass into a bag in the freezer, too. When she has five carcasses she'll make a batch of chicken stock. At the same time she'll make vegetable stock. Today isn't a stock-making day. While the laundry washes, she'll start making food for the freezer for the fortnight. Once the laundry is done, she'll hang it out. At some point she'll do the Hoovering and clean the bathrooms. Another batch of washing will go on. Usually, she has the girls while she's trying to get things done. Usually, she will be keeping them busy while trying to organise the house so they can maybe go and do something in the afternoon. Usually, she does this all alone because Scott is in bed with me.

Tami continues to push clothes into the washing machine and without raising her head says, 'No thank you.'

'It's no trouble. I'd love to do it,' I say.

She raises herself to her full height, slams shut the

porthole to the laundry, and concentrates on setting the dials, on pouring the powder in the drawer, on pushing the 'start' button. 'I said no thank you.'

'I want to help out,' I explain. 'Take my mind off things.'

When Tami rotates to regard me for long silent seconds, I forget for a moment who I am, what I am facing, and I see my friend. She looks horrendous. That's not me being bitchy, that's me being concerned. Her hair is pulled back into a ponytail and shows that her face is a greyish-brown, and a mass of blotches and pimples. The dramatic weight loss is apparent on her cheeks, her neck, her shoulders . . . her entire body. She is swamped by the Goonies T-shirt she has pulled on, the jogging bottoms that are sitting on her hips like baggy clown trousers were once figure-hugging and flattering. *When was the last time you ate?* I want to ask her. *When was the last time you took care of yourself?*

'Do you really want to help out, or do you want to go back to playing replacement mummy to my children?' she asks.

I wasn't expecting that. Like that moment back when she told me she knew Scott and I were lovers, I wasn't expecting her to say that. I don't know what I was expecting, what I thought would happen if I stayed here, but not this. I suppose I hoped she would hold my hand. She'd ask me if I wanted to talk, would let me express my feelings and fears, would sit with her arm around me and reassure me. Maybe she would encourage me to cry, to unplug the bottle of terrors that are inside me and release them.

'I, erm, it wasn't like that,' I say.

'It was exactly like that. From day one it's been like that. You wanted my husband, my house, my children when they came along. I thought your interest in us was because you were on your own and needed a family, that's why I kept encouraging you to become part of our lives. That's why I didn't mind Scott going to the football with you, coming over to do odd jobs for you, going for a quick drink with you. I thought . . . I thought you were my friend and all along you were after my life.'

It honestly isn't that simple. Remember how I sort of told Rufus that I wanted that love at first sight thing? That I needed to find that with a man who, when I looked into the future, I'd know we'd be together? I had that with Scott. That very first time we met, I felt a pull towards him that I had never experienced before. As he spoke, I knew I wanted him to be talking about me like that. I wanted him to call me amazing, to be quietly euphoric that I was having his baby, and starting a new life together. I didn't set out to get him, but I did love him from afar. I wouldn't have done all this if I didn't love him. 'Tami—'

'That's why you hated Mirabelle, isn't it? She saw right through you.'

'I know you won't understand this,' I speak carefully, knowing how much this will hurt her, 'but I loved him. Since . . . Since we met, I fell in love with him and I never wanted to hurt you. I *was* your friend, it *was* genuine. I just loved him, too.'

Even before anything began I used to feel sick sometimes visiting when he was at home because I was terrified she would see how I felt about him. I used to crave seeing him, though, *anything* to be around him. If not him, the girls because they were a part of him. Sometimes it was enough to be around Tami because she had been with him. It scared me how much I wanted him, wanted to be with him. When we started our affair I was frightened every day that he would end it. That he would choose Tami, or that his guilt would kick in. I was never relaxed, never stable about us. I had to keep myself available, play games by telling him about other men to keep his interest, do things I'd sworn after my husband left I wouldn't do again because of how degraded, dirty and worthless they made me feel. I hated myself for it, but I would have done anything to keep him, I did do anything to try to keep him. I did everything he asked me to.

'Well, as long as you loved him, that's all right then, isn't it?' she says.

'No, Tami, I didn't mean it like that.'

'When's your next appointment?' she says in reply.

'Wednesday. Further tests, pre-op information.'

'What time?'

'Ten.'

'Fine. I'll book a taxi for nine o'clock. Driving into Brighton at that time will be an exercise in the hell that is parking, otherwise. We can go to a café until it's time to go in. I'll make sure the girls can have tea at a friend's house in case we're not back in time.'

'You're still coming with me?'

'Did I ever have any choice?' She stares at me while awaiting my answer.

We all have choices. Every single one of us. Some of us are too blind to see them. Some of us don't make use of them. Some of us don't use them correctly. And some us are completely robbed of them because we are trapped in a situation we can't escape. We still have choices, though.

I lower my gaze and turn to leave the room. 'I really did love him,' I say quietly. I don't know if she hears me but she does not reply. Or maybe she does. She must have because I hear in my head, *Why was your love so important it had to destroy someone else's life?*

Beatrix

Call me? Bea x

'Bix, are you going to live in our house forever?' Anansy asks.

I am taking them to school. Tami asked them if they wanted me to, and they said yes. She was doing it for them, I knew that. And me, I suppose. She knows that although my motives were not pure originally, I do love them. Right now, I need my life to be filled with love. No, I haven't heard from Scott in case you're wondering. I'm tempted to send him a text telling him what's really happening. See if that will shock him into getting in touch. I don't want to think badly of him, I know he's under immense pressure, but I need him. I need him to come here and make it better with his presence and his love.

I'm sleeping in the master bedroom. Clearly she didn't believe me when I said we hadn't done it in the house, we hadn't infected their home with what she obviously thinks of as our treachery.

You see, *I* should feel that what we did was treacherous, but I don't. I'm a terrible person for not feeling horrendously guilty but I simply can't summon it up. Maybe it's the diagnosis, maybe it's because we didn't do it to hurt her. It did hurt her, but we didn't sit there and go, 'Let's make love in front of the fireplace the weekend she takes the girls to visit her folks because that will really traumatise her.' We did it because we wanted to express how we felt about each other with our bodies.

'No,' I reply, 'I'm not going to live in your house forever.' Anansy's hand fits into mine perfectly. Cora is too much of a big girl to hold my hand, except when we cross the roads, when she has no choice in the matter. 'I'm staying until I feel better. I don't feel very well at the moment and your mum said I can stay until I feel better.'

'If Dad gets a bit sick do you think Mama will let him stay until he feels better?' Anansy asks.

'That's not how it works when you get a divorce,' Cora says to Anansy. There was a time when she would have been frustrated and cross with her sister, she would have snapped at her. She is being kind and gentle here. 'That's not how it works when you get a divorce,' she says to me, in case I didn't know.

'Mama didn't say they were going to a dee-vort,' Anansy replies. 'She said Dad was on business for a very, very long time.'

'Do you even know what a divorce is?' Cora asks her.

'Yes!' she says. 'I do,' she says to me. 'I honestly do.'

'I know you do,' I say. I think my bra is too tight – my breath seems to have trouble expanding my lungs, allowing air into them.

'Mama said when they know when Dad's coming home they'll tell us,' Anansy says.

'That's what adults say when they mean someone isn't coming home. They say, "we'll see" when they mean "no" and they say "when we talk about it we'll tell you", when they mean it's already happened.'

'That's not fair,' Anansy says. I've learnt over time that when she says that she actually means, 'That's not right.'

'It is. Isn't it, Bix?' Cora asks, drawing me back into this argument. This argument that I caused.

Maybe Tami didn't have the purest motives for letting me take the girls to school, after all. Maybe she wanted me to see this devastation close up, maybe she wanted me to experience for a few minutes what it felt like to be her and dealing with two children whose dad has gone.

'That's not fair, is it, Bix?' Anansy asks.

They used to call Mirabelle 'auntie' like she was a relative, and I used to love that they didn't do that to me. I was their mate, I was their Bix. Now, when they call me it, it cleaves a knife through my core. I am not their friend, am I? I have done some terrible things to their family. I stop in the middle of the street, lower myself to their level.

I pull them into a hug. 'I love you two,' I say to them. I release them and they both look confused. 'I didn't have a dad growing up.'

'Everyone has a dad,' Anansy explains. 'Otherwise you wouldn't have been borned.'

'She's right,' Cora says.

'Yes, she is. I mean, my dad left when I was very young.'

'Why, were you a bad girl?' Anansy asks.

'Were you?' Cora adds, suspiciously.

'Would you not eat your dinner?'

'Did you draw on the walls?'

451

'Did you break your mama's favourite necklace and hide it down the side of the sofa?'

'Did you spill drink in the car when your mama told you to be careful?'

'Did you break your sister's favourite doll and then pretend it was someone else?'

'I didn't do that!' Cora screeches, rounding on her little sister.

'You did, you did, you did!'

'I didn't, I didn't, I didn't.'

I only wanted to reassure them, give a pep talk that would make them feel loved and wanted; reassure them that their lives would turn out OK even if their dad was away. I wanted them to know that Scott would never do what my dad did – he wouldn't leave for someone else and then refuse to pay for his child or even to see them. He wouldn't reject his offspring every time by saying her mother was the town bike and he had no way of proving she was his; Scott would never say, when confronted with DNA evidence, that he had no room in his life for her no matter how old she is when she tries to contact him. He wouldn't make her feel worthless.

I watch Cora and Anansy bickering, and I'm reminded of the time I rowed in the street with my best friend from school.

Twenty-seven years ago

Eilise Watford was a redhead like me. We both got called 'ginger snap' and we didn't care. We didn't care about anything because we were best friends and we lived on the same road. We used to walk to school together and we'd walk home together. And sometimes we were even allowed to play out front together. Last summer we'd spent lots of time outdoors when Eilise's mum went to visit her sister in Wales who'd had a baby. My mum looked after me and Eilise when Eilise's dad was at work and we always had her over for dinner. Sometimes Eilise was allowed to stay over and we slept in the same bed.

That day, when we were walking to school because we were big girls now and we were allowed to go to school together on our own, she called my mum a bad name.

'Don't say that about my mummy,' I screamed at her and grabbed handfuls of her hair, pulling at it. I'd heard the big children who smoked in the park call one of the girls that word and laugh at her and she'd cried and run away. 'Don't call my mummy that!'

'She is! She is a whore!' Eilise screamed back, trying to get my hands off her head. 'My mummy said so. She kissed my daddy so she's a whore.'

I clawed at her, feeling my short, ragged nails touch her face. I wanted to get her eyes, I wanted to hurt her like her word had hurt me. Her hands pulled at my clothes. We screamed at each other, no words, just screaming, and then Mr Johnson who lived in the house we had stopped in front of was pulling us apart.

'Stop this at once!' he said, holding us apart. He was big and strong and was practically holding us off the ground. 'You're nothing better than common street trash. I shall have both your mothers tan your hides.'

He dragged us both back to our houses. My house was nearest to his so we stopped there first. When Mum opened the door she was shocked that I was there, being held firmly by the neck by Mr Johnson.

'What the devil?' she said.

'Fighting in the street,' Mr Johnson said, sounding very cross. 'The pair of them. I'm going to take this one home. I hope you tan her hide.' He let me go and marched Eilise off to her house.

'Bea, what do you think you're doing?' Mum said, snatching me into the house but checking the road to see who was looking. I didn't care who was looking.

'She called you a bad name!' I screeched at her. She had to know it wasn't my fault.

Mum frowned at me, not understanding. 'What bad name?' she asked.

'She said you kissed her daddy. She said you were a—' I heard our creaky backdoor open, and creak shut again as the latch went. My eyes doubled in size because someone was in the house. I heard footsteps in the backyard. I was wrong: someone was leaving. I'd only just left for school, who could have been in the house?

'Bea,' Mum said, pretending she didn't hear someone going out the back.

I ran. I couldn't get my legs to move fast enough to get me upstairs but I tried. I knew who had been in the house. Even at nine I knew that Eilise wasn't going to be my friend any more. And I knew it was all my mum's fault.

'Do you think we can hold off on the arguing until I get you into school?' I say loudly to Cora and Anansy. 'We don't want to be late.'

Cora looks at Anansy and she shrugs in reply. 'Suppose so,' Cora says.

'Yes,' Anansy adds. 'Suppose so.'

At least I haven't got children. At least they'll never feel about me how I used to feel about my mum sometimes.

16

Fleur

From The Flower Beach Girl Blog

Things I want to do before I die (in no particular order):

See the big Jesus in Rio.

Paint every toenail on my feet a different colour.

Spend time in Italy learning to cook authentic Italian food.

Have sex on a beach. Any beach will do, it's never been a specific one.

Dance naked in the rain. (I got that one from that song.)

Donate a month's wages to a charity. (Have to get a full-time job first.)

Maybe get married.

Maybe, possibly have a baby.

Earn enough so I never have to work after the age of thirty-five.

Understand my mother.

I've been a bit distracted. By sex. By that wonderful, all-powerful thing called sex. It might be love, but at the moment it seems to be sex that is the main reason for my distraction. Sex with Noah, obviously.

It's not new to me, sex; I am not a fresh cherry, nothing like that. I've been doing it since I was eighteen. That's what I told her, Mirabelle, Mum, anyway. (To Dad, I'm obviously a virgin.)

459

I knew that she'd done it younger – obviously she did because I exist – but she would flip if she thought I'd done it younger. Like, say, at fourteen. I didn't. Like Dad ever let me out of his sight long enough for *that* to happen! I was sixteen and he was safe. Like, you know – *safe*. Nice. Didn't rush me, didn't do anything I didn't want. Safe. He was a boy who was in his second year of university, and he thought I was older. By that I mean he *said* he thought I was older when Lariska's brother got hold of him, but he knew I wasn't. I didn't look it, I didn't talk it, I might have acted it a little, but at the end of the day we both got something out of it.

And they've been all right since then. A couple of 'goods', a couple of 'mind-blowings' – that's the session not the whole thing – and a couple of 'so darn amazings I couldn't speak afterwards'.

What Noah and I have, though, is *sex*. It needs to be said in a soft, sultry voice to emphasise how exquisite it is.

It's beautiful. So beautiful I ache when I think about it. I feel echoey, as if the absence of him and us being physically together reverberates throughout my whole body, right down to the littlest cell. My body doesn't feel right without him.

I think he feels that, too, by the way he takes my hand, kisses my neck, twirls my hair around his forefinger. We struggle without each other. Which is going to be a bitch because I'm not leaving Brighton. I can't. And he's just taken a huge contract for the next year based up in London. He can work remotely for a few weeks, but he needs to be in London. His whole life, his whole family are there. He's a family man, and I left my family. I left my family to find my family.

Either way, Noah isn't moving down here because some girl he met is staying here.

'What's going on in that whirling mind of yours?' he asks. He strokes over my bare stomach and my body instinctively moves towards him, craving his touch. 'I can almost see the wheels turning. What are you thinking through?'

'You. Me. Us. What happens when I find out what happened to my mother. How soon afterwards you'll move back to London.' You see, that's what makes this sex so different. It's the honesty that comes with it. Before, it's always been about playing that game, holding back, not being *that* girl. With him it was like that in the beginning, but now it is easy, necessarily honest.

'Don't be getting ahead of yourself,' he says. 'One day at a time until we know what happened to your mother.'

'I can't help it. I think I'm staying here. I can't imagine living anywhere else now. You love London, don't you?'

'Brighton's growing on me,' he says. 'I've been thinking about commuting.'

'Living here and going up there?'

'Yeah, I don't see why not.'

'You'd want us to live together?' I ask. 'Because I don't know if that's a good idea.'

'No, I don't think that's a good idea, either. It's been good, this, though. Being in this hotel together all this time.' His hand moves lower and the ache becomes a pleasurable pain that yearns for us to hook ourselves together.

'Let's talk about this again when I know what happened to my mother,' I say. His fingers are still working lower, reaching for me, my body is longing to be with him.

461

I'm blatantly ignoring the fact that I may never know what happened to her. Especially since *nothing* has happened with the investigation. They know nothing more than they did when I first got here, they have no new leads or clues. I get the impression they're not looking very hard 'cos they think they know who did it.

I have two new phones and one new number. I turn on the phone with my old number once every day to get messages from my dad, the other phone is the one I use now. I still can't talk to Dad. Maybe one day, but not at the moment.

The thing I have to get my head around right now, though, is finding the courage to go into the house where my mother was murdered.

Beatrix

Just a quick text to let me know you're OK would be nice.
Bea x

This café, a five-minute walk to the hospital, is rammed, the tables are crammed close together to get as many people in there as possible, and there are still people standing by the counter, lurking, waiting for anyone to move even a fraction so they can take their place.

We don't speak, Tami and I. Those hand-holding chats I was sort of hoping for haven't materialised. I have dinner with them, she puts the girls to bed, and I tidy up the kitchen. She goes to her office – yes, every time she opens the door I feel a trickle of shame – and stays there for hours. Well, at least until I have returned to my room. I have watched television, I have read the entire internet on my phone, I have tried to count the number of piles there are in the carpet. Anything other than think about Wednesday, today. Even if she could bring herself to speak to me, what would I say?

I can't tell her I am scared. That's not the person I am. That's not my role in this drama I find myself in. In this drama, I am the scarlet woman. I am the marriage wrecker. I am the whore. I have no feelings beyond carnal, man-stealing ones, nor any right to any other type of feelings.

463

Everything that Tami says to me seems to be punctuated with the W word. I remember when Cora was first learning about reading, she would add silent letters onto words without your knowledge so I-Spy would become a game of randomness: something beginning with G could as easily be 'table' as it could be 'glass' because of the silent 'G'. Tami does this with sentences: 'Your dinner's ready [*whore*]'. 'Do you have any washing you want putting in [*whore*]?'

To be honest, her long-suffering betrayed wife act is starting to PISS ME OFF.

I've done wrong, yes, but I didn't do it on purpose, I didn't set out to hurt her. She really does need to start getting over it. I have bigger things to worry about. And I can't focus on that because I've got Mrs Betrayed Wife sitting opposite me. As I become more agitated, more wound up, I start to stir the coffee in my cup a little more forcefully. A lot more force-fully, actually. Until I'm bashing the cup hard.

'Is there a problem [*whore*]?' Tami asks.

'No, no problem.'

She returns her gaze to her cup. I return to abusing mine, satisfied when she raises her gaze again. 'What's the matter? You've clearly got a problem. Why don't you share it and save us all the passive-aggressive crockery abuse [*whore*]?'

'I'm . . . this is a really tough situation and you're acting as if it's nothing.'

'How am I supposed to act?'

I shrug. *Not like this. Not like I'm evil,* I think.

'If you don't know, how am I supposed to? The thing is, I can't give you absolution and make you feel better about the choices you made.'

Am I asking for absolution from her? I don't think so. I just need a friend. People drift like clouds in your life, they may stay around for a while but slowly and surely they drift out again when your life experiences don't match up.

I do not need absolution for falling in love with a man who fell in love with me. I just need a friend. And Tami is it because she hasn't drifted out of my life.

'I don't want absolution, I just need a friend.'

'You're not sorry at all, are you?' she says.

'I am sorry I hurt you, but I honestly didn't mean to,' I reply. I am sorry for the pain, for the disruption, but I am not sorry for falling in love. How can I be? You can never be sorry about falling in love. 'I couldn't stop myself from falling in love with him. You really can't help who you love.'

'No, you can't help who you love. But you can help how you behave,' she says, the incredulous look hasn't left her face. 'You really aren't sorry for what you did at all.' She shakes her head again. 'What am I doing here? I must be insane.' She offers me a close-lipped smile and stands. 'I hope your appointment goes well.'

I'm not going to beg her to stay. I'm not going to let her blackmail me into being here with me. If she can't get over it, she can't get over it. But I need calm and stability right now, not drama and tantrums. I need Tami.

She knows that. She knows I need someone who will stay level-headed as they explain what comes next to me. As they put items into my body, take tests, take samples, prod and poke and practically drain me. I need someone to sit with me. To tell me, even if it is silently, they will be there. My body is not my own any longer. It has been taken over by

465

cancer. *Cancer*. It is about to be invaded by the people trying to stop it spreading. I am on the side-lines, watching, learning, trying to understand. I am a woman wandering around in the dark wilderness who needs a guide, or at least a companion who will not panic, who will be there as I start this journey.

I do not understand much of what is happening to me. I do not understand much of what is going to happen to me. I do know that I do not want to go through his alone.

I need Tami. She knows it. She's going to use it.

But is she? Tami's not like that. The fact she has spoken to me at all, has come here with me today, is testament to her *not* being like that. She didn't have to come. I stare at the café door through which she left. She didn't have to organise a taxi, pay for it and then sit here with me, a few hundred yards from where I am about to become a cancer patient.

I was an ordinary person, now I am about to become a cancer patient.

I need Tami. It's selfish and it's wrong, and I shouldn't have hurt her. I shouldn't have betrayed her trust. I shouldn't have even asked her without asking her to be with me. But I need her. The cloud that would not drift away.

A man in a navy blue suit darts across the space from the counter to our table and takes the seat she was sitting in. He smiles sheepishly at me. I glare at him return. He responds with a half shrug and sips his coffee while avidly reading his mobile phone screen.

My eyes go back to the door and I watch her weave her way through the tightly placed tables and chairs as she comes back to me. The cloud that will not drift away.

She stands above the man in the navy blue suit sitting in her seat and glares at him. He looks up at her, then at me, and decides the seat is not worth it. As quickly as he appeared, he is gone again. Tami pulls her chair away from the table and faces it away from me. 'Don't speak to me,' she says. 'The moment you speak to me is the moment I'm gone for good.'

The relief brings tears to my eyes. I'm not going to be alone. Not speaking is a small price to pay to not be alone.

Beatrix

I've gone into shock again.

I am sitting here, listening to this doctor talk, and my mind is not grasping onto anything for very long. He has talked about numbers and stages and gradings. He has talked about surgery, radiotherapy and chemotherapy. Most of the words slip in and out of my head straight away, like I am trying to hang on tightly to wet soap – impossible to grasp for any length of time.

It's the word 'chemotherapy' that sticks in my head. It's that which I know about with the word cancer. Your hair falls out. I know that. You have to wear wigs or scarves. I've never really looked that good in a scarf. That's a stupid thing to think right now, isn't it? When I have so much more to worry about, to think about, to prepare for, I focus on that. Which proves what I've thought all along: I'm not grown up enough for this to be happening to me. I need a few more years of life, experience, before I am forced to face this.

I haven't heard the other word, yet. The word that you always associate with the words breast cancer. I have been waiting for it, I think. Waiting, expecting. It's coming soon, I can feel it. Like I felt this was not going to turn out to be a cyst, I feel that other word coming.

My heart leaps in fright when I feel a hand around mine.

I look down and it's her hand. She has carefully encircled my hand with hers, and now is slipping her fingers between my fingers. I stare at our hands. Linked. Together. She hasn't even looked away from the man who is still talking. On the other side of me is sitting the specialist nurse from the other day. She sat with me for a long time replying to questions I didn't know I needed to know the answer to. I haven't actually remembered the answers to any of them. The only thing that stuck in my mind was that I had an appointment today at ten o'clock. Everything else was white noise.

'There'll be no need for a mastectomy, then?' Tami asks. My head turns to her.

'No. We think a wide local excision will be sufficient.'

'And you think it is a stage one, grade one cancer at the moment given its size and location?'

'Yes. We will be able to find out after the surgery which stage it actually is and whether it has spread to the lymph nodes in the armpit by carrying out a sentinel node biopsy. If this proves to be positive we will remove those nodes during the same procedure.'

'After the surgery, what happens then, treatment-wise?'

'A lot of that will depend on the actual stage and grade of the cancer, as well as whether it has spread or if it has remained localised. We will also be able to determine whether it is oestrogen-receptor positive or not. If it has receptors it will most likely respond well to hormone treatment. Once we have all these pieces of information we will be able to map out the best course of treatment.'

Tami is talking because I can't. She is asking questions,

essentially asking the doctor to repeat information he has already given so I will maybe hear it this time. I will take it in. I will understand that this is really happening.

Every night I pray: *Dear God, Please don't let this be happening. Thank you. Bea*

'Ms Carenden, you are a fit, healthy young woman and it seems we have caught this at a very early stage. All these factors will count in your favour. You will need to undergo more tests and pre-op prep.'

He's talking to me again. He is talking to me and I am listening. For the first time since this started, I am listening and I am listening properly.

She has anchored me here by taking my hand. She has stopped me from floating away, from retreating into denial and pretending this is not happening.

'What will my breast look like after the surgery?' I ask and she, my friend, my anchor, tightens her fingers around mine.

Tami

'I'm sorry I hurt you, Tami,' Beatrix says to me in the taxi home.

She is not apologising for real, she is engaging in Beatrix Doubletalk. What she really means is: '*How did you know to ask all that stuff? How did you know that if you got the doctor to repeat it some of it might sink in? Why did you hold my hand?*'

The answer is clear: I know her. She may have been faking it all these years, befriending me to try to steal my life, but I wasn't faking with her. I know her. I know she has been in denial and won't have found out any information because she's trying to believe it's not happening; I know that with Beatrix it takes several goes to get most messages across; and I know that physical touch grounds her. It's what she constantly craves to make her feel real. Sometimes Beatrix thinks that if she isn't held then she will disappear, that no one will believe she is real.

'I thought I told you not to talk to me,' I say.

Tami Doubletalk: '*I know you. Even though you've done this terrible thing, I still know who you really are.*'

If I had trusted myself enough to believe Mirabelle, to accept that I knew her just like I knew Beatrix, Mirabelle might not be … And I might not be stuck in this waste-land of waiting for the next piece of the jigsaw of my

471

memory to reveal itself and tell me exactly what I did that night.

'Sorry,' Beatrix mumbles and returns to staring out of the window at Brighton and our way home.

Fleur

From The Flower Beach Girl Blog
The thing I'm most afraid of:
Many things scare me. I'm not a person who is scared of everything, scared of the world, but I do have a healthy fear of rats, big-arse spiders and being trapped on the Tube.

The thing I am most afraid of is love. When you say you love someone you are giving them licence to hurt you. That sounds cynical and bitter, but think of all the bad things people have done in this world that are because of love. Think of all the people you have loved that have hurt you. Love is like the emotional equivalent of a free pass to bad behaviour. People think they can hurt you and it's OK because they did it out of love. Or they think they can lie to you because they love you and wanted to protect you. Or they think they can leave in search of love and never come back.

Love scares me. It terrifies the life out of me. Think about this, yeah? Who would you hurt in the name of love?

Noah told me last night that he loved me. He whispered it into the nape of my neck before he fell asleep. I pretended to be asleep and not to hear. I don't want him to say it again. I don't want to be afraid that now he's said it that will be it. He'll hurt me and I'll have to accept it because he loves me.

Beatrix

She was here when I stayed in the night before surgery, she was here before they took me down, and she was here when I woke up. She had food, an iPod with movies on and a card drawn by Cora and Anansy, covered in hearts and orders to 'get well soon, Bix' in what looks like every colour crayon they own. They've also stuck on the inside pictures of the three of us in the park, at the beach, in their living room at the house. It is a behemoth of a card, and sits propped up on the bedside cabinet because there is nowhere else to put it.

I have red hair in those pictures, and one of them was taken when I wasn't sleeping with their father.

The lymph nodes were clear, apparently, so again, another plus point. Another sign that everything is going to be OK. The surgeon described to me that day I first came with Tami what my breast was likely to look like afterwards and he described it to me again before I went under. He said it would look like I had a very slight dent on the left side of my cleavage.

It's done, there is a piece of me missing, taken to save my life. I used to be whole and complete, now I am missing a piece.

I should be grateful that it wasn't a bigger piece. I should be grateful that it looks like it will be a stage one, grade one cancer and I may not even need chemo and radiotherapy.

I should be grateful for all these things. And I am. But ... Why me? I am not supposed to ask that, I know. I am supposed to look on the positive side and stay strong. I am supposed to look this thing straight in the eye and tell it I'm going to kick its butt. I am scared. How am I supposed to deal with this fear?

'I think you should tell your mother,' Tami says, during this visit. She farms her children out to any of their friends who will take them in and feed them, like a dog owner off on a jaunt, so she can come here and be with me. *Me*.

'Not going to happen,' I say, trying to move, but the tug of my itchy stitches, the press of the heavy-feeling dressing, halts me.

'She has a right to know,' she says.

'Erm, no, she doesn't.'

'It would break my heart if Cora or Anansy went through something like this and they didn't tell me. I would move worlds to come and be with them.'

'Remember how the specialist nurse said to be careful who I told because people's reactions could have a negative effect on me? My mother's reaction would have a negative effect on me.'

'You love your mother, though. You've always said you were very close.'

I glance down at my blanket, a white waffle thing that doesn't really keep me warm. 'Yeah, well, there's close and there's close.'

'I still think you should tell her,' she says.

'When my husband left me, I rang my mother in tears. I had no one to talk to and I needed her to tell me it was going to be all right. That I wasn't to blame and that I wouldn't be on my own forever. How hard would that be for a mother to say to her child? Whether she meant it or not, I needed to hear that. Instead she was devastated that all the people who had come to the wedding would know that I hadn't managed to make it work. That she would be the mother of a divorced woman. That people would look at her and think she set me a bad example. And then she started to intimate that I hadn't worked hard enough to keep him, then she outright said that because I hadn't given him enough sex he had to look elsewhere. All in the same phone call. I love my mother to bits, but she's not the person to rely on if you need emotional support.'

Tami has retreated, she is tight-lipped after hearing what my mother said to me about the end of my marriage. She is poring over her marriage like you would a sandbox your contact lens has fallen into, searching furiously for it, looking for clues. She is also back to thinking I am The Devil. Maybe she never stopped thinking that, but right now her body language says she is wishing herself away from me. 'I wish you could understand that I did it because I love him,' I say to her.

At those words, she inhales deeply and glances away in irritation. I do not speak because I know she has something to say. 'No, you didn't,' she eventually states, still staring out of the window. The whole world is going on out there, while I am in here, recovering from surgery and speaking to my love rival. She looks like she is far away, in another land.

She sounds like she is talking to me from overseas, her voice drifting slowly and calmly through the air to me.

'Don't tell me how I do or don't feel,' I say to her. I will not be patronised by her. No matter what she is doing for me, I will not let her tell me I don't know what I know. 'I love him.'

'Love him?' She turns on me, anger flashing up for the first time. 'You don't know him, how can you love him?'

'Just because I haven't known him as long as—'

'Who was the first girl he kissed?' she cuts in.

'I–I don't kno—'

'Jemmy Tanton, when he was fourteen, down at the local bus station. How many times did his dad put him in hospital?'

'What? I knew he had a difficult childhood but not that—'

'Five. How many times has he been arrested, not including the most recent incident?'

'What? He's been—'

'Seven. Once for drunk driving, the other times they did it because he's a Challey. What's his middle name?'

'He doesn't have—'

'Keir. After his grandfather, but he tells everyone he doesn't have one because he hates it.'

'What would he have wanted to call the baby I miscarried if he'd been a boy?'

The air catches in my chest, it sits there, hard and painful. She had a miscarriage? They went through that together? He never told me. He never told me any of this. 'I ... I don't—'

'Kade. And a girl?'

I shake my head. I don't know. Of course I don't know.

'Igrayne. How many times has he been married?'

'Twice?' I guess.

'Once. To me. Do you believe me now? You didn't love him – the real him – because you don't know him.' She stops speaking, returns to looking out of the window. 'Turns out, neither did I. And I've known him more than half my life. More than half his life.'

She's right, I don't know him at all. That doesn't mean I can't love him. That I didn't love him. That I don't love him.

'You can't love someone you don't really know. You fancied him, you were attracted to him, but in the nine years of friendship, you never even scratched the surface of who he was. Admit it: you wanted to have sex with him. It's allowed, you know, women are allowed to have sex without love. I think you're deluding yourself that you did it *because* you loved him.'

'I think you're deluding yourself that we didn't have a real connection that led to us being unable to help ourselves.'

'Yeah, you're right,' she says.

What? 'Don't patronise me, Tami. You weren't there, you don't know what we had.'

'I said you're right,' she repeats.

'Stop it. I know why you're being like that.'

'I'm not being like anything. I don't want to argue with you. And you're right, I wasn't there, I don't know what it was like.'

'You're only saying that because I'm in this hospital bed. If I wasn't, you'd be tearing strips off me like you were a minute ago.'

'I shouldn't have done that,' she says.

'Yes you should,' I try to shout at her, but my throat is

sore, dry; quietening my outrage. 'Of course you should. I did something terrible and I'm trying to explain why I did it.'

'You're not telling the truth, are you though? You're using all the reasons you used to give yourself permission to do what you did. The truth is, you wanted sex with him. He was with someone else so you had to tell yourself the only reason you would ingratiate yourself with someone to get their husband is because of love. Because love is your "I can do whatever I want" pass, isn't it? Never mind his wife, he can't love her, she can't love him, she can't be having sex with him so I can move in.'

'You weren't having sex with him,' I remind her.

'That's where you're wrong, he wasn't having sex with me. I wanted sex but my sex life pretty much came to an end when all Scott wanted was porn sex.'

'You're saying he only wanted me for sex, porn sex at that?'

'No,' she says. 'I'm saying I don't want to talk about this any more. Not with you. Not with anyone.'

'Now you're the one not telling the truth. It wasn't about porn sex, was it? You're rewriting history to make sense of why he went looking elsewhere.'

Her gaze is unflinching and direct. 'I liked sex with Scott. It was about intimacy and fun and adventure, and, yes, about expressing our love. And you know what, I would have been happy to try new things. To have explored the kinkier side of sex. But I was never consulted in that. Scott wanted it, Scott did it. If I didn't feel comfortable with something, he just sulked and moaned and cold-shouldered me until I gave in. If I didn't give in, he wouldn't touch me for weeks – it was sex his way or no way.' She continues to eviscerate me with her stare. 'And, maybe it was different with you, maybe he went back to who he was, but you know what, I got tired of being manipulated into trying things that always made me feel dirty and degraded and disgusting.' She stops, her face momentarily agonised. 'Did he ask me – *ever* – what I might want to try? Or what my fantasies were? Did I ever get the chance to make unilateral decisions about our sex life then become unpleasant if I didn't get what I wanted? No. No. And No. Why would I want to have sex with someone who treats me like a breathing blow-up doll and makes me start to hate sex? I love sex. Just not with Scott any more. And as I refused to be his doll . . .'

'He found someone else,' I finish for her. 'That's what you were going to say, isn't it? He found someone else to be his blow-up doll and that someone else was me.'

'I don't want to talk about this. You're supposed to be positive and think about the future. None of this can be doing you any good. This wasn't the conversation we were meant to have. You were meant to agree to think about telling your mother. But if you don't want to, you don't want to. I'll come and pick you up when they discharge you tomorrow, OK?'

I nod at her, not really listening. She has set me off. Down this road. Down the road of doubting Scott, doubting what he truly felt for me. I heard about their relationship from both sides, but his seemed more plausible for what he was doing, what we were sharing. While hers seemed more plausible, full stop. I dismissed it, though, because Scott was not a terrible man, he wouldn't lie to get me into bed.

'I'll see you tomorrow,' she says, quietly. She is shaken by the conversation, too. She hasn't spoken of those things before. She has kept them locked inside her, a tainted treasure trove of the things that trashed her marriage.

As she stands and stretches her body, I notice she is still losing weight, still not eating properly or taking care of herself. She used to be curvy, filling all her clothes in all the right ways. She used to have the body shape I always wanted. I loved my body but I often coveted hers. Now there is much less of her, but I can still see the curve of her breasts. They are perfect, complete. She doesn't have a part of her missing.

'When was the last time you had sex with him?' I ask her.

'I don't remember,' she says.

'I'll assume it was last week, then,' I say petulantly.

'About six months ago.'

He told me over a year ago. He told me there'd only been a slight overlap in him sleeping with both of us. It was a huge overlap. He lied to me.

'I'll see you,' she says.

'Yeah,' I reply, wondering now what else he lied about.

Two months ago

'God, I've missed you,' Scott said to me as soon as he entered my flat, reaching for me. I stepped back, twisting my body away from him and heading for the living room.

'What's the matter?' he asked tiredly as he followed me.

'What's the matter? How about you and Mirabelle for starters?'

He sighed, heavily, his fingers moving up to pinch the bridge of his nose.

'And that's your answer is it?' I said. 'Nothing?'

'Do you really think I'd go near her? Especially when I have you?'

'I saw your wife three hours ago, she seems convinced,' I stated.

He became agitated, couldn't settle, couldn't sit, pacing the living-room floor, his hands constantly running themselves over his hair, his eyes unable to focus or alight on anything too long. I said nothing, waited for him to calm down and reassure me that it wasn't the case. 'If I wanted this shit, I'd go home, talk to my wife,' he proclaimed.

This was shit? What did he think was going to happen? That I'd hear all that from her and simply melt into his arms the second he walked through the door? From the sound of the conversation I had with her, she had given him anything *but* shit. Besides, I was not her. Wasn't that the point?

'Feel free,' I said, throwing myself onto the sofa and folding my arms.

He hesitated, shocked and blindsided by my reply. Sometimes, he obviously forgot who I was. He dropped to his knees, came across the room to me like that, prostrate and contrite.

'I'm sorry, I'm sorry, it's such a stressful time.' He arrived in front of me, took my hands in his and lowered his head to look into my face. 'Forgive me?'

'Did you have a fling with Mirabelle?' I asked him, unwilling to relent until I knew everything.

'No, for God's sake! As if I'd go anywhere near her. I told you, didn't I, that she was hassling me? I told you when I got tough with her she'd say I was sexually harassing her. Not even I could imagine she'd do this.'

'Why did you say all that stuff then to *her* about you and Mirabelle? It sounded so true.'

'You know how she is, how she's so hot on women's rights. You know she's more likely to believe Mirabelle than me. And you know Mirabelle's a man-hating bitch. She's all but convinced the police I did it. You have to believe me that I never would—'

'Of course, of course,' I cut in. 'I just didn't know what to think when I've got her sobbing her heart out on me.'

'I know, I know, I feel awful I had to do that to her, but it was the only way to stop myself getting sent down for something I didn't do.'

'Do you promise nothing happened between you?' I sounded like a teenager begging assurances of eternal true love and fidelity from her spotty boyfriend.

'I swear on the girls' lives,' he said.

That caused me to pause, to draw back from him: someone once told me you can always tell a liar by their willingness to swear on someone else's life. *Especially their children's.* Craig had done that – sworn on his children's lives there was no one else – when he left his wife. Scotty wouldn't do that, though. Only an evil man would do that. I wouldn't have fallen in love with an evil man.

'I like your hair,' he said, reaching up and gently tucking it behind my ear. 'I knew you'd look amazing as a blonde.'

'I didn't do it for you,' I said, defiantly, again shaving years off myself in the maturity stakes. 'I did it because I fancied a change.' As simple as that. He didn't *own* me, I would never

484

just up and change something as fundamental about myself as my hair colour for a man. I fancied it, so I did it.

'I know, but I'm glad you tried it. You look incredible.'

'Don't look so bad yourself.'

'God, I missed you,' he breathed.

'I missed you, too. That's why I didn't like you not texting me.'

'I didn't like hearing about you meeting some random man at the airport. Did you fuck him?'

'No, but I could have.'

His face tightened. 'Great, how's that meant to make me feel?'

'Scotty, when you're free to sleep next to me every night, and when I know you're not going to be sleeping next to her for the foreseeable, I'll stop finding other men to do that with.'

I watched the large mass of his Adam's apple move up and down as he swallowed, pushing down his jealousy and frustration. 'We'll be together soon,' he said. 'I promise.' A salacious grin spread across his face. 'Now, I think it's time to check whether the thatched roof matches the downstairs carpet,' he said.

In one movement he was upright on his knees. He grabbed me by the hips and pushed me back onto the sofa. I giggled as in another fluid movement he was hitching up my skirt, tugging off my knickers and making love to me with his mouth.

As my orgasm subsided, and I relaxed backwards against my white leather sofa, he shifted to undo his trousers and then his hands were on my hips again, twisting them to turn me over. I knew immediately what he was doing. I didn't want that. I wanted to enjoy our reunion without *that*. I started to struggle a little, my hands gently pushing at him to stop. Since the baby talk he'd respected what I'd said and had dutifully 'suited up' each and every time without prompting – until this time. I continued to gently resist until he paused for a second and stared down at me, begging me not to be like her, not to let him down by denying him what he wanted. What he wanted was to come inside my body without a condom and without the risk of getting me pregnant.

I stopped pushing, ceased my half-struggle and let him turn me over, giving him silent permission to continue. I was attached to him, I was his, and I desperately wanted his baby. I'd never wanted anyone's baby before – no, not even my husband's. That's why I loved Cora and Anansy so fiercely, they were half his, and if I skipped into the future when we were together properly, they could also be half mine. I wouldn't convince him we should try for our own baby by fighting him on things like this.

I acquiesced because when you love a man you sometimes do things you don't especially enjoy or even like to make him happy; to make him stay. And sometimes you stop your struggle for the same reason that I did: I didn't want to be like her.

Tami

I like to come to these appointments with Beatrix.

It's a strange thing to think but it's the truth. I like to come because it humbles me by reminding me what life really is. It is the people who sit in the waiting area at the oncology department. It is the woman sitting alone with a small rise of skin where her eyebrows should be, a beige, red and cream floral scarf tied around her head, knotted on the side, the long tail forwards over her shoulder, huge silver hoops at her ears, who has immersed herself in the open book on her lap. It is the man whose skin is weathered, wrinkled and aging even though he does not look much older than me, sitting in silence beside his companion, both of them seemingly lost in thought, but so close their biceps touch. It is the young woman with the pink wig, surrounded by four of her pink-wigged friends, giggling and chatting like they would if they had gathered at someone's flat for a girls' night in. It is the woman whose fingers are knitted through her husband's while they both read on their mobile phones. All of them, *all* of them are what life is. Life is out there, on the street going about daily business, and it is in here, sitting, waiting.

Whenever I walk into the waiting area with Beatrix, we take a seat and we take our places in a part of the world where life is measured by understanding the need to use, fill, enjoy, *embrace* every tick of the clock. We are there, being reminded that the true beauty of life is the living part.

Mirabelle. *Mirabelle*. She is on my mind constantly. I wish I could remember. I wish . . . I wish Mirabelle and Fleur hadn't been so hideously robbed of time together. I always look around at the other people in the waiting area and remind myself what the desire to live is all about. Then I think about Mirabelle and Fleur. And then I pledge to myself not to waste a single second of what I have.

Beatrix

It's not as big as I thought it would be. How it felt under the dressing was like they had taken away half my breast. Even though I could see they hadn't, it felt like that.

I hadn't been able to look when the district nurse had come out to change the dressing and remove the drain. I'd been too scared of what I might see, and too terrified of not being able to handle it. The area around the dressing is calming down now, it was bruised, such a deep purple it almost looked black, with tinges of blue and yellow and red. Under the dressing seemed a vicious, dangerous place and I did not want to see. I had enough reality drip, dripping itself into my life, I did not need to see that before I was ready.

Today, I am seeing. I am ready. I have taken the requisite deep breaths. I have a full-length mirror in the corner of the room and I have Tami standing in the other corner of the room, by the door, as if she wants to escape. She's been pretty inscrutable this past week. We haven't had any big chats, it's all been neutral where she helps me to the shower, brings me food, lets the girls come in to say goodnight, and reminds me to do my arm exercises.

You would not think that I had betrayed her. She is still wasting away, though. Something is eating her up. I do not know what, but I know deep, unrelenting guilt when I see it. What she has to feel guilty about I don't know.

You can see what I'm doing, can't you? I'm thinking about other things so I do not have to open my eyes and look down. I do not have to see what has been exposed to the air. I can feel air on it, cool after the wound has been protected all this time by the dressing.

In goes another breath, another moment of steeling myself, and I look down. It is a thin, slightly jagged line that runs about 5cms across the left part of my cleavage. It's nothing, really. Not when I was expecting a crater.

I resist the urge to touch it, fascinated at the marked skin and the bruising that has not completely disappeared. I am fascinated because you couldn't tell. You couldn't tell that something that came out of a space that small could have brought about the end.

'It's not as bad as I thought,' I say to the nurse. She nods. My eyes move to Tami. 'It's not as bad as I thought,' I say to her.

She is pressed up against the wall, her lips curled tightly inwards, her face an ocean of tears. Is it the scar? Is it how close I came? Or is it that I am naked to my waist, making the pictures of what I did with her husband more vivid and real?

I turn away from her. As I walk the few steps to the mirror, I hear and feel rather than see her slip out of the room.

Beatrix

This is what I found out today:

It is a stage one cancer because it is smaller (just about) than 2 cms and it hasn't spread to the lymph nodes.

It is a grade two cancer because the cells are growing at a moderately fast rate.

It is oestrogen-receptor positive.

I will need to have radiotherapy as well as chemotherapy.

I will also need to be on a hormone therapy probably for five years.

I will need regular visits and check-ups probably for the rest of my life.

I will have to revisit the whole baby thing because oestrogen-receptor positive cancers make pregnancy 'complicated'.

I have to be told things several times before they sink in.

I can hurt someone so badly she looks like she is being eaten alive from the inside out and she will still hold my hand while I listen to the hard bits.

17

Fleur

The inside is completely different to the outside. From the outside, the house is old and stuffy, but from the moment you open the door, it hits you, this place is modern; everything new and expensive.

One time I said to her that I felt bad about her spending all that money on a car for me when I couldn't drive it and she said, 'Who else am I going to spend my money on?'

She obviously had a lot of money. I knew that, there's a lot of it in her will, but this shows that she must have earned a bomb because her house is mint.

It's taken a while for us to make it here because I've been waiting to hear if they had anything new in the investigation. But nothing has changed: they have a suspect and are still gathering evidence. After a few days of pretending that situation might change, I knew I couldn't delay any longer and I had to come to her house.

I was sort of expecting to feel something, like maybe her spirit or something would be hanging around or I'd feel her when I opened the door to walk in. I'd taken Noah's hand the moment I pushed the door open, needing him to be with me, not to let me go.

He was nervous, too, although he tried to hide it. Neither of us knew what to expect, or what would happen or how I would feel. I'd wanted so desperately to come here over the years, but I didn't dare ask. She never offered, either. But now I know my father, Dad, has been lying to me, I wonder how many times she asked over the years if I could come and stay for the weekend. For half term. For the summer holidays. How many times did he turn her down before she gave up?

We hold hands as we walk down the tiled hall, black and white tiles that look antique but are new. We instinctively go down the corridor instead of going upstairs. That's something we'll tackle soon.

There's an odd quiet in the house. It's more quiet than you get with empty houses. Maybe that's what I thought would happen, instead of feeling something there, it's knowing there is something missing. The heart of the home has stopped beating and you can sense it in the air.

The first room we come to is a large living room. I gently push the door open, almost expecting to see her on the sofa, sitting there, with a book or maybe a cup of tea or even a glass of wine, although she never drank around me. There are two leather sofas, a large rug, a couple of side tables. And that picture. I've never seen it before, I've never known it existed, but it feels like it should be here. Her house wouldn't be complete or hers without it. We don't dare go into the room, that'd be like walking into the deepest recesses of her heart or something. We both stand on the threshold and look. We do that for every downstairs room. The other room down there is a study, it has a wall of books, the shorter wall has shelves that are lined with work files. There is a computer on a glass-topped desk, and a printer on the corner of the desk. We move on to the kitchen. It is longer than it is wide, but it is a big space with all chrome and shiny appliances and gadgets. When we have looked at everything from the threshold, we both return to the staircase.

'You don't have to do this now,' Noah says to me.

'If I don't do it now, I'll never do it,' I say.

I feel sick. Properly, properly sick as I put my foot on the bottom step. I don't know where the bathroom is. I don't know if it's the first room we'll come to or if it's the last. I'm crushing Noah's hand, I know it, but I'm feeling sick and if I don't squeeze tightly I might actually throw up. My feet are like giant's feet and make a very loud sound on the stairs even though there's carpet.

At the top of the stairs we stop. There are five doors all leading off from the oblong corridor. I have to do this bit alone, I realise. It's good having him here, I've needed him, but I need to see where she died on my own so I can assimilate it. It won't be real if I don't go in and see it. And it won't mean anything if I let someone else share that burden. He didn't know her, he didn't have that messed-up relationship I had with her.

'Can you . . . Can you wait here while I find it?' I ask him.

'If you're sure,' he replies.

I'm sure. I'm not sure, I'm sure, but I don't want to do this wrong. I don't want to bring a stranger into the place where she spent her final moments. They were minutes of terror and horror, I guess, and that is private, that is not something to share with someone who didn't know her. I want to think it is not something to share with someone who didn't love her like I did, but I'm still struggling to feel

I did love her. I'm still trying to convince myself that I do feel it, that it's all stuck behind this grief and anger. I have anger that I have been robbed three times: first by Mirabelle, then by my dad and now by whoever has done this. I have been robbed three times of the same thing, the same *person*. And with this last robbery, this crime committed against me as well as her, I'm never going to know the full her.

At the first door, the door to my left, a short way down the corridor, I close my hands around the brass handle and hold my breath as I turn it and push. Nothing. It is stuck. I try again. No, it is locked. I exhale all at once. I don't think anyone would have locked it after the police had gone, but that policewoman in charge of the case said on the phone that I could go into the house and they'd left it as they found it. So maybe they did. Maybe this door was always locked, but I do not see a key anywhere. Would they really have gone to the trouble of locating the key and then locking it and putting it back where they found it?

That's thrown me. We're going to have to go through the house looking for the key now. We'll have to move stuff and destroy the house that she created, the home that she had so carefully made.

I walk to the next door and turn the handle, not expecting it to open. It does, though, and behind it is a bedroom. The way it is set up, the formal way the bed is made, the chair sitting in the bay window with guest towels folded upon it, says it is not a room that is used very often. Again, did the police check in here? Did they examine every inch of the place to find clues, because it doesn't seem like it. It seems as if they've tidied up to a professional standard.

'We weren't sure but didn't think you would want to come in after the investigation so we told the cleaner she could come in after we'd gone.' The policewoman said that, didn't she? I wasn't really listening, I was too busy freaking out that I was finally going to go into the house.

'The cleaner's been,' I say to Noah.

'That explains why it's so tidy, then,' he says.

The next one is the one I'm dreading. I know what will be behind it when I open it, I know that it's going to be the one. Inhaling deeply, my fingers close around the brass handle and I turn. The door doesn't creak or nothing freaky like that, it swings back smoothly on its hinges and the white rushes out to fill my line of vision. The walls are tiled in white, the floor is tiled in black and white. Against one wall is a huge glass shower cubicle with a wall-hung sink beside it. Directly in front of me is a large old-fashioned window, and then on the other side of the room, against the wall is a large roll-top bath. It is white with large chrome taps.

I take a few steps into the room, my heart is running in my chest. It's trying to escape. I think I'm shaking but I can't be sure because I'm not sure if I feel anything any more. I take a few more steps ... stepping ... stepping ... and I am in front of the bath.

I used to talk to her in the bath. When it was only her and me in the house and she wanted to take a bath, I would bring my storybook and sit next to the bath and talk to her. Sometimes I would read to her, making up the story as I went along, and she would help me and laugh with me when the most implausible things would happen. She'd sometimes splash me and I'd laugh as the droplets of water rained down on my face and shoulders and hair.

I drop to my knees beside the bath. I close my eyes as I touch the smooth, cold side of it.

I remember ... I remember the sound of the water splashing as she used a red flannel to clean herself ... the radio as it played soul music outside on the landing ... the smell of her rose water soap filling the air ... the heat from the steam because she liked her baths hot ... the sound of her laughter as I told her the dog had flown to the moon ... her long fingers as they curled around the edges of the bath right before she stood up ... her voice as she'd say, 'Hand me my towel, please, Fleury-Boo' ... the happiness of being allowed to help and saying, 'Here you go, Mum' ... the feel of the scratchy towel as I took it off my lap and handed it to her ... her becoming a giant when she stood up to wrap the towel around her body.

I remember. I remember every second of it.

'Hand me my towel, please, Fleury-Boo,' she says to me. I open my eyes, looking for her, looking for my mum. Her voice was here, surely she should be too.

She's not. It was an echo from my memory.

I take in the bath again. My fingers stroke slowly along it. My throat is too full, my heart is caving in, my eyes are too heavy.

'Here you go, Mum,' I murmur.

'Thank you, Fleury-Boo. Thank you.'

Tami

Fleur's boyfriend, Noah, rests the picture against the wall in the hallway, then immediately flexes his fingers at the strain that carrying it put on him.

'I really can't accept this,' I tell Fleur. 'It's too much. It should be yours.'

'It is mine. I want you to have it, though.'

'But, Fleur—'

'The thing is, Mrs C, I hate that story. Yeah, yeah, I know hate isn't the opposite of love and it suggests an on-going emotional attachment,' she glances at Noah when she says this, he must have tried to reason with her, too, 'but I hate it. I hate that story and I hate that picture. It reminds me that my mother left me. That she'd rather be there, in the picture, on some fantasy quest, than to stay with me.'

'I'm sure it's not that simple, Fleur. Life's not that simple.'

'Sometimes, it really is.'

'She loved you.'

'So? She loved me but she still left me. She had no part in my life until I was grown up. I'm starting to, you know, be cool with that. We all do what we gotta do. But I still hate that picture and that story. Yeah, she probably changed her mind and tried to come back, but some mistakes are just too big.'

Yeah, they are, I think. 'Look, I'll keep it for you. I wouldn't feel right, accepting it, so I'll keep it for you. Wherever I am, the picture will be too until you want it back.'

'You sound like you're going somewhere,' she says.

'Get off me! Don't touch me!' Chocolate-brown silk. Raised voices. Flailing, fighting arms, kicking legs. Mirabelle's face. My body burning with an incandescent rage.

'You just never know what's around the corner.'

'True.' Another look at Noah. I'm glad she has him. I'm glad she has someone. 'But if I could give you one bit of advice from, like, someone who knows – don't leave your kids. I know you wouldn't but, you know, just don't.'

I smile at her.

'Get off me! Don't touch me!'

I'm not sure how it was for Mirabelle in the actual moment when she left her child all those years ago, but I know that for me, I may not have any choice in the matter.

Beatrix

'Hello, TB.' He is so calm, so quiet, so relaxed.

I shouldn't have answered the phone, it's not my house after all, but it was automatic: a phone rings, you pick it up, don't you? Well, I do.

And it was him. *Him.*

He sounds ... Normal. His voice, his tone, causes me to catch my breath, then to drop the phone.

'Tami?' his tiny, tinny voice squawks from the receiver on the carpet. 'Tami? Are you there?'

Bending slowly, my trembling fingers reach for the silvery-grey handset and place it near my ear. Not actually to my ear because I don't think I could stand to have his words reverberating directly through my body.

'I know you don't want to talk to me right now, but I need ... sorry, what I need isn't important. But I'd *like* to speak to you. I miss—' I click the red telephone hang-up button. I can't listen any longer. With a shaking hand, I return the handset to its cradle, staring at it, seeing his face. The lines that make up his manly, powerful features: his straight nose, his set lips, his brow above those chocolate-maple eyes, his hair styled carefully off his face.

He did not sound like a man in pain; so mired in his own private version of hell he has not been able to reply to my texts, answer my calls (not even when I have sneakily with-held my number). He will not speak to anyone at work who does not give their name and reason for calling.

Scott sounded like a man who missed his wife. A man in love with his wife. *'Never mind his wife, he can't love her, she can't love him.'* Isn't that what Tami said? Never mind that he was married, I lied to myself that it was OK what I was doing because *I* loved him. I defended myself, I defended him, I defended what we did by saying it was love, we couldn't help ourselves, Tami was deluded because she couldn't accept that.

I'm the one who's deluded. My hand goes to my chest, to the site of my scar, to where the weight of the world seems to rest. I'm the one who's been in denial about what I did, who I really am.

The door opens and she sticks her head around. Her gaze rests momentarily on my hand, on the way I am holding myself together.

'Are you in pain?' she asks. 'Do you need me to call the doctor?'

I shake my head. It's here now, dispersing through me like dye dropped into water, spreading out through me, staining every part of me as it moves. Guilt. Guilt at what I've seconds ago done and what I've done in the past.

'Are you sure?' she asks, stepping into the room. She avoids coming into this room as much as possible. It's sort of become my living room because the children either play in the kitchen or in their bedrooms or in the garden. I wonder what happened in this room that has made her consign it to a never-visited zone. I used to avoid this room before I started to stay here because of the pictures of family life it held on its walls. Now I sit here and drink in those pictures, trying to believe I will be seeing them for years to come, that things will work out for me.

I am in that stage between appointments when I am recovering from surgery and waiting for chemotherapy. I am euphoric and exhausted often in the same spaces in time. I am here. I keep reminding myself of that. I am here. And now, my guilt is here, too.

Tami stands uncomfortably in her own living room and stares at me.

'Did I hear the phone?' she asks.

I say nothing, but my eyes dart to the phone in its cradle, the image of Scott's face evaporated but the memory of hearing his voice, discovering the way he really spoke to her, really felt about her, lingering like a heavy, cloying perfume that will take time to disappear. I press harder at the scar, at where the weight of the world lives, at where the guilt has started.

Her eyes go from me to the phone then back to me before moving on, like they always do eventually. She knows.

She knows I picked up the phone and it was Scott. She's probably wondering what I told him, if I begged him to come back to me. If it's only a matter of time before he is at the door claiming me. 'Don't answer my phone,' she says calmly and not unpleasantly.

'*Sorry*,' I mumble. '*Sorry for answering your phone. Sorry for sleeping with your husband. Sorry for trying to manipulate you into leaving him. Sorry for ruining your life. Sorry for everything. I am truly, truly sorry.*' Except I don't say those things. I don't say the single word. I don't say those sentences. I'm not sorry enough to breathe in her presence right now. I'm not even sure I'm sorry enough to carry on living.

Tami

Something is different about her. I noticed it when I walked into the living room and she was standing there, clutching her chest, her body so rigid it seemed capable of shattering if I breathed too hard in her direction, looking as if she had just been diagnosed with cancer all over again.

She'd been talking to Scott, I realised when I asked about the phone. He's the only one with that number, so she must have been. I don't know what he said to her, I don't know if he told her off, or said he'd never loved her, but it's as if her spirit – whatever it is that has kept her going so far – has been peeled away by a sharp knife, leaving her with nothing. Leaving her with the shell of the person who doesn't make it down to breakfast or any other meals any more, and barely raises her head when I take meals up to her.

I think she's given up.

That selfishness, that denial about what their affair was about, that constant arguing we were doing was driving her. It's evaporated. All I can see is a person who is sorry, a person disintegrating under the weight of her guilt.

She's given up.

I need to speak to Scott, to find out what he said, but that would mean speaking to Scott. I still can't manage that. We text and email about the girls, but we don't speak. I can't talk to him. His voice would sound the same, and he'd call me TB and arrange his words in sentences that I found so familiar and comforting, and normal, I'd only have the truck-smash sensation all over again when I put the phone down. Anyway, who rings her husband to find out what he said to his mistress to make her give up on life? Me, apparently. Because this is the life I have been placed in. This is the life I've got since Mirabelle died and I have been battling with my own guilt demons.

I think she's given up on life.

And I don't know if I'm strong enough to find out how to make her live again.

The Rose Petal Beach picture is in front of me. The way Mirabelle said she knew the artist makes me think now that they were probably lovers. That's why the picture is so intimate, the shape of her body so accurate, so precise. The person who had captured Mirabelle on this canvas knew her so well, had loved her so completely, they could put into the image something unique and precious. Every stroke is an act of love, a sonnet to the perfection they saw as Mirabelle.

The ache of missing her unfolds inside and I have to close my eyes as the suddenness, the enormity of it yawns throughout my body.

Mirabelle would have wanted to live. She would have given anything to live. The split fingernails, the state of the bathroom, the bruising on her body that DS Harvan told me about say that she fought as hard as she could to live. Her terror at what was coming must have been huge, insurmountable. Drowning, her lungs filling up with water each time she was submerged, the pain of fighting, the horror of knowing that she couldn't stop what was happening to her.

Knowing, as she died, that she would never see her daughter again. She would be permanently leaving behind her baby girl.

Her face becomes clear in my mind, in the space where the chasm of missing her is, and I see her smile, I see her skin, the curls of her black hair, the look in her eyes that made her Mirabelle. Gone. It's gone. She's gone.

And now we have Beatrix.

She's given up on life.

If I had believed Mirabelle, would her death still have happened?

'Get off me! Don't touch me!'

There's nothing I can do realistically to 'save' Beatrix. But I can help her. The question is, do I want to help her? She has helped me. Having her here, in my life, in my house, has held back the devastation, like Moses holding back the mighty, raging waters of the Red Sea. The pain and horror and sorrow, the deep wound is still there, but they are transmuted, frozen, waiting for the time they will be allowed to flow again. There is a time limit, of course, on how long I can defer the crash, but at the moment it is a divine luxury to be able to think, feel, breathe without being mentally and emotionally devastated.

Beatrix has given up on life. If I do nothing, it will be me who helped to kill her. It will be another death on my conscience; another splash of blood on my soul.

The shaking is back as I reach for the phone.

A second after I hit the dial button the line clicks to connect.

'Hello, Scott,' I say before he can speak. I need to delay hearing his voice for as long as possible because as soon as I do, I will become undone, like the threads of my life that have already been unwoven, I will come apart. 'I think we need to talk.'

'Hi, TB,' he replies.

And I am undone.

Tami

'Beatrix.' How many times have I said her name since I found out? I've avoided saying it because her name was synonymous with the role she had in cleaving our lives apart.

I can tell I haven't said her name too often because she stops staring at the window and refocuses on me. This room is a pit now. She has left it to go to the toilet, to go for a shower and to come back. She has been wallowing in bed, staring at the window, sometimes with the television on, sometimes with the radio on, mostly there is silence. I don't know if she has been surfing the internet on her phone, but I know that mostly it is quiet in here. As quiet and still and darkened as you would imagine a mausoleum.

The blinds are always closed, firmly shut against the outside world. Light seeps in, of course, light is like life, it will not give up until it absolutely has no choice, but this room is dark, and it is quiet and it is still. The air has not moved in a long time, it has become stained, infected with the smell of sleeping bodies and food. It is stagnant. And I'm not going to put up with it for a moment longer.

Even though I have her attention, I stand and go to the window. I tug on the blinds cords to let in light, to let in the outside world, and then my fingers fumble for the catch, to open it, to let in some air, some new life.

511

'Nggghhhh,' she groans. 'Don't.' She moves in bed, shies away from the light, pulling the covers over her head, disappearing from the freshness that has instantly started to wake up the room. There are security latches stopping the windows opening more than an inch or two, and if I didn't have to go back to the bedside table to get the key, I would throw them wide open letting the world around us cleanse this room of the staleness within.

'Beatrix,' I say again, the word mottling on my tongue, as I return to my seat beside the bed.

She slowly lowers her barrier of covers, to look at me again. Surprised that I have said that word, her name, again.

'He loved you,' I say. I don't lie. I don't lie unless ... 'I, erm, spoke to him. And he loved you. That doesn't mean he didn't love me as well, but you know ... *Scott*. You know he's complicated. He loved you. I know he did.' Unless I have to. Unless I have this huge, terrible thing that I need to make up for in any way I can.

Moving as if she is in great pain, she eases herself upright in bed until her upper half – covered in a grubby, off-white vest that I recognise as her yoga top – is completely exposed. 'Why are you saying this shit to me?' she asks.

'Because ... Because it's the truth.'

'No it's not,' she says, her face twisted in disgust. 'Of course it's not. What are you doing?'

'I'm ...' I begin.

'I fucked your husband, remember? For nearly two years. In this bed. I fucked your husband and I fucked you over, and I know it wasn't because he loved me. It was because he could and I would. So why are you saying this shit to me?'

512

I'm shaking. I thought I could do this and I thought I could be strong. But the shaking is back. The *need* for a drink is back. The feeling of fear at what I think I have done is back. 'Because it's enough. There's been enough loss and I want it to stop. You've given up because you think he didn't love you. I need you to go back to fighting and looking after yourself and believing you can get through this. You know, Mirabelle . . . She had no choice in what happened to her. But you do. You need to . . . Just live, Beatrix, don't give up. I can't lose you, too.'

She stares at me, her forefinger and middle finger pressed against her trembling lips. 'What is wrong with you?' she snaps. 'Why can't you just hate me and be done with it? I did a horrible, horrible thing to you and to your family. If it was me, I would have put my foot down when I saw you in the road, not slowed down. I would have ripped out every hair on your head and scratched your face off. I remember how much I raged when I found out what my husband had been up to. I remember the unquenchable anger I had in me. But you . . . You won't hate me. WHY DON'T YOU HATE ME?'

She thinks I'm being a saint. I am not a saint. I am a person who is scared. I am scared of what I'm capable of. I am scared of the memories that are being pieced together from that night. I am not a saint, I am simply scared.

'I do hate you and I hate what you did,' I say to her. 'But I hate the thought of you dying more. It really is that simple.'

She stares at me for a few long, tense seconds. But it isn't until she disintegrates in tears that I realise that, without even trying, I've hurt her more than I thought possible.

513

Beatrix

'I do hate you and I hate what you did,' she says to me. 'But I hate the thought of you dying more. It really is that simple.'

The thing is, I am meant to pass away peacefully in my sleep from natural causes aged ninety-nine. I am meant to be surrounded by my beautiful brood; I am meant to be holding the hand of the man I love, who will pass away within days of me because he can't contemplate remaining on Earth without me. I am meant to be a mother and a grandmother and I am meant to have lived a fabulous, fulfilling life.

They caught it early. I know this. The prognosis is EXCELLENT (even though there are no certainties in this world). I know this, too. I am almost fully recovered from surgery. I am fit. I am young.

In the grand scheme of things, I am doing well, better than a lot of others with my condition.

In the small scheme of things that is my life, I am sitting in a bed bent so far forwards my forehead is almost making contact with my outstretched knees, my arms are around my waist, and I am crying. My body is rocking as it is racked with agonised sobs. Five little letters have done this to me. Five letters beginning with D.

That is the first time anyone has used the D word about

me in relation to this. They talk around it, they use words like 'prognosis' and 'mortality' and 'stages' and 'grades', all to avoid using the range of D words that mean the same final thing. I am dying. My body is attacking itself and I am dying.

I am dying.

I. AM. DYING.

I haven't accepted that. Why would I when we don't talk about it? When we can't stand up and look that word in the eye. Not in this context. How many times have I disrespected the range of D words by merely throwing it in with a jumble of phrases about something frivolous and unimportant: *'I was so embarrassed I could have died.' 'I'd die for another piece of cake.' 'I looked like death warmed up.'* I never meant it. I never understood it. It was never truly relevant to me. Why would it be when I am young and healthy? When things like *that*, you know, the D stuff, happen to other people. People like me do not get these sort of test results other unfortunates do. They're the people whose misfortune and misery you absolutely understand and feel for; their pain and hurt churns you inside because you completely understand what they are going through. And, you're so deeply affected by their plight you keep them in your thoughts; you say a prayer if you're that way inclined; you cross your fingers and hope that it all works out for them to beat the odds no matter how slim.

BULL SHIT that you understand. You have *no* idea.

I had no idea.

I had no idea until it happened to me.

And even then, *even then*, the D words were off limits. They were caged away from me, everyone careful not to use them, everyone stopping their sentences rather than utter the ultimate taboo to me. It wasn't going to happen as long as no one spoke of it.

Now she has spoken it. She has said it. And everything is falling apart.

'I'm sorry, God, I'm so sorry. I didn't mean ... I'm sorry. I'm so sorry.'

'It's not your fault,' I sob.

'I'm so sorry.'

She's sobbing now, horrified she has broken the taboo.

'God,' she is digging the heels of her hands into her eyes, 'what is wrong with me? I'm sorry, I'm so sorry.'

'Tami, I ruined your life, please stop saying sorry.' I can't bear it, you know? I can't bear how noble and kind she is. Kindness is so underrated. She has sacrificed so much of herself to help me out and she still has the decency to be devastated. I can't bear it.

'Do you know why you and Scott hurt so much?' she says suddenly, her sobs subsiding.

I don't want to talk about Scott, especially not now. Especially when I've just realised I. AM. DYING. But do I get to choose what I do and don't want to talk about? Maybe I would if I hadn't been such a selfish bitch pretty much my whole life. I shake my head.

'It,' she inhales deeply, drawing on her courage, 'it was because I wondered if you were the type of woman he's always actually wanted.' Her tear-stained eyes are heavy and tired. Without warning she stands and then climbs onto the bed, resting her head on the pillow next to me as she curls up and faces me. 'It made sense that you and him were having an . . . *affair*. I've wondered on and off for years when he was going to find someone else.' She inhales and exhales deeply again. 'Scott was never my type. The policeman who's been investigating what happened to Mirabelle? He's more my type. But I got swept up with Scott. Not by him. Just with him. I'd known him so long, he was such a good friend. He cared about me, I cared about him. I fell in love with him over time despite him not being my type. I've always wondered if it was the same for him.

'And then you came into our lives. All cool and free and into football and the same music. And white, of course. Like the girls he used to go out with. His family wouldn't have had an issue with you. Your family wouldn't have had a problem with him because they wouldn't know he comes from a family of criminals, like my family knew and had issues with.

'Me and Scott, we were Romeo and Juliet. Which meant it was always bound to go wrong, no matter how much we believed we could rewrite the ending. So, it made a horrible kind of sense he went with someone he found it easy to be with.'

'You. Scott. The pair of you obviously chose each other because you wanted to be together,' I admit.

'And he chose someone else. You.'

I rest my head back and stare at the ceiling. I've been doing a lot of thinking since that conversation with Tami in the hospital, since I heard his voice, since he tried to tell Tami he missed her, and I've come to the conclusion that I have been deluding myself.

I have been lying to myself that he loved me, that what

he felt was anything other than finding another person to fuck because his wife was sick of being used. Please believe me, it didn't feel like that. Not all the time. Sometimes, yes. But isn't that what relationships are about? They aren't always about equality and respect. Or are they? Is that what a good relationship is about *all the time*? Don't people sometimes behave badly? Don't you have to sacrifice a little of who you are to make the person you love happy?

I have been in denial, lying to myself so I could believe him. Whether I loved him or not, I accepted his version of their relationship because it suited me to believe him. It made it OK because he wasn't getting much sex at home, and what he did get was nothing beyond missionary. I often quietly acknowledged that he was probably exaggerating, that in conversations we had she would mention things she'd done in the bedroom, and since she'd been with him so long, she must have tried them with him. His story didn't work if I examined it too closely, so I was always careful to leave it alone.

Denial. I have become incredibly well-versed in denial, don't you think?

That's why I ignored how tired I felt. The inexplicable weight loss – nothing major – just enough to notice that I wasn't in good condition.

That's why I ignored the lentil-sized lump I'd noticed in my breast a long time ago. It was a cyst, it was my imagination, it was nothing to worry about.

Until it's the size of a large blueberry and mostly visible on my cleavage.

Until it's cancer.

I'm excellent at denial. And it's almost cost me my life. It's absolutely cost me my best friend. She's taken the time to get to know me. To understand me. And I . . .

'He didn't choose me,' I reply. 'As I said before, he did it because he saw an opportunity and he worked out that I would go along with it.' He worked out I was a weak person who would put love – or at least the illusion of love – before a friend. 'I could have been anybody.'

'That's a comforting thought.'

Did you notice what she did there? I've seen her do it a million times with Cora and Anansy: distract and divert to calm down a tantrum or hysteria. Nine times out of ten it works. Like it's worked now.

'You know why I went into a depression?' I say to her. I want to reach out and trace my fingers over the lines of her face. I want to tell her to take care of herself. That whatever it is that is eating her up is not worth it. Nothing and no one is worth losing your health over.

'Because Scott called me when he hadn't called you,' she says flatly.

'No, because when he called he sounded nervous. He sounded desperate to speak to you. He said he missed you before I hung up.' I lick my parched lips, I've stopped putting on the lip salve that I'm meant to. I've stopped doing a lot of things I'm meant to because I don't really care any more. It's not important to look like a woman any more, it's far more important to feel like a woman, to feel alive. I don't at the moment. I don't feel alive. But I don't feel the other thing, either. 'I realised what we had wasn't some big, grand love, it was a grubby little affair. I was a grubby little other woman

519

who thought the scraps of someone else's husband were all I was worth. Even if that hadn't been the case, I'd been waiting for the man I was sleeping with to leave his wife. Leave my friend and her children like that was nothing. Those few seconds on the phone made me realise what a terrible person I had become.' I swallow, my throat sore and dry like my mouth. 'And then I realised I hadn't become that person, I *was* that person. I've always been that awful type of woman who would do anything to make someone love me.'

Tami says nothing for a moment or two, digesting what I have said. Then she says, 'I think we're all capable of doing terrible things and then telling ourselves it's OK because it's for love, me included.'

I turn my head to her. 'I don't believe that for a second.' My smile sends pain shooting through me from the cracks in my lips.

'Despite what you think, I am not Saint Tami. I have done something terri— I am not Saint Tami.'

'Now I really don't believe that.'

She smiles but I can see something is sitting there in her eyes. Something is torturing her and I don't think it is simply her husband's affair.

'Tami, if you ever want to talk about what's going on with you . . .' When she focuses her gaze on me, the distrust she feels for me plain on her face, I look away and stop talking. It's too late for that. Once upon a time ago, when we were friends, I could have asked her what was hurting her so badly, she could have relied upon me for support. Now . . . She has to deal with whatever is eating her up on her own. I'm so ashamed about that.

'I'm dying,' I say to her after a few minutes.

'I know,' she says.

I've said those words out loud and it feels OK, actually. Not good, nowhere near the realm of good. Just not bad. Not horrific. I have said those words. I have accepted them for now, because tomorrow I may not be able to handle them. Tomorrow I may be broken by them. Or tomorrow I may be buoyed by them. I may embrace the concept and go about trying to live every single second of my life to its fullest. But in the here and now, I am OK with saying those words to another human being and simply sitting with them.

She reaches out, her fingers briefly touching the edge of the palm of my hand that lies on the bed before she withdraws again. 'But we all are in our own ways, so you can be living as hard as you can at the same time, too. You can try everything you can to get well because it doesn't have to happen right now.'

'Yeah,' I say.

'Yeah,' she says.

And we spend the next hour in complete silence.

18

Tami

'Thank you for agreeing to see me.'

I haven't heard him sound so humble in years; even when he was regretful – apparently – about being caught cheating he still had the edge of Scott The Arrogant about him.

I nod.

'As I explained to you on the phone, Mrs Challey, your husband wanted to meet you with me here so it would be a safe space for you both to talk.'

My eyes go to the brown-haired man in his fifties sitting in his comfortable chair.

'You're free at any time to stop this meeting and to leave,' he continues. 'If Scott says anything you don't agree with or wish to comment upon, feel free to. If you're not comfortable saying it yourself, you can ask me to mediate for you. If I see that you are showing any signs of upset or distress, I'll ask you if you want to carry on or I'll end the proceedings to protect you.' He pauses, presumably to allow what he has said to sink in. 'Does that sound acceptable to you, Mrs Challey?'

'Tami. Call me Tami,' I say. 'And, yes, it sounds fine.' Obviously I'd rather not be here at all, but those aren't the choices I have, are they? I opened the door to speaking to Scott when I called the other day about Beatrix. I could have shut it again, but not when we have to discuss him seeing the children and money and divorce in detail.

He didn't pressure me at all, he simply asked if I'd come along and meet his therapist, and allow him to tell me the truth about what he'd done. I'd gone to say, 'I don't want to see you ever again,' and instead, 'OK,' came out. And then I was talking to his therapist about what was going to happen.

The room we are in isn't small, but it is intimate, comfortable, homely. The sort of place Scott would normally have hated being in. He liked everything shiny, new and minimalist. How he must have *hated* our house.

'If it's OK with you, Scott would like to start talking,' the therapist says.

'Fine,' I utter. I don't plan on saying much.

I'm avoiding looking at Scott. Since I arrived I've kept my gaze towards the window, slightly to the left of him so his shape is in my line of sight, but I can't make out any of the details of him. If I see those details, I'll start reshaping and reforming him in my head, visually sculpting him until he is the person I want him to be, the man I thought I'd married, instead of the person he is. The man I married doesn't exist any more, I'm still not sure he ever did.

'Thank you, as I said, for agreeing to see me,' Scott says. 'I've been seeing Dr Bruwood since I left the house and he suggested it might be time for me to try to talk to you. I've wanted to speak to you, but have had to stop myself because that would all be for my benefit instead of yours.

'First of all, I'm not going to try to persuade you to take me back. You did absolutely the right thing in asking me to leave, I would never have started the process of helping myself if you hadn't done that. It's probably saved me. I had crossed so many boundaries ... I'm sorry, that's the most important thing I wanted to say. I'm sorry for what I put you through. I'm sorry for lying to you and cheating on you and manipulating you. And for the rest of it.

'Since I left I've signed up for a perpetrator's programme. It's hard.' From the corner of my eye I see him nodding, confirming to himself that it is difficult. Of course it is, accepting what you are. 'It's really hard. I've only done one session, but I've had to accept that I'm no better than men like my father and my brother. I always thought because I didn't threaten people for money, that I didn't go on the rob or didn't beat the children, that I was better than them. I'm not. And I'm doing everything I can to change that.

'I've also been talking a lot to Dr Bruwood about my porn addiction and how it affected me. I'm starting to realise it completely altered how I saw women, how I thought about women. I basically saw all women in terms of what they could do for me, sexually. I stopped seeing women as human beings, just as orifices. I also believed sex was all about how I wanted it, how I thought sex should be, what I was entitled to do ...'

He wants me to look at him. He wants me to connect with him, I think.

Scott continues, 'I thought I could do whatever I wanted whenever I wanted. I've been doing a lot of thinking about how I decided that what I wanted was going to happen no matter what.

'I'm sorry for how I made our sex life, for the resentment I showed towards you for not wanting to do the porn stuff.

I'm sorry for not even contemplating that you have a sexuality that is as important as mine. And I'm ... *so* sorry ... for what I did to you that night.'

The memory of the night of yes that felt like a no wells up, and immediately my body becomes rigid with the reverberations of those feelings. The confusion, the horror, the pain. I shut my eyes, trying to hide from what is coursing through my veins, then my eyes jolt open – it's much more real in the dark. Confusion, horror, pain send shockwaves through me again.

'Mrs Challey, Tami, are you OK?' The therapist's voice is calm and gentle. 'Would you like to stop?' The man who I had been lightly mocking in my head sounds so concerned, so sweet. It brings me back to the present, banishes the memory and its feelings back to where it came from. In the past. Firmly, securely in the past. 'Would you like to stop?' he repeats even more gently.

'I don't want to talk about that,' I say through my rigid mouth. The memory is gone but my body can't relax, it can't immediately let go of the residual emotions.

It's because he's said it, admitted it wasn't right or fair. All this time, the only other person who was there carried on as normal so I had normalised it in my head, convinced myself that I was the one who had misunderstood and overreacted, not him. He is telling me that it wasn't me, I was right to feel as I did. It was him. He had ... It was too complicated to unravel in its entirety but he used my yes, my consent, to brutalise me. He used my love for him and our family to pretend it was nothing out of the ordinary. If I hadn't stopped sleeping with him after that, he would have carried on and got worse ... I shudder. I saw the videos, I know where things could have ended up. I remove the thought of that from my mind. I cannot think about it any longer and go back to normal life. Another time I will deal with that, another time I will process it.

'Would you like a drink of water?' Dr Bruwood asks. He really is a nice man, I shouldn't have teased him, even in the privacy of my own head.

'No. I just want this over with.' I sound hard now.

'I'm so sorry, TB. I didn't think how bringing that up might affect you. I'm such a fool ... Look, one of the other things I wanted to tell you was that I went to the police. I told them the truth about Mirabelle. What I did, how I lied.'

I whip around to him. 'What?'

The shock of what he's just said is transmuted by the shock of seeing him properly. He looks ... like Scott again. He's lost the polish and sheen that encapsulated the man he has been these past few years. His hair has a gentle, slightly unkempt quality that looks like it was held under the shower for a few minutes then allowed to dry. Gone is the harsh cut, one of the preened creations he'd progressed to. His face is lined and lived in, he has a few open pores on his cheeks, his skin tone is uneven and healthy looking instead of fake, smooth and unnaturally glossy from his almost fanatical use of products. His fingernails are scraggly and chewed instead of manicured and perfect. He's wearing an old T-shirt of his that I'd 'borrowed' originally because it smelt of him, and kept after a few washes because it felt of him against my skin. It was a reminder of him, the real him, when I was living with the other him. He's also wearing jeans he bought for fifteen pounds at Liverpool's Saturday market when we went up there to see his sister one time when the children were young. (She'd been surprisingly welcoming but had made it clear we weren't to tell their parents she'd so much as seen us.)

He's looking me over, too. Seeing if I have changed, what's different about me. Trying, I guess, to see if what has been happening has altered me physically. It has, of course it has. The past few weeks have been life-changing, and life changes are always worn on your body – inside and out. 'You did what?' I repeat.

'I went and told the police the truth. What's the point in doing all this work on myself, trying to change, if I can't tell the truth about what I'd become?'

'What did they say?' I daren't ask what the truth is in case it is as bad as I fear.

He looks down at his hands, his body now a different shape as he holds it in a different way. Shame. Before he held himself in honesty and openness, now he holds himself in shame. He links his hands and then unlinks them. 'That policewoman, Harvan, told me that because the statement had been retracted and she's . . . *gone* it was too late now for an attack of the guilts, as she called it. She said she wanted to prosecute me for wasting police time and lying to the police. And they're very close to uncovering the evidence that will prove you were the murderer, not just there that night, and when she does so, she's going to do me as accessory before and after the fact.'

My body recoils; they still think they can prove that I did it. That I am capable of that. I still can't prove that I didn't.

530

'Why didn't you tell me that they thought you did it?' he asks quietly. 'She said you're their only suspect but wouldn't say why. Why didn't you tell me any of this?'

'Why didn't you tell me you were sleeping with my friend?' I reply, still shaky from the knowledge the police haven't given up on pinning a murder on me.

He inhales deeply and lets the matter drop by lowering his gaze. When he raises his gaze to me again, I can tell by the colour of his eyes that I am seconds away from hearing terrible news, I can tell by the way he has paused that he's about to reveal something so atrocious I will want to throw up. 'I've been unfaithful before,' he says.

I turn away again, my eyes focusing on the window as this latest truck strikes me without slowing; it is a full-force hit, square on the body.

'More than once but by different degrees,' he continues. Can't he see I'm already down here, can't he see that I was going to struggle to get up, why has he put his foot on the brake to stop and is now reversing to hit me again?

'I didn't . . . just start with a full-blown affair, there were different incidents over the years that allowed me to believe I could do it and get away with it. First it was a couple of flirtations, they weren't doing any harm so I didn't think anything of them.' *Wham! He's hit me again and has now applied the brakes and is coming for me again.* 'Then came a few more flirtations that I took a bit further with texts and emails and naked pictures.' *Wham! Brake. Reverse.* 'Then it was a couple of kisses with one of those people.' *Wham! Brake. Forwards.* 'I always stopped for a while afterwards, told myself I was being stupid risking everything like that when I loved you

531

and the girls. Often you'd mention something about one of those women, and I'd convince you that you were being jealous and paranoid.' *Wham! Brake. Reverse.* 'But when you let it go, I guess I thought it can't have been that bad, I wasn't going to get found out, so when the opportunity arose I did it again. But then, it was the next step – a couple of one-night stands on business trips.' *Wham! Brake. Forwards.* 'After each of those I swore never again. I didn't want to hurt you like that. I'd made a legitimate mistake and I needed to pull myself back and recommit to you. Make it up to you even though you never knew.' *Wham! Brake. Reverse.* 'And then, things took another step when I had a three-month thing with . . .'

'With the American woman who came over to find out about how the company worked,' I find myself saying. I *knew* he fancied her, I *knew* from the hour I spent with her when she dropped by before they met other work colleagues for dinner, she fancied him. But when I mentioned it he said I was paranoid, a jealous, nagging wife who was putting one and one together and coming up with sixty-nine. He'd been really proud of *that* joke, had chuckled to himself for weeks about it.

'Yeah,' he breathes. *Wham! Brake. Reverse.*

I can picture her, all long auburn hair, perfect white teeth, flawless skin, laughing at me as she sat astride him, fucking him. The little housewife she'd looked down her nose at when she sat in my home. *'Gee, your house is beautiful. You must be so dedicated to keep it that way,'* she'd said, moving a cushion on the sofa to the position she obviously thought it should be. I can see him, too, guffawing at how pathetic I'd been sitting there after serving them wine and not having a clue what their practically coded conversation was about.

'I'm sorry,' he says. 'For all of it. It's all bad, it's all terrible. I have behaved appallingly. I have treated you appallingly.'

'Why did you tell me that?' I say, unable to look at him. 'You could have gone the rest of your life without telling me that. I wish you had gone the rest of your life without telling me that.' I cover my eyes with my hands, pulling air in and pushing air out of my lungs as fast as possible to stop myself breaking down.

'I didn't want to tell you,' he says, his voice weighted with regret. 'But I had to because I had to let you know all the facts of your life before you make any decisions. I lied to you for so long, I need to be honest even though I *know* this will be the end. I have hurt you so badly, and you didn't even know the half of it. I'm sorry. I can't think of anything else to say except sorry.'

That *word*. I *hate* that word. It means nothing – just like anything, if you say it enough times it loses all sense, all meaning – but people say it all the time. People say it to me all the time. It is a combination of letters that has no meaning attached to it if you are having to repeat it several times over several occasions.

I hate that word with a passion.

'I love you,' Scott adds in a whisper. 'I wanted to say I love you. I never stopped loving you, I just thought what I wanted was more important than anything.'

'That makes it worse,' I say in my head. *'You loving me and still being capable of all those things, all those deceits and lies, it*

makes it worse. It shows that love is meaningless to you. How can you do that to someone you love? How?'

My tears are too much for me to speak through. And what is there to say? But why am I crying anyway? It's not as if he could ever come back, as if I could ever live with him again. This is simply confirmation of information – that we're over – that I already knew. Why am I crying? Did part of me hope that it would work out? That he could somehow undo his addiction, his behaviour, his arrogance, his *crime*?

Or is it that there is more of my marriage to be rewritten, more of the thread of my life to be unpicked and rewoven? Is it because I thought I knew it all, and in the end, it was only the tip of the iceberg of his betrayal?

I pick up my bag, my fingers closing around the cotton handle and finding an odd comfort in its familiarity. I stand and look directly at my husband. He meets my gaze with tears in his eyes.

I cannot speak right now. I cannot speak at all.

Without a word to anyone, I turn and leave the room. There are no second chances to be given here. Maybe a part of me came for that, maybe a part of me hoped that if he had done all the right things – even though I had no real idea what those right things were – I could learn to forgive, learn to forget.

That's not going to happen.

Beatrix

Hi Scott. I know you might not reply to this. But I'm going to say it anyway. I need closure. I need to speak to you and to see you to say the things I didn't get the chance to say before she found out about us. I think it's only fair. You don't get to walk away from this just like that. I feel like such a bitch doing this after all she's done for me, but I need to speak to you. I need to know if I meant anything to you. I know I didn't, but I'd like to hear you say it. Because I feel used. And, yes, I probably used you too to make myself feel better. To make myself feel like the years aren't advancing as quickly, to feel like I'm more desirable and sexy than a woman who seems to have it all. But, please, talk to me. With all that's going on in my life I need to make sense of these things. I need to stop assuming I know what was going through your head and find out for certain. I fell in love with you. You said you loved me too. Please, just talk to me. Please. Bea x

Tami

'Are you happy now Scott?' I say, returning to the room.

My whole body is aflame. I reached the bottom of the stairs, my hand on the doorknob to let myself out, when my whole body ignited and the slow, burning rage of the past few weeks became a rampant inferno of anger. I could barely contain myself and took the stairs two at a time to get back here.

'Are you pleased with yourself now that you've unloaded all that stuff onto me? What am I supposed to do with all this information? How am I supposed to cope knowing that you've basically shat all over the last five or six years of my life?'

The nice man in the corner does nothing, does not speak, does not protest, does not try to mediate.

'I've now got to go back and put on a happy face for your children because it's not their fault their father is sexually incontinent and their mother was too stupid to dump him the second she found him looking at porn and basically starting a sex life away from her. I don't know how I've been able to look my daughters in the face knowing I've still talked to you when you regularly orgasm to women being raped and abused on film.

'Oh and let's not forget I've got to cook and care for your

mistress because after what you did to Mirabelle and what happened to her, I'm too scared to be angry at another person in case they die on me, too.'

I throw my bag on the floor in frustration, pleased that it causes Scott and the nice man in the corner to jump in alarm.

'Are you happy now?' I ask again. 'While you get to fart about talking to your little mate here, and going on counselling courses to try to address your behaviour, I've got to carry on with every-day life. And who do I talk to, huh? Mirabelle? She's dead. Beatrix? She's dying and the last time I spoke to her she was manipulating me to try to split us up. My family? They already hate you, I won't get a word out before they start plotting to have you killed. That's it. My support network of one. Me. Because I was so busy all these years raising our family, looking after our home so you didn't have to worry about it, earning a wage so all the financial responsibility didn't fall upon you but fitting it in around you and your wonderful career, there is nothing left for me. It's been all about you for years.

'All of that was bad enough, hard enough, and now, you've unloaded the contents of your head onto me so you feel better. What am I supposed to do with it? How am I supposed to feel? Tell me that, how am I supposed to cope and feel and carry on when my life has been a lie?'

'It's not been a lie,' he says.

'SHUT UP!' I scream at him. 'Just shut up. I can't even get angry without you butting in and telling me how it is from your point of view!' Anger is not attractive, it is not feminine, it is not what women like me are meant to feel or

537

show. But my God it feels good. I'm liberated, free of the shackles of expectation that have been binding me since all of this began. I'm not supposed to get *this* angry. I'm supposed to have a mini-meltdown, supposed to shout a bit, maybe cut up his suits, drink a little too much, eat ice cream, gather my girlfriends around me for emotional support and then I'm supposed to step back and be dignified. I'm supposed to inhabit the higher ground and not react. But, the reality is, I have so much rage inside me I could smash things, I could punch Scott into the middle of next week, I could commit murder.

'If you weren't the father of my children I would never see you again. I would be happy for you to rot in hell. I HATE YOU!' All the veins in my face and neck stand out as I scream that at him, and he shrinks back.

'If you were so unhappy, so unfulfilled with our life, why didn't you leave?' I have reined myself in again enough to speak at a shout. 'Why didn't you walk away? The girls? You were hardly there anyway, you'd probably see them more if you left. The house? You could have had the stupid place, the girls and I would have been fine elsewhere – even though it was my money that made it possible for us to buy it. What, you stayed for the image of a family? You could have found someone else who didn't mind the porn sex and having to go out of her way to look good all the time, and the constant, low-level disrespect. If everything was so horrible that you had to behave so badly, why didn't you just leave? Huh? Why?'

'Because it wasn't horrible,' he mumbles. 'It wasn't horrible, it wasn't terrible, you did nothing wrong.' He stares down at the carpet. 'I just wasn't satisfied with what I had.

I didn't want to leave but wanted the excitement of sex with someone new ... And ... I wanted to have what you call porn sex. It wasn't you, it wasn't awful. I wanted an adventure and I thought I could get away with it.'

'Is that what you think I deserved? To be treated like that?'

His head moves slowly back and forth. 'No. I suppose I expected you to put up with it because my mum put up with all the stuff my dad did for the good of the family. She was never going to leave, no matter what he did. I never wanted to be like him but I think I sort of expected you to be like her.'

'Oh, yes, that's right, I forgot, you had a hard time growing up so you get to treat the whole world like shit.'

'I'm sorry.'

'Oh, fuck off, just fuck right off.' I turn to the nice man in the corner. I want to tell him to fuck off too. He's probably the reason that Scott has managed to connect the dots enough to be honest and to open up but he's still the one that Scott talks to; his mate who knows all his secrets. He hasn't done anything to me, though, so I hold my tongue. I snatch up my bag, grateful that nothing has come out, and spin towards the door. My hand grasps the brass doorknob and throws it open, not caring that it slams against the wall, and I race out into the blue-carpeted corridor, then down the rickety staircase again. I slam the door onto the street behind me, not caring that I'm probably disturbing the other people getting therapy in other parts of the building.

I run down the street, away from this stupid place where more of my life has been erased and rewritten, not bothering to stop and check before I cross the road. That's always been my problem, following the rules, doing what's right, caring how what I do will affect others. Maybe I should take a leaf out of Scott's book, out of Beatrix's book, out of Mirabelle's book and please myself first. Then sit back and expect everyone else to fall in line.

'Tami!' I hear Scott's voice somewhere behind me. I can't speak to him right now. If ever. I run a bit faster, away from the direction my car is parked. I've probably got a ticket by now because I only put an hour on the meter. I thought I'd hear what Scott had to say then would leave and be back in my car within the hour.

I tear into the little patch of green surrounded by fencing that sits among the old regency buildings of this area, my bag flying wildly on my shoulder as I round the corner. I'm hoping the shrubs will hide me. I turn back to see if Scott has seen me, if he'll follow and will try to talk to me. Just as I turn back, I collide with the solid form of a body.

A pair of hands grab me and hold me firm. I look up at this latest obstacle in my path. The rage pumping through me halts, then goes into overdrive. If there is anyone I do not want to see right now apart from Scott, it is him.

'Mrs Challey?' His voice is rich and deep, like hot coffee on a cold, bleary-eyed morning. 'What are you doing here?'

Beatrix

Scott. Please. I would really like to talk to you. I'm not going to try to start things up again, I just honestly need closure on what went on between us.

Tami

I tear myself from Wade's grip and back away a few steps.

'What are you doing here, Mrs Challey?' he repeats.

'It's a free country, I can be anywhere I like,' I reply. I'm cheeking the police and I don't even care.

'True,' he says.

'What are you doing here?' I reply.

'I live around here,' he tells me. Straightforward. I'd expected, after my reply, for him to cheek me back.

'Right,' I say. 'See you then.' There is a bench and I want to sit on it, but I think once I do, all the anger and rage will pool around my feet and I will lose the impetus to do anything including walk back to my car. But I have to sit, anyway, since the adrenalin dissipating in my veins is making my legs jittery. I make my way to the bench, grateful that Scott obviously didn't see me – if he did he'd probably be here now. Talking, explaining, repeatedly using that stupid, meaningless word.

Cradling my bag on my lap, I inhale. I'm not that far from the sea, I can hear it in my mind's ear, I can definitely smell the salt in the air. I lean my head back, close my eyes and think of a bench on a beach, the sea behind it. Calm, rippling steel-blue water, orange sunlight dancing upon the tiny peaks of ripples. I hear the gentle, crooning swish of the waves on the beach, the languid bobbing motion of moving water.

This is my perfect fantasy beach, no bloodied footsteps turning to rose petals, no searching for a lost love. On my beach there is nothing but serenity and peace.

'You seem upset,' Wade says, sitting down beside me.

I open my eyes, force myself to sit up. 'Do I?' I reply.

'Yes, Mrs Challey.'

'Well, I can see why you're in the plain-clothes division, you're pretty sharp.'

'That I am,' he says.

I give him the side-eye, wondering if he is really clueless or if he is taking the piss.

He continues to stare straight ahead, idly swinging the plastic carrier bag with the name of a local convenience store on it between his hands. Taking the piss, of course.

'I've just seen my husband,' I say. 'It didn't exactly go well.'

'Want to talk about it?' he asks.

'That depends, are you going to use whatever I say against me in a court of law?' I reply.

'If I had to I would,' he states.

'Well then I don't want to talk about it,' I respond.

'I saw your husband the other day, as it happens,' he says, swinging and swinging his half-full bag. I wonder what's inside, what a man like him would be buying from a local grocery shop in the middle of the day.

'Yes, he told me,' I say.

'It's not often a person will come in and confess to a crime when they've got away with it.'

'You sound like you think he deserves some kind of medal.

543

How about not doing it in the first place, or is that too radical a concept nowadays?'

'I'm not saying that your husband is a good guy or that he doesn't deserve to be punished for what he did, I'm merely saying in my experience in dealing with these matters, very, very few people confess when they don't have to.'

'OK.' It's gone; the adrenalin from my anger has leaked away and I feel deflated, like someone has let all the air in me out and I am a flaccid shell of a woman, sitting on a bench in the middle of Brighton, feeling sorry for myself.

'After Harvan had left the room, your husband was also asking what I thought about those perpetrator courses,' he continues. 'He wanted to know if I thought they were worth doing and if they worked because he's doing one at the moment.'

'What did you say to him?'

'I said I was cynical. I've known a lot of men go on those courses in my time – a lot. Most of them are there because the Court ordered them there. Others are there because their wives or girlfriends make it a condition of their relationship continuing. Like I say, I've seen a lot of men go on those courses – well over a thousand – and have met maybe two or three who were "cured", by which I mean they don't go on to reoffend in the time I continued to know them.'

Alarmed, I turn to look at him. 'That's shocking.'

'Not if you think about it. Few of the men who go on those courses want to change. They don't think there's anything wrong with them. It's the world and the woman who "drove" them to it that's at fault. They only go to fulfil a condition of their sentencing or to get their wives to shut the hell up. They don't need to change. Why would they when it's the world's fault and not theirs?'

'So that's it then, no hope for Scott,' I say in despair. No hope for me trusting him to put the girls first, to be the parent they're going to need in the coming weeks if I'm forced to do what I think I'm going to have to do.

'Now I didn't say that, did I?' he corrects. 'I said I was cynical. The men I know who didn't reoffend are the ones who went there voluntarily as well as having personal therapy. They wanted to change. They followed the programme to the letter, they didn't think they knew best or try to trick anyone. They made the effort to learn what was being taught. Those are the men who do well. It's a point in his favour that he's signed up for it off his own back. It's another point that he came and confessed.'

'Things must be bad if you're trying to give me hope about my husband,' I say. 'That maybe he is capable of redemption after all.'

'We're all capable of redemption, Mrs Challey, whether we take the opportunity when it's offered is what shapes our lives and our character.' I can feel his gaze on me: fixed, sharp, knowing. 'But that also means we need to recognise the chance of redemption when it's offered.'

'I didn't kill her,' I want to say to him. *'I don't remember properly what happened that night, I know I had scratches and bruises but I know I wouldn't kill her. I might have felt enough rage to possibly do it, but I don't think I could do it. The way I miss her, the way I ache for her, tells me everything I need to know. I may have been there that night, but I didn't do it. I couldn't have done that to her. I couldn't have left her lying in a bath of bloodied water*

545

with her fingernails ripped off, her heels bruised, her face slack, her body lifeless.'

'I'll leave you to it,' Wade says, standing up.

'Yes, thanks. I feel a lot better now,' I reply.

'Good. But you think about what I said about redemption, won't you?'

'I will,' I reply, offering him a tight smile. 'I definitely will.'

Beatrix

You're not being fair. Just call me or text me. Anything.
I just need to know what you were thinking. Is that too
much to ask? I think you owe me that at least.

Tami

Scott is waiting by my car by the time I return to it.

Under my windscreen wiper sits a plastic envelope with a green and white form inside. A parking ticket. In the grand scheme of things, it is pretty insignificant, but if Scott wasn't standing here I'm pretty sure I would be curled up in a ball on the ground, ticket in hand, howling at the injustice of all of this.

'Your house keys,' he says, holding out the slender Tiffany keyring fob that holds five different keys. 'They fell out of your bag. Normally Dr Bruwood would have called you to return them instead of inflicting me upon you, but he's absolutely terrified of you now.'

Unbidden, a vision of Dr Bruwood cowering behind his clipboard, quaking in his brown clothes while I rant and rave, comes into my mind and brings a small, vague smile to my face.

'He said he's seem some partners get angry before, but he's never seen anyone lose it like that.'

Our fingers brush together, briefly exchanging heat as I take the keys from him. I used to love those little, inconsequential, accidental touches we shared. They were the tiny but neces-
~y connections we reserved for each other, that reminded
~ow together we were. Another thing stolen from me.

548

'Are you going to divorce me?' Scott asks as I return my keys to my bag. I have to bin that keyring now, of course. He bought it for me when he went to New York for work. No doubt shagging that American woman. That is what is so complicated about all of this: there are so many little, minuscule things that connect us that will be reminders of the relationship I thought we had. The keyring, his favourite mug, my slippers he helped the children to choose last Mother's Day, even the wooden Bienvenue (welcome) mat that lives outside the front door that we picked up in France the weekend of our fifth anniversary. Our house is crammed with tokens of our life together.

'Yes, Scott.'

His body crumples a little, his face openly showing his disappointment.

'I knew the answer, couldn't help hoping . . .'

I lower my gaze to the pavement. His trainers are the ones the girls gave him for his birthday two years ago. I'd seen him looking at them when we were in town and, unusually for him, he hadn't immediately bought them, so I had, in consultation with Cora and Anansy. We'd presented them to him at his surprise party. It'd been easy to get him out of the way for a couple of hours in the morning and when he got back the house was primed for the party.

'Do you remember that surprise party we threw for you?' I say to him. 'I really wish I'd taken a picture of your face when I told you what was happening.'

I feel him smile at the memory but do not raise my head to see it. 'How you managed to organise it and invite fifty people without me finding out, I'll never know.'

'Cora and Anansy said it was the best party they'd ever had – mainly because of how many sweets they got away with necking. And anyway, they say that about every party, so I shouldn't get too big-headed about that.'

He touches my arm and doesn't take his hand away again. 'It was a fantastic party, you have every right to be big-headed about it.'

Without making too much of it, I tug my body away from him. His hand lingers in the space between us, obviously wanting contact again. He can't have it, of course. 'I don't really know why I brought that up,' I say.

'Sometimes I get reminders of things we've done in the past, often little things, and I want to talk about them with you, it feels natural to do that.'

That's exactly why I did it. I didn't know that until he said it, but that's it.

'The thing about all of this that hurts the most is what I let you do to me,' I say. He returns his hand to his side, sensing that no more contact is going to be forthcoming. 'What you said about your mother putting up with anything really struck a chord because it's what I've been doing. I would think something was wrong, I would question you, you would put me down, tell me I was paranoid, jealous, controlling, whatever, and I would shut up, even though I knew that I wasn't the problem. I trusted you before I trusted myself. Like, when you were shagging that American woman. I knew something was wrong, you were so normal but so different at the same time. I got really down about it and went to the doctor and she prescribed antidepressants. She asked a few questions about my home life but I told her it was all fine because you had told me it was. You had convinced me I was the problem.'

'Why didn't you tell me about the antidepressants?' he asks, shaken.

'I didn't take them. I almost did, but it didn't feel right to. I knew something was wrong in my world but I didn't know what so I assumed it was me. I told myself that I would see it through the next couple of months and if it was no better, I'd start taking the tablets. But you obviously stopped shagging her and went back to being you so I stopped feeling depressed.'

'Jesus, I had no idea,' he says.

'Let's be honest, Scott, if you did have an idea would you have stopped? Confessed? Would you have told me that you were the problem not me? Or would it have become another thing to use to put me down so you could carry on with what you were doing?'

'I don't know how to make this better, how to fix this,' he says, despairingly. 'I'm doing everything I can think of, but I don't know if it'll be enough.'

'You can't fix it,' I say, finally looking up and catching his eye. We hold each other's gaze, something we haven't done in so long. We've looked at each other but there's always been something hidden, a barrier between us; now we are open, now we are honest with each other. 'Our marriage is over, you know that. There is no fixing it.'

'I don't want that to be true,' he says, sadly, his voice swelling with tears.

My tears are not far away, either. It really is the end for us. I break our visual link and root around in my bag for my car keys.

'Once I've finished the programme and have had more therapy, would it be OK to sort of ask you out even though we'll most probably be divorced?'

That stops me. 'You don't want me, Scott, I'm not enough for you.'

'I do and you are. No matter what happens next, I'll never stop loving you. I'm getting help. I'm going to make sure this never happens again.'

'I believe you,' I say to him. 'I know you're trying and that's brilliant for you as a person and as a father to the girls, but me ... I can't ... I just can't.'

Scott inhales and exhales deeply several times. 'OK,' he concedes, 'I understand.'

'You do? *Really*?' Scott never concedes. He may pretend to because he has bigger fish to fry or decide he'll get what he wants by other means but Scott never concedes. Even before he became the stranger.

He nods. 'I don't like it, and I'm struggling not to try to manipulate you into at least thinking about going on a date at some point in the future, but I'm not going to do that because I understand. And you're right.'

'Thank you,' I reply. I open the car door and get in, but before I shut the door, he speaks again.

'Thanks for coming today,' he says. 'I'm sorry it was so awful for you.'

I give him a short nod.

'Kiss the girls for me,' he says. 'And tell them I love them.'

'You can tell them yourself. You can take them out for lunch on Saturday, if you want?'

'Really?' His face shows a thousand shades of joy and my

heart swells at the memory of the man who cried as he held both his daughters after they were born. It swells further at the memory of us taking it in turns to sleep the first month after Cora was born so one of us could watch her because we were too scared to take our eyes off her for even the shortest second. We did it again with Anansy even though we knew what to expect. My heart almost explodes with the memory of the man who said we should have the due date of our first inscribed on the inside of our wedding rings.

I nod. 'I'll ask them where they want to go and will drop them off to meet you.'

'Thank you,' he says, the happy smile still on his face. 'Thank you so much.'

I have to leave before I break down. This is the Scott I married, of course. And the other Scott murdered him.

Beatrix

She's sitting in the dark at the kitchen table, a full glass of water in front of her. She is fully clothed with her dressing gown over the top of her clothes, almost as if she'd meant to get changed for bed but had forgotten to, but still put on her dressing gown anyway. From the light in the corridor I can see the troubled frown on her face as she stares into space, not even acknowledging me as I enter the room.

Dressed in newly acquired pyjamas, I pull out a cream padded chair and sit down opposite her.

'Are you OK?' I ask her.

She takes her hands away from the glass, curls them up and places them in her lap as she sits back in her seat. She refocuses her gaze on me and manages one of those close-mouthed smiles of the Not OK.

'No,' she says to me. 'I'm not OK.' She rubs her hand across her scrunched-up eyes. 'But, old news, old traumas. Or rather, old news that keeps getting added to.'

She refocuses on my face, and a small smile develops on her lips as the mournfulness in her eyes deepens. 'You're going to add to that old news now, aren't you?' she says.

I look down at the table, ashamed. Thoroughly ashamed of myself because that is what I'm going to do. I can't lift my gaze from the table. I stare at it, noticing for the first time how it stands out in the kitchen because it is cheap. Not cheap as in 'cheap and nasty' – it's a very nice lightwood veneer – it's simply not handcrafted and top of the range like a lot of the kitchen. I'm sure it's from the early days when they didn't have much money. When they were mainly relying on Tami's wage to support them.

I feel so completely wretched for what I've done, but I couldn't stop myself. He's like an addiction, something I am powerless around. 'I'm weak,' I say. 'I'm weak and needy. And I hate myself for what I've done. I texted Scott. I needed closure with everything going on, I just wanted to end that chapter of my life properly so I can move on.

'I begged him to get in touch with me. I needed to hear from him, to hear what he had to say about everything. I couldn't help myself. I'm so sorry, I don't ever want to hurt you again, I just wanted to know. There are so many uncertainties in my life right now I suppose I wanted to grasp something that would make me feel as if I was standing on solid ground again. I'm sorry.'

She stares at the glass in front of her. Is she going to glass me? If I were her, I would. I probably would have a long time ago, to be honest. She takes a sip of water, and the way her face grimaces, it's not water. It's a tumbler of vodka or maybe schnapps. Carefully she settles the glass on the table.

'I understand,' she says. Slowly her eyes move up towards me until they settle on my face. 'I really do. I understand what it's like to be addicted to a person, to be weak around them. I was the same with Scott for a long time, so I do understand. Don't feel bad, OK? Just concentrate on your recovery and getting better.'

She must be angling for sainthood or something. I can't bear it. I suppose I told her because I wanted a reaction. He's ignored me, of course, and I wanted some acknowledgement that what I was doing was right, that I was owed an explanation from him. Yes, it's selfish of me to be asking that of her, but I think I'm entitled to be a little selfish right now. If, when you're in my situation, you can't think of yourself a little, I don't know when you can.

'You have to leave, you know that, don't you?' she says. 'You can't stay here any more. My fears have been irrational and they've forced me to make unwise decisions and accept the unacceptable.' She smiles sadly at me. 'I know you're scared, Bea. I know you're terrified for the future, but I can't take care of you any more. It's not good for me. I'm falling apart. I'm trying to hold everything together and it's stupid. I can't start to get over what's happened if you're here. I knew that and I accepted it. It was killing me, confusing the girls, but I thought I could do it to help you get better. But I can't do that if you're going to bring him back into your life. I can't support you in that. You have to leave.'

I have just been thrown off a cliff. With no warning, no chance to prepare myself, I have been thrown away and cut adrift. The cliff face in front of me is too sheer for me to even contemplate climbing, and that is if I can swim through these rough, choppy waters to make it back to the shore in the first place. She is leaving me alone. She is letting go of my hand when it seemed as if she was *always* going to hold on.

'If you want, I'll still come to your appointments with you,' she says.

But what about the nights of going to sleep knowing I'm not alone in the house? What about hearing the girls charging around getting ready in the mornings? What about taking them to school? What about the feeling of being part of a family? That has been helping me to find my footing in this new world I have been set adrift in. She has thrown me off a cliff and has only flung a toy life preserver as support into the rough seas beside me. I don't need someone to come to the hospital with me, I need a family around me to help me heal.

'I'll go in the morning,' I say.

'OK,' she says. She stands after pushing back her chair, the sound of it scraping at the inside of my ears.

She moves to the sink with her glass and after staring at it for a long, tortured moment pours it away. Rinsing the glass in a dribble of water, she turns it upside down to drain in the sink.

'Night,' she says on her way out of the kitchen.

'Night,' I mumble back.

I need a family. I've always needed a family. That's why I tried to take hers.

19

Tami

This is the first time I've been running since Mirabelle died.

It hasn't felt right to do it.

The laces feel unfamiliar between my fingers as I double-tie the knot on my left shoe. I always put that one on second. Mirabelle was left-handed so I think that's why she always put her right shoe on last. You could tell by the slightly less secure-looking bow she tied that one in. First bow you're always careful, always more conscientious about doing it right. Second bow you get cocky, you've done it before so don't need all that care and attention.

After this run, I am going to the police station.

I've remembered almost everything about the night Mirabelle died.

After this run, I am going to the police station and I am going to confess what I did that night.

20

Beatrix

This woman, this *receptionist*, has no idea how much I hate her. I hate her voice, her manner, her whole existence. She's the one who used to say 'soon' to me whenever I asked when Scott would be returning to work in those first days when he disappeared. She's the one who gleefully screens his calls now. For two days I've been dealing with her and her attitude. I thought it might be easier in person. It's actually worse in person because she can see me and look down on me.

I would look down on me, too, I have to accept that. I look ordinary. Yes, I know you never thought you'd hear those words from me, but it's true. See, my roots are growing out so I've got a halo of orange-red developing on my crown. The natural wave is returning to the rest of my hair so I'm not as sleek as I used to be. My complexion is pale, not touched up and brightened by make-up. I am dressed for comfort rather than display: baggy jeans, a T-shirt and this voluminous suede jacket my husband left behind, as well as comfy knickers and bra.

I can't be bothered with the other stuff right now. I can't face squeezing into a skin-tight skirt so it shows off my waist, I can't bring myself to pick up a make-up brush and create perfection. I can't be bothered to blow-dry or GHD my hair straight. This is me, just as I am. Ordinary.

Guess what? Ordinary ain't too bad: I have had a few men – men who would never normally look at the me I used to be – do a double-take. And I feel comfortable now that I'm not constantly on show. Ordinary, though, is not what this receptionist respects.

If I was dressed how I used to, she might not be so dismissive. She might not think she's got the right to treat me like I am nothing.

She really has no idea who she is dealing with.

'I would like to see Mr Challey and I *will* see Mr Challey,' I tell her.

She sits with her headset and her straight, smoothed and conditioned hair and gives me the 'good luck with that' eyebrow and says, as patronisingly as possible, 'That really won't be possible, Madam. Mr Challey really is extremely busy at the moment.'

'Fine. In two minutes I am going to start taking off my clothes. Every minute I am standing here I will remove another item of clothing until I am naked.' I look from her to the glass front of this building – this area is very visible to the outside world. 'Then I am going to start screaming the place down. Yes, the police may well come and take me away, that security guard over there may be able to eject me from the building, but not before I have brought A LOT of attention to your company. You might want to tell Mr Challey that I said all that.' I raise my hand and look at my imaginary watch. 'And just so you know, I haven't had a wax in *a very long time.*'

The Über Receptionist has never been taught how to deal with this. She keeps looking from me to the security guard who is sitting by the door, pretending to have not heard the threat. He doesn't get paid enough to wrestle with mad women. Especially ones who are promising him a bit of nudity. I remove my jacket and dump it unceremoniously on the ground.

With pursed lips she pushes a button on the desk in front of her. 'That's Beatrix Carenden, in case you've forgotten,' I remind her.

Tami

Detective Sergeant Harvan would like to kill me.

Normally, I'd expect her to look as if she wanted to lock me up and throw away the key. The look on her face, however, is telling me that she could reach across the table and put her hands around my neck and squeeze until I am dead. I get the impression that her position in the police force has been damaged by Mirabelle withdrawing her statement. It probably doesn't help that she hasn't found Mirabelle's killer – and the best they've managed is someone voluntarily coming forward to help them with their enquiries. I get the impression that DS Harvan doesn't like people making her look bad. Detective Wade seems a fraction less affronted. Maybe he thinks that his pep talk the other day finally woke me up to the fact that I had to tell the truth, but he's still internally outraged at the gall of me withholding information the last time I was here.

They both sit opposite me, and they have both made their statements for the tape of the date and the time and who is present. Harvan's yellow pad has a blue, clear-cased Biro on top of it in front of her, her hands are clenched together. Wade also has a yellow, lined pad in front of him but he has his pen in his hand. He is the listener, she is the questioner. I am the talker.

I don't have a solicitor because, really, what would be the point? I just want the truth to be known. To unburden myself.

'I still only remember most of what happened that night,' I say to them, staring down hard at my hands resting on the table. My hand still feels bare without my wedding ring. 'But I remember most of it now. So, if it's OK, I'll tell you what I do remember and then you can decide what to do next.'

The girls are with my parents in London, staying for the weekend, maybe longer. That depends on what happens next. I wanted them away from here when I did this. If they keep me in, I will call Scott and tell him. And even though he's only partway along his journey to being a good man again, he'll have to move back into the house and take care of the girls. Live his life around them as I've had to do all these years.

I suppose I am a 'flight risk' so it's unlikely I'll be released on bail. I am not under arrest, so I have not been formally advised of my rights to say nothing that may be later used against me in a court of law, but I have been told that if I am later arrested and charged, anything I say now will be used to build the case against me. Basically, they are telling me I'm allowed to 'incriminate' myself as much as I want right now and I can't say they didn't warn me when I decide to do the wise thing and get a solicitor.

'I was very drunk that night. I don't often drink, so more than two bottles of expensive wine on an empty stomach and frazzled nerves went straight to my head,' I say by way of a beginning. I'm not sure how I'm meant to begin this so I'm starting here. I may need to go back, I may need to skip very far forward, but this is where I am starting this: my confession.

Tami

I'm not sure how I'm meant to begin this so I'm starting here. I may need to go back, I may need to skip very far forward, but this is where I am starting this: my confession.

I was very drunk that night. I don't often drink, so more than two bottles of expensive wine on an empty stomach and frazzled nerves went straight to my head.

I only mention it was expensive wine because it came from Scott's personal collection. It's obscenely expensive and rare, and I opened both bottles at the same time because he had hurt me and I knew the quickest way to hurt him was through his pocket. I didn't intend to drink both bottles, I just wanted him to see them there on the table and know his precious wine hadn't gone on an important person but little old me. The stupid, clueless wife he'd been cheating on. Even better if it was left out and spoiled.

I was so angry. I suppose I should admit that. I thought at the time that Mirabelle had betrayed me. We were meant to be friends, really close friends, I'd trusted her with so much of myself – things I didn't even tell Scott, nor Beatrix. I genuinely thought Mirabelle had had an affair with my husband and she wanted him to leave me. It was all Scott's fault, but he was trying. Or that's how he painted it to me – he was trying, we were trying to fix our relationship, mainly for the sake of the children. I was deluding myself, I've accepted that now. But Mirabelle had suddenly been the reason for everything going wrong.

I know that's not right. It wasn't her fault, even if she had been sleeping with him, it was all down to Scott. There's a particular kind of hatred that grows inside you, though, when the other woman has made herself a part of your lives. When she has insinuated herself into your heart and mind, into the hearts, minds and lives of your children, and all along has been laughing at you behind your back. What else would she have been doing but laughing at me if she had the capacity to betray me like that?

I sat in the kitchen drinking and brooding and obsessing, that rage building until I was out of my chair and creeping out of the house without any shoes on.

I wanted to talk to her, to see if she could make me understand why she had done it. It was stupid to go there because I wasn't rational, I wasn't sober, and if I am honest I wanted to hurt her as much as she'd hurt me. I'm talking about then, of course, all that I knew then, not what I know now.

What I remember most is the feel of the pavement under my feet. It'd been raining earlier in the day so the pavement was still that earthy damp of not-quite-evaporated rain. I felt every stone underfoot, but I must have been sober enough to avoid stepping in any bird droppings, which are rife in our road.

She opened the door and I was awestruck as I often was when I saw her. You've met her, you know that she's that special kind of beautiful woman who is completely comfortable in her skin. She was in her silk dressing gown, with her big fluffy slippers on, her hair was bunched up on top of her head.

She looked so normal. She'd been sleeping with my husband for months and months and yet she looked so normal. Serene. Beautiful. She shouldn't look so normal and balanced and everything I wasn't. I wasn't jealous so much as angry for being made to feel second-best, if that makes sense? She didn't do that, I just felt like that after everything – after all the time we'd spent together, talking and sharing and being friends. After she'd encouraged me to take up running, and put myself first every once in a while, and have the confidence to be myself despite what the world around me was saying about being a mother and a wife and a woman, all along she'd been after my husband. She'd been worming her way into my life.

She sighed when she saw me, then looked away over my shoulder as if seeing if there was something more interesting out on the street. 'Yes? What do you want?' she asked, hostility in her tone. *She* was being hostile to *me*?

'I want you to tell me why you did it,' I slurred.

She stopped looking over my shoulder and concentrated on me. 'You've been drinking?' she said, suddenly full of concern. And then she looked down at my feet. 'And you've got no shoes on. Oh God, Tami, what are you doing to yourself?'

'Stop pretending you care,' I said to her, I was swaying at that point.

'Come in here,' she said and before I could properly protest, she took hold of my arm, pulled me into the house.

'Get off me!' I screeched at her, pushing her off. 'Don't touch me ever again!'

She let me go and I fell into the wall, which I was glad of because it was solid and I could hold onto it to keep me steady.

'I need to know why you stabbed me in the back,' I remember saying.

'You can believe whatever else you like about me, but I wouldn't do that to you,' she said. 'Especially not with him.'

'Why would he lie?' I said. That was when standing became too much and I collapsed.

She shook her head at me, looking so sad.

'Maybe he's not lying about what he's been up to,' she said, 'just who with? Maybe that's why you're so willing to believe what he's told you because deep down you know he's got someone else?'

'I saw the text messages,' I said to her.

'What text messages? I never sent him any text messages. If you knew how much I hated him you would know that I wanted nothing to do with him so there's no way on Earth I'd send him text messages.'

'"I know it's wrong but I can't help feeling how I do. I know you're married, but I'm willing to wait. I'd wait a life-time for you to be ready to be with me properly. It'll cause a lot of hurt, and I'm not proud of that, but I love you",' I said to her. 'You wrote that, didn't you?'

She stood there blinking at me, obviously shocked that I'd seen the text messages, horrified that I remembered enough to quote them; she didn't know they were burned into the very fabric of my being.

'You need to leave, right now,' she said and started to pick me up.

I didn't really want to be picked up, I was drunk and I felt perfectly happy sitting on the floor with the world not spinning. 'Get off me, get off! I told you not to touch me!' I was hitting back at her, kicking out so she would leave me alone. 'Don't come near me! Go away! Don't touch me!'

That was where the memories ended originally. The next thing I could remember, the next memory I could hold onto with any certainty, was waking up in bed fully clothed with no shoes or socks, a raging headache, cuts and bruises on my hands and forearms and the sense that something very bad had happened.

When I heard about the violence involved in her death, and remembered the rage in my body and mind, recalling that the last thing I knew for definite was that I'd hit out and kicked at her, I thought I'd done it. Then the memories came back, in flashes and feelings and déjà vu-like moments. As they came back I stopped being scared of them and instead grabbed at them, held them close and added them to the other patches in my memory until I could recall whole chunks of time. I don't remember all of it. I do remember that after a while she stopped trying to get me up, she stood back and looked down at me with abject despair.

'I don't like to see you like this,' she said.

'How am I supposed to be when it's all gone wrong?' I asked her. 'Tell me why you did it in words that I can understand and I'll feel better. This hit-by-a-truck feeling will go away, I know it will. I just need to understand why.'

She sat down next to me. I rolled my head along the wall, my neck felt very bendy because I was so relaxed, and looked at her. She looked back at me. 'I can't tell you that, because I didn't do it.'

Mirabelle was a kindred spirit. I think we both felt lost in the world sometimes. What's to say I wouldn't do what she did if I fell in love? I always thought I knew what I would do in any given situation, but when I found out my husband had cheated on me I hadn't chucked him out. What's to say if I met someone I fancied enough, I wouldn't break my wedding vows, decide that getting laid was more important than staying faithful to my husband? Maybe I would have been Mirabelle in that situation?

I stared into her eyes and she into mine. No, I wouldn't do that.

'Let's, for argument's sake, go along with this ridiculous idea that I had an . . . *"affair"* with him. Why are you willing to accept something so hurtful and deeply disrespectful? Why would you stay with him? Especially when it's someone you know? You're teaching your daughters damaging things about relationships.'

'Don't talk about my daughters, they're nothing to you.'

'They're everything, actually,' she replied. 'They're the reason I . . . He did it, Tami, and I'm sorry you can't see that. But I retracted my statement because I knew it would take the hardest toll on Anansy and Cora. They don't deserve to have their lives ruined by everyone knowing their father is a rapist, but hey, should I have bothered if they're being forced to live within what must be a hideous atmosphere?'

'You don't know what you're talking about.'

'Actually, I do. I completely know what I'm talking about. Did you grow up in a family where your parents showed each other they loved and respected each other or did you grow up with parents who slept in separate rooms, hardly spoke to each other, made nasty little comments about each other, would glare at each other, and would remind you every day with their relationship that when one person in the marriage is selfish and self-serving and entitled, everyone has to kow-tow to them because that's easier than upsetting the status quo?'

Mirabelle knew which type of home I grew up in because I trusted her with that. I opened up to her like I hadn't done in many, many years and told her the truth about what growing up was like. I told her about my father who could be lovely to us but would fly into uncontrollable rages; I explained about my mother who could be so caring and nurturing but would just as quickly become cold and unavailable. I opened up to her with things I hadn't even told Scott because Scott's home life trumped all others; no one's home life could be worse than the Challey home life.

Mirabelle knew this, she had understood this and had constantly told me that it wasn't my fault. It was things like that that made me trust her, and which made her betrayal so total.

'Do you remember how you swore you'd never put your children through what you went through?' she said to me. 'Do you remember how you promised yourself that you'd teach your girls that being a single parent is better than being a marginalised, unhappily married one?'

'Please stop talking.'

'OK, I will. But you stop talking, too. And we can sit here and pretend for a few minutes that none of this has happened, that you don't think me capable of betraying your trust, and I can pretend I don't mind you not believing I was almost raped. Let's sit here and be two friends who can sit in silence and not mind.'

We sat in that near silence, both of us staring at the wall opposite.

'Do you remember that time that woman asked us if we were sisters?' I asked her. 'And you told her we were actually lovers and she nearly fainted in shock?'

She gave a small giggle, one of those ones that would always set me off and we would end up incapacitated with laughter. 'Why did you think about that?'

'At the time, it seemed funny, now it's just an example of how easily you can lie and sound plausible.'

Her silence was shocked. It's hard to explain but she was clearly hurt by what I said, and that should have given me a little satisfaction but it didn't – I felt wretched.

'You know, I did sort of lie to you about something,' she admits. 'If you think of me not having the chance to tell you everything as lying.'

My head swung to look at her.

'He stopped,' she continues. 'He'd ripped my clothes, and was fumbling with . . .' She paused and took a couple of deep, steadying breaths. 'It wasn't only the phone ringing that helped me get away, he stopped himself. It was as if something snapped back in place and he came back to himself. His eyes, all the while he'd been . . . They'd been glazed over and vacant. Then he was there again. And he looked . . . I don't know, shocked with himself. Then the phone rang. He took his eyes off me for a second and I kicked him and ran.'

'He stopped?' I said. 'Did you tell that to the police?'

'Yes, of course I did. But it didn't negate what he did to me. He still hurt me, terrified me, he still penetrated me with his fingers – which is sexual assault. And which is why the police arrested him.'

I covered my mouth with my hands as bile mixed with expensive wine came rushing up my throat. I knew she was telling the truth. I just knew. And my whole reality started to cave in. He'd done it.

That was the terrible thing that happened, that was probably why my memory abandoned me, I didn't want to face that. I didn't want it to be true, so I turned my thoughts away from it, I escaped back into the drunk haze I was in and tried not to leave.

'You believe me now, don't you?' she said because Mirabelle was like that. She could see into my soul sometimes. It often felt she knew me better than I knew myself, and that she had known me all my life. That's why I had been drawn to her, I think. For how she made me feel.

I concentrated on breathing through my nose, getting oxygen in so I wouldn't throw up.

'I'm so sorry for what he did to you,' I said when I could get myself under control. 'And I'm sorry I didn't believe you straight away.'

Even as I was speaking, my mind was screaming about the text messages. They must have been having an affair, I realised. And then he got rough, he did that to her and she ended it. Or maybe she finished it because she felt so guilty, her text messages did say she felt guilty, and he didn't like it. Tried to get her back with seduction but things got out of hand, he got too rough and almost ended up . . . He didn't finish it, she did. He still did it, but then so did she. She still had an affair with him.

'I have to go,' I said, wondering how I was going to get up when I felt like throwing up, plus my legs were made of sponge and my arms were made of jelly.

She smiled sadly and shook her head. 'You still think I slept with him, don't you?' she said. 'Even though you believe he did what he did, you still think we were having an affair.'

'I saw the messages.'

'There were no—' She broke off from what she was about to snap at me and was suddenly on her feet and then dragging me upright. 'You know, Tami, there were all these things I wanted to tell you about myself that I haven't. I've felt so guilty keeping them from you. But now . . . I'm glad I didn't tell you. And you're right, you have to go.'

I held onto the wall for support and watched her through the haze that was descending.

'Go,' she said, sternly. 'Nothing I say is going to change your mind, so go.'

'Why won't you explain about the messages? If you weren't sleeping with him, then why won't you tell me about the messages? I know you wrote them. If not to him, then who?'

She glared at me. 'Goodbye, Tami,' she said, then turned and swept up the stairs in that imperial manner she had. 'Shut the door on the way out.'

I wanted to go up after her. I wanted to get her to explain about the messages because they were the only thing that didn't make sense in her version of events. And they were the only things that made sense in his version of events. Why wouldn't she explain?

But then a wave of drunken tiredness crashed over me and I couldn't stop myself from swaying, nearly toppling over in the process. I needed to leave. I could talk to her another time.

I hadn't even thought about how I was going to deal with Scott now I knew that he had done it. Like I said, I think I shut that horror away so as not to have a complete breakdown.

I don't remember how long I was there. I do remember tripping over the doorstep on the way out and instead of putting my hands out, I put them up to my face so I scraped the back of my hands and bruised my forearms. I cried with the pain and the anger and the hurt of everything, I remember that, but I picked myself up. After that, I don't remember much at all. I don't remember how I got home. The next thing I do recall is waking up in bed fully clothed and barefoot, like I said. I had a sense that I had seen Mirabelle the night before, but I couldn't remember it clearly. And I had a newfound revulsion for Scott. Even though we were waiting for counselling that he had never actually arranged, I could barely stand to be near him but I didn't know why.

And that's it. That's what happened that night. I've only just remembered so many of the details. As soon as I recalled almost everything, I knew I had to come in and tell you.

I can't control what happens next, if you want to formally arrest me then that's what's going to happen.

If you want to ask me any questions, feel free. I'm sure that's what you were always going to do but I sort of think I should make it clear that I'll answer anything.

Beatrix

'I can't believe you've done this to see me,' he says after shutting the door to the conference room he's hustled me into.

He once screwed me in here. I look around the room, which overlooks the huge courtyard one level down where they used to have summer drinks. The glass is tinted and mirrored so you can't see in, but you can see out. I remember watching our reflection as he kissed my neck, ran his hands up and down my body and then gently guided me forwards over the long, oval table that has microphones coming out of the seat places. *'I'm going to enjoy meetings in here all the more, now,'* he'd said as he moved quickly inside me, the fear of getting caught by one of the security guards adding to the excitement of doing something so forbidden.

'I had to do this so you would see me,' I say to him. We couldn't go into his office today because it is glass-walled and everyone can see in. People will talk if they see him lower the blinds. And I'm guessing it would get back to Tami that I was here.

He looks so different from the last time I saw him. Less polished, more like . . . More like the man I met in the street that day he was moving into our road. This is how Scott looked when Tami said her vows. He radiates decency, kindness, tenderness. He would look after you and listen to you, and be there when you needed him. He dressed in a smart but understated way, he didn't bother making sure his hair was perfect before he left the house, it just had to be neat. I sort of prefer the one I fell in love with. I liked this one, don't misunderstand, but the other one, he had more presence, more arrogance the world had to notice – no one walked past the Scott Challey who fell in love with me and didn't need to look again. He drew attention to himself with an impressive ease. And, most importantly, the new Scott Challey was a bit of a bastard and I liked that in a man. I craved men with an edge.

The man in front of me, although lacking the stance and presence of the real Scott Challey, has a face that is set with anger, he has eyes that are staring through me. He doesn't want to be here with me. It might surprise him to learn I don't want to be here, either. But he wouldn't reply to my texts, he wouldn't answer the phone. He won't talk to me so I've had to make him.

'What do you want, Beatrix?'

'That's how it is now, is it? It's all "Beatrix" and "what do you want?"?' I come closer to him, reach out to put a hand on his chest. I want to connect myself with him, he is a whole person, someone who is breathing and living, who hasn't had to have a part of themselves removed so they've got a chance at life. Physically, I've known the whole of him, I've kissed almost every inch of him, so I want my body to remember what it feels like to be with someone whole who I was once whole with. I want to touch him in a way I haven't been able to with anyone else. Just touch him to see if I can remember what it feels like to be complete again. 'You used to call me Bea in that low growl, you used to look at me like I was the most beautiful woman who ever lived. Remember?' He steps backwards, away from me, not allowing contact. Then takes a few more steps away to severely mark the gap between us.

'What do you want?' he asks again.

I turn my fingers into the palm of my hand, shock pumping through my body. I only wanted to touch him. I didn't want anything else. I couldn't do anything else even if I wanted to. But touching, making contact with another human, feeling their life under the skin of your palm, those are the things you need. *I* need.

Maybe he doesn't understand, maybe he doesn't know.

'Did Tami tell you that I've—'

'Yes, yes she did. And I'm still shocked, and pretty impressed, that you actually moved into our house so she could look after you. After everything we put her through.'

'It wasn't like that,' I say to him. I want to put my hand over my scar, to protect myself, that damaged part of myself, from this. This is not how I expected it to be. None of this is how I expected it to be.

He closes his eyes, rubs across them with his forefinger and thumb. Just like Tami did the other night. 'I'm sorry,' he says. 'I know it wasn't like that. It must have been awful for you. And terrifying. I hope you're doing OK now and that you'll make a full recovery. And, yes, I'm glad you had someone who could be there for you. But it shouldn't have been Tami. She shouldn't have had to look after you after the terrible thing I did to her and you helped me to do.'

'You can't help who you fall in love with,' I say to him. 'We didn't set out to hurt her, we just fell—'

'No,' he cuts in. He looks anxious and pained as if he regrets already what he hasn't yet said. 'No, Beatrix, we didn't fall in love. It wasn't like that. I liked you, I like you, but no, nothing more.'

'I don't believe that. You don't behave with someone how you did with me if you're not in love with them. Remember, I was there. I know you loved me and you said so.'

His sigh is long and laborious, designed to delay what he says next. 'Beatrix, I'm a selfish man. I'm going to therapy and I have had to admit that I am a selfish person. I am selfish, entitled and a disgrace as a human being. I am struggling to deal with all these truths. But be honest with yourself. When you look back over what went on between us, if I was as truly in love with you as I claimed to be, why did I never leave my wife? I am selfish, my needs and wants always come first, why wouldn't I just walk out to be with someone who allegedly made me happy?'

'The children, you told me so many times, you didn't want to leave your children.'

'If I loved my children so much, why wasn't I spending all my spare time with them instead of sneaking off to screw around? I didn't just cheat on Tami, I stole time away from my children as well. And I used them to get what I wanted – sex – without ever having to commit to you. I told you, I am a disgraceful human being.'

'I don't believe you. I think you're saying all this to get Tami back. I think you've panicked at the thought of not seeing your girls every day and you'll say and do anything to get your wife to let you come home.'

'Tami's divorcing me. She's not going to take me back, under any circumstances. She's told me that and she's right to. I've lost her and much as it hurts in ways I had no idea I could hurt, it's what I deserve.'

'But if you're not getting back together, why haven't you called me? Why . . . ?'

He lowers his head, embarrassed. He really wasn't going to call me. He really wanted nothing to do with me. He would have ended things by not speaking to me again. Even though I was ill and he knew it, even though we'd been together for nearly two years, longer if you count the build-up, he would have never seen me again.

He doesn't love me.

He never loved me.

The Earth is splitting in two, right beneath my feet. I can feel the vibrations of the seismic shift, I can hear the groan as it is rent asunder, I can sense I am about to fall. I have nothing to hold on to, nothing to stop me from falling into the underworld. I betrayed my best friend for a man who never loved me. Who used me. Who lied to me. And, worst of all, colluded with me in lying to myself. No wonder the world is falling apart. I have ruined everything on a poisoned promise. Even when I was being wheeled into the operating theatre I thought I had to get better so he and I could be together. Even as I told Tami I was a terrible, selfish person who would do anything in the name of love, I thought of the future Scott and I would have together, how we would cuddle in bed someday and look back on this awful period of our lives and how we eventually came through it. Even, *even* when I fell into that depression, I had visions of telling him about it and him taking me in his arms, kissing my forehead and telling me he'd never ever make me feel like that again.

I have been living on a promise written on water, I have been pinning my recovery and my hopes for remission on a man who has already proved himself a liar and a cheat. Instead of relying on me, I relied on someone else. I nearly sacrificed my life for love. And it wasn't even real love.

'You've cheated on Tami before, haven't you?' With the world splitting in two I can see so much more clearly.

He nods without raising his head. Can't face me. Can't look me in the eye and admit he lied and lied and lied. Spineless prick.

'Did you tell Tami about the others three days ago?' I ask him.

He sharply raises his head, because I'm talking about her, of course. It's always been her. *Always*. He just didn't realise it until she was no longer his to have whenever he chose. 'Yes, why?'

This is the real reason why I came to see him. It wasn't for closure, it wasn't to see him and to get him to remember what he felt for me – it was because in my flat of silence and loneliness I kept seeing her face. I kept thinking how broken she seemed. I kept thinking of the woman who had literally held my hand through the hardest few weeks of my life sitting in her kitchen, looking as if she was about to fall off the edge of the world. I came here for my friend.

'Because, and this is the reason I came to see you, three

nights ago I came down to the kitchen in the middle of the night and she was sitting in the dark with a tall glass of what looked like neat vodka or schnapps.'

'Was she all right?'

'No, she really wasn't. I was actually scared for her,' once I got over my horror at being asked to leave, 'because she looked so distressed and haunted. She said something about old traumas being added to, I didn't really understand what she meant until now. And then I told her about texting you because I needed closure. Added to Mirabelle's death I think she's under so much strain she might break down or even harm herself.'

'How has she seemed in the past few days?' he asks frantically.

'I don't know, she asked me to move out that night.'

'What? And you just left her like that? What is wrong with you? And why didn't you tell me this before?'

'I don't know, but it could be something to do with the fact *you won't answer your fucking phone*,' I reply, with the silent [*Cockhead*].

'Oh, Jesus Christ, I've got to speak to her.'

'Yeah, you do.' I hook my bag on my shoulder and slip my hands into my pocket. My fingers close around a pebble that Anansy brought me back from the beach once. It's smooth. It must have been on that beach for more lifetimes than I can imagine, being smoothed and weathered by the sea and nature. Stroked and bashed. It's about the size of the lump and area they removed from my breast. Small, but incredibly significant.

I'd said thank you to her and had put it in my pocket to

return to the beach because she didn't know the importance of leaving things in nature as you found them, of not upsetting the balance by removing things. But that's what nature does all the time, it takes things away from you all the time and you're supposed to work out if it's for the best or not. I had to have part of my breast taken away to keep me well. I've had to have Scott taken away because he was never mine in the first place.

And I've had to have my complacency taken away to remind me that I need to embrace everything I've got: I can't rely on anyone else wanting me to live as much as I do. I've got a life, I need to live it.

'Thanks, Beatrix,' Scott says, and means it.

I nod at him as I go through the door. I nod so I don't reply with a not-so silent, *'Whatever, cockface.'*

Tami

'Now here's what I don't understand, Mrs Challey,' Detective Sergeant Harvan says after hearing my tale. 'You stayed with a man who was accused of rape. How on Earth can you live with yourself?'

'I don't know,' I reply. 'I thought they were having an affair and I thought she lied out of revenge for him ending the relationship. When I found out the truth I asked him to leave.'

'Was Mirabelle dead by then?' she asks.

I glance down at the table, start to worry at the space where my wedding ring should be. 'Yes.'

'Did you kill her?' Detective Wade asks.

'No.' I don't sound as forceful or as angry as an innocent person should when I say that. But I am innocent.

'Shall I tell you what I think happened?' Harvan says.

I nod.

'I think that you were very drunk and very angry. But because you'd decided to make it work with the rap— sorry, with your *husband*, you had no choice but to take that anger out on Mirabelle. So you got tanked up and went over there maybe not to kill her, maybe simply to talk. And let's say that it did all happen the way you said it did, I don't think you left after she went upstairs. I think you were still raging and went upstairs after her to demand an explanation for the text messages. She dismissed you and that enraged you. You grabbed hold of her and tried to push her head under the water. She fought back, maybe even hit you in self-defence, and you lost control. After all, here is the woman who had ruined your life, apparently slept with your beloved *husband*. And now she was hitting you.

'I think you pushed her head under the water to teach her a lesson and when she came out fighting, promising to tell everyone what you had done, you knew you couldn't let her do that. You thought of your children and how they'd already been traumatised by seeing Daddy carted off by the police, now you were going to be taken away as well, so you realised the only way to shut her up once and for all was to finish what you had started.'

I am shaking my head throughout her monologue, horrified that she can see it like that. Does she really think that someone would carry out a killing so easily?

'That's not what happened,' I say.

'Sounds more than possible to me,' Detective Wade chimes in.

'That's not what happened. I left. I didn't go upstairs.'

'What would you say if I told you we found evidence of you not only going upstairs but also into the bathroom?'

I stare directly at her and then move my gaze to him. Bluffing. I know bluffing when I see it. Especially after being told green was red for so long by Scott, I have to trust my own judgement first and everything else last. 'I'd ask you why hadn't arrested me, even now, when I've admitted to having been in the house the night she died.'

They have that finishing each other's sentences thing going on then, but with looks this time. They are wondering if the stupid housewife-type person sitting in front of them will eventually fall for their bluff or if they should give up on it.

'I'll tell you what we'll do now, Mrs Challey,' Detective Sergeant Harvan says.

'Because there's no doubt at all in our minds that you killed Ms Kemini,' Wade says.

'We're going to go back over all the evidence we have with a fine-tooth comb, we are going to find something proving once and for all that you're the one who murdered Mirabelle. In fact, we're simply going to find proof that you were in the bathroom. And then we will arrest you, Mrs Challey. Be prepared to spend a very long time in prison.'

'You won't find anything because I didn't do it.'

'We'll see, Mrs Challey,' Wade says.

'We'll see,' Harvan finishes.

'You can go now,' Wade says.

'But it'd obviously be extremely unwise to book any sudden holidays or trips away from Brighton,' Harvan says.

'And trust me, we will know if you do.'

'My daughters are in London,' I say.

'Well you'll have to find a way to get them back without you actually leaving Brighton,' Wade replies.

'Good luck with that,' Harvan says.

I have a new burden upon my shoulders. I am free, I know I didn't kill her. Talking about it had put the final few pieces into place. But she is still gone. And she died knowing that I didn't believe her. That is the sort of pain that will stay with me for ever.

'I didn't do it,' I say at the door. 'I could never do that.'

I shouldn't have expected any more than the silent contempt I receive in reply.

Tami

Outside the police station is my husband.

I pause at the top of the stone steps, wondering if he is real. If he isn't then I do not know who has magicked him here because it was not me. He is pretty much one of the last people I want to see right now.

'What are you doing here?' I ask, remaining on the steps.

He approaches me, a troubled frown upon his brow, his mouth a straight line of worry, his whole demeanour tense and anxious.

'Beatrix came to see me at work,' he says without lingering over his mistress' name in the way I would expect him to. 'She was worried about you and thought I should check you were all right. She was scared you were going to harm yourself. She said the last time she saw you, you seemed so haunted. I've never seen her so concerned before. It terrified me.'

'How did you know I was here?'

'I've been trying your mobile for ages, and then I called the school to find out how the girls seemed and if you'd said anything to them or if anyone at the school had spoken to you this morning. When they told me the girls hadn't come in, I panicked. I had this sudden flash that I'd never see you again. I called your mother and basically dragged it out of her. The girls are fine, by the way, so you don't have to worry about them.'

I haven't told my mother the truth about what Scott has done, just that he's working away for a bit because we haven't been getting on. I could feel a grandmother-class 'I told you so' building up behind her face and had slipped off my kitchen stool and went running in to speak to the girls before it detonated all over me. My mother was expert at making one 'I told you so' so comprehensive it would cover all the tiny little moments I hadn't listened to her in the past as well as any that might arise in the future. I told her I had to go to the police station to talk to the police about my friend who had been murdered. I told her that the police had questioned lots of people but because I knew her so well, and I had seen her on the day she died, they wanted to talk to me for a bit longer. And I didn't want to rush things to get back to pick up the girls from school. I didn't tell her that it was probably me that did it because I didn't know for sure if I had or I hadn't. I didn't tell her I had to tell the police what I knew because it was eating me up inside.

I'd hugged the girls as if it was the last time I would see them outside of a prison, but didn't say any big dramatic goodbyes because I didn't want to scare them.

When I was eleven years old I spoke to the boy version of the man I was going to marry for the very first time. I often wonder what would have happened if I hadn't told him he could be whoever he wanted to be, he didn't have to behave like a thug just because his brother did. Would he have gone to university? Would we have become friends who became lovers who became a couple who shared a loss that made them pledge their futures to each other? I often wonder if Fate would have found a way to make our paths cross and cross and cross again until the fabric of our lives was so intertwined with each other we'd end up where we are now. Him guilty of the most appalling behaviour, me suspected of murder.

I wonder if there would have been any way for Scott and I to have lived a life without each other in it?

He comes closer to me and my body suddenly aches with the longing to be in his arms, inside the small space in his heart I want him to have reserved for me. It would be so easy to melt into him, let him take away my burden. Easy and complicated: every time I forget, I'm reminded again that he did this. He brought our lives to this point. He is the one who began my life and led it to here.

'I know I'm the last person you want to do this,' he says, 'and I know this wouldn't be happening if it wasn't for me, and I know it doesn't change anything between us, but come here.' He pulls me into his arms. I don't resist or try to push him away, I disintegrate. I come undone on the outside just as I've felt all this time on the inside. 'Pretend I'm someone else,' he whispers against my hair, drawing me closer. 'Pretend I'm someone else and let me look after you for now.'

I hardly notice I'm crying until his arms tighten around me and he hushes me while carefully and gently stroking my hair. 'I thought I'd done it,' I hear myself sob. 'All this time I thought I'd killed her.'

21

Tami

A long time ago

'How did you end up in Brighton?' Mirabelle asked me.

We were cooling down after a run, stretching against the wall outside her house. I pressed my toes against the wall while stretching my heel down to extend my hamstrings. 'Same old story,' I said.

'You followed him down here?' she asked.

'No, I was offered a job down here. The branch of the multinational company that TLITI was a part of back in the day needed someone who had worked in London to go there. They offered it to me, but I was going to say no because of Scott. And Scott couldn't let me do that so he transferred his MBA down here.'

'He followed you? Wow, I can't imagine him doing that.'

'You're not the first person to say that. When he started working at TLITI most people couldn't believe it; by the time I left, the story had kind of got changed to he was looking to do his MBA down here so I asked for a transfer and we came together.'

'Doesn't that piss you off?'

'No,' I replied.

'Why not? It would me.'

'Because he knows the truth, and I know the truth. He

was feeling insecure, worrying that following me down here made him look weak and love-addled to junior employees – which is all bullshit, by the way – so he started to fudge the facts of the story. I'm not bothered, like I say, we both know the truth as do the people who employed me. But, you know what, just because someone says something doesn't make it true. And they can say it as many times as they want and it still doesn't make it true.'

'I suppose that's the best way to look at it.'

'How did you end up in Brighton?' I asked her. She stopped stretching and instead hopped up onto the wall that ringed her driveway. I did the same, sensing I was in for a long story. I loved Mirabelle's stories. She had a way of talking that made me escape into what she was saying, disappear into her tale.

'I was at a point in my life when nothing seemed to be going well. I'd been married for a while and ... I suppose I'd lost myself. Lost who I was, really. Then I heard about a friend of mine who had moved to Brighton and who had vanished. I came down on the train to look for her. Mad, huh? I had no real idea of what Brighton was like, how big it was, where anything was, I just had to come here to find her. I think I thought that the beach would be like the one in the story. She was the one who told it to me, by the way.

'I had to leave at the end of the day and I hadn't found her. So I did it again the following week. I kept coming down here on day trips to try to find her. This went on for months, until there was a delay on the trains one day and I couldn't get back to London in time to be where I needed to be. My husband went crazy, and quite rightly so. I hadn't told him what I was doing. That's what I meant, that time you asked if I'd cheated on my husband. I hadn't exactly, I simply kept a huge secret from him, which was like cheating, really. In my case it wasn't with a person as such, more the search for my friend and with this place. I fell in love with Brighton a little more every time I came here.

'He was so angry that I'd been doing this behind his back so I stopped for a while, I promised him I would behave and would put all those stupid thoughts of finding my friend out of my head. I asked my husband if we could move down here, make a fresh start. I was sure things would be better, easier, if we moved here, but he said no. His life, his family, his work were in London and he was suspicious, of course, about why I wanted to move.'

She turned her head and looked at me, tendrils of hair she'd tied back in a ponytail hung down beside her face as she smiled at me.

'It was in my veins, you know. Brighton. The salt-tainted air, the sound of the gulls, the boom and crash of the sea on the shore. It was like a heartbeat, like my heartbeat.' She paused as her eyes glazed over. 'So I left. I told him it was only for a little while, it was until I found my friend, cleared my head, found a bit of who I was again. Because I was lost, Tami. I'd spent so long trying to fit in, trying to be someone I wasn't, that I had no idea who I was any more. I think you can relate to that, being a mother, can't you? Do you sometimes want to escape from everything and get to a place where you sit and be who you used to be? Or even try to be who you used to be without all the expectations of daily life?'

'I suppose I do. Well, I did until I started running.'

'He told me if I left it was forever, that I could never come back. I said that was a chance I had to take and he relented, said if I wasn't gone for too long he would give me the time I needed. I'd been asking for support and space to be me for so long and he hadn't been able to understand or give it to me until I said I was leaving no matter what. There's irony for you.'

She stopped looking at me then, focused on the mid-distance, in the direction of the other red-brick houses that sat on the opposite side of the road.

'Leaving was one of the hardest things I've ever done. I cried so much and panicked that what I was doing was the wrong thing. But I had to. I reminded myself of that every day: if I had stayed I would have disappeared because I wouldn't have been true to myself. As time has gone on, I've realised how selfish that was. That decision ... It was all about me and that's fine when there aren't other people involved, but when there are ...'

'Did you find your friend?'

'Yes and no. I found out what other people thought happened to her, but no one knew for sure. So I sort of kept looking. Then, I don't know when but I stopped searching. I think sometimes I see her, but it's always the her who was the age the last time I saw her, if that makes sense? I keep seeing young her, not the her she would be now.'

'Did you ever decide to go home?'

'Yes. I kept in touch, called almost every other day. I wrote letters, I sent postcards, I went to visit. But I left it too late. When I tried to go back it was too late, too much time had passed even though it was only a year at most. He didn't want me back, he'd managed perfectly well without me.'

'How did that make you feel?'

Her agony consumes her face for a moment, then it is gone, whipped away to be replaced by the Mirabelle face I'd come to know. 'I made a mistake. I can say that now. For a long time I blamed everyone and everything for not understanding, for not being patient, for not putting their lives on hold so I could "find myself". I shouldn't have stayed away for so long. I got caught up in the new life I had, in myself. And that's the thing I've never been able to figure out. Should I have stayed and died every day in tiny increments until I woke up one morning and there was nothing left of me, or should I have done what I did and left so I could live again?'

'I guess you'll never really know because you made a choice.'

'What would you have done?'

'Me? I don't know. I can't imagine leaving if Cora and Anansy were in the equation, but I can't imagine leaving just Scott, either. He's too tied up in the fabric of who I am, I suppose.'

'That's what I was looking for down here. That person who was tied up in the fabric of who I am. I'll never forget the moment my husband shut the door in my face. It nearly broke me. It did break me when I saw— When I saw the devastation I'd caused. It was always so easy to convince myself of what I was doing when I didn't have to experience the fallout up close.'

She rubbed her hands together as if trying to warm herself.

I was getting cold, too, despite the heat of the day – the sweat on our bodies was drying and we hadn't stretched properly as part of our cool-down.

She continued, 'It was the making of me, though. I tried so hard to come back for a long time, but he refused to even let me through the door. So, I took a good hard look at myself, and decided to change myself. I had to get a proper job and smarten myself up and make myself a person who could cope and was worthy. So I enrolled in college down here, I did a degree, I did an MBA, all the while doing as much work experience as I could get. I worked bloody hard to get where I am.'

'Yes, it really paid off.'

'No it didn't,' she said with the most heart-tearing smile. 'I'm still alone, Tami. I'm still apart from the person I love most in the world. I came here looking for someone who was part of the fabric of who I am, I stayed here chasing love and fulfilment when I had it all along at home, I just didn't know it. I try not to let it get to me, but you know, sometimes it does.'

'He still won't have you back?'

'"Coming back is not an option," as he once told me. "We have to find a way to move forward."'

'Is it because you wanted him to be the father of your children and your pregnancy didn't work out? Is that why you love him so much? I remember when it happened to Scott and me, I felt so empty afterwards and I wanted to be filled up with another baby almost immediately, but then I didn't ever want to take that risk in case it happened again. But it made me cling like crazy to Scott. I'm not sure where we'd be if that hadn't happened, but I couldn't imagine life without him after that. I needed him so much because he was the only other person who could come close to understanding what I felt. No one knows this, but it was Scott that suggested we have the baby's due date engraved inside our wedding rings so I know he thought about our baby, too. I can understand why you were so bonded to him if that's it. Is it?'

'In a way,' she said quietly.

'You lost your baby?' I asked, reaching out to rub her back.

She exhaled in a deep, pain-filled way. 'I can't talk about it.' She started to hyperventilate. 'What I did ... How I let her down.' Her inhalations and exhalations increased in speed and strength. 'I see her face every day ... I think about her all the time ... Everything I do is for her, about her ... Oh God, oh God.' She threw her hands up and covered her face. Her breathing becoming a series of short, sharp in-breaths and short out-breaths, until one huge in-breath and then a longer, calmer out-breath. 'I can't think about it. I lost her because I wasn't where I should have been. And I can't think about it.'

I took her hand and forced my fingers between hers, then curled my hand around hers, linking us and bonding us, telling her I was there for her.

'I know I act like I'm not bothered about most things, that I'm strong and life is for the taking and I can do anything, go anywhere but ... On the inside I feel frozen. Without her, I feel frozen.'

My arms went around her, pulling her to me. She rested her head on my chest, and I felt her relax a little so I pulled her closer still, tightened my grip around her. Without thinking, I kissed the top of her head, like I would Cora and Anansy if they were hurting.

When I think about the baby we lost, I hurt, but to lose a child who I got to know, whose face I learned every line of, whose breathing I'd become accustomed to as I heard her go to sleep at night, whose smile could lift me from the deepest pit I was in ... It doesn't bear thinking about.

'I'm sorry,' she said, pulling away. 'I'm OK now. I'm OK.'

'You don't have to be all brave, you know? It's OK to fall apart sometimes.'

'Yes, Tami the Perfect, of course it is.'

'Me? Perfect? I wish! I strive for perfection, that is true, I achieve "meh" if I'm lucky.'

'Yeah, right. I've seen you with your children, I know what you're really like.'

'No, you've seen me with my children when they are co-operating. You haven't seen me standing in their bedroom screaming like a banshee because they won't stop making noise and get ready for bed. You haven't seen me hiding in the downstairs loo, crying because I can't cope. It's a bit easier now that they're older in some ways and I haven't had the feeling of wanting to walk out and never come back for oohhhh, two hours, thirty-seven minutes.'

The smile that rose on her face was like the sun coming up over Brighton – warming and beautiful. 'Have you really wanted to walk out and leave it all behind?'

'Yes. I think all mothers do. No one tells you about the hard bits, do they? You hear about the sleepless nights and the no time for your relationship, but you don't hear about

606

the no time for you to think about what you want in life. You don't hear about the being scared you're doing it all wrong and harming your child. You don't hear about how it physically hurts when your child hurts and you'd do anything to stop their pain. You don't hear about the absolute terror of looking in the mirror one day and realising the person looking back at you is not the person you thought you'd see and you have no clue what happened to the woman you thought you were.'

'You get it,' Mirabelle said as her smile became wider. 'You really do.'

She reached out, stroked her thumb gently across my cheek, a little like Scott used to do in the days before we became an established couple and we used to find any excuse to touch each other. 'You remind me of my friend who I came to Brighton to find,' Mirabelle said, removing her hand from me but not her steady gaze. 'I sometimes wonder if you're a reincarnation of her.'

'Nope, one of a kind, me. Didn't you hear, they broke the mould when they made me.'

Her laugh was like that first taste of buttered hot toast, so perfect and fulfilling you had to restrain yourself from eating it all up in one go. I wanted her to keep laughing, to keep filling my ears with that divine sound. 'Can you hear that?' she said to me.

'What?'

'The water, the sound of the tide coming in.'

'No,' I said, but I could. I could hear the gush of water rushing to the shore, covering the sand, rising ever higher. The world around me was brightening with each rush of waves, the buildings were fading and the world was being replaced by a beautiful blue sky that only existed in my dreams. The sun was a huge, orange-yellow ball up in the heavens and all around us there was sand and pebbles and palm trees with stout, solid trunks. From the sky it started to rain, red, red and more red. Falling on our shoulders, our heads, our bodies, the beach. The sand on which we now sat was becoming inundated with red petals. Soft, silky red rose petals.

I turned to Mirabelle. 'We didn't have this conversation, did we?'

'I think we did,' she said.

'But how would I not remember all that stuff about Fleur?'

'Or maybe we didn't,' she replied.

'Tell me, did this happen?'

'I can't tell you that, you have to work it out for yourself.'

'But—'

'You know what to do, Tami, don't you?'

'I don't.'

'Course you do, you know everything because you're the mama. Come on mama. Mama. Mama. Mama? Mama!'

Anansy is standing in front of me, holding the handle and body of my favourite mug in two separate hands. 'It was an accident, Mama, it was an accident,' she says.

I swallow against the dryness in my mouth, trying to get my bearings, to find a path of reality I can climb back onto.

'I'm sorry, Mama,' Anansy says.

'I know,' I say, sitting up. My head feels like it is being fed through an apple press. That memory felt like a dream, and that dream felt like a memory. There was something in it that nagged at me. It's been nagging at me for an age. But did I have that conversation with her? It felt like I did. I remember sitting on the wall outside her house, but we did that so often. Although I'm sure I'd remember the occasion where she broke down and told me about the daughter she lost.

'The thing is, Mama, I might have made a bit of a mess,' Anansy says. Cora is at a friend's house for the night and I was meant to be with Anansy, but she'd wanted to play in the living room and I was too tired to keep my eyes open.

'Where?' I say, looking around the kitchen.

'Now you have to promise not to shout,' she says.

'I can only promise that I'll try not to shout very loudly,' I reply.

'The teddies needed their late, late breakfast,' she explains. 'So I had to take the Cornies into the living room. It was to Anansy's Restaurant. I'm sorry, Mama.'

All things considered, there isn't that much mess. Just half a packet of cornflakes crushed into the carpet, a bit of milk split on there, too, but my favourite mug did not survive and, of course, I've had to come into the living room to sort everything out. I still have an aversion to this room. It is where my life started to unravel. It is where my life began all that time ago.

'I'm sorry, Mama,' Anansy says.

'It's fine,' I say, still a little sleep-addled as I bend to start to gather up the orange flakes littering the oatmeal-coloured carpet. If the carpet was sand and the cornflakes were red, it'd be like picking up rose petals on The Rose Petal Beach.

'What did you dream about, Mama?' Anansy asks as she gathers up cornflakes with me.

'I dreamt about going to The Rose Petal Beach, like in the story Auntie Mirabelle used to tell you.'

'Oh. Was she there?' she asks.

'Yes, she was, actually.'

'That's nice. Did you have a nice time?'

'I did.'

There are parts of that conversation that remind me of something. It has been niggling my mind for a long time. Something is missing. Something that has been staring me in the face is missing.

Putting the detritus from Anansy's tea party in the bin, the picture of The Rose Petal Beach catches my eye. I walk up to it on my way back to Anansy. I look over the form in the picture, so lovingly painted.

'Oh, Mirabelle,' I say as my gaze rests on the rose petals in her arms. I stare at them and stare at them, and then my gaze moves to the hand I can see. A bare hand crammed with rose petals. A bare hand.

The tingling starts in my scalp, but it is all over my body seconds later. I know who did it. I know who killed Mirabelle.

Fleur

Mrs C was really shocked when we showed up with that picture.

It was the first thing I changed about the house. Not that I'm fixing to live there or anything, I couldn't stand that picture being there, knowing it was the reason she left.

I'm feeling it now. Since I was in that bathroom and all those memories came pouring in like a swollen river that's broken the walls of a dam, I could feel. Noah says it was the shock wearing off, that I'd been protecting myself from completely falling apart by convincing myself I didn't feel what I was feeling. I'd think he was right if I didn't now feel like this. If the pain wasn't so bad sometimes I cried from the hurt, not from her not being there.

I stay in bed most mornings wishing I could have one more day with her. I'd really talk to her then. I'd ask her why she left. How she could stand to leave. And I'd ask her if she could be my mum again. If she could be my mum instead of the woman I became friends with. Most mornings I shush Noah as he is about to speak, and he knows not to say a word because I am wishing. I am wishing on the life I should have lived. I am begging for something that was obviously never meant to be mine.

The picture had to go. That story was the original thief

that stole my life, and I didn't want reminding of it every time I went there to pack up. I knew Mrs C would appreciate it. I wasn't sure if she knew or not that the woman in the picture was so obviously my mother. I didn't tell her or anything like that. I wasn't sure how she'd feel about having my mother up on her wall after everything, but I know in my heart that's where that picture is meant to be.

We've been through the house looking for the key to the room with the locked door. We called the cleaner who cried about Mirabelle and said she'd never had a key to the room and had never cleaned it, then we called the police who apparently put it back where they found it but couldn't tell us where that was exactly. 'As much help as a toothpick in the rain,' Noah said after *that* conversation and I'd looked at him funny 'cos I had not a clue what that meant.

So, our next course of action is to break down the door.

'Are you sure about this?' Noah asks again.

'Yes,' I say. I'm so not sure. It's technically my house but it's still her house. I keep thinking she's going to turn up any minute now and shout at me 'cos I've got rid of her picture and I've broken down the door to her secret room.

It takes him four goes to manage it and he's hurt his shoulder and his pride at the same time. 'My hero,' I say to him and he tries to tickle me in retaliation but his damaged shoulder stops him grabbing me as I half-stumble into the room. It's not the mess I expected. The covers on the bed have been pulled back, and there are no guest towels on the chair in the bay. It's a nice, homely room with a nice, flowery duvet on the bed, and a huge rug with daisies on it. Daisies are my favourite flower. This room has curtains when the other rooms have blinds, these curtains are a royal blue. Royal blue is my favourite colour. Beside the bed is a lava lamp. I loved lava lamps when I was younger, wanted to start up a collection of them but had no space in my tiny room. The walls are painted a duck-egg blue. I had that blue on my walls when I was a little girl. This is my room.

I know it's my room not because of these things that make up the room, but because it has pictures of me on the walls. My school photos have been put into a large chrome picture frame with white card separating the different images, all in chronological order, so there I am at six, with pigtails, then at seven with one big puff of hair tied back in a pony-tail. Dad's friend's wife hadn't remembered it was school photo day so she'd let Dad do my hair. At eight I've got two big pigtails with puffy ends instead of plaits because I liked it. At nine I have my hair really short because Dad didn't know what to do and so took me to the barber and asked him to cut it. I cried and cried. At age ten my hair is a big, puffball afro and I'm smiling at the camera like I think I'm the cutest ten-year-old ever. (I did look cute, though.) At eleven, my hair is back on my shoulders because Mirabelle had shown up at school in my lunch break and begged one of the black dinner ladies to give me the products she'd brought and explain to me how to use them. That's when I started using coconut oil. At twelve, my hair is loose and down by my shoulders. At thirteen, I have a side-parting and my hair is falling mysteriously over my eye. At fourteen I am hiding behind my hair and you can barely see my face.

I didn't know she had these. There are other pictures framed and on the wall: four-year-old me and her, playing at the beach; me at five serving her tea in our minuscule back yard; her holding me when I am a tiny baby. They're old pictures, reddish from time, but she has blown them up huge and hung them on the walls. And then there are the pictures from recent years of me she has taken with her mobile: me in my car grinning at her; me sitting outside a café in Lewisham with her big sunglasses on my face; me looking back at her over my shoulder as I'm about to walk away; me just smiling at her across the café table. The quality of the pictures isn't brilliant, but she has had them enlarged and hung on the wall as well. The whole wall is taken up with photos of me.

'You were cute,' Noah says.

My heart is beating really fast looking at these photos. I want to run around tearing open the drawers and the wardrobe, frantically searching for what else she had of my life locked up in here. I move to the large, mahogany wood set of drawers sitting beside the window and pull open each drawer. The first is full of towels, the second full of sheets. The next two are empty, but the final drawer is full of official-looking letters. I sit where I am crouching and start to open them. They're letters from my schools. Letters for school trips, consent forms, open evening dates and times, photocopies of my school reports – the originals are back at my dad's place somewhere – even my exams timetables.

'I don't understand,' I say aloud but I do. She asked the schools to keep her updated. I wonder if she told them she'd left? I wonder if she confessed to that and told them she couldn't come back so all she wanted was to know about me? She wanted school photos and copies of my school reports. That's why she knew when to turn up after my last exam. That's why she knew to come back when Dad broke his agreement. It was her, wasn't it, who told the head and Ms Devendis to work on my dad to let me go on the school trip in the first place?

She was there, all along. She was a part of my life from afar.

'I was important to her,' I say to Noah.

His familiar, comforting presence returns to me as he crouches down beside me. He puts his arm around me. 'Of course you were,' he says.

'But don't you see,' I say to him, showing him the pieces of my past I hold in my hands, 'she did think about me, all the time. She tried to be a part of my life in any way she could.'

'I know,' he says. 'Babe, the stuff you've found out, the stuff you remembered by yourself, all this stuff, it's been telling you she was desperate to be a part of your life. She did love you. She was your mum.'

'My mum.'

Mum. I roll the word around my tongue. Mum. Such a small word that means something huge. Mum.

She was my mum.

I look at the picture of her holding me, when I am tiny and wearing a pink, towelling babygro and she has her hair plaited straight back in canerows. She's not grinning at the camera, she's looking straight down and smiling at me.

'Mum,' I say to the photograph. I've said it a few times, I know. But this is the first time I've truly meant it.

22

Tami

'It was you, wasn't it?'

I am standing in the presence of a murderer. Someone who has purposely, knowingly, *intentionally* taken a life. It wasn't to relieve suffering, it wasn't to save their or someone else's life, it was to put an end to someone. To unmake them, to end them. I do not know how someone could do that.

'Mrs Challey,' she says to me, smiling as warmly at me as she did in the police station the first time we spoke. 'A pleasure to see you as always.' I'm momentarily thrown, but then I see it, the look sliding across her face and sitting in that hollow space behind her eyes. She knows what I'm here for. She indicates with her slender hand to the seat across from her.

I had found her sitting at a table placed on the shingle not far from a small beach-hut café stand. Not many people come down here because its location right beside where the fishing boats come in means by the time the sun is this high in the sky the smell of fish is powerful and pungent.

She has her hair loose, sunglasses on top of her head and a book in front of her on the little plastic table. When I see her normally she is dressed in a suit; today she has jeans on, a pretty floral top, and a brown suede jacket – her day off, obviously.

'Please, have a seat,' she continues in the same warm, welcoming tone, removing her glasses and indicating to the empty chair opposite her. My eyes are fixated on that hand. The hand that killed Mirabelle.

I hesitate. This is a public place, there aren't that many people admittedly, but we're in full view of the man wearing the food-stained apron in the hut. A few people are on the water's edge in deckchairs, fishing rods dangling hopefully in the shallows. She won't do anything here. No, her style is killing in private. Murder most discreet.

Still hesitant, I lower myself onto the plastic seat. She smiles at me again. Was she smiling as she held Mirabelle under the water, or was she screaming abuse and hatred? Or was there nothing, was it simply another thing to do?

'I'm just catching up on a little reading,' she says, indicating to the book that lies face-down on her table. I can't stop staring at her hands. They are smooth and slender, her nails short and neat. 'So, how can I help you?'

'It was you, wasn't it?' I repeat.

She fixes me with a look, her head slightly to one side as she weighs up what to say to me. I haven't looked at her properly. She was always in the background, but looking at her now, I can see what Mirabelle fell for. She has a lived-in face, the sort of face you wouldn't mind waking up to every morning. It has been shaped by a hundred thousand smiles, moulded by displaying affection. If I didn't know she was a killer, I would think she was beautiful, in the way that ordinary people are.

'I don't know what you're talking about, Mrs Challey,' she states.

'So many little things have been niggling me, things that didn't feel right. First it was you knowing who I was the first time you came to my house. You didn't ask who I was, I could have been anyone, but you knew who I was.'

'Hello, Mrs Challey. Is your husband in?'

'And then, that time outside Mirabelle's house, the way she got shirty with you and Wade for your double act. She was jealous, not annoyed, jealous that you had this private world going on without her.'

'Do you two do a double act on the stage or something? Because what you're doing – all the finishing of each other's sentences – it's not endearing, it's not funny, it's irritating.'

'And in the police interview room, you asked if I went to Mirabelle's house to check if she overslept because you knew I had. You were most likely there.'

'Did you go to her house and check?'

'And you knew Scott looked at r– extreme pornography because Mirabelle had told you in detail the things he described to her. That's why you put the thought in my head to go and look.'

'Does your husband masturbate to rape pornography? You sound very sure, have you checked?'

'You told me yourself at the funeral that the killer was almost definitely there.'

'*You'd be surprised how often the killer will show up at the funeral.*'

'And when I came in and told you what had happened the night she died, the way you kept forgetting to call her Ms Kemini and kept slipping into Mirabelle, like you knew her. You said her name like someone who loved her would. Detective Wade never once made that slip.'

'*But because you'd decided to make it work with the rap— sorry, with your husband you had no choice but to take that anger out on Mirabelle.*

'And then there's the main thing: my wedding ring. You knew what the date stood for. The only person I have ever told about that was Mirabelle and that was because I thought she'd lost a child. The only way you could have known about that is if she told you; Mirabelle knew about secrets, she would never have told that to anyone unless it was someone she loved.'

'*Well, not our Wade, here. But I, I recognised it because it is so unusual. And then, of course, there is the unusual inscription. Not your wedding date, I gather. What is it? First date? A special birthday? First declaration of love? First fuck?*'

'I saw her picture, the woman without a ring on, and I realised that was it. That was what had been niggling me. You knew too much about me for it to have been just another case to you.'

In response Detective Sergeant Harvan – I don't even know her first name – says nothing. She smiles at me benignly.

622

When I do not say anything either, she says pleasantly, 'What is it you're expecting me to say?'

What was I expecting? A confession? Denial? Something in between?

'I don't know, to be honest. Actually, I want you to tell me why. I've seen those texts she sent you, she was completely in love with you. Why would you kill her? How could you?'

Detective Sergeant Harvan is silent for a long time, then slowly she meets my gaze. 'I had this friend once,' she says, slowly, carefully. 'She was happily married with two children. She had a great job and pretty darn amazing life – on paper. My friend felt dead inside, she told me. She had the perfect life, but it felt like the light had gone out of her.

'And then, one day, when she's out running, trying to get away from it all, she sees the most beautiful person in the world. They run past each other for weeks, only noticing each other, then the smiles, then the nods. My friend said she started to live for that part of her day, that moment when the most beautiful woman in the world would smile at her and lift her whole day.'

'I live for your smiles. They make everything worthwhile.'

623

Erica

Tamia Challey stares at my hands. She's fixated on them, probably imagining what I have done with them. I never could understand what Mirabelle saw in her. She is dull and frumpy, a modern-day Stepford wife who doesn't even realise she is one.

'My friend was scared of what was happening,' I say to her. I have to keep reminding myself not to speak too slowly and carefully because, apparently, she doesn't like it when I do that. 'My friend had never felt like that about a woman before. She'd always been into men, and she still was in a way, but this woman was incandescent. A goddess in an ordinary world. Eventually they got talking, they'd stop in the middle of their run, wherever they crossed, and would sit on the beach and talk, and the talks got longer, the runs got shorter.'

'You know the best part of my day is when I see you. It has been for weeks. You're really funny.'

'And my friend knew she was falling in love with this beautiful, unique person. They had so much in common, they liked the same films, the same music, they laughed at the same things. And, the day the beautiful runner woman casually

624

brushed her hand against my friend's, my friend thought her life was over and was about to start at the same time.

'Why don't you come over to my house for a coffee? It's not that far from here. You can explain to me again in detail why I need to get a better pair of trainers than these bad girls on my feet.'

'Then the runs stopped and they met at her house, always in secret because no one could know, what with my friend being married and no one knowing that the beautiful woman was gay. My friend said the first time she was brave enough to kiss the beautiful woman they were sitting on her sofa, staring at the picture of a story that meant a lot to the beautiful woman, and she did it. She turned, shaking, shaking like a leaf, and leant over and touched the woman with her lips. My friend said she'd never felt anything like the heat, the electricity, the passion spinning through her veins. It'd never been like that with a man. Not even her husband who she loved dearly.'

'I thought you'd never kiss me. I wasn't sure if you were interested. I've wanted to kiss you since that first time we passed and you turned around and looked at me while running backwards. I thought that was so cool. If I'd have been a bit braver I would have chased after you right there and then.'

'If I had the slightest clue how I felt I'd have let you catch me.'

'A few weeks later, when they went to bed, my friend thought she was going to die afterwards. She finally, finally understood about love and sex and what it felt like to be satisfied. Complete.'

'I only realise now that I've never made love before. I'm still tingly from what you've done to me.'

'I've never made love like that before, either. You're everything to me.'

'But she's got children, hasn't she? My friend can't up and leave her husband because she wouldn't be able to see her children every day. And that would kill her. So she sticks around, falling deeper and deeper in love, having the most amazing sex, and feeling for the first time that she knows who she is.'

'I hope you realise how much I love you.'

'Deeper and deeper my friend falls until, one day, she notices that the beautiful woman has had her head turned. She just senses it, you know, like you do with the people you love. Something's changed and she's not quite sure what.

'Until the beautiful woman mentions a name, someone who she can now go running with because, of course, the beautiful woman can be seen with whoever she wants and she can flirt with whoever she wants. She can do whatever she wants, but my friend, my poor friend, has to keep up appearances in her life: perfect mother, perfect wife, perfect employee.'

'Tami's great. You should meet her sometime. We can all go to a bar or something one night. I've convinced her to come running with me once a week.'

'Is she the one married to that Scott character?'

'Yes, but she's lovely, really she is.'

'I think you should stay away from her. If he's bad news, she will be too.'

'She's not at all like that. Truly. When you meet her you'll see what I mean.'

'The beautiful woman doesn't even think what it's like to have to sit on the sidelines and watch as she starts a friendship with this new running partner. And my friend, who'd been so happy, who'd felt alive again, started to realise that she was scared. Scared of losing the beautiful woman and scared of losing her family. But then, the beautiful woman starts to tell her about the problems she's having again with the man at work who's connected to this new running partner.'

'He's been OK-ish since I became friendly with Tami, but since we started going running, it's like, BANG! he hates me again. It's worse than before. Nastier, more threatening without it ever being overt. He's started with the porn scenarios, too.'

'I think you should do him for sexual harassment.'

'I love my job.'

'Yeah, and he'll get sacked and you can keep your job.'

'Right, because that's what happens all the time. Women aren't painted as lesbo, humourless troublemakers if they report a bloke and he isn't seen as a good man who went a bit too far with the jokes and should be given a slap on the wrist. Can you tell I've been here before?'

'That's when I know that it's going to be OK after all. Because why would the beautiful woman even think about taking

627

anything further with the running partner when she's being harassed by the running partner's husband? But no, it's not all right. The beautiful woman is so enthralled by the running partner, she can't give her up. Not even when the running partner's husband tries to rape her.'

Tamia Challey's whole body contracts in horror. She doesn't like to think about it, does she? She knows he did it, but she likes to pretend that it was OK to continue to sleep in the same bed as a rapist. She needs to tell herself she didn't know, she didn't think him capable, she did the right thing in the end. Stepford all the way.

'The beautiful woman was almost destroyed by that. I spent so much time holding her while she cried about what happened and what to do. She didn't want to hurt her running partner, but she didn't want him to get away with it. Especially when the running partner had no idea. So she got up the courage to report him. I . . . My friend made sure she got the case, she wanted to prosecute the man who had done this to the beautiful woman, to the love of her life. She knew it would be the end, too, of whatever was going on between the beautiful woman and the running partner.'

'If you had seen her at the beach crying her eyes out . . . Poor Tami. I feel awful.'

'It's him who should feel awful. And her, if she doesn't know what a criminal she's sleeping with.'

'She's known him half her life. How's she supposed to understand what he's really like? I mean, the man had the due date of the baby they lost to miscarriage engraved on the back of their wedding rings.

How is she supposed to believe a man who can be that thoughtful would do this?'

'Men like him don't just do this out of the blue. I see it all the time. It starts off with small deviant acts that get worse and then as they get older – and in his case more successful – they just don't bother to hide it because there are less sanctions against him. None of this is your problem, though, you have to concentrate on doing what's right for you.'

'But no, the beautiful woman can't go through with it. She can't stand what the investigation is doing to the running partner. She doesn't back out for herself, for me and how much pressure I'm under, but for the running partner. The worst part is what it does to m— to my friend. My friend begs her to change her mind, to think about what it'll do to her career: her bosses never wanted her to go after such a well-known businessman even if he was guilty because the things he was into – the extreme porn, the womanising – were things they dabbled in as well. But my friend pursued him because it was the right thing to do and now she was going to have to watch him walk away Scott free. Ha-ha. Did you see what I did there?

'The beautiful woman won't change her mind. All she cares about is the running partner, the running partner's children. The beautiful woman hasn't behaved very well in her distant, distant past so she's trying to do something right. She doesn't want to destroy an innocent person and her children like she did once before. What about me? What did I ever do to her? What did my children ever do to her?'

'And that's why you killed her?' Tamia Challey asks, the

picture of innocence as if this isn't all her fault. She doesn't get it, does she? She doesn't understand what life was like for me – falling in love for what felt like the first time in my life, finally understanding what that part of me that was missing was about. I wasn't broken, I wasn't odd – I simply hadn't met the right person. I was watching everything slip away from me: my job would be unbearable if I let him get away with it. All the men who looked at me with suspicious eyes because I wouldn't join in the blokey banter and I wouldn't turn a blind eye to stupid, sexist 'jokes' would be making comments about me being a man-hater; they'd feel justified in calling me a man-hating carpet-muncher (they called me that because I wouldn't flirt with them) who had it in for a decent bloke who liked a bit on the side, which wasn't a crime.

Tamia Challey doesn't see that while the beautiful woman was trying to save the running partner's family, she was ruining my friend's life.

'It couldn't go on. My friend was desperate. She kept trying to make the beautiful woman see sense. That's what happened. She was only trying to make her see sense. But the beautiful woman wouldn't. She kept saying this was her chance to atone for what she had done in the past. How she had let down the one person she had loved with all her heart and so now she was trying not to ruin someone else's life, even if it meant the end of her own.'

'If I stop those girls from hurting, from having to go through the hell of a police investigation and a trial, maybe it'll be OK. Maybe something in the universe will shift, everything will be righted and

she'll love me again. Like she did before. She'll look at me how she used to and I'll finally have her back. I wish you could understand, she is everything to me, I want her to love me again. I'll give anything for her to love me again.'

'I . . . My friend knew the beautiful woman was talking about the end of her professional life and of her life on Providence Close, but my friend realised that it really should be the end. She had gone around to see if the beautiful woman was all right, if she could change her mind, and there she was, barely dressed, and letting the running partner into her house. She wasn't even discreet about it. While my friend waited for the running partner to leave, she thought about what the beautiful woman was going to give up and she realised it wasn't enough for the running partner to lose everything material, she had to know what it could feel like to lose everything.'

'You're not listening to me. I need you to make a new statement. Say they threatened you, say you were scared of how it would hurt Challey's children, say anything, I'll say I saw her leaving just now—'
   'So you were out there. Have you been watching me?'
   'Not how you mean.'
   'Which means yes.'
   'Will you stop changing the subject? My bosses want to go after you for wasting police time, this is serious. You need to go back on the record.'
   'You're not listening to me. Which means there's no point talking to you any longer. I'm going to take a bath.'

'No, you're— Put your dressing gown back on. Get back here. Don't you walk away from me. Don't you ever—'

I try to forget what happened next. I try not to think about it because it could have gone differently if she had listened. Everything would have been better for all of us if she had done the right thing.

'Arrgghh! What are you doing? You almost pushed me under then. Can you leave? I have nothing more to say to you.'

'Well I've got plenty to say to you.'

'I don't want to hear it.'

'Who do you think you are? I've put everything on the line for you – at work and at home.'

'I know, I know. I'm really grateful but—'

'There are no buts in this. I will do anything to protect my career and family, and if that means hurting you, that's what I'll do.'

'Hurting me? Are you threatening me? I think your bosses will take a very dim view to that, don't you? I think you should go before you get yourself into any more t—'

'She really did love y— the running partner. She had every chance to live, but she gave up her life for you. I'm sure you're very pleased about that.'

Tamia Challey is staring at me with those doe eyes she must have used on Mirabelle a thousand times to turn her head. The look turns slowly to disgust. I liked it better when she was that tiny bit afraid of me.

'She didn't mean me,' Tamia Challey says quietly, scorn now added to her disgust. 'She meant her daughter, Fleur.

She wanted her daughter to love her again. Leaving her was the very bad thing she did in the past. I'm guessing she thought that if she could somehow balance the cosmic scales, do something for my children, she'd be allowed to be a bigger part of her daughter's life once more.' Tamia Challey takes an age to blink, to shake her head a fraction, to wind her fingers around her bare ring finger. She isn't moving in slow motion, the world is. The world has slowed down with what she has said.

'You never bothered to ask what the very bad thing she did in the past was, did you? You thought it was some crime she committed so you didn't ask in case you were forced to report her. It's ironic that you were so hard on me for being in denial about the man I love when you essentially did the same about the woman you loved.'

Tamia Challey is lying. She has to be.

'What's even more ironic is that you've behaved exactly how Scott used to – only concerned with your needs, your wants, your sexual satisfaction. You just assumed Mirabelle meant me – another potential lover – because that's what you would mean. That's what you would do.'

Tamia Challey shakes her head at me again, still in slow motion. *Her daughter.* The words are crawling around my brain, eating through my mind like maggots devouring a rotting corpse. I have seen that, of course. I have seen that and hundreds of other things just as terrible, just as disgusting. And that is what is happening inside me at the moment. She was doing it to get her daughter back.

When I saw that room at her house, which was basically a shrine to her daughter, I'd been as stunned as anyone who didn't know her. But I knew she was a free spirit, that in a divorce she would have been brave enough to leave her child with her dad.

'Did you ever even ask about her life away from you? Her hopes, her dreams? What had happened in her past? Or was it all about what she did for your life, your sexuality, your this, your that? You, you, you.'

Every trace of fear has been erased from Tamia Challey. She is talking to me as if I am just anyone. 'Careful you don't topple off that high horse of yours, Challey, it's a long way down.'

'Oh I know. I know.' She stands, obviously ready to make her sweeping exit on a dramatic one-liner that is meant to put me in my place.

I could never understand what Mirabelle saw in her. Every time I encountered her I was surprised again that she had Mirabelle enraptured. Mirabelle was like the air you breathe. She was the woman who you could not live without once you became involved in her world. She was so beautiful, her body divine, her mind incredible. I could not lose her once she was mine. I could not let her go. Not for anyone. Not even for Mirabelle herself.

Why would Mirabelle want Tamia Challey? The best answer to that Tamia Challey could come up with was that she didn't, that everything she did was for her daughter. That made sense. Everything made sense if you looked at it through Tamia Challey's eyes.

'No high horse,' she says. 'But I don't have to live with being a murderer.'

Is that it? The best one-liner you can come up with?

Who would want to look at the world through Tamia Challey's eyes?

I roll my eyes at the drama queen and pick up my book again. I can do this. Tamia Challey has every reason in the world to lie about who Mirabelle was doing it for. Why wouldn't she? She knows that no one has anything on me, and she knows that *she's* the reason Mirabelle is dead. If I was her, I'd lie and lie again. Everybody lies, especially to themselves.

Tamia Challey was trying to hurt me in the only way she knows. I don't care if it all made sense once she said it. Why Mirabelle said more than once she felt awful about what we were doing to my family. Not awful enough to stop it. But if she really was doing it for her daughter then that would put a different spin on things. I might even have understood if she had explained why she was doing it, but to let me believe it was Tamia Challey, even as I held her under the water . . .

This would have turned out differently if Mirabelle had been honest with me. This is Tamia Challey's fault, of course, and she has to pay for that. When they found her ring, I thought it was a gift from the heavens. I could put her in the house on the night of the killing. But she managed to wriggle out of that one. I will make her pay for this. I will.

'Wade!' I say when he approaches the table and sits down where Tamia Challey sat. 'What are you doing here?'

He stares at me as if I am a stranger, his face stern and serious. He is like a brother to me, we work almost without words – we know what the other is going to say, we can guess what tangent the other is going to go along. I haven't liked keeping the other side of me away from him, but he wouldn't understand. He understands facts, he understands motives, he does not understand passion and love and the need to save yourself no matter what the price.

'I told her she was crazy,' he says, his tone has that evenness he uses when he starts an interview with a suspect. 'That's why I told her where you'd be. Crazy woman with a messed-up life trying to mess up everyone else's life, too. I told her to go and talk to you and that I would stand over there out of sight because it was going to be a short conversation. I told her, afterwards, she was going to be arrested for wasting police time and attempting to pervert the course of justice.'

'She is crazy. She does have a messed-up life.'

'I watched her sit down. I watched as she didn't get up. You didn't tell her to go away. You talked to her. You *explained*. She didn't even say anything to me as she left, she simply looked at me like she had stared in the face of The Devil. You know what that's like, we've done it enough times.'

'You've got it all wrong, you know, Wade. I admit I did know Ms Kemini outside of the case. It wasn't the wisest move to—'

'I don't want to hear it,' he interrupts, rising to his feet. He removes his handcuffs from his belt and places them on the table. 'We can do this the easy way or the hard way.'

'Wade, this is ridic—'

'I mean it, Harvan, I don't want to hear it. Stand up.'

'No. This is all a big—'

His hand is on my biceps then, dragging me to my feet.

His handcuffs are in his other hand, then one half is linked around my wrist, the other is linked around my other wrist.

'Erica Harvan, I am arresting you on suspicion of murder and attempting to pervert the course of justice. You do not have to say anything, but it will harm your defence if you do not mention when questioned something you later rely on in court. Anything you do say may be given in evidence.'

This is all a huge misunderstanding, Wade will understand. He may not completely comprehend passion and love and fear, but he'll understand this in the end. He really will.

23

Fleur

Mrs C has asked me to meet her here, at the beach.

It's my most favourite place in Brighton and I'd love to spend all my time here if it was possible.

We've been sitting here in silence for quite a while, she has something to tell me. I could tell by the way she spoke on the phone, by the anxiety on her face as she walked towards me, and from the fact she's started shaking.

I don't want her to say whatever it is she's going to say. I want her to keep it inside because I'm only just adjusting to this world where Mum is gone and I can call her that without hesitation. It's an odd place. The anger doesn't burn as hard, the feeling of being robbed isn't as potent. I'm starting to feel normal, I think.

'I know who killed your mother,' Mrs C says, as gentle as a bird's wing through the air. 'I'm sorry. I'm sorry that it happened. And I'm sorry to be the one to tell you. But I thought you might prefer to hear it from me rather than the police.'

'So it wasn't you?' I say with the faintest wisp of humour. She shakes her head. 'No, sweetheart, it wasn't.'

'Just checking,' I say, my voice all high and bright. 'OK.' I'm trembling as I reach into my inside pocket for a cigarette. Proper, full-on shaking. How I'm supposed to light it with this shaking I have no idea. I manage to get a cigarette out of the packet, but then I put it back in again. I don't want to smoke. I don't want to do anything, least of all hear what Mrs C has to say.

'Who was it?'

She puts her arm around me, holds me close like Mum used to do when she was reading me a story and we would snuggle up on the sofa. I'd move as close as I could to her and wish the story would go on forever so I wouldn't have to move away from her. Mrs C holds me close as she tells me the story of my mother's death. She tells me who. She tells me why. But she doesn't tell me what I can do about it. And she doesn't tell me how I'm supposed to live with knowing this thing. And she doesn't tell me that it's going to stop hurting and horrifying me one day. But she does tell me this: 'Your mother was one of the most wonderful people I've known. She did wrong but she knew that and she was still an incredible human being. I loved her so much. I wish I'd been half as brave as she was and even a fraction as brave as you are.'

My voice won't work to let me speak.

'I brought this,' Mrs C says, reaching into her pocket and pulling out a large sandwich bag filled with rose petals. 'I thought we could sprinkle some on the sea and wish her well upon her journey.'

I face Mrs C. My head is a whizzing mass of confusion. 'I'd like that,' I say. 'I'd really, really like that.'

24

Three Weeks Later

Beatrix

**Dear Me. You can do this thing. All my love to all of me,
Beatrix x**

'I'm ready,' I say to her.

'Right. Come on then, let's go,' she says.

I hesitate, despite thinking I was ready. I look around the hallway to my flat, knowing that the fridge is stocked, the bedroom has clean sheets, extra duvet, a stack of DVDs, an even bigger pile of books and magazines, a water jug, comfy pyjamas instead of the on-show lingerie I used to wear. I have the phone. I have the huge television regifted from my best friend's living room. Everything is ready, but I feel I am looking around for the last time.

'I'm scared, Tami,' I confess.

'I know,' she says. 'And you're also being incredibly brave.'

'I don't feel it.'

'You are. You can still be scared when you're being brave. You *can* do this,' she reassures. 'Besides, what's scarier, first chemo appointment or your mum coming for an extended visit?'

'*Don't!*' I hiss at her, but I also laugh as she knew I would. 'I'm actually now tempted to go get back into bed until it all goes away. Mum included.'

'When does she arrive again?'

'You know full well she arrives the day after tomorrow.'

'Yes, I do.' She picks up her bag, then my bag and opens the front door, then she turns back and holds out her hand. 'Come on.'

My hand slips easily into hers and I step outside after her.

Slowly, I shut the door behind me, knowing that the next time I open this door, the next stage of my life will have begun.

Fleur

From The Flower Beach Girl Blog

Things I wrote on the postcard I sent to my dad today:
Dear Dad. I love you, but please stop calling me. I can't speak
to you right now. I will be coming back soon to see you and
we can talk then. For now, I'm living with Mum's best friend
and her family. I'm going to apply for art college down here.
I have a boyfriend and he's moving here, too. Most import-
antly, I'm going to try to be happy. Please be happy, too. I
truly, truly love you. Fleur x

25

Three Months Later

Tami

'Shhh, we mustn't wake the clouds,' Anansy whispers.

The three of us are on the beach, looking up at the sky again.

'We still don't know where they sleep,' Cora says ever so quietly.

'I do,' I say softly.

'Where, Mama?' they both ask.

'At The Rose Petal Beach.'

'With Auntie Mirabelle?' Cora asks.

'Yes.'

'That's a lovely place to sleep,' Anansy decides. 'Have fun with Auntie Mirabelle,' she calls quietly to the sky.

'Yes, have a nice time,' Cora adds.

The shadow that falls over us causes both girls to squeal in delight and scramble to their feet. 'Dad!' they shout in unison, the hush needed for the sleep of the clouds forgotten. They throw themselves at him, as if they haven't seen him in an age, when it was only four days ago.

He gets down on his knees and hugs them close. He does this now: he shows how much he loves them, how devoted he is to them. It's not words and showy gestures, when he has them for the weekend he spends the entire time with them. He plays with them, does their homework with them, cooks and cleans for them. He proves every day that they are his priority.

He's still in therapy, he's still on his perpetrator course, he's still trying to be a better man. I get to my feet, brush myself down and retrieve my coat.

'See you later,' I say, kissing each of their heads, lingering on each one because, while walking away from them for the weekend is getting easier, it still hurts. There's no other way to describe it. It hurts. But that's part of my new life. 'Have a good time.'

'See you later, Mama,' they chorus, well versed in this ritual. 'We will.'

'We'll call you later,' Scott reassures.

'Yes, great,' I say, as well versed in this ritual as the girls.

I begin my way up the pebbles back to the promenade, the ache growing deeper and stronger. It never really, truly stops until I am with them again, until that is the longest time I'll go without seeing them every day.

'Oi,' Scott calls suddenly.

I stop, turn back to him.

He tips his chin up at me, like he did all those years ago.

It's over for us, but we have Cora and Anansy, we have the memory of our first, and we have the life that existed before our story started to be unwritten. We're bound together for ever by those things. And by the love I had for him that I know will never completely go away.

My face creases in a smile, like it did all those years, too.

I glance up at the clouds as I saunter towards home. They roll on by without a care in the world, maybe heading for a sleep at The Rose Petal Beach, maybe just drifting to another part of the planet.

I can do that now: drift, without a care in the world.

26

Mirabelle

Not very long ago

I'm closing my eyes really slowly in the hope I can freeze-frame the world. And once it's done, once it's paused, I'll know my lover will still be out there somewhere, and our lives won't have passed each other by.

The ice-cold sea slaps against my shins, and even though I don't want to, I know I have to open my eyes again, I have to come back to where the world is still turning, moving, going on.

The people who are on Brighton beach will see me here in the sea, a perfect red rose in my hand, and they'll wonder what I'm doing, or they'll think I'm really quite mad. I am. Of course I am. But I need to be here and I have to do this because I can't freeze-frame the world.

Each petal of the rose comes away from the stem after the gentlest of tugs, and I keep on pulling until the spindly green stalk is bare except for the tightly curled inner bud, which is folded like tiny arms around its shiny red heart. Once my hand is crammed with dark red petals that I must be careful not to crush, I step further into the waiting sea.

I shut my eyes, ever so slowly, and try again to freeze-frame the world. I want it to work, I want the world to stop, because I can't believe this is all happening to me. I can't believe my life in London is over, and now I have been banished – entirely by choice – to Brighton, to be beside the sea. I open my eyes, stare out to the horizon, in the city where I lost my lover; the place where my life is about to begin again.

I move deeper into the sea, the water hungrily soaking my dress, robbing my body of heat. And carefully, slowly, I release the petals in my hand. I want to be brave like her, the woman in the legend of The Rose Petal Beach.

I want to be able to do what she did and pledge my life to finding my lover. She lost her beloved at sea and, without a second thought, she went to the deserted island where he was last seen and she promised to search every inch of it until she had found him. As she walked her feet were cut by the sharp pebbles of the beach and because her love was so rare and wondrous, so deep and beautiful and pure, every drop of her blood turned into a rose petal, until the beach became a blanket of perfect, red petals.

A few of my petals dance out of my hands, floating away on the breeze, the others spiral downwards onto the foamy water and are immediately carried out on the retreating waves.

After she had walked every step of the island, the woman lay down on her beach, her rose petal beach, and slipped into her final sleep. And in her sleep, her endless sleep, she found the man she had been looking for.

I want to be as strong as the woman from the story instead of trying to freeze-frame the world. I want to promise I'll do whatever it takes to learn the truth about my lover's life and death.

But standing here, I know I can't, it's not in me to follow through with such a quest – I'm just too scared that my lover was murdered, and the same thing is going to happen to me.

Now

Have you heard the story of The Rose Petal Beach?

Do you think it's a story worth dying for?

Have you heard the story of The Rose Petal Beach?

If you have you'll know I left my life in London and came to Brighton to find my first lover, the person who showed me who I was meant to be.

Have you heard the story of The Rose Petal Beach?

If you have you'll know that in the end it wasn't my lover I died for, it was for *her*, my baby, the only person who has ever mattered to me.

Have you heard the story of The Rose Petal Beach?

If you have, you'll know there's only one thing left for me to do: to lay down here on my petal-covered shore, and start my endless sleep.

Have you heard the story of The Rose Petal Beach?

I hope so. I want it to do for you what it did for me – make me believe you should never give up because you'll always find what you're looking for.

The Rose Petal Beach
About the Book

The Rose Petal Beach, my eighth novel, is the story of Tamia Challey and what happens to her when Scott, her husband, is arrested for a hideous crime. Tami's life starts to unravel as she discovers that everyone around her has to some degree been lying to her so she has no idea who to turn to or who to trust. I hope you've read the book so that this doesn't give anything away.

My inspiration for the book came from the numerous news stories there have been over the years about prominent, powerful, *married* men who have been accused of hideous crimes or affairs. While the spotlight has been on the man, I've always been fascinated by the impact of this scandal on their partners. The wives of these men seem to be judged on/by whether they stand by their man or whether they leave, and that's what I wanted to explore – how an ordinary woman would cope if this sort of situation came crashing into her life. How would I cope if this sort of thing happened to me?

Of all the couples I've written about, I think, with the possible exception of maybe Nova and Mal from *Goodnight, Beautiful*, Tami and Scott's relationship has effected me the most of all. I feel so much for them, for the *Romeo and Juliet* nature of their love; how no one wanted them to be together but they overcame all that. Even after I typed the last word of the book back in June 2012, I was thinking about them, replaying conversations, trying to work out where it all went wrong and remembering how they fitted together for so many years.

When I was re-reading proof pages of *The Rose Petal Beach* for the paperback version – once a book has been in hard-back and is reformatted to fit the smaller size of a paper-back, you have to check the text is in the right place – I happily experienced the falling-in-love-again part of Tami and Scott's relationship, then had to live through the upset of the destruction of their marriage all over again, too. That may sound odd, because I did it to them, but reading it so long after initially writing it, I was gutted. All my charac-ters are like real people to me and when they hurt, I ache too. When they're sad, I want to cry for them. When they're happy, I need to laugh, too.

I believe that's the point of being a writer, though. If I didn't feel moved by what I've done to my characters, if I didn't feel that everything that happened to them had happened to me, I wouldn't be doing it right.

Once I had finished reading the proofs of *The Rose Petal Beach*, I went back to the chapters, passages and sections I had edited from the novel (in this case, more than 50,000 words) to remind myself of the other good stuff that happened to them that I didn't have space for in the book. I've included one of my favourite 'deleted' scenes below. Hope you enjoy it.

Dorothy x

PS If you would like to read a free eBook accompaniment short story to *The Rose Petal Beach* called *Beside The Rose Petal Beach*, you can visit: www.dorothykoomson.co.uk

The Deleted Scene
from *The Rose Petal Beach*

Tami

Twelve years ago

From here, my place in what would have been my childhood bedroom if my parents hadn't dismantled the room the second I moved out, I could see out over my parents' garden, and the houses that were on the other side of the railway track. I could see parts of the track that weren't obscured by trees, and I could see over the gardens of the next five house to the left my parents' terrace.

Also, I could see the sleek black and white feathers of the magpie that had landed in the upper branches of the tree at the bottom of the garden. It perched perfectly still, watching the world going on around it. *One for sorrow.*

I stared at it and tried not to let it shave anything off the excitement bubbling up inside me. Today was the day. My eyes strayed to the dress hanging on the back of the door, nestled safely inside its large, black plastic cover. I didn't need to see it to know what it looked like. I could describe every crease, every sequin, every line of boning. And I could tell you that there were 102 small, ivory silk roses around the hem of the dress, and 68 small, ivory silk roses around the top of the bodice. My fingers had stroked each one as I counted them after my mother sat up sewing them on. They were secured with six stitches through the tiny, white pearlescent beads she'd put at the centre of every rose. I'd wanted red roses, wanted to make my dress stand out, but she'd said no, it wasn't the done thing, so I had to accept these.

My eyes strayed back to magpie. It hopped down to a lower branch, looking very pleased with itself, oblivious to what it was doing to me.

One for sorrow.

'*I'm getting married today, you git,*' I wanted to scream at it. '*I don't need you hanging around. There's already enough sorrow clinging to the edges of our lives, trying to nudge its way in, trying to overwhelm our happiness, I don't need any more, thank you very much.*'

I should look away, but I couldn't. It was like the sentinel – the reminder that Scott's family were officially boycotting the wedding. Every last one of them. He didn't have much to do with them, especially now we lived in Brighton, but he had thought, truly believed, that they'd come to his wedding. They'd put on a show and pretend to the outside world they were happy about the choices their youngest son had made. He clung to that idea, really holding on tight. Several times, when he was talking about maybe having his father do a reading and having his brother as an usher and his sister's daughter as a bridesmaid I wanted to ask him if he knew his family at all. What *I* knew – from the rumours and from what he had told me, and, of course, from getting 'verbal' from his brother in the street – was bad enough. Even if they had considered showing up, did we actually want them there? I hadn't said anything, just dutifully sent an invite and waited for the inevitable fall out.

Scott was still shaken by it: his mother called to tell him not to send invites to events that might as well be his funeral, his brother swore he'd turn up and teach us all a lesson on the day, his father apparently lamped his mother one for the idea of his son marrying someone like me, and his sister said she couldn't come because of what would happen to her if the rest of them found out.

'It doesn't matter,' I'd told Scott over and over. 'And the last laugh is on them anyway because I'm absolutely changing my name to Challey. If they'd come, I'd maybe have stayed a Berize to appease them, but now, nah, changing. See how they like that.'

That made a smile surface on his face whenever I said it, and it was the best I could do. They hurt him, repeatedly, but he plainly loved them.

The magpie changed its mind and hopped back to the higher branch, obviously preferring the view up there.

One for sorrow.

My family were outwardly fine, accepting, excited. Privately, away from Scott, they all – *all of them* – asked if I was sure. If I really wanted to marry someone like him when the world was full of men who came from non-racist, non-criminal families. Even the fact he had been to university didn't change the fact he was a Challey. I told them that I was sure, of course I was. Nothing could part me from him. We were like parts of each other, pieces of the same machine – we did not work properly without each other. He was The One. He was My One. I was doing the right thing, I was sure of that. I absolutely wanted to marry him. I absolutely wanted to be with him forever. His life was my life, my life was his life. Our lives were interwoven, our hearts were inseparable.

I felt the grin spread across my face, my eyes closing as I thought about him and our life. About our lovely little flat in Brighton, about waking up to the sound of the sea. Sunday mornings walking on the sea front, even when he'd come back late after a shift in the bar and was exhausted. The nights when we crossed paths with me coming in from work and him going out to work, pausing to kiss and cuddle and wish we had more time. The notes he'd leave me in bed, his favourite being 'crumbs', because I was always complaining about him putting crumbs in the bed. And that moment every night, when he would climb into bed and curl up around me. We had a good life. Getting married, making it official, was the next logical step. The step we would have taken even if things had worked out with . . . with the baby.

I opened my eyes again, ready to stick my tongue out at the magpie, but found it had been joined by another magpie. They sat beside each other, their heads resting together for a moment or two, enjoying each other, then they began hopping from one branch to another branch, following each other, never wanting to be far away from each other's orbit.

Two for joy.

I knew it. I knew I was doing the right thing. *Two for joy. Everything is going to be perfect, I know it is.*

The Rose Petal Beach
Reading Group Questions

These questions might help get a reading group discussion on The Rose Petal Beach *started.*
Warning: contains possible spoilers!

1. Who was the character you identified most with in the book? Why?
2. Who was the character you disliked the most? Why?
3. Why do you think Tami is so horrified by what Scott is accused of? Why do you think she was unsure as to whether he was innocent or guilty?
4. Do you think Tami is weak to have let Scott stay after what he confessed?
5. Have you ever been betrayed like Scott betrayed Tami? If you have, did you react how you thought you would? If you haven't, how do you think you would react?
6. Were you shocked by what was revealed about Mirabelle and her life before she met Tami? Do you understand why Mirabelle kept her secrets for so long?
7. What were Tami's reasons for doing the things she does towards the end of the book? Do you think you could have done what she did?
8. Do you think Tami and Scott could repair their relationship?
9. How do Tami, Scott, Beatrix and Mirabelle change throughout the course of the book?
10. What are the main themes of *The Rose Petal Beach*?

read your heart out with
DOROTHY KOOMSON

Sign up for exclusive news, extracts and to be the first to hear all about Dorothy Koomson's next novel at www.quercusbooks.co.uk/dorothy-koomson

www.dorothykoomson.co.uk

You Tube /dorothykoomson

@dorothykoomson

f www.facebook.com/pages/Dorothy-Koomson

Quercus
www.quercusbooks.co.uk